CW01500618

Blood Caste

Shylashri Shankar is an award-winning author, researcher, food historian, and political scientist. Her non-fiction book, *Turmeric Nation: A Passage Through India's Tastes*, received the AutHer Award for best nonfiction in 2021. Her debut *Blood Caste* won the 2022 Spotlight First Novel Award and was also longlisted for the 2022 CWA Debut Dagger. She lives in New Delhi with her husband and cat.

BLOOD CASTE

SHYLASHRI SHANKAR

CANELOCRIME

First published in the United Kingdom in 2025 by

Canelo Crime, an imprint of
Canelo Digital Publishing Limited,
20 Vauxhall Bridge Road,
London SW1V 2SA
United Kingdom

A Penguin Random House Company
The authorised representative in the EEA is Dorling Kindersley Verlag GmbH. Arnulfstr. 124, 80636
Munich, Germany

A CIP catalogue record for this book is available from the British Library.

Print ISBN 978 1 83598 202 0
Ebook ISBN 978 1 83598 195 5

This book is a work of fiction. Names, characters, businesses, organizations, places and events are either
the product of the author's imagination or are used fictitiously. Any resemblance to actual persons, living
or dead, events or locales is entirely coincidental.

Cover design by Jet Purdie

Printed and bound in Great Britain by Clays Ltd, Elcograf S.p.A.

Look for more great books at
www.canelo.co | www.dk.com

I

For Appa and Amma

Cast of Characters

The Muslim Ruler of the Deccan

His Imperial Highness Mahbub Ali Khan, the VI Nizam of Hyderabad

Sir Khurshid Jah: Premier Noble

Nizam's City Police

Commissioner Colonel Derek Ludlow

Deputy Commissioner Mir Akbar Jang

Acting Chief Inspector Soobramania (Soob, Subbu to his family): An officer in the British Viceroy's Imperial Criminal Investigation Department who has stayed on after completing a secret assignment to snuff out an insurrection against the Nizam.

Sub-Inspector Kamran Shah

Head Constable Muhammad

Sub-Constable Akeel

The Residency

British Resident Sir Trevor C. Plowden

The Residency Police

Commissioner Robert Hankin

Inspector Bill Wilberforce

Head Constable Thomas

The Baigs

Niloufer Baig: Married to Nawab Zulfikar Baig

Nawab Zulfikar Baig: Niloufer's husband and father of Ali and Imran

Ali Baig: Elder son and heir of Nawab Zulfikar Baig

Maryam Baig: Ali's wife

Mohsin Baig: Ali and Maryam's son

Imran Baig: Zulfikar's younger son

Parveen Baig: Imran's wife

Devi: Nursemaid

The Royal Visitors

Grand Duke Alexei Alexandrovich: The Tsar of Russia's brother

Henry James FitzRoy, Earl of Euston

Lady Ariel Falloner: A distant relation of Queen Victoria

The Templeton Household

Arthur Templeton: Publisher of *The Jasoos*

Phoebe Templeton: Arthur's American heiress wife

Edith Whittaker: Phoebe's companion

The Parsis

Dr Shiraz Daruwalla: Soob's best friend Cyrus's widow

Friya Daruwalla: Shiraz's mother-in-law

Aunt Gul Jamasjee: Niloufer Baig's mother

Dr Currimbhoy: Parsi doctor, head of Afzulgunj Hospital

Soob's family

Soob's grandfather, a scholar of Sanskrit

Soob's grandmother

Rohini: Soob's late wife

Srinivasan (Cheenu): Soob's late brother

Natraja: Soob's nephew ward

Others

Dr Dora Board: English doctor, head of the zenana wing of Afzulgunj Hospital

Vahid Baig: Editor of the *Deccan Gazette* and a third cousin of Zulfikar Baig

Mukesh Lal: Jeweller

Tathachari Iyengar: Lawyer and President of the Deccan Brahmin Society

Ram Rahim: Street urchin

Mallu: A Hindu gardener's daughter

Fatima: A Muslim gardener's wife

Chandini: Templeton and Ali's favourite dancer-prostitute

Sikandar Khan: Commander-in-Chief of the Nizam's army

Abdul Huq: Gunrunner and scammer behind the Deccan Rail Scheme

Sobha Singh: Niloufer's guard

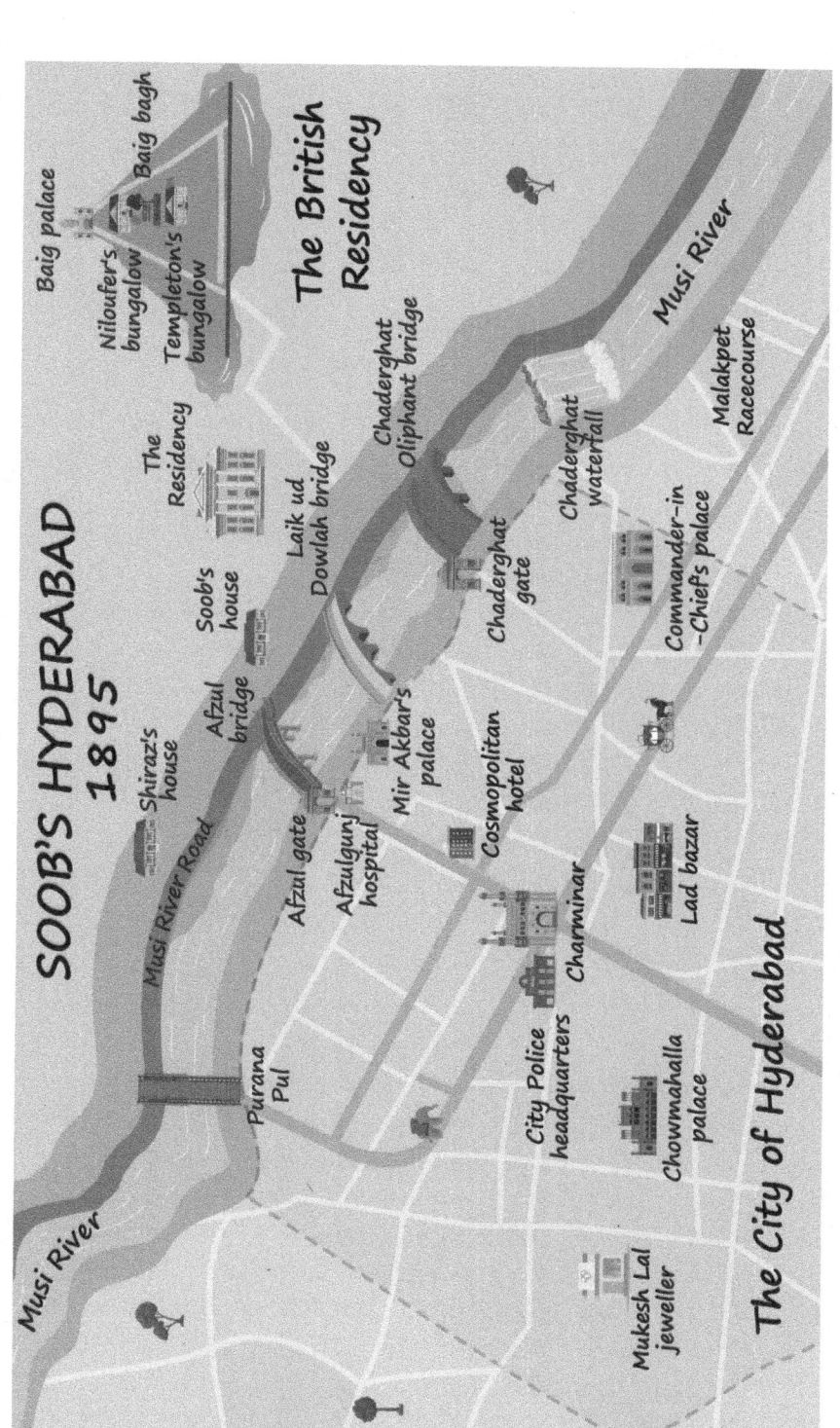

SOOB'S HYDERABAD 1895

Musi River

Baig palace

Baig bagh

Niloufer's bungalow

Templeton's bungalow

The British Residency

Shiraz's house

Musi River Road

The Residency

Afzul bridge

Soob's house

Laik ud Dowlah bridge

Chaderghat Oliphant bridge

Afzul gate

Afzulgunj hospital

Mir Akbar's palace

Cosmopolitan hotel

Chaderghat gate

Chaderghat waterfall

Musi River

Malakpet Racecourse

Purana Pul

Charminar

Commander-in-Chief's palace

City Police headquarters

Lad bazar

Mukesh Lal jeweller

Chowmahalla palace

The City of Hyderabad

Chapter One

22 June 1895

When Soob first saw the body, he thought it was a dog. In the dim light of dusk, looking over to the bank of the British Residency from under the city bastions, he'd glimpsed something caught on the rock weir across the Musi River. Leashed by streamers of algae and ribbon weed, it looked set to crash into the foaming waters of the cataract.

He'd been out looking for a rare purple frog in the mudflats between the Laik ud-Dowlah and Afzul bridges. A bluish-pink water balloon, one of his constables had said, with small arms and legs. So after a tiresome day spent fending off contrary orders from the Nizam's courtiers and the British officials, here he was, ready to pounce on anything that bulged purple – when he found himself staring at a trapped dog in the weir. *Or was it a child?*

He plunged in. The water came up to his knees, pouring over the top of his military riding boots. Strong unexpected currents clamped his ankles, but he pushed on, thrusting through the silken sludge of the riverbed. The green tether snapped as he neared, releasing the object. He lunged to grab it before it shot over the boulder and into the waterfall.

'Oi, what's that?' A stocky washerman in a loincloth splashed up to him from the city side, brown water lapping his chest.

'Only a gunny bag,' Soob yelled above the crack and boom of the water, his fingers gripping rough coconut fibre.

'Ooh, salaam, Chief Inspector.' The dhobi's betel-stained lips beamed. 'It's a great honour to meet the esteemed sahib who saved us from big, big troubles.'

Soob gave a nod and let go of the sack. Something soft and clammy slapped his wrist.

A hand – jutting from the sack's mouth.

The rope tie slithered into the foaming waters. The sack teetered. Soob dived forward onto the ledge and, seizing it with both hands, hauled it over the rock face. The top of the sack gaped, and inside he saw a head tipped to one side in the low light – dark hair cropped close to the skull and brown rock weed splayed on the face.

'Hai, hai!' The dhobi clutched his elbow. 'Is he dead, Chief Inspector?'

A miracle it'd be if he wasn't, Soob thought, staring at the deep gash across the throat, a cut all the way to the bone.

The bundle jerked at a sudden gush. Damn it! Another dam had burst upstream.

'Quick, help me,' Soob snapped.

The washerman gulped a breath, ducked into the rushing waters and emerged again clasping the bottom hem of the sack.

Soob turned towards the city ramparts.

'It'd be easier to go that way, Chief Inspector.' The dhobi jerked his chin at the paddy field on the British Residency bank.

Holding tight to the sack in the rough wash, Soob forged on, not bothering to reply. On that side controlled by the British Resident, the Nizam's City Police had no authority. As for the Residency Police, this victim with his wheat-coloured skin and calloused fingers – a poor native – was unlikely to warrant much attention.

Not that the Nizam's side was much better, Soob reflected drily. A fistful of *halli siccas* would suffice as blood money for this man's family. In the two weeks of an undercover assignment to snuff out an insurrection against the Nizam, it was clear to Soob that while the British and the city's wealthy nobles and merchants could count on the whole machinery of the state, the poor had no one. For his authority to prevail, the body would have to be towed to the city side.

By now they'd reached the mudflats, and as they picked their way through foul-smelling puddles, three urchins emerged from the gloom and followed them.

Soob stopped by a black granite boulder close to the city wall. 'It's dry here.'

He gently laid the body on the flat top. The sack's mouth opened and reddish water rolled down over his Hessian boots and the dhobi's bare feet.

'Fetch the constables from Afzul Gate,' Soob told the boys, closing the folds to hide the sight from them. He found coins in his pocket and flicked them a copper each.

'You're bleeding, Chief Inspector,' the dhobi said. 'Very, very sharp, those rocks are.'

Soob glanced down at his tunic. It was ripped, and his chest burnt like fire. It could wait. 'Later,' he said, and opened the sack's mouth.

In the iron-grey light, dusk turning to night, he gently lifted the algae off the man's face. His fingers brushed against soft down, causing him to stiffen. It was a woman – brutally butchered. Her nose had been sliced off, a hollow sat in place of the left eye. Muddy water trickled from the cavities.

'Hai Ram!' the dhobi gasped. 'It's a woman. She must've betrayed her husband.'

Soob's jaw tightened. He'd come across this reaction, here and in England during his time at Scotland Yard. How anybody could blame this poor woman for her own murder... No point wasting his breath, though. He jerked his chin towards a rock a dozen feet away and told the dhobi to sit there.

With the light dimming rapidly, he noted the other details. No earrings, though her ears were pierced with holes around the rim for loops of silver or brass. And oddly enough, no bangles, not even glass ones, when custom here frowned upon bare wrists on a married woman as causing misfortune to the husband. She hadn't been robbed, though: no ragged cuts in her ear lobes and no welts on her wrists.

He studied the short hair on her crown. Only Hindu widows were shorn of their hair and stripped of their jewellery; that is, if they weren't burnt alive on their dead husband's funeral pyre.

'Looks like a widow, Chief Inspector,' the dhobi piped up from his rock perch, a wad of tobacco lodged in one cheek, his small eyes glittering with excitement. 'It seems to me she didn't serve her husband's family with due respect. Cut her up well and proper.' He transferred the wad to the other cheek. 'But why go to all this trouble? If she didn't behave herself, then they could just throw some kerosene on her and strike a match. I know your Brahmin caste doesn't follow this custom, Chief Inspector, but this is our way.'

Soob ignored the babble. In a few moments it would be pitch dark. Bracing himself, he gently peeled away the coir sticking to her body. A coppery scent of blood and raw flesh caught in his throat. She had been stripped, and not just of clothes. Black holes gaped in place of her heart, liver and stomach.

Then something else caught his eye. A darker marking on her inner elbow. A tattoo of the Aum symbol, sacred to Hindus, though it had not protected this widow.

His fingers curled into fists as he stared into the black hue of night. Mutilated corpses he'd seen before, most recently in his previous assignment, a Goddess Kali cult in central India. He would never get used to the sight. But these wounds bore an altogether different signature. Such clinical inhumanity he'd seen only once before: at Scotland Yard. In the photograph of Mary Jane Kelly, the last victim of Jack the Ripper.

Chapter Two

Soob looped his horse's reins around an iron post at the entrance to Afzulgunj Hospital and lifted his gaze to the grand sandstone edifice. Built for poor subjects by the ruler's great-aunt, the irony of bringing someone from a hovel to die in a palace had evidently escaped her, he thought.

The police carriage and the half dozen City Police constables on horseback had brought two white-robed attendants sprinting up with a trestle stretcher. They paled at his remonstration – 'Careful, she's been badly cut up' – and gingerly lifted the bundle, one clutching the folds of the sack's mouth now tied with a rope.

Soob followed the stretcher bearers, noting his men's dismay with a sardonic eye. In a courtly society that set such store by appearances, their status came from him, their superior. High officials should not stoop to such a menial task as ushering some poor victim to the morgue, their frowns said, and what's more, it was bound to diminish the prestige of the City Police. But if he hadn't come in person, this poor widow would be dumped in some corner to be buried in a pauper's grave. Exactly what the killer had wanted.

Damned if he was going to enable it, Soob thought, cutting through the crush of patients and their carers in the atrium. Murder was rare in the city even though no man stepped out of the house without a gun or at least a knife stuck in his cummerbund. That's what the deputy commissioner had told him in his first briefing two weeks ago. And unsolved murders were rarer still, what with everyone sticking their noses into the affairs of their neighbours. Despite the pains the killer had taken to hide this woman's identity, in his experience, murderers always left clues.

Crossing a courtyard, they now arrived at the mortuary barn, its air thick with the smells of straw and carbolic acid and the buzz of tiny winged insects and kerosene lamps.

A stout middle-aged man stood by a trestle table in the middle of the spacious room, wearily wiping his hands with a cotton towel. Soob was relieved. Dr Muzaffar Khan's skill as a pathologist was just as good as Head Doctor Currimbhoy. Dispensing with the usual fifteen minutes of niceties, and shrugging off the tut-tutting about his bloodied tunic, Soob came straight to the point.

As the attendants placed their burden on the trestle table, the doctor's sharp eyes traced the places where the coir jutted out at odd angles, as if he could see the broken limbs and gaping holes. After dismissing the attendants, Dr Khan untied the knot, and lifting the coir from the body, carefully cut the burlap. A cross breeze nudged the kerosene lanterns strung above on a rope, the play of their shadows heightening the grisly effect. The doctor stiffened, but continued with his examination. Then he turned to Soob.

'She died sometime in the afternoon. The blood is still sticky because the fast-flowing water has not allowed it to clot properly.'

The doctor pointed out a marked difference in the cuts: precise and clinical on the right side, and jagged on the left, all made with a knife. Possibly the same knife. He picked out another detail – the woman's hair had been cut short; it wasn't natural hair growth from a shaved head.

'See the uneven cut and the split ends? A natural growth would have tapered ends, like in a paint brush. It could be a ritual, you know.'

'One or two killers?' Soob asked, trying to make sense of the shorn hair.

'Two, perhaps. One of them was clearly skilled – almost as if a teacher showed a student how to do it. But believe me, Chief Inspector, this is not a cadaver from our medical school. Those are given a proper funeral – a burial for the Muslim corpses and a pyre for Hindus. Our students treat the bodies with respect. They certainly would not cut the throat and stab the body. And certainly not that.' He pointed to the stubs of her middle toes. 'Why?'

'To make it difficult for us to find out when she was widowed,' Soob said grimly. A widow had to remove the silver band married Hindu women wore on their second toes. 'Cutting her hair would also fit in with this logic.'

'You mean he didn't want us to see how pale that skin was, and how long she'd been widowed?' Dr Khan asked, ashen faced. 'Ya Allah! What an inhuman fiend! I pray he suffers terribly when his head is crushed under the foot of the executioner elephant. Find him quickly, Chief Inspector.'

'I intend to, Dr Khan.' Soob strode out, slamming his way through the morgue door and out into the courtyard.

He raged at the killer as he mounted his horse and galloped down the main avenue to Charminar. Candles shone from the sixteenth-century monument marking the cardinal centre of Hyderabad, and from its four minarets started the main avenues dividing the city into quadrants. Soob slowed down by the south corner. Dr Khan's observation about the two types of cuts seemed to indicate two killers. They had thought of every eventuality, taken precautions, possessed a logical and clinical mind, and were capable of carrying out the grisliest of mutilations.

He dismounted at the City Police Headquarters, a two-storey building painted the green of a Koran with more windows than walls. Lanterns shone from the downstairs windows and from his upper-storey office.

The Afghan Rohilla contingent stationed below Charminar's vaulted dome let out a stentorian cry, stamped their feet and saluted him. Soob gave a nod and handed over the reins to a constable who'd hurried to meet him.

Inside, he paused to tell the duty constable to summon the riverside patrol, then took the stairs up to his office.

The lamp buzzed from the bookshelf along the near wall. In the breeze wafting through the bank of floor-length windows, a fistful of chits tamped down by a thick green file fluttered from the teak-wood desk. He eyed them with acute disfavour. More 'requests' from noblemen recommending yet another 'brilliant' son for the Nizam's detective force. After foiling an insurrection against the Nizam, a secret mission for the Imperial Criminal Investigation Department, he'd made the fatal mistake of agreeing to the ruler's request to stay on and set up the force. He had not anticipated that the local nobles would find him, a Scotland Yard-trained man, worthy enough to school their progeny, train them as detectives in order to spy on rival families. Here, older sons inherited the title and the ancestral properties, while their younger brothers eked a living running the family's spy networks. He ought to be thankful, he supposed, that they didn't know he was a high ranking officer in the ICID. Nobody did, apart from the Nizam and the British Resident.

He ran an eye over the other notes – more conflicting orders on the state guests' security arrangements. The last thing he needed right now. Scooping the lot, he dropped them in the bin.

He leaned back in his chair and let out a deep breath. It was going to be another long night of work, but then he was used to it, welcomed it even. Your office is your real wife, Rohini used to tease him. They'd married late – she seventeen to his twenty-four – when their horoscopes had matched. Despite his objection to using something so nonsensical to fix such a life-changing event, he and Rohini could not have been a better match, her gentle nature a buffer to his stubbornness.

A clatter sounded from the wooden stairway, announcing the captain of the riverside patrol who entered and saluted.

Soob issued his command: 'Find out if the slum dwellers on the riverbank saw someone throw a sack in the river this evening – around dusk.'

With a glance at Soob's bloodied uniform, the shrewd-eyed veteran nodded and left.

Soob began unbuttoning his tunic. Another knock. Sub-Constable Akeel peeped around the door, his wide eyes bearing a worshipful gleam that had made the boy the butt of much teasing from the hardened ex-mercenaries. Soob had tried to fob him off, but each time it felt like he was kicking a pup.

Akeel held out iodine and a roll of cotton gauze. 'With the compliments of the constables, sir.'

Soob took them, surprised at his men's concern for an acting Chief Inspector. It was common knowledge that he was a temporary appointee until his predecessor, who'd been wounded, returned from the hospital.

Dismissing the youth, he peeled off his wet tunic. The iodine stung as he cleaned the clotted blood and worked the antiseptic into the wounds, wincing at the sharp burn. A deep cut across his rib looked like it might need stitches, but it would have to wait. He wrapped the bandage around his torso and knotted it, then changed into a clean khaki shirt and pants he kept in his bottom drawer for emergencies. He could do little about his wet feet apart from emptying the reeking river water from his boots into the spittoon behind his chair.

Another constable hurried in with a telegram, apologising profusely for having misplaced it. In the hiss of the hurricane lamp on his desk, Soob read the missive from his grandfather.

'Cholera in Madras STOP Arriving Hyderabad STOP 23 June Deccan Queen 2nd class.'

That was tomorrow. His grandparents and nephew, his only remaining family... their impending arrival evoked mixed emotions.

He rose to his feet and went across to the window. Tinsel strung between the avenue lamps crackled in the breeze. A mosquito dived at his chest, scenting blood. He flicked it absently with the paper.

He'd stayed on in Hyderabad and agreed to the ruler's request partly to avoid the difficult conversation he knew needed to be had with his grandfather. An assignment at Scotland Yard had taken him to London in October 1892, triggering an automatic excommunication from his Brahmin caste. A Brahmin had to make a ritual prayer to the sun daily from land. Impossible, of course, during his sea voyage. The expectation had been that he would perform an atonement rite on his return.

Rohini's death while he was away, seven months and nine days ago, had changed everything. By refusing her the last rites because of his own excommunication, those callous priests had condemned a devout soul to an unholy death. He would never return to his caste – that's what he had told his grandfather.

Deep down, though, he blamed himself. He felt he was responsible for Rohini's death. He had not considered her feelings at being shunned as an outcaste's wife, and had failed to sail back promptly on learning of the miscarriage and her subsequent decline. Instead, he had put his work first, staying on in London to help nail the Ripper.

Chimes sounded from the clock in Charminar's first tier. Its eleven beats accompanied a thunderous cry: 'Hail!'

Soob jerked away from the window as the Rohillas below stamped their feet and roared the obligatory salute reserved for nobles. Damn it! He couldn't pretend he hadn't seen the bejewelled grandee gliding past on a richly caparisoned elephant, considering they were at eye level and within touching distance. It stopped outside his window and the nobleman, reclining on a park bench strapped with thick ropes to the elephant's back, looked at him expectantly. No matter what they expected, he wasn't about to make fawning bows to pompous nawabs. Tomorrow he'd get curtains made.

At his brusque nod the nawab glared with outrage before moving off, leaving in his wake a stomach-curdling stink of sweat mixed with rose attar.

A tap on the door and the riverside patrol captain entered and saluted again.

'That was quick,' Soob said.

'Only three men were around, sir, picking up the last of their belongings,' reported the grey-haired Deccani, born and bred in the city. 'They didn't see anyone throw a sack into the river. Their families and the rest of the slum have already moved to the field inside the city walls.'

Theirs was an annual monsoon exodus, the captain added, when the rain-fattened river submerged the mud huts. While on the other side of the city wall, the nawabs would be safe and snug in their palatial edifices, Soob thought with a frown, as the captain saluted once more and left.

He returned to his chair and drummed his fingers on the table. Dr Khan had put the time of death sometime that afternoon. She must have been killed elsewhere, though, not beside the river, a noisy thoroughfare during the day. More likely the killer had brought her body at dusk, after the riverbanks had emptied of people, buffaloes, elephants and camels, indicating someone who knew the local environment.

The sack's position on the rock ledge indicated it came from the Residency side. The Musi River, he had been warned, waned and swelled between ten and twenty metres depending on rainfall. The present sluggish current wouldn't have carried the body far. The killer must have released it in the deserted patch under the Chaderghat-Oliphant Bridge. There were no slums on that stretch: only melon, cucumber and paddy crops cultivated by locals on dry patches. The high paddy grass would have hidden the killer's tread to the water's edge.

Thanks to infernal politicking, the City Police couldn't question anyone in the British Residency without the Resident's permission. Worse still, Soob had little hope of getting approval in the current situation, with the British gunning for control over law and order in the Nizam's territory. But the 'Saviour of the Deccan' intended to cash in the favours both sides owed him. Had the insurrection succeeded, the Nizam would be dead, or at the very least deposed, rendering the British hold over the Deccan shaky at best. He picked up the bell and shook it.

A constable entered, and Soob told him to find the deputy commissioner, a nobleman who'd be out at some soiree or the other.

Propping his elbows on the table, Soob gazed out at the yellow glow of the street lamp. Though these mutilations bore a strong resemblance to the Ripper's victims in Whitechapel, it couldn't be him. Two years ago, as part of a secret Whitehall investigation, he had hunted down the cold-blooded killer, a constable in the Metropolitan Police. It was hushed up by the top brass to save face, and Soob had kept his silence for the sake of the constable's young family.

But he had shot dead the Ripper.

Chapter Three

A woman's agitated voice came from the stairwell, and its familiar lilt lifted Soob's spirits. Shiraz, his best friend Cyrus's widow, another reason he had stayed on in Hyderabad.

She came rushing in, a pink scarf trailing from her dark hair pinned in a bun, a frazzled Muhammad in hot pursuit. Soob's lips twitched. The head constable had strict views about a woman being veiled and cloistered at home. Shiraz flouted every one of them regularly. She was one of only two woman doctors in the city *and* only the second Parsi woman to obtain a medical degree from London.

Despite her hospital attire – a full-sleeved navy cotton blouse over a long skirt with a sari's pleats – her delicate features might evoke to the undiscerning some gentle Persian princess in a miniature painting. In reality, she was nothing like that, and Cyrus wouldn't have fallen head over heels in love with her if she had been. It was her take-no-nonsense-from-anybody attitude and her kindness that had attracted his best friend and sparked Soob's own admiration for her.

'What's wrong?' he asked, rising to his feet.

She thrust a sheet of yellowed paper in his hand. 'Niloufer is missing.'

'Cyrus's young cousin? The one who recently married the nawab?'

She nodded. 'Aunt Gul sent this. I was working late at the hospital.'

He read the note from Niloufer's mother.

> *Shiraz,*
>
> *Niloufer hasn't come home from a dinner party at Mrs Templeton's next door. They said she left at 10:30 to walk back alone. The nawab is ill. We have searched everywhere. Come quickly, and please bring Chief Inspector Soobramania.*
>
> *Gul*

He glanced out of the window at the clock on Charminar. Almost a quarter past eleven.

'Why no carriage and no guard?' Every man here, noble or otherwise, caged their women and never let them out without an armed escort.

'Niloufer hates having servants hanging about.' She gripped the edge of the table in a convulsive movement. 'Only a small park is between the two houses. It should've taken her only a couple of minutes to walk home.'

He wasn't sure if it was something to worry about. As the wife of a wealthy nobleman, Niloufer would have a fleet of servants and guards watching over her, even if they hadn't accompanied her.

'Where does she live?'

'In one of her husband's bungalows by the Baig lake – in the British Residency. Hurry, Soob.'

He hesitated. 'Who are these friends?'

'Arthur Templeton is English. He publishes *The Jasoos*, a gossip rag. His wife, Phoebe, is American. Niloufer met her a couple of weeks ago.'

'Maybe she left something behind and went back to their house.'

'But the note says she left their house over forty minutes ago and they've searched everywhere.' She frowned. 'Look, Soob. I wouldn't normally worry, especially with Niloufer. She is my dearest friend and I know what a madcap she is. But with her husband ill, she wouldn't have gone off gallivanting at this time of the night. Something's wrong.'

He picked up the oilskin pouch with his identity papers from the desk and strode around to her.

A cry came from the stairway.

Head Constable Muhammad twisted around in the doorway as a boy slid past like an eel. His kurta and pyjama smelt of the river – wet plants and rotten eggs. Muhammad surged in after him.

'Wait, I know him,' Soob said, holding the boy's shoulder. 'Ram Rahim, what's the matter?'

Tears shone on mud-streaked cheeks, wide eyes urgent. 'Come quickly, huzoor. He was cutting her throat.'

'Sir, he must be lying.' The HC shook his fist at the boy. 'You rascal!'

Even if he hadn't found the river victim, Soob would still have believed Ram Rahim. He'd rescued the street urchin from a pack of feral stray dogs the previous week and, as far as the boy was concerned, had saved his life. Gratitude, in Soob's experience, evoked honesty. Besides, just because someone lived on the streets didn't mean they were dishonest. He had found more lies among the wealthy than among the poor.

It had taken a great deal of pluck for the boy to enter a police station with such a story. And a great deal of trust that Soob wouldn't clap him up in prison when they found the body.

'Where, Ram Rahim?'

'Baig bagh.'

'Soob.' Shiraz's voice trembled. 'That's the park next to Niloufer's house.'

She flew to the door.

—

Soob hoisted the boy onto the saddle and sprang up behind as Shiraz scrambled into the open phaeton under a sky thick with thunderclouds. Accompanied by seven Rohilla Afghan constables, he galloped down the gauntlet of two-storey shops-cum-residences with shuttered windows, through a street smelling of sugar and cinnamon, then another with the stench of civet and dirt. Finally, loop-holed battlements rose in front of him, above the high granite archway of Chaderghat Gate.

'Permit?' demanded a soldier in an olive green uniform. Pikes and long muskets glinted against the grey stone wall behind him. 'Oh, sorry, Chief Inspector.'

No one could enter or leave the city between the cannon shots at eight at night and four in the morning without permission from a superior. Soob showed the pass signed by the deputy commissioner.

The tall wooden door creaked open.

A dozen oil lamps lit Chaderghat–Oliphant Bridge as their cavalcade thundered across, past the ornate iron poles festooned with yellow and silver tinsel. On the Residency side, they had to stop again and a contingent of British soldiers in light blue uniforms surrounded them. Precious minutes ticked by as Soob spoke to their commander. His permit from the Resident, which he used only in emergencies, was accepted, though they were saddled with an escort of a dozen pink-cheeked cadets.

Angling right, they sped along a broad, well-lit asphalt street. Within ten minutes they were galloping up the Baig hill; below, a dark lake curled around them like a bean. A high hedge loomed to the right, ending at the iron grill of a park gate.

'Guard,' Soob shouted, reining in, while a constable removed a lantern from the saddlebag and lit it.

A man emerged from the gate hut yawning, hitching up his pyjama with one hand, keys jangling from his cummerbund.

Another constable hastily dismounted, snatched the keys and opened the lock.

They rode in, Soob's ears straining for cries over the crunch of hoof and wheel on the gravel path. At a T-junction, Ram Rahim, who'd clung on silently, pointed right.

They raced to a banyan copse and emerged into a clearing. Ink-dark branches pressed in around them, skeletal limbs caging what looked like a fountain with a porpoise leaping into the sky.

Something lay by the basin.

'Stay here, Ram Rahim,' Soob said, leaping down.

His men dismounted amid a clatter of hooves and the constable hurried over with the lantern.

'But huzoor, it wasn't—' The boy gave a gasp.

Yellow light from the lamp spilled on a mutilated and bloodied body.

Chapter Four

The dead girl's skin was the colour of wood smoke. Curly dark hair spread out, a wreath cocooning her head. Soob leaned back on his haunches and took a deep breath.

She couldn't be more than seventeen. About five feet tall, painfully thin, wrist bones jutting from the full sleeves of a faded cotton blouse. Calloused feet peeped from the frayed edge of the petticoat. Glass bangles, green and red, some broken – shards on bloody gashes marking her stomach. A burgundy cummerbund coiled around her neck, one silken end covering her left eye.

By his shoulder, Shiraz breathed out, 'It isn't Niloufer.'

But if this poor young girl wasn't Niloufer, then Niloufer was still missing. He snapped out the orders to his men. 'You five, search the park for a young woman, and you two, stay back and mind the English soldiers.'

'Soob, is it the same madman who killed the other woman today? What if… Niloufer…' Her trembling voice trailed off.

Soob crouched next to her, wanting to hold her hand to comfort her, but the men were watching. He didn't reply. She could well be right, but to speak it out loud would only add to her distress.

'My men will find her. Shiraz, I need your help before the Residency Police show up. Can you examine her?'

She raised her head and gave a nod.

Soob detected a whiff of the hospital beneath the pungent aroma from the kerosene lamp set on the fountain rim. He leaned in and sniffed near the dead girl's face. Not iodine or phenyl, but definitely something connected with the medical profession.

He pushed the lamp further away. 'Shiraz, smell here. Anything familiar?'

She sniffed. 'I can't make it out. I don't have a good sense of smell.'

A nightjar's rhythmic cry blared from the trees behind them as if it had been startled.

Soob glanced over his shoulder to see the British cadets drifting towards them.

'Halt!' he said in English.

The cadets took a deliberate step forward, the glint in their eyes declaring they weren't about to take orders from some native employed by the local ruler. Well, he'd see about that.

At his order, metal snicked, and the two Rohilla Afghans stepped into the cadets' path, swords raised.

The youths retreated hurriedly to the glade's edge – clearly, they'd been warned about the City Police 'ruffians'.

He turned to Shiraz who had raised the bloodied dupatta from the girl's abdomen and was examining the wounds. 'Has she been molested?'

She glanced up at him and paled. 'Oh, god, I hope not. But she won't be a virgin, she's old enough to be married.'

'She's unmarried. That's a half sari.' He pointed to the petticoat and the cotton dupatta and blouse Hindu girls wore before their marriage. But Shiraz was right. This girl ought to be married, unless there was a defect in her horoscope. He gazed at the gentle curve of her cheek. Would her parents feel relief along with their grief? An unmarried girl her age was seen as a burden and bad luck, especially if she had younger sisters.

He brushed away the tiny black flies hovering over the face. The scarf dipped and lay oddly over the left eye. He tensed, knowing what he would find.

'Look away, Shiraz,' he said, and lifted the silk. A sure hand had carved out the eye leaving few ragged edges, and matched the mutilations on the right side of the river victim's body, where the cuts on the left side had been coarse and clumsy.

Shiraz whimpered and lurched away, retching as she made for a palmyra palm some feet away.

Clenching his teeth, Soob pushed the silk from the neck. A gash curved from ear to ear. Again, the Ripper's victims in Whitechapel rose in his thoughts. Five of those women had had their throats cut from left to right; a neckerchief had been looped around one, Annie Chapman. In four, the soft parts of their stomachs and arms had suffered many stab

17

wounds, and in two, other organs had been sliced out and displayed. Their names and faces were tattooed in his memory.

Was someone copying the Ripper?

There were far too many discrepancies, though. The Ripper had focused on the neck, breasts, abdomen and the genitalia, not the eyes. But here the killer had gone for the left eye – why?

'Sorry, Soob,' Shiraz said, dabbing her lips with a handkerchief as she returned and huddled by him.

Their gazes met, and he gave a nod. Shiraz was no stranger to death, but coming up against a brutal murder was not the same as a patient dying of natural causes.

She bent back to her task.

The mournful beat of a drum came from the hilltop palace. The Baigs must be high nobles, he thought. Only such families were allowed to have a timekeeper who beat a hide drum. It was looking to be a difficult business. He hoped his men would find Niloufer quickly, alive and unharmed.

'She's a virgin.' Shiraz leaned back on her haunches. 'Thank god, she wasn't molested. But why did he kill her, Soob? She has no jewellery, no money – nothing to rob.'

A question to which he had no definite answer. But it seemed all too likely it was the same killer or killers who had murdered the girl in the river.

The clop of hooves drew closer. They were out of time, and his constable's 'Halt' in Urdu didn't deter the cadets.

Soob leaned in and picked up the lantern. Large fan-shaped shadows swooped down on them and away as the palm leaves rustled, the breeze picking up.

'What are you looking for?' Shiraz asked as he slanted the light on the mosaic paving stones.

'Blood spray when the murderer cut her throat.'

She lifted the girl's head. Blood pooled under the neck, and a crust had formed on it. 'He laid her down and then cut her throat. Why didn't she struggle?'

He bent and lifted the girl's hand. The fingers were stiffening. 'Rigor mortis has begun. How long has she been dead?'

Shiraz clasped the calloused fingers and moved them. 'Over two hours.'

'Between nine thirty and ten, then.'

The timing was off, it didn't match Ram Rahim's account. The boy had reached the police station at half past eleven, a whole hour later than when he ought to have come. He stared into the dark shrubbery: there was another possibility.

'Huzoor,' Ram Rahim whispered from a few feet away.

'Stay there,' Soob said. 'Don't come closer.'

A constable grabbed the boy's shoulder and lifted him like a dog.

'Don't hurt him,' Soob snapped. 'Let him go. Ram Rahim, get back to the city and meet me there later.' He'd be safer there.

Hoofbeats and yells snaked through the rustle of the leaves. His men's whistles repeated from every corner of the park. Only one whistle, not three. They hadn't found Niloufer or the killer. It had been a long shot.

Boots and hooves clattered towards the fountain.

'What in the blazes are you doing here, acting Chief Inspector Soobramania?' A heavy-set Englishman in a light blue uniform dismounted, his plump cheeks flushed with outrage. Inspector Wilberforce of the Residency Police.

Ram Rahim dashed up and tugged Soob's sleeve. 'It wasn't her, huzoor… it wasn't here.'

Soob's heart sank. Had this been the victim Ram Rahim had seen, Niloufer's disappearance might well have had a harmless explanation. But it seemed all too possible that she was dead.

Lantern in hand, ignoring Wilberforce, he barrelled through the shrubbery, with Shiraz close behind. Ram Rahim disappeared into a mound of feathery kochia plants and Soob followed, emerging onto a gravel path. On the other side, kochia shrubs were lined up like large black cannonballs, and beyond, an ink-dark lawn rolled to the park boundary.

'Here, huzoor, they were right here,' yelled Ram Rahim from up the path, rummaging through the gravel as if he expected to find her body.

Soob lowered the lamp and searched for signs of an attack. Something glinted from the grass verge. He picked it up, and it pricked his finger. A shard of glass. More broken bits were piled up in the thick turf, as if someone had gathered the fragments of the broken lantern and hidden them there. Shiraz's pale face, eyes anxious and dreading, bored into him as he steeled himself to ask Ram Rahim the questions that would deepen her distress.

'Where were you?'

'There.' The boy pointed to a grass mound twelve feet away, by a path coming from the rear end. Having entered through a hole he'd hacked in the back hedge, Ram Rahim was hurrying to the gardener's tool-shed where he liked to shelter on rainy nights. 'I heard clinks like glass breaking, followed by grunts.'

With the moon cloaked by thick clouds, the boy couldn't have seen anything more than shadows. Soob asked anyway, and got the boy's disconsolate confirmation.

'But huzoor,' Ram Rahim said, tugging his arm. 'I can describe the killer's shadow. He wasn't very fat or very thin.'

'How tall?'

The boy's eyes darted between him and Shiraz. 'Taller than hakimji, but not as tall as you.'

Between five foot three and six feet, then. Not much to go on. The average Deccani man was five feet and a couple of inches, and the women much shorter. But it wasn't unusual to find taller men among the mercenaries and nobles whose forefathers hailed from Turkey and Arabia.

'Could it be the park guard?' Shiraz asked.

'That fat lout.' Ram Rahim spat on the gravel. 'Of course not. Everyone knows he snores away the whole night.'

'How could you tell it was a woman being murdered?' He put his hand on Shiraz's arm, feeling her tremble as she too hoped for an answer that would show Ram Rahim to be mistaken about a second murder.

'The moon came out, I swear, only for a moment. The clothes looked like a woman's. That's when I saw a knife. It cut her throat, it did, I swear. I must've cried out. The murderer jumped up and ran towards me, and I legged it.'

Shiraz's nails dug into his bare skin. 'Soob, it must be Niloufer. Where is she?'

A whiff of lemon flower came with a gust and faded into the lantern's pungent odour. He shone the light on the nearby shadows. No lemon tree. The scent wafted from a grass mound on the other side of the path. It had begun to drizzle.

'Did Niloufer wear a scent?' he asked, moving towards it.

20

'K… Kanaga of Japan.' Her voice trembled.

'Smells of lemon?'

She nodded, unable even to get the word out.

'Hold this, Shiraz,' he said, giving her the lamp. 'Stay back.'

Stepping up to the kochia bush, he parted the feathery leaves, readying himself for the iron tang of blood.

'Niloufer,' Shiraz breathed by his side. The lantern wobbled, throwing light and shadow on the body.

For a moment, seeing the aquiline nose and high cheekbones, it looked like Cyrus lying there. Even in death, Cyrus's cousin was beautiful. Beads of rain shimmered in the dark hair braided around her head. Satin slippers poked out of the organza skirt gathers, their scuffed fronts testifying to the struggle Ram Rahim had witnessed. They'd remained on her feet though, tied with ribbons to her ankle. Here too, the bloody gashes on her stomach bore witness to a frenzy. That her face and eyes were intact probably owed more to Ram Rahim's interruption than to any restraint on the killer's part.

Hot oil scalded his arm. Soob winced and noted the lamp's handle dangling from Shiraz's fingers, its safety door open. He steadied it, closed the door, and taking it from her, set it on the gravel path.

Shiraz fell to her knees and, clutching Niloufer's wrist, felt for a pulse.

His breath caught in his throat at the telltale sag in the wet silk around the neck. Though he knew little about women's fashions, or men's for that matter, the red of her fitted organza skirt clashed with the scarlet cummerbund around her neck. It couldn't be hers.

'Shiraz…' He couldn't get the words out.

'Huzoor, did you find her?' The boy's whisper merged with the shush of the drizzle.

Soob turned swiftly. 'Ram Rahim, go and fetch the English inspector. Yell in Urdu from the bushes and then slip out the way you came. Wait for me at the police station.' Wilberforce wouldn't think twice about arresting the boy for murder. He shoved a hand into his pocket and pulled out a couple of coins. 'Get yourself something to eat at Irani's.'

Lightning skittered on the horizon; thunder rumbled.

'Niloufer… Niloufer…' Shiraz shook her friend's shoulder as if trying to wake her.

He crouched next to her and lifted the silk on Niloufer's throat.

She turned her face into his shoulder. 'Sweet Niloufer. She was waiting with the family when I came with Cyrus's ashes. So sweet she was... hugging me, not letting me go. Who could hate her so much?' Her body shook, racked by sobs.

'Shiraz,' he said gently. 'I'm so sorry to ask, but can you please examine her before Inspector Wilberforce gets here?'

She tensed, then dashing away the tears with the back of her hand, looked up and nodded.

Dark half moons under Niloufer's nails, clipped and well shaped, caught his eye as Shiraz flexed the fingers. He couldn't imagine this fashionable woman attending a dinner party with dirty fingernails.

'Soob, rigor mortis hasn't started. Niloufer was killed after the other girl.'

'A little after ten thirty?'

She gave a jerky nod, swallowing a sob.

'Can you remove one of those dark bits under her nail, Shiraz?' He took out an empty matchbox from his pocket, cupping his other hand to shield it from the rain.

Her fingers shook as she complied. The fragments looked to him like leather from a glove – perhaps to protect the murderer's hands from being scratched.

A large diamond sparkled from Niloufer's left ring finger. Little white balls bobbed on the grass blades as the rain began splattering down. Pearls. Even to his untutored eye, they glowed with a deep lustre.

'Soob, it wasn't robbery. He didn't take her jewels. Maybe Niloufer came to the other girl's rescue. She could've heard her cry out.'

It had occurred to him too. 'But the park gate is locked, Shiraz.'

'Oh, so stupid of me.' She pressed her temples with her fingers. 'There is a side entrance to the park opposite the Templetons' back door. Niloufer has a key.'

He slanted the lantern's light on the flattened stalks. 'Where is her reticule?'

'She never carried one. It'll be in her pocket.' A sob escaped her as she patted at the side of Niloufer's skirt. 'Here.' Between her thumb and forefinger dangled a small iron key knotted with a blue ribbon.

He rose to his feet and pocketed the key, his ears picking up the crunch of gravel drawing closer. 'Shiraz, deal with the inspector. I have to check something.'

'What the hell are you two still doing here?' Inspector Wilberforce charged up. 'Tripping over dead bodies! Who in God's name is this one?'

Chapter Five

'How in God's name did you find this body?' Wilberforce demanded.

This was the last straw. First, the bloody Brahmin had sent his men to clomp their clumsy feet in the evidence. Now he was interfering with another dead body. Wilberforce's eye ranged over the victim, snagging on the kneeling woman. She shared the corpse's slight frame and fairer skin. Though not a beauty, the lady's fine eyes had a fire to them. He was about to give her an earful for the hash she'd surely made of the clues when he caught sight of the silk scarf looped around the victim's cut throat and the lacerations on her stomach. His blood fizzed.

'Bloody hell! It's Jack the Ripper.'

Wilberforce's nemesis had followed him from the soupy fog of Whitechapel, across the rough and choppy waters of an unending ocean, through the dusty plains and humid jungles and parched fields of the Deccan to this blistering hellhole of Hyderabad. It was thanks to the Ripper that he'd had to resign from the Metropolitan Police and move to this godforsaken colony in the first place. On the night of the multiple murders in Whitechapel, he and his beat partner, John, had popped into the pub for a pint. If only he hadn't stopped for another one and let John cover for him, they could have nabbed the Ripper. Those Investigative Committee bastards had hinted that John had used him for an alibi. Or perhaps he was John's accomplice? And with his poor partner driven to suicide by the unjust accusations, he knew the actual culprit was still at large. Among the police and the powers that be, blame had been pinned on his conveniently dead partner, and the whole affair swept under the rug to remain a mystery as far as the public were concerned.

'Ah, so you think the Whitechapel killer carried out this murder.' The Brahmin didn't seem surprised.

He hadn't realised he'd spoken aloud. Of course, this smooth native, never a hair out of place, was in London two or so years ago, hanging around at Scotland Yard. He would know about the Ripper. And with the story splashed in all the native newspapers – *the Nizam's guests, the Grand Duke and the Earl of Euston, members of the Hellfire Club, were questioned in the Ripper murders* – every Tom, Dick and Harry here did too. His superiors could do little about these rags, all huddled under the ruler's protection.

'What do you mean, Inspector?' the lady asked in a clipped tone. 'Do you really think the Ripper came here all the way from London to kill my husband's cousin and that other poor girl? Why on earth would an Englishman murder Niloufer?'

Her words rang an alarm, snapping Wilberforce out of his thoughts and slapping the scowl back on his face. If the Ripper turned out to be British, it could scupper their plan to seize control of the City Police. The Nizam's wily courtiers would have a field day bleating that the threat to his subjects came from the British. And he knew which sap would be in the doghouse! Best to shut her up sharpish.

'And who are you?' he demanded.

'Dr Shiraz Daruwalla.'

He eyed her with disapproval. He'd heard rumour of this lady doctor who had joined the city hospital a few months ago. In his book, a woman had no business carrying on in a man's profession, least of all in medicine. Entering strangers' homes at odd hours, being in their bedchambers no less, hobnobbing with all manner of men and even touching their bodies, that was the lot of a doctor. A woman's place was at home with her children, keeping a clean house, putting hot food on the table for her husband. This one, he recalled now, was a widow and childless.

'What exactly was your cousin doing in the park so late at night, madam?'

'Niloufer lives on the other side of the park,' she said coldly. 'Practically next door. She attended a dinner party at her neighbour's house. She must've been walking back.'

'Through the park? Alone? Where is her guard? This is a wealthy neighbourhood, and she's evidently a rich woman.' He pointed to the scattered pearls and the large diamond ring glittering from the victim's finger, half-buried in the wet stalks. 'Why didn't she walk back on the road? Was she meeting someone in the park?'

Her fine eyes narrowed. 'Niloufer was not a loose woman, sir, if that's what you are insinuating.'

Wilberforce stood his ground. It was odd behaviour, and she knew it. Rich native women got up to all kinds of mischief within their cage of four walls, but they couldn't wander alone in the dead of night, and certainly not in a park. Not with the guards posted to watch over them. It struck him, belatedly, that the victim wasn't veiled and neither was the doctor, her scarf all sodden and crumpled on her shoulders.

'Is the victim a Muslim?' He had a vague recollection that the lady doctor belonged to some other religion.

'No, she is a Parsi like me,' she snapped. 'Married to a Muslim.'

'Where is the husband?' he asked, raising his voice over the rumbling thunder.

'Nawab Zulfikar Baig is a nobleman, Inspector,' she said in an icy tone. 'This park is named after him. He owns the houses on this hill and the very ground you are standing on.'

The name didn't ring a bell. Not that Wilberforce had bothered to mug up on the names of the nobs here, most of them ungodly long. His pulse quickened, though. Well, well, well, a local nob, rich enough to travel to London during the Ripper's carnage. He'd give the husband a good working over, but – hang it, he'd need the commissioner's permission.

'Where is this nawab then?'

She glared at him, lips firmly shut.

'Nawab Zulfikar Baig is ill,' the Brahmin said, still crouching by the victim.

'I find it curious the good wife wasn't at her husband's bedside, then.' Soobramania had been nosing around the body all this while, an indignant Wilberforce realised. 'Both of you, step away from the corpse.'

They obeyed, retreating to the gravel path. Wilberforce stepped on the now flattened grass stalks, and squatted by the corpse. The silk scarf he unwound from the victim's neck was long and had a padded middle like the other one – longer than the neckerchief the Ripper had tied on one of his victims. He sniffed. Smelt lemon and blood.

'Is the scarf hers?' If his hunch was correct, it wasn't.

'Umm, Inspector, it is a cummerbund,' the Brahmin said.

The bugger was right, damn it.

'Like the one you natives wear around your waist to hang your knives and swords.'

'And like those you Englishmen wear at dinners and balls,' came the Brahmin's rejoinder, much to his annoyance.

Wilberforce ignored the comment and repeated his question, but the lady did not respond.

'Shiraz, please answer the inspector,' the Brahmin said, to Wilberforce's surprise.

'No,' she said, scowling. She pointed to a gauzy red strip jutting from the corpse's hip. 'That is.'

His heart beat faster. It belonged to the killer. In this small city, it should be a walk in the park to trace the merchant who'd sold the scarf.

'Where was her dinner party?'

The lady doctor had closed her eyes and seemed to be praying, the rainwater streaking down her pale face.

'At the residence of Arthur Templeton, the publisher of *The Jasoos*,' the Brahmin answered, pointing in the direction of the house. 'It seems Mrs Templeton and Mrs Baig were friends.'

Phoebe Templeton friends with a local? Not bloody likely. Wilberforce had downed gin and tonics with her husband at Secunderabad Club often enough for him to know the man was no fool. In his one and a half years of policing here, Wilberforce hadn't met a single native who could be trusted not to stab a fellow in the back; friendship was impossible between the two races and he knew Arthur shared his view wholeheartedly, often mimicking the fawning drawl of the Nizam's courtiers. More likely Mrs Baig had mistaken politeness for friendship.

It struck him that they hadn't answered his initial question, and he repeated it. 'How in God's name did you find this body?'

The Brahmin's explanation about some stunted, grubby urchin being an eyewitness made him burn up with rage.

'For pity's sake, man, why didn't you say so earlier? It didn't occur to you that this urchin could be the killer?'

'It isn't Jack the Ripper then?'

Though the Brahmin's tone was expressionless, Wilberforce knew when he was being mocked. He ignored it and signalled his Anglo-Indian head constable lurking in the gloom.

'Thomas, take three constables and search for this urchin. He is a witness.'

The capable Thomas saluted and left, and the remaining two constables stood at attention on the path.

'What did the boy see?' Wilberforce asked, his eyes noting the position of the body and the fact that she was hidden in the bush. 'Did he describe the killer?'

To his surprise, the Brahmin explained the sequence of events. Had their roles been reversed, Wilberforce wouldn't have been so obliging. He had no intention of sharing the credit for nabbing the Ripper, certainly not with this sodding busybody.

The description of the killer gave him hope. Most was unhelpful, but the height could match the Ripper's described by an eyewitness during that investigation. 'You two leave now, and take your men with you. Constable, escort them to the city gate.'

'Inspector Wilberforce, I suspect the other victim lived nearby,' the Brahmin said. 'She isn't dressed in finery to meet someone. It's more likely she was taken from her house, perhaps when she used the outhouse. Please send the constables to check the servants' quarters on this street.'

Wilberforce was livid. The cheek of the fellow, telling him how to do his job! And his tone said he didn't expect Wilberforce to bother about the poorer victim. Did he know about his days and nights as a constable, patrolling the lanes of Whitechapel during the Ripper's butcheries, looking out for destitute prostitutes, Jewish refugees, Irish hustlers and all the riff-raff of London?

'And, Inspector, get your men to check the entrance in the boundary wall on that side,' the Brahmin added, pointing towards Templeton's house.

'Why didn't you tell me earlier, damn it? The killer will be long gone by now. You can be damned sure I'll be having words with your commissioner.'

Two short whistles sounded.

'The side entrance,' the Brahmin said, shooting forward on the path.

'Not so fast, acting Chief Inspector,' Wilberforce said, springing up. 'Constable, watch them.'

Chapter Six

Seeing Soob take a half step behind the awful English inspector, Shiraz insisted he go. 'I'll be fine,' she said. 'The constable is here.'

As he sprinted away into the pitch-dark, the ashen-faced young Deccani dragged his gaze from Niloufer's body. 'Sir, wait. You have to stay here! Oi—' and he hurried after Soob.

'Don't go, constable,' she called out.

She must not be left alone with Niloufer's body. Their religion would not permit it. For a Parsi, two people had to attend a dead body, and there must be two pallbearers and two priests for the death rites. Any other way just wouldn't do. Niloufer might have converted to Islam to marry, but she was a Parsi through and through. She had still celebrated Parsi festivals, still performed Parsi rituals and had never seen herself as a Muslim. Her spirit would surely want the correct death rituals to be followed scrupulously.

'Constable, please come back.' She felt a presence, as if Niloufer's soul itself was pleading through her.

Still kneeling, she clasped her dear friend's hand and found herself chanting a prayer, as she'd once done with grave fervour every night before going to sleep, a prayer she had cast off after losing Cyrus and their baby. Opaque eyes, their life's bright spark snuffed out, stared back. Something about the glazed calm of Niloufer's expression tugged at her memory. The face of the young girl by the fountain had a similar placid cast. Could the killer have drugged them first before killing them? The idea took root in her mind and refused to go away as she stroked Niloufer's hand, catching the fading warmth of the skin.

A tingling sprang up on the back of her head, the pinpricks spreading like wildfire down her neck, jaw and back. The palpable sense of someone or something watching her.

A twig snapped.

Flesh and blood. She shot to her feet and spun around, heart racing, mouth dry.

The killer. He must have circled back. The sound had come from the undergrowth on the other side of the path.

'Who's there?' Her voice came out in a quaver.

Fat raindrops plunged down, the lamp's flame sputtered.

Please don't go out. Please.

A shadow slid through the darkness of the bushes, a coiling, crooked silhouette that wove its way closer, gravel crackling.

Some instinct buried deep within her welled up, rising to an urgent command.

Run, it said. You can't die like this. But her body only juddered, fixed to the verge. Her heart thudded like it would crack open her chest. She opened her mouth to scream. Nothing came out.

The snap of pebbles drew closer.

'Hakimji, where is the Chief Inspector?' a voice said. It came from behind her.

The shadow stilled.

The lamp snuffed out.

Soob's constable, thank god. Her legs gave way, and she sank to her knees.

'There's someone in those bushes opposite me, constable,' she said in a thin, trembling voice unlike her own.

The constable plunged into the undergrowth, the snap and rustle growing fainter as she gulped in deep breaths.

The wind picked up, and from the corner of her eye she caught a flitting movement. Oh god…

You will not die like this. Get up!

Something pushed her to her feet and drove her forward.

'Constable, quickly,' she yelled, rushing towards it, fingers curled into claws.

Soob's man pounded up behind her. Charcoal dark clumps met her searching gaze. The dark mass had disappeared. Had she imagined it?

The Rohilla constable seemed to think so. He re-lit the lantern under the makeshift canopy of her scarf (rainwater was the culprit, not oil), his glance, half-questioning and half-contemptuous, one that men reserved for hysterical women. *No, I wasn't imagining things*, she wanted to say, but a small part of her wondered.

'Come, Shiraz.' Soob emerged from the gloom, the rain now pummelling his bare head. 'Quickly, before Inspector Wilberforce returns.'

'Did you find the killer?' Should she tell him about the shadow? What if she had imagined it?

'No, but the side entrance – it's a door – was open.'

Then the killer must have fled. Better not tell him about her fears, she decided.

'Soob, we can't leave until two people are with her.' Her explanation of the Parsi custom arrested his steps. He doused the flame, and after instructing the Rohilla to round up the others and escort Shiraz's coachman to Niloufer's house, drew her to a kochia bush.

'Soob, there's an opening in the hedge between Niloufer's house and here,' she whispered, as they waited for the English inspector. 'We can go through there. Her gardener made it in—'

A crunch sounded further ahead, and he tugged her arm, but Shiraz lingered until the lanterns bobbed closer.

'Where are those two? Find—'

Torrential rain tore through the clouds pelting them hard and fast.

Chapter Seven

Wet leaves licked Soob's face and arms as he squinted through sheeting rain at the opening Shiraz had described in the high *Duranta erecta* hedge between Niloufer's garden and the park. He ducked in, dead wood snapping under his boots, the wild sounds of the storm gentling in the thick middle as he re-lit the lamp. Brown twigs and green leaves glowed in the dense web around them, and raindrops twinkled above, fat and pendulous, splattering down when he straightened his head.

'Don't move, Shiraz,' he said over his shoulder. 'I want to see if Niloufer or the killer came through here.'

But there were no threads or scraps of material stuck to the sides of the tunnel: the gardener had done too good a job at smoothing the wood so that neither sleeve nor hair would snag.

His neck prickled. A sound. A muffled sneeze? He eyed the other end, hidden in the deep vale of darkness.

'Soob—' Shiraz stopped as he raised a finger to his lips. The sound came again, a sniff. He lunged forward, hurtling through the tunnel, slamming into a muscular body, driving it back and out the other side. Before the intruder had time to react, Soob had the man flipped and pinned, lying face down in the mud.

'Soob, are you all right?' Shiraz stepped out armed with a stick she must have managed to pry from the hedge.

'Hakimji,' the man grunted.

The light fell on his face.

'Soob, it's Sobha Singh. Niloufer's head guard.'

The man's turban sat crookedly on his head as he struggled up, a dagger and a knife thankfully snug in his cummerbund, his thick moustache and beard splayed like a black mask on his cheeks.

'It wasn't a fair fight,' Soob said in Urdu, helping him up.

The Sikh's shrewd eyes in a weathered face gleamed with approval at Soob as they huddled inside the opening. 'You did that very well, sahib.'

Soob gave a nod. 'Did anybody else come through here apart from us?'

'No, sahib. I've been watching since the whistles and noise in the park.'

'Did Mrs Baig go this way to the dinner?'

The Sikh shook his head. 'I escorted the begum on the road when the timekeeper beat the drum seven times.' He explained that he'd returned to his post and waited for Niloufer's summons, but when it didn't come, her mother had sent him there and the Templeton guard said she'd left with a lantern a few minutes before, at half past ten.

'Did the park guard see her?' Soob asked.

Sobha Singh scowled. 'Bastard was asleep. We looked everywhere: on the road, the lakeside, everywhere.'

'What about the park?' Soob asked, cursing the man for ignoring such an obvious location.

'No, sir.'

'Why not?' Soob would have tried there first.

'The begum's mother said she would not enter the park at night.'

Soob glanced at Shiraz, eyebrows raised.

'Niloufer promised not to,' Shiraz said in a strained voice. 'You see, she was planning a gothic garden in her husband's palace and wanted to see the Champa grove silhouette in the moonlight. She entered it one night last week and the park guard saw her lantern and raised an alarm. There was a bit of a to-do about it in our community. Aunt Gul was furious and made her promise never to do that again. Niloufer never breaks... broke a promise.' Her lips wobbled.

But she had. Ram Rahim had heard the lantern break inside the park and they had seen the broken glass near Niloufer's body. The killer had not attacked her in the lane.

'Who knows about this entrance?' Soob asked.

'Only the gardener, us guards and the begum's family, sahib. It was made ten days ago. We were commanded to keep it a secret and we have. I can vouch for my younger brothers, the other two guards.'

'Then why is there no screen on the other side?' The man-sized hole would be visible to all and sundry in the daylight.

33

'But there is, Soob,' Shiraz said.

'Wait here.' He returned to the park side, and stepped out, oblivious to the rainwater gushing down his face and arms. Grasping a part of the hedge, he tugged. Not here. He did it again to the left of the opening. A section came away. Twigs tied together, cleverly made to merge with the living hedge, and light enough for a petite woman like Niloufer to lift.

Brushing the water from his eyes, he returned to them. 'Would Niloufer have set the screen to one side and forgotten about it?'

'I don't think so. Niloufer told me she made sure to put it back each time. Could it be the killer, Soob?' Shiraz said in English.

'Have you found the begum, hakimji?' The guard's shrewd gaze took in Shiraz's woebegone expression as she gave a nod, and his face tightened. 'What has happened to her?'

'Was she expecting to be harmed?' Soob asked.

The man did not meet his gaze.

'Sobha Singhji, you can speak freely to the Chief Inspector.' Her teeth chattered, more from shock, Soob thought, than the cold. No need for her to remain in the rain. He opened his mouth to tell her so, but the guard interjected.

'The begum told me to hire an extra man two days ago.'

'Niloufer met her two stepsons for the first time at lunch that day,' Shiraz said in English. 'Surely they—'

The hard drum of the rain snatched away her words. There was no point in staying here and getting wetter. Taking the whistle from his belt, Soob handed it to the guard.

'My men are in the stables. I'll have them informed to assist you if they hear the whistle.'

He knew, though, that the killer was probably long gone.

Chapter Eight

A keening cry came from the sitting room. Soob stood in the sconce-lit corridor, steeling himself to face a bereaved mother. Though it was Inspector Wilberforce's task to officially break the news to Niloufer's mother, Soob could not let her hear it that way. The lady had asked for Soob, and had trusted him to find her daughter alive and unharmed.

Despite all the times he had spoken to victims' families in his ten years as an Imperial Criminal Investigation Department officer, the ferocity of their grief never became easier to face. Nor would he ever rest easy with the questions he must ask, forcing them to relive their torment. He always tried – unsuccessfully though – to couch his questions so that the family did not hear in them blame for not having taken better care of a daughter, a sister, a parent or son.

Shiraz came out and beckoned to him. Taking a deep breath, he strode to the sitting room. It was furnished in hues of pink: a rose glass chandelier lit up the pink and cream upholstery, delicate watercolours of wildflowers and ferns dotted two walls, and opposite the door, blush-coloured curtains draped a bank of shuttered French windows, all evoking a restful elegance. Finally, Soob forced himself to look at the grieving mother.

She lay crookedly on an embroidered chaise longue, her gaze fixed on the stucco ceiling. It was like seeing a flesh and blood ghost of Niloufer. The same eyes, the same high cheekbones. Mrs Jamasjee wore the muted colours of a Parsi widow: a long full-sleeved white blouse and a beige sari with one end covering grey hair pinned in a bun. Niloufer's father, a famous lawyer, had passed away three years ago. That's when Cyrus had first mentioned the family to him.

As he approached, uttering condolences that he knew were trite and inadequate, her fingers gripped Shiraz's hand, the mottled skin stretching tight over the knuckle. Tremors wobbled through Shiraz's frame; he wished to have spared her this, but he knew she wouldn't have it any other way.

'Thank you for coming, Chief Inspector.' Her English came in a thin tone as she struggled up, pressing veined wrists on the stiff silk. 'Please be seated.'

He chose a wooden chair, not wanting to ruin the silk upholstered ones with his rain-soaked khaki pants.

'How did my Niloufer die?' The stony gleam in the lady's eyes demanded the truth.

Shiraz swallowed hard and looked away.

He'd always been honest with a victim's loved ones. They yearned for the truth and deserved to be told, no matter how gruesome the death. Not knowing was worse for them. A factual account coming from him would be vastly preferable to reading the sensationalised stories in tomorrow's newspapers.

He told her in a gentle tone.

She pressed her fists to her eyes, shoulders sagging, and in the silence, rain pounded like grit flung at the glass.

'Niloufer didn't suffer, Aunt Gul.' Shiraz's voice cracked. 'She was drugged, she didn't feel anything.'

Mrs Jamasjee turned to him, a question in her dry eyes. She had not been able to shed a tear, he realised.

He gave a nod. Who was he to deny a mother this crumb of comfort? Shiraz could well be right, and if confirmed, it would be another deviation from the Ripper's method.

Her shoulders stiffened. 'What do you need to know to find my daughter's murderer, Chief Inspector?' she asked, folding her hands into a tight fist.

This hard tone he'd heard before in the voices of other fathers and mothers, a tone that carried the implacable resolve to see their child's murderer hunted down and brought to justice.

He confirmed with her Niloufer's movements that day: she spent the afternoon reading, pottered in the garden at teatime when her husband's note was delivered. The nawab had informed her that he had food poisoning and had urged her to carry on without him. Niloufer had complied reluctantly and had been expected back by ten thirty. She hadn't taken a reticule or a lantern.

'The nawab doesn't live here?' he asked, thinking it highly irregular for a nawab to countenance his bride living in a separate house.

'No.'

'Nawab Zulfikar lives in the palace on this hilltop,' Shiraz explained.

Odder still was the fact that the nobleman's soldiers didn't seem to be combing the hillside for their mistress. He asked when the lady had sent word to him.

To his question, she looked away, her veined hands plucking nervously at a thread on an embroidered cushion.

'Did you send word?' he probed in a mild tone.

She raised her chin and shook her head. 'Why did I insist on my Niloufer's attending the dinner? She didn't want to go. But Mrs Templeton has been very kind to her – came round for coffee twice and asked Niloufer over. This was the first time they'd invited her to dinner. New friends would be good for my Niloufer, I thought. Our community has taken her marriage badly. They want to excommunicate my Niloufer. Oh god! Why did she have to meet that accursed man?' The words tumbled out as if she'd repeated them to herself many times in the past couple of hours.

'Have they been married long?'

'One month and two days,' she said bitterly. 'They met at the Resident's ball last month and he pursued her.' *Shamelessly*, her tone said. 'The nawab is so much older than my Niloufer. He is fifty-four and a widower.'

The large age gap didn't surprise Soob. This need to find and cherish innocence was not uncommon among wealthy and powerful older men, here and in other parts of the world. The more jaded they were, the more they craved youth and spontaneity. More often than not, though, they ended up crushing that young spirit. Usually it was the parents who forced their young daughters into the marriage. Not in this case, though. Why, Soob wondered, had the beautiful and rich Niloufer braved the anger of the Parsi community for a Muslim man old enough to be her grandfather, when she could have had her pick of suitors?

'I pleaded with her not to take such a hasty step,' Niloufer's mother carried on, as if she'd divined his thoughts. 'Her three older brothers tried to reason with her, but Niloufer wouldn't listen. That daughter of mine never does. Within a week of their meeting, they were married.'

The Sikh guard had stated that Niloufer had hired extra guards after meeting her stepsons. On enquiring about the nawab's children, the lady said there were two sons in their thirties. 'The elder one is especially furious about the marriage,' she added. 'Was it him, Ali Baig? These nawabs do all kinds of things and get away with it. That's why I asked for you, Chief Inspector. You are Cyrus's friend and ours, and you will see to it that justice is done.' She drew out a handkerchief tucked into her sleeve and began pulling at it.

The stepsons weren't the only suspects, he thought. There was one more.

'What were your daughter's relations with her husband, Mrs Jamasjee?' he asked. 'Had they quarrelled?'

She would have liked to say yes, her expression said, but the facts were against her. 'No, the nawab treated her like a treasure.'

'Then why didn't Niloufer live with him in the palace?' he asked, still puzzled.

She stiffened. 'Understand this, Chief Inspector. My only daughter will not be caged in a dingy room with no windows. Harems are worse than prisons. I told the nawab it wouldn't do at all when he came to ask my permission to marry Niloufer.'

Her determination to get her own way seemed to be something she'd passed on to her daughter. He asked, 'What did he say?'

'What could he say?' she said, back straight, lips clamped in a tight line. 'He had to agree. But he insisted we live here, in one of his houses. I had to shift from my home in Secunderabad cantonment.'

Soob asked about the other aspect that had puzzled him. 'When your daughter visited Mrs Templeton, did she take a carriage or did she cut across through the park?'

'She walked. Carriages and palanquins made my Niloufer feel like a caged pigeon. My Niloufer loved the park. Every morning and evening she was there, and sometimes during the day when she was upset or annoyed. That's where she met Mrs Templeton for the first time and found a friend in her – both of them were plant-mad. I expected them to send her home in their carriage or, at the very least, provide an escort. I should have sent Sobha Singh earlier. How could they be so callous, Shiraz?'

Eyes ablaze, Shiraz opened her mouth to say something, then shut it again.

The Templetons' behaviour had raised his ire too, but he banked it for now and asked about the hedge opening. 'Who knows about it?'

'The guards and us.'

'Her husband?'

'Yes, but he didn't like it.'

'And his family?'

Her troubled gaze met his. 'I don't know,' she said, looking upset. 'I shouldn't have let her make that entrance. But nobody could say no to Niloufer. Gardening and plants, that's all she cared about. She never listens to anyone.'

'Mrs Jamasjee, you mentioned Niloufer walked in the park when she was upset,' Soob said, noting the chilling slip between the tenses. 'Could she have done that last night? Worried about her husband's health?'

'It was only food poisoning,' she said. 'He wasn't on his deathbed. And she promised me she wouldn't enter the park at night. My Niloufer never breaks a promise.'

'But she was found in the park, Mrs Jamasjee,' he said gently. 'Is that why your guards didn't search there?'

She squeezed her eyes shut. They were still dry, he noted. 'Oh god, they could have saved her from the killer. It is my fault.'

He went over to the sideboard, picked up a silver jug and poured her a glass of water. With trembling hands she raised it to her lips, his own cupping hers to steady it. Shiraz made to take over but he shook his head.

Then, setting the glass on a shell coaster, he took out the park key from his pocket. 'Is this Niloufer's?'

She glanced at it dully and nodded.

'Thank you, Mrs Jamasjee,' he said, rising to his feet. 'I'm deeply sorry for your loss. If you can think of anything else, please tell Shiraz, or send for me.'

Shiraz followed him to the corridor. 'You're hurt, Soob.'

He glanced down at the red patches on his shirt. 'Just a scrape.'

'Let me bandage it at least.'

'I'll see to it later. You should change out of those wet clothes. You'll catch a cold.'

'Will you come tomorrow and tell me what you've found out?'

'I will,' he said, pressing her hand. 'Try to rest.'

In the portico, the rain having petered out, Soob waited for the attendant to fetch a constable from the stables, filling his lungs with the fresh scent of washed leaves. What could have drawn Niloufer into the park so late at night? Not a cry from the young girl – she'd been killed around half past nine or so when Niloufer was still at the dinner. Perhaps Niloufer had been upset about the nawab. It might have driven the promise out of her mind. Soob decided to speak to the Templetons about their guest's mood at the dinner. But first, he had to find the other victim's family who, his instincts said, surely worked in one of these mansions. Niloufer had the might of the Residency Police tracking her movements; the other girl had nobody.

Chapter Nine

Having issued the order to his men to remain hidden in the stables, Soob hurried to Niloufer's gate to warn the guard. 'Tell the Residency Police we've left.' His eye traced the conical foliage of the asoka trees on the other side of the asphalt road, tapering high into the sky. 'Is the lake behind those trees?'

'Yes, huzoor.' The Sikh was a younger version of Sobha Singh, sporting a similar soft wispy beard.

It felt significant to Soob that the bodies had been left in a park where they would undoubtedly be found in the morning, when they could have lain unnoticed for days in the water meadow, hidden by tall rushes.

'Thomas, find the City Police Chief Inspector and his men,' Wilberforce shouted from the park. 'I'm going to the victim's house. It's next door, the lady doctor said.'

The whistles hurried Soob's steps across the asphalt to a tree trunk. He ducked behind it as Wilberforce rode up, followed by three constables on foot, one heading for Niloufer's house and the other two moving in his direction.

He didn't need a lantern. Since Rohini's death, night had drawn him often to the Koovam River in Madras, to tramp through hues of black and grey, the question playing over and over in his head: why hadn't he rushed back from London when Rohini's health had been so critical? Now, as he dodged from one tree trunk to the next, shielded by the dark, guilt ate at him. He made his way down the gentle slope to an alley that joined the back lane. From there he proceeded up again.

Thatched roofs rose to his left, the outhouse and the servants' quarters, behind boundary walls low enough for the killer to vault over and grab someone. He crept on in a crouch, hugging the wall, slush muffling his boots, the air heavy with the green tea scent of reeds and fishbone water fern. Tall rushes swayed on the other side and hid the lake, the only sounds here the shush of the gentle drizzle and the cries of the bullfrogs.

The first four doors were bolted from inside, and all was dark beneath the thatched roofs. It was the same with the Templetons' house. Hooves and boots clattered in the alley by the park and Soob crossed over to the lake side, continuing in the shadow of the trees. A lamp bobbed, coming towards him. A Residency Police constable sent to check with the servants. Soob devoutly hoped that the constable had been despatched before Wilberforce's men had started looking for him.

'Constable.' He stepped into the man's path. 'Is anyone missing from the servants' quarters of these homes? I'm helping Inspector Wilberforce with the investigation.'

The middle-aged Deccani eyed his khaki shirt and pants, the whistle raised to his lips.

More whistles sounded from the park. The constable's eyes skittered there.

'Quick. Is anyone missing from the servants' quarters?'

Something in his voice and steady gaze must have persuaded the man of his authority.

'No, sir. All the back doors are locked and everyone is asleep. The two houses near the palace are empty.'

'Wake them up, constable, starting from the house next to the Templetons'.'

The man saluted, and Soob strode on. Near the top, a stifled sob came from one of the empty houses. On the other side of the chest-high wall, a small shadow, a child most likely, huddled against the mud wall of the outhouse. Next to it was the black outline of a hut.

He pushed the back door, but it didn't budge. He pressed harder, and it swung open. Stuck, not locked. No creak, though. He ran his fingers over the hinge, and they came away sticky with oil. The bungalow, dark behind a large lawn, did not look inhabited.

The sob came again. He stopped a few feet away, wishing he had a lamp to reassure the child that he wasn't a monster.

'Little one, I am a policeman. I won't hurt you.' He spoke in a calm voice, the one he used with frightened animals. His boot sank into the slop of the toilet. Taking a step to the side, he squatted on his haunches so as not to loom. He made out two thick pigtails. It was a girl, not much older than his nephew Natraja.

She gave him a terrified glance, the whites of her eyes showing, and curled herself up, her palms shielding her head as if she had done this many times. If he were ever to lay his hands on whoever had harmed this child...

'I won't hurt you, little one. I can help. Is your sister missing?'

She stilled.

'Did she come to use the outhouse?'

'How did you know?' A whisper.

'What was your sister wearing?'

She hid her face again in her hands.

'Was it a half sari, light brown colour?'

She shrank back.

Soob leaned back on his haunches, ignoring a sharp twinge from his injury. 'What's your name?'

The child peeped between her fingers, but didn't speak.

A bullfrog croaked from the lake, giving him an idea. Would it work? It had with Natraja. Couldn't hurt to try.

'That's an owl's hoot,' he said.

The child stiffened.

The croak came again.

'Yes, definitely an owl.'

'Frog,' she whispered.

'No, it's an owl.'

'No, no, a frog,' she said, removing her hands from her face. 'My pet frog makes that sound.'

'Oh, then you should know. That's very clever of you. What's your frog's name?'

'Hanuman.'

'And what does Hanuman call you?'

'Shanti.'

'And your sister?'

'He doesn't speak to Mallu. She's afraid of him.'

'But you aren't, are you, Shanti?'

'Of course not. Hanuman is a very sweet frog.'

'I'm sure he is, Shanti,' he smiled. 'My nephew is your age. He loves frogs.'

43

She mumbled something.

Shouts and whistles came from further down the hill. He was running out of time, but this child couldn't be rushed.

'What did you say?'

'Pet frog, does he have one?' she whispered.

'No, but I'm sure he'd love to see yours. But first, shall we find Mallu?'

A sniffle and a nod.

'Tell me what happened.'

The story tumbled out. Mallu had been the last to use the toilet at her usual time of half past nine when the timekeeper beat the drums. Shanti had woken up and found her sister missing, so she'd come out to look for her. Mallu was indeed in a light brown half-sari – the victim by the fountain. Soob expelled a breath.

'Is the back door bolted at night?'

'Yes,' she whispered.

'But it was open when I came,' he said. 'Tell me, Shanti, does your back door creak?'

'Yes.'

'Your father oils the hinge?'

She shook her head.

Mallu had not been picked by chance. The killer had been watching her.

'Whose house is this?'

Shanti explained that an English family lived here, but they had gone away, and the other servants had left too. Only her father, a gardener, remained to look after the plants for Nawab Baig.

Glassy eyes shone from the toilet door. Soob waved his hand, and the creature scuttled away. An empty bottle tipped over and rolled towards him. He picked it up and sniffed. Arrack. That would be why Shanti hadn't woken her father. A loud snore came from the hut.

'Shanti, you are a very brave girl. Fetch your mother and bring a lantern.' He waited till she shot into the hut, and then rose to his feet.

After a few minutes, a woman shuffled out, a lantern quivering from her fingers. Her careworn face, a black eye and the welts on her arms told a familiar story of drunken rages and beatings. Though this family lived in better conditions than slum dwellers, their isolation posed a real danger for the mother and the children. The law saw them as the man's property. In a slum, there was at least the possibility of a kind neighbour intervening to stop the beatings. Not here. Since a man could legally do what he liked with his property, the police would never intervene to protect a woman or her children.

Taking the lantern from her, he set it down and identified himself. He was sure the dead girl was Mallu, and now, in a gentle tone, he told her about her daughter.

She stared back as if she didn't understand. Suddenly, she crumpled. He caught her shoulders and lowered her gently. A thin wail pulled out of her and she beat her fists on her chest. More shadows emerged from the hut, two children and an old lady.

The snores paused then resumed at a raucous pitch.

He picked up the lantern and strode into the small room smelling of damp, alcohol and sweat. A thickset man lay sprawled by a dung-smeared wall. Seizing hold of a leg, Soob dragged him out, letting his head bounce on the uneven floor and bang on the brick doorstep. He didn't want to subject Shanti or the mother to the task of identifying Mallu. It would have to be the father. He worked on the man, hauling him to his knees and shoving his head in the pail a good few times until his cries grew strident.

'Sir, what's all this noise? What happened?' the constable asked from the doorway.

More boots thudded his way, coming from the park end. Soob bit out a brief explanation and slipped out into the lane.

'Who's that?' a voice yelled. 'Oi, stop.'

Soob sprinted to the boundary wall of the Baig palace.

Chapter Ten

Wilberforce took a deep swig of whisky, the fiery warmth burrowing into his stomach, blunting his rage at how the victim's mother had treated him. His fingers tightened on the leather armrest. As if it were his fault her wayward daughter hadn't been taught better morals. To top it all off, the blooming Brahmin had stuck his oar in again, getting there first and nattering to her about Lord alone knew what else. His men were out combing the streets for him and his ragbag of mercenaries, a waste of time when they should be looking for the killer.

Ignoring Arthur Templeton's glance at his muddy uniform and boots, he cracked his back and stretched out his legs on the fancy carpet. Phoebe was rich enough to afford a dozen armchairs and silk thingummies. It was no skin off his nose if a few more got ruined.

'What a godawful night! I wish we'd never laid eyes on that dratted woman.' Arthur poured himself a generous shot, emptying the crystal decanter on the sideboard, and tipped it down in one gulp.

His third in the past ten minutes. Still, a man who has been informed that his dinner guest was murdered outside his house bloody well deserved a drink.

'Why didn't you send Mrs Baig home in a carriage?' Wilberforce asked.

'You think I didn't suggest it? I should've insisted.' Arthur stared gloomily at his empty glass.

'Your other guests, who were they? When did they leave?'

'General Rowbottom, Colonel Hancock, Fraser and Smith. They left with their wives around ten fifteen.'

Wilberforce knew them. They could be dismissed as suspects, but not because of their good names – in his book, the more respectable a man was, the higher he ranked as a probable Jack the Ripper. But the timing absolved them: they couldn't have made it back from their houses in time to kill the victims. The Brahmin's urchin had seen Mrs Baig murdered at ten forty or thereabouts. With her body that much stiffer than the rich victim, the other girl must have been killed earlier. He'd get his constables to confirm their alibis.

'Tell me more about Mrs Baig,' Wilberforce said. 'Where is the husband? How did he let her out of the harem? Or did she do a bunk?'

In the seventeen months he had been here, he'd seen all kinds of devilry from the natives — and from his lot too, if he were honest. It wouldn't surprise him if the husband were in on it.

'Baig married her last month,' Arthur said. 'He was supposed to come but fell ill. Have you met him? A suave and wily chap. Some relation to the former prime minister, I believe.'

'He lives where?'

'In a massive pile of brick and marble at the top of this hill. Owns all the houses here, mine included, and keeps a palace in the city. One of the wealthiest landlords in the Deccan.'

'No room in the palace for the new wife, I suppose!'

Arthur opened the cabinet and took out another decanter filled to the brim. He poured a generous shot, and returned to his chair.

'Phoebe wouldn't tell me,' he said, taking a gulp. 'The sons, I suspect, opposed the marriage. They are much older than Niloufer — Mrs Baig. Didn't want their inheritance to be frittered away on a young bride. Reminds me of when my old man got involved with a Russian countess. I hired a private detective to trace her family, and the father turned out to be a fishmonger from Birmingham. Pater was furious with me and packed me off to the colonies. The best thing he ever did for me.'

From the way he spoke, you'd think Arthur came from royalty. Not bloody likely. Wilberforce's enquiries with friends at the Metropolitan Police had dug up a silk merchant of middling means for a father. No doubt, though, Arthur had done very well for himself. Marriage to an oil heiress and now cosying up to the Nizam's old tutor, a very powerful man and rumoured to be the moneybags behind Arthur's newspaper.

'Who are these stepsons?' They sounded promising suspects.

'Ali and Imran. Ali Baig is friends with the Grand Duke and the Earl, the Nizam's guests.'

Oho, so the Baigs moved in very high circles… like the Ripper. The blooming higher-ups would nag him to solve Mrs Baig's murder quickly, not what he was looking forward to. Ali Baig's name sounded familiar. He frowned and ran a finger along the rim of his glass.

'I find it peculiar that the nawab doesn't mind his bride swanning about with strange men,' he said.

'She is a Parsi, not a Muslim. They're fire worshippers from Persia. Fled with their sacred fire when the Muslim invaders toppled the Sassanians sometime in the tenth century and some sailed here to the Bombay coast.'

There goes the club bore again, Wilberforce thought, eyeing the pristine books behind the glass doors of the bookcases ranged along two walls. He'd bet Arthur had never opened most of them. Probably read one book and mugged up useless tidbits. Arthur was notorious in the club for doing that.

'Never mind about that. Don't Parsis have harems?'

'No.' Arthur leaned forward. 'Can you make it go away?' He jingled the coins in his pocket.

Wilberforce eyed him coldly. In his entire career as a policeman, he had never taken money to look the other way in a murder case. For other things, maybe, but not for murder.

'Murders don't go away, Arthur. But you have nothing to fear. It was simply an unfortunate coincidence that you were the last to see her.'

'What do you mean?' Panic flashed in his eyes. 'The guard saw her at the gate. I said goodbye in the foyer.' He had started to slur his words.

Wilberforce's instincts flared up. Templeton was too nervy by half, considering it was the murder of a native. An uncomfortable thought wriggled in. Arthur had been in London in 1888 and 1889 when the Ripper went on his rampage. He pushed down the thought.

'No need to get defensive, Arthur,' he said, shooting a thoughtful glance at his red-faced host. 'She was a beauty, though.'

'Didn't notice her looks,' Arthur mumbled.

Patently untrue. Perhaps Arthur had made a play for the woman and been fobbed off. Everyone knew he had a glad eye and indulged it when Phoebe wasn't looking. That could be why he was nervous.

'I have my beauty in the brothel, the divine Chandini,' Arthur added, glaring at him.

That wouldn't preclude him making a pass at Niloufer, however. 'Sure one of your guests didn't drop her home?'

'Left after them.'

'How much after?'

Arthur blinked and frowned.

'Half an hour?'

'No, no… ten minutes, tops. Chatting with Phoebe.'

They had the whole dinner to talk, yet women always seemed to find something urgent to discuss during their goodbyes. Clara, his wife, did that. Drove him mad.

'Why didn't you see her off at the gate?'

Arthur stiffened. 'Had to finish an article.' He tottered to his feet and over to the sideboard, and with a shaking hand poured himself a glass of water from an enamel jug. Gulped it down in one.

Wilberforce stretched out his leg, his boot slicking a black mark on the white marble fireplace surround. 'Did you?'

'Did I what?'

'Finish it?'

'What?'

Wilberforce eyed him sharply. 'Another girl was murdered in the park. A poor one.'

Relief washed across Arthur's face. 'Oh, Nilouf… Mrs Baig wasn't the target then. Who was it?'

'We don't know. One of your servants isn't missing a wife or a daughter, I suppose?'

'Think not. They'd be wailing and beating their chests by now. Any suspects?'

Normally he wouldn't be cagey about a native's murder, but his policeman's instincts told him to keep mum. 'We're still investigating. I have to speak to Phoebe. Is she asleep?'

'No need to wake her now. I'll tell her in the morning.'

The shutters rattled in the wind. Should he insist on seeing her? What if the victim was meeting someone in the park and had confided in Phoebe? 'Was the Baig woman Phoebe's friend?'

'No, no, not a friend. Just a neighbour. Phoebe thought it would be a nice gesture to invite her and the nawab to a dinner party.'

Wilberforce's shoulders relaxed. That was all right then. Mrs Baig, being a native, had misinterpreted Phoebe's politeness for something more. But if they were mere acquaintances, why would Mrs Baig stay on to chat? Arthur's nervousness also did not strike the right note seeing how he was usually so full of himself.

Ali Baig! Wilberforce slammed his glass on the coffee table. His memory had been worrying away at why the name sounded familiar. Now it came to him. Ali Baig, a student at London University, a Hellfire Club member, and a suspect in the Ripper murders. Crammed with Irish and British toffs, the club was notorious for its bloody rituals and initiation rites. Raping, mutilating and murdering young women. Sick bastards all. The current version, they claimed, was tamer, but in Wilberforce's book, it was still a blooming shop of horrors.

'Didn't Ali Baig study in London?'

'Maybe…'

Wilberforce shot to his feet, heart thudding, mouth dry. He had found the Ripper.

Chapter Eleven

Blazing torches at the palace gate and the boundary wall illuminated three dozen Sikh mercenary riders armed with muskets. A few pairs of shrewd eyes in battle-marked faces flitted between Soob and the yells from the back lane. They wouldn't turn him in; not much love lost between them and the police.

He eyed their uniforms and his pulse quickened. The high nobles here had a colour assigned to their house by the Nizam to be displayed on the banners and clothes of their soldiers, servants and slaves. The uniform's burgundy hue matched the cummerbund knotted around Mallu's throat.

On the other side of the filigreed iron gate, a soberly dressed man around his own age of thirty-two was speaking to a heavily armed chieftain. Seeing Soob, the man gave a quick bow.

'I know why you are here, Chief Inspector. I was expecting you. The head of my security force has told me about the murder of my father's second wife.' Worried eyes took in the bloodstained shirt. 'I am Imran Baig, the younger son of Nawab Zulfikar Baig.'

Soob had realised it was going to be difficult to catch the stepsons off guard, especially with the commotion at the park. It wouldn't have hurt for things to go his way for once, though.

Imran Baig was a pleasant change from the hirsute, gaudily clad young nobles he'd encountered before. With clean-shaven and regular features, Niloufer's younger stepson had the air of a sober and reliable treasury official. He even dressed like one, in a dark angharkha and slim-cut pyjamas, although his shoes, long-lipped and in maroon leather, had seen better days, with scuff marks on the back and tips. The only sour note came from the rose attar scent billowing from the nobleman.

'Excuse me, Chief Inspector.' Imran Baig turned to the chieftain. 'Tell the doctor my father has collapsed. He must accompany you immediately.'

The chieftain saluted and rode away with a dozen horsemen, muskets and swords jostling against their saddles.

Soob's ears picked up the sound of riders coming up the hill.

'Please excuse the interruption, Chief Inspector,' Imran said smoothly. 'We found out about her death some fifteen minutes ago. The valet informed my esteemed father, who unfortunately collapsed. I was furious with the man, but what to do? He is fiercely loyal to my father.'

'Your father has been home the whole evening?'

'Yes, I sat with him for a while. The prawns at lunch didn't agree with him. He asked me to send a note to his new wife asking her to go on alone to their dinner engagement.'

The resonant timbre of Inspector Wilberforce's bark, carrying from lower down the hill, hurried Soob into the driveway. A green tunnel of leafy boughs arched overhead, the gravel path lit by a dozen oil lamps strapped to iron posts.

Imran Baig followed, looking puzzled at his haste.

'You were with your father the whole evening?' Soob asked, stepping into a pool of shadows, away from the blaze of the torches.

'Well, I left him briefly around nine and had my dinner.'

The alibi could be confirmed once Head Constable Muhammad found someone working for the Baigs among his relatives employed as cooks, maids, footmen, soldiers and chamberlains in the homes of nobles, courtiers and high officials.

Imran Baig stopped under an oil lamp and observed him with clinical detachment. 'Am I a suspect, Chief Inspector?'

'Should you be?'

'Chief Inspector, my eye!' Wilberforce's voice bellowed from the gate. '*Acting*, that's what he is. That blooming Brahmin has no authority here. Let me in.'

Imran Baig turned back to the gate. 'Who is that man?'

'Mr Baig, why do you think you are a suspect?' Soob resumed his questioning, ignoring Wilberforce's remonstrations.

The nobleman hesitated, his eyes flitting to the gate where the mercenaries were stolidly lined up.

'I'm going to be frank with you, Chief Inspector,' Imran said as they walked. 'We lost our mother five years ago and my father didn't marry again until now. Neither my brother nor I approved of his marriage to such a young girl, and a Parsi too. But nobody should have to die in such a ghastly way. I wouldn't wish it on my worst enemy.'

'So you know how she died.'

'She was attacked, I understand.'

As they passed under a lamp, ignoring Wilberforce's shout, he described the wounds.

Imran's face lost colour. 'What a terrible way to die. My poor father. Thank god he doesn't know the details. It'd finish him off. He was besotted with her.'

Muslim noblemen usually had many wives. In fact, as Shiraz had once remarked, they seemed to collect women like horses, and treated their horses better than their women. So why was this man surprised by his father's second marriage?

'Mr Baig, did the marriage shock you?'

'My esteemed brother perhaps, but not me. It surprised me, being so sudden. I didn't know what to think. Whether his new wife was after his...' His voice trailed off.

'Money.'

Imran inclined his head.

The tinkling sound of a fountain grew louder, drowning Wilberforce's now faint protests.

'And your brother? Why was he shocked? He didn't approve?'

'It's not my place to convey my esteemed brother's sentiments, Chief Inspector.'

Such deference, Soob thought, was ironic in the context of the Deccan's bloody history, where it wasn't uncommon for a brother to kill a brother when it came to claiming power and riches. In fact, scarcely two decades ago, the present Nizam's uncle had mounted a failed insurrection against his own elder brother.

'Where is your brother now?'

'At the Resident's ball in honour of his friends, the Earl of Euston and a Grand Duke of Russia.' Imran's tone was colourless.

'You didn't go?'

'I'm not important enough to be invited – not that I enjoy social engagements, or gambling for that matter. In truth, I'd rather be catching up on new ways to improve our estates' yields. Our lands begin at the edge of the Residency.'

This nobleman was a definite oddity: the social slur hadn't bothered him, and he appeared not to be interested in his kind's usual hedonistic pursuits of dinners, balls, nautch girls, races and cockfights.

Palm fronds rustled above, showering them with raindrops as they turned the corner. The wet bandage lay heavy on Soob's ribs.

'The estates will come to your brother, won't they?'

'Yes, but my esteemed brother finds such matters tedious. So I administer them.'

'Is that why you live here and not in the city, to be closer to your lands?'

'Why do we deliberately subject ourselves to British laws, you mean? It can't be helped. My great-grandfather was told by a Sufi saint to build a house on this hillock. So here we are.'

They had reached the fountain in the forecourt. The palace, a grand marble edifice, rose up ahead, its Palladian pillars lit by torches, lending an air of classical grandeur.

Imran cleared his throat as they mounted a dozen wet steps. 'The guards said another girl was also murdered, Chief Inspector? Who is she?'

He stopped under a semi-circular arch with stuccoplaster of lime. Beyond, a burly doorman in a burgundy turban stood guard to one side of a carved teak door.

'Mallu lives two houses away, and her father works for your family. Do you know her?'

'Of course not. So that's why you suspect us! It's ridiculous, Chief Inspector. I can see why you think we have a motive with our step-mother, but not this girl. My servants will vouch for me; that is, if you think their word is acceptable.'

Clearly Imran Baig was intelligent enough to understand that an alibi provided by those whose fathers and forefathers had served his family would carry little weight.

A brougham bowled towards them, its gold-edged wheels tossing and crunching the wet gravel.

'My esteemed elder brother has arrived.'

Ali Baig vaulted down without waiting for the footstool. In skin-tight black pantaloons, a silver-spangled frock coat with a matching cummerbund, and buckled shoes studded with diamonds, Niloufer's elder stepson could not have been more different from the quiet and unassuming Imran.

'Who are you?' Ali demanded, bounding up the steps.

He frowned on seeing Soob's shirtfront, and at Imran's introduction, panic flashed in his eyes. 'I don't need your help. Get out.'

Soob examined him with a narrowed gaze. What help did he fear from the police?

'If I may speak, esteemed brother, the Chief Inspector has brought bad news. Our stepmother is dead.'

Ali stiffened, then a sneer appeared on his lips. 'What was it? Syphilis?'

Imran drew a sharp breath.

'Kindly tell me where you were this evening,' Soob said in a grim tone.

'None of your business,' Ali snapped.

'Esteemed older brother, if I may speak, she was murdered,' Imran hurriedly interjected.

'That woman had it coming. Wandering around in our park alone, going here and there without an escort. Was she murdered in Baig bagh?'

'You knew she liked to walk there?'

'Everyone did. It was the talk of the town. My father is too doting a husband to tell her to behave herself and act like a respectable lady of decent upbringing. Is that where she was killed?' Fierce eyes examined his face. 'I thought as much. Good riddance.'

Along with relief, his ear caught an edge of fear in Ali's tone.

'Did you know about the hedge entrance?'

Ali looked puzzled, and at his explanation, said it didn't surprise him.

'And you, Mr Imran Baig?' Soob turned to the younger man who had been regarding his brother anxiously.

'Oh, he wouldn't know if I didn't,' Ali said, as Imran shook his head.

Soob raised an eyebrow. Not likely for the scions of a family with a whole stable of spies, he thought.

'I suppose, though, you must have a key to the park?' Soob asked.

'My father has one.' Ali's frowning gaze took in the guards assembled at the foot of the stairs. 'Imran, where is the sardar?'

'Esteemed brother, I sent the chieftain with his battalion to fetch the doctor.'

'How dare you expose everyone to danger.' Ali tore into his brother and gave him an earful, ending with, 'Why didn't you tell me about our esteemed father's collapse immediately?'

Soob interrupted Imran's apologies. 'Mr Ali Baig, you haven't answered my question. Where were you tonight?'

'My dear sir.' Ali drew himself up, but still came only to the level of Soob's chin. 'I disliked my father's wife, but not enough to murder her. I was at the Resident's ball with my friends.' A vein began pulsing by his left eye. 'By the by, do tell me about the body you fished out of the river earlier today. Who is she? What did she look like?'

A question that was both peculiar and interesting. Why would a Muslim nobleman be interested in a poor Hindu widow?

As he described the mutilations and the absence of jewellery, he watched Ali Baig closely. And at the mention of her shorn hair, the nobleman's tense frame visibly relaxed.

'Is someone missing from your household, Mr Ali Baig?'

'No.'

In Ali's eyes there had been a momentary flash of something. Fear or despair or both, Soob wasn't sure.

Men on horses thundered up the carriageway, a grim-faced Inspector Wilberforce in their midst. Ali glanced at them and turned on his heel. Soob watched him go, wondering again what help Ali feared from the police, and why with such experienced mercenaries and a spy network at his beck and call, this arrogant nobleman was frantic about his family's safety. And, above all, had someone gone missing from his household?

Chapter Twelve

This pile of marble was enough to make the Grand Panjandrum himself feel measly and beggarly. Through buzzing black specks, a scrum of mosquitoes having taken the place of rain, Wilberforce made out three men at the top of the stairs. Two he recognised, one being the ruddy Brahmin. Interfering fellow, sneaking around, alerting every suspect, especially this one. If the Ripper escaped him this time, it would be more than words the so-called Saviour of the Deccan would have to suffer. The sight of the second man, all togged up in silver, striding in through the ornate stucco doorway, sent him galloping up the steps.

'Ali Baig, stop!'

The toff whipped around.

Wilberforce bounded up to him. 'You are a member of the Hellfire Club and you were questioned in the Whitechapel murders, were you not?' He wasn't about to mind his tongue with a mass murderer.

He caught the Brahmin's sharp twitch from the corner of his eye. Gladdened his heart, it did. So he didn't know everything, after all.

'Esteemed brother,' the shorter man with a clean-shaven face said in a quiet tone, 'surely you are not still a member. You promised.'

'Shut up, Imran,' Ali Baig snapped from the entrance. 'Who the hell are you?'

He'd got his man – the haughty sneer was familiar from when they'd brought the bastard in for questioning during the Ripper's massacres. His influential friends had got the man's name expunged from the investigation records. And these friends, he now realised, were now here in Hyderabad – the ruler's guests – and the murders had started again.

'Inspector Wilberforce of the Residency Police. Where were you tonight, Mr Ali Baig?' He noted the silver cummerbund and the knife stuck in it. If he could just search the fellow's wardrobe and question his valet about any missing scarves – they might well match the ones on the victims' necks.

'None of your business, Inspector.'

Already, he risked an official reprimand for coming to a nobleman's home without written permission from Commissioner Hankin. Might as well be hanged for a sheep. 'You had reason to hate your stepmother, so I am asking you again, where were you tonight?'

'That woman wasn't *my* anything. She deserved what was coming to her. Imran, see to it they leave immediately.' He strode into the palace leaving behind the scent of tobacco and lemon, and Wilberforce had to let him go. Manhandling him under the eye of all these ruffians was foolhardy. He'd get his man, though.

Wilberforce turned to the younger stepson, who wore the same disdainful sneer these high-up toffs reserved for tradesmen. Hang you too, he thought, and bit out his question. 'What does your brother mean?'

'Ask him yourself, Inspector,' came the cheeky reply.

'He said he was at the Resident's ball, Inspector Wilberforce,' the Brahmin said in a cool tone.

'I'll be having words with you, acting Chief Inspector,' he replied through gritted teeth. 'I'll thank you to hold your tongue for now, if you'd be so good.' The three nobs were together and likely up to their murderous tricks, he thought, dragging his gaze back to the stepson.

'And you, Mr Imran Baig, where were you between nine and eleven tonight?'

'At home, Inspector,' the fellow said in a haughty tone. 'My father is unwell.'

'Summon your brother. This is a murder investigation, lest you forget, and you live under British jurisdiction here.'

'Do you have written authorisation to question us? No, I thought not.' Imran snapped his fingers, and half a dozen ruffians leapt up the steps.

As the torches illuminated the colour of their uniform – the same as the cummerbund on the first victim – Wilberforce's fingers gripped the baton on his belt. The sudden halt in the Ripper's murders pointed to a sailor or some visiting foreigner as the culprit, a view shared by his fellow Metropolitan Police constables. Now he had finally found the killer, nothing and nobody was going to stand in his way.

Wilberforce raised his whistle.

A brawny ruffian slapped down his arm. He clenched his fists. He'd love to give him a black eye.

The Brahmin stepped up and put his hand on the soldier's arm. 'I'm sure you, Mr Baig, would want us to find your stepmother's killer,' he said in a smooth tone.

To Wilberforce's annoyed relief, the stepson raised his hand. The soldiers stepped back and waited.

'Go ahead, Inspector,' the Brahmin murmured.

The cheek of the fellow, giving him permission to do his job! 'Mr Baig, your stepmother was much younger than you. How did you feel about it?'

'Why should I be upset over my father finding love again?'

Wilberforce would be right miffed if his father showed up with some young strumpet for a new bride. This lot could expect to have dozens of young stepmothers; their religion insisted on multiple wives.

'Were you and your father in London with your brother?' He could well imagine them helping Ali in the Whitechapel bloodbath – and in tonight's murders. He wouldn't be excluding the nawab until the so-called ailment could be confirmed.

'Yes, we went a little later, in November 1889. Why?'

Long after the Ripper slayings, he noted. 'What were you doing there?'

'I, like my esteemed brother, was enrolled in natural sciences at Imperial College. Why do you ask?'

A few months ago, it would have surprised Wilberforce that the local nobs sent their sons to study in London. But no longer. Not after hearing of architects, astronomers and inventors among this lot here. The brother and the father could not have been Ali's accomplices then, but it didn't mean they couldn't have killed tonight.

'Your brother was there for how long?'

'From February 1888 to January 1891.'

Throughout the Ripper's butcheries, he thought with grim satisfaction.

'Does your brother wear an astrakhan hat?'

'In this heat?'

Wilberforce didn't care if he sounded mad. An eyewitness in White-chapel had seen a toff in such a hat, a black tie with a horseshoe pin, button-over boots and a large gold chain across his waistcoat. 'Does he?'

The Brahmin shot him a shrewd glance.

'In London, yes. So did I, my father and many others.' Imran Baig's tone was of someone soothing a crazy horse. The fellow then raised an eyebrow. 'You're surely not implying that my esteemed older brother is the Ripper, Inspector Wilberforce? Let me inform you my brother was not charged then. He just happened to be a member of a club that came under suspicion.'

Another half dozen horsemen clattered up with a chubby light-skinned older man whom Wilberforce recognised as Dr Currimbhoy. The doctor dismounted with the assistance of one ruffian, and then hopped up to them, hailing the Brahmin like a long-lost friend.

Imran snapped his fingers and the mercenaries surged in. 'Excuse me Inspector, Chief Inspector, I have to accompany the doctor.'

Dismissed like a pair of button sellers, Wilberforce fumed as he marched down the steps, hustled by the soldiers. His horse was waiting at the foot, the reins with a mercenary on horseback.

'Follow me, acting Chief Inspector,' Wilberforce said, mounting his horse. The Brahmin walking behind like a peasant would serve him right for sneaking in like this. Make the fellow stew a bit.

As they left the palace, though, the Brahmin's unfazed demeanour as he trudged alongside got Wilberforce's goat. He wheeled his horse around and glared down his nose. 'What the bloody hell do you think you are doing? Traipsing about, mucking up my clues. This is a murder investigation. Two murders, and by Jack the Ripper too.' He stabbed his thumb towards the palace.

'The Ripper was caught, Inspector Wilberforce,' came the Brahmin's smooth reply. 'Ali Baig is not him.'

'Why not? You heard his brother. He was in London during the bloodbath. And whatever rumour you heard about the Ripper, toss it out. He is alive and blooming well here on a killing spree. Where the hell are your men? I will personally see to it you—'

'Inspector Wilberforce, I found the other victim's family,' the Brahmin said in a cool tone.

'What? Where?'

'The girl's name is Mallu, her father is a gardener, and she lives there.' He pointed to a gate they had just passed. 'The killer knew her – had been watching her.'

'Yes, Ali Baig again.' He vaulted off his horse, coming nose to nose with the Brahmin. Feeling one hand curl to a fist at his side, he spoke through gritted teeth. 'Are you going to leave on your own two legs, or do you want to be carried out?'

The fellow didn't turn a hair. Looking him in the eye, he took out a whistle and blew it thrice.

'I'm on your side, Inspector. I want to find the killer. There are several suggestive points. Both the victims live in this street. Mallu was taken from her outhouse at half past nine, and Niloufer was somehow lured into the park at half past ten. Both may have been drugged, and the killer may have a key to the park. The killer is trying to copy Jack the Ripper.'

By now a dozen of his men had gathered around them. Wilberforce was all set to have them grab the Brahmin and rough him up when his ear caught the sound of hoofbeats.

'And Inspector Wilberforce,' the Brahmin continued in an annoyingly even tone, 'I would suggest treating every person here as a suspect, including the Templetons. Did Mr Templeton tell you if there was any unpleasantness with Niloufer Baig at the dinner?'

How had the man leapt to this conclusion? Granted, Arthur's nervousness had rung an alarm, but with Ali Baig they had clearly found their murderer. He'd better put a sock in it.

Eight horses, one riderless, came through the gate. His heart sank at the fright in some of his younger constables' expressions as they faced the City Police ruffians. In a fight, there was no doubt about who would win. They would never be able to live it down, being thrashed in their own backyard.

He cleared his throat and held his ground.

'I know what you're trying to do, acting Chief Inspector Soobramania. You want to finger an Englishman. Arthur had nothing to do with the murders. Mrs Baig left at half ten and refused to let Arthur escort her home. Ali Baig is our main suspect and I'll lay odds he doesn't have an alibi either for half past nine or half past ten. I have my doubts about the younger brother too. Looking after a sick father! Pah!'

One ruffian held out the reins of a horse, and the Brahmin vaulted on, much to Wilberforce's relief. They were going to leave without making trouble.

'Stand down, constables,' Wilberforce said, and HC Thomas translated. Everyone knew, though, it was only to save face.

'What about the Nizam's guests? Weren't they suspects too in the Whitechapel murders?'

The Brahmin's parting shot, as he and his men rode away with the Residency Police constables on their heels, left Wilberforce more uneasy.

The bastards had been up to no good. Then... and now.

Chapter Thirteen

Soob leaned out of his office window and hailed Ram Rahim. The tuneless whistle stopped abruptly and the boy shot into the police station.

The boy had spent what remained of the night curled up in the entrance of a mosque across the street, too wary of the other policemen to accept Soob's offer of a bed on his office couch. He'd seen to it that the boy had a good breakfast: half a dozen alu parathas and dal.

When Ram Rahim burst into his office, Soob handed him a note for the British Resident. Since Inspector Wilberforce had barred him from entering the Residency, he had no alternative but to send a private request, which Sir Trevor Plowden would accede to from a high-ranking undercover officer of the Imperial Criminal Investigation Department.

The sun warmed the air as he rode down the silent avenue to Cosmopolitan Hotel where he'd put up since his arrival two weeks ago. There he bathed, rebandaged his wounds, and had changed into a fresh set of clothes when the boy returned with a chit. The request had been granted.

Now for a trickier task, which Soob wasn't looking forward to. With the commissioner down with malaria, Soob had to convince the deputy commissioner, a nobleman who loathed the British, to send an official message to the British Resident offering the City Police's help. Worse than chivvying a temperamental racehorse into the stables, he thought, dismounting outside the deputy commissioner's palace.

A footman garbed in sepia, the nobleman's family colour, ushered him to the audience chamber. A few minutes later, Nawab Mir Akbar Jang strolled in, his chubby face wreathed in a smile displaying four gold teeth. His bushy sideburns merged with a moustache, a fashion started by his distant cousin, the Nizam. The nobleman's gaudy attire was true to form: a red brocade sherwani over cream silk pyjamas, shoes embroidered with silver thread, and rows of giant pearls draped on a broad chest. Such flamboyance had fooled many into bracketing the deputy commissioner as a harmless dandy. They didn't realise the toothier the smile, the more dangerous the man.

'Welcome to my humble abode, Chief Inspector V. S. Soobramania.' Mir Akbar waved him to a chair upholstered in gold, blue and sepia brocade.

Soob stifled a snort, and cast a jaundiced eye on the gilt-edged blue silk furnishings, their French theme being all the rage among the local aristocracy. Decorative displays of scientific instruments was another fashion these days. Seeing the rose in a test tube that must once have held urine or blood, his lips twitched.

Mir Akbar launched into a description of a dessert he'd sampled at a soiree hosted by the Nizam, no less, his voice rising over the bird calls that wafted in through the French windows framing a manicured lawn.

'Sir, we have a problem,' Soob interrupted.

An attendant garbed in a short sepia angharkha and black pyjamas entered with a silver bowl of water and a towel, followed by another one holding a tray with glasses of water and sherbet.

Soob refused both attendants, having little patience or time to waste on the tiresome local custom of engaging in inane pleasantries and sipping undrinkable sherbet before business could be broached.

'Sir, this is urgent.'

'My dear Chief Inspector,' Mir Akbar began, with a tone of disapproval. 'At last night's banquet—'

'Our control over law and order in the city is in danger.'

The nobleman stiffened. 'How?'

Soob succinctly laid out the events of the previous night: the murders, the suspects and his conjectures.

Mir Akbar sighed and slumped in his throne-like chair. 'This Jack was caught? Then why does the English policeman think it is this Jack?'

'Because of some similarities in the way the women were killed, sir. Someone is copying the Ripper, and not very well at that.'

'Then this murderer must know about the London murders, yes? And if he was there at the time, it is unlikely to be a Deccani, thanks be to Allah, since few have travelled to London. It must be an Englishman.'

We are fortunate indeed that this Jack is their business, not ours. I see no need for us to interfere in their problem.'

'Sir, Mr Ali Baig was in London at the time of the Ripper murders, and was a suspect then. He is their main suspect in last night's murders. His stepmother is one of the victims.'

'The Parsi girl.' Mir Akbar tugged his sideburns. 'That's not good. They'll surely cook up evidence against Ali. Is this a British plot to seize control? That is what we have to ask ourselves.'

'It would be to our advantage, sir, if you could send a note to the Resident offering our help.'

Mir Akbar gazed at him, a shrewd gleam in his eyes. 'I like the way you are thinking, Chief Inspector. We can influence the course of the investigation, make sure the English don't pin the blame on us. But will Sir Trevor Plowden agree?'

Soob knew what Mir Akbar was asking: *Is the British Resident your patron?* Here, more so than in other places under direct British rule, *everyone* was somebody's man. With his success in foiling the insurrection, the local grandees saw him as having the ear of the two most powerful men in the Deccan – the Nizam of Hyderabad and the British Resident. They were unsure which of the two was his patron, while taking it for granted that one of them must be. For Soob, being answerable to rival powers had its advantages: it helped him be nobody's man, and he intended to keep it that way.

'Sir, if the Resident rejects our offer and they find a Deccani culprit, we can point out that we wanted the killer brought to justice.'

Mir Akbar tapped his chubby fingers on the gilt armrest, clacking his gold rings. 'No, no, Chief Inspector. That would not do at all. You are aware of the threat we face. His Exalted Highness is understandably anxious.'

Soob inclined his head.

'I cannot emphasise enough how imperative it is that we find this English killer.' The nobleman eyed him sharply. 'Your task is simple. You must hunt among foreigners who've arrived recently. I can think of two myself. Know this: I will back you, however powerful they are.' He stroked his sideburn with a manicured nail. 'We are depending on you to do the needful. And Chief Inspector Soobramania, don't bother the Baigs. I can vouch for them.'

Though Englishmen headed the two wings of the Nizam's police force – the City and District police – they still reported to the Nizam. If blame for the murders rested with a local, they both knew the British Viceroy would use the pretext to seize formal charge of the province's law and order. It would be the prelude to bringing the Deccan under direct British rule, a Damoclean sword dangling over the heads of every one of the five hundred native rulers in India. The only way the Nizam's courtiers could circumvent it was by ensuring that the killer was an Englishman, and even better, a relation of the Queen. Though Soob had been expecting some such command – to pin the crime on the visiting Grand Duke and the Earl – it didn't stop the familiar irritation pricking his insides. He knew how to handle it.

'Of course, as soon as you give this to me in writing… sir.'

'You should do as you see fit, Chief Inspector,' Mir Akbar said smoothly. 'I am merely saying do not let anybody go just because they are powerful.'

'You may depend on it, sir,' Soob said drily, 'that no matter if it is a nobleman or someone else, I will bring them to justice.' As he'd expected, panic flitted across the courtier's face when he added, 'They may arrest Ali Baig this morning, sir.'

'The request shall be sent immediately.' Mir Akbar picked up a silver bell from the desk and shook it violently. Then, recovering his composure, his smile became toothier, his neck swelling like a puff adder over the glistening brocade collar. 'I don't need to tell you, Chief Inspector Soobramania, any command must come from me. You are not from here, you don't know who is working for whom. Commissioner Colonel Ludlow is an Englishman. That's all I am saying.'

Don't bother about the English Commissioner and don't trust him. He will leave, but I'll still be here, so be my man, not his. Mir Akbar never tired of making this point each time they met.

'Oh, and Chief Inspector, congratulations on ensuring that the British Resident will take the City Police's help.'

His lips twitched at his superior's glee in thinking he had pinpointed Soob's patron.

Noting his amusement, the nobleman stiffened, doubt creeping into his gaze.

THE JASOOS

A GRAND WELCOME FOR THE ROYAL GUESTS

23 June 1895

Grand Duke Alexei Alexandrovich and Henry James FitzRoy, the Earl of Euston, arrived in Hyderabad yesterday morning. The Grand Duke, a brother to a Tsar of Russia, and whose sister is married to Queen Victoria's fourth son, travelled here in His Highness, the Nizam of Hyderabad's personal railway carriage with his friend, the Earl of Euston, the son and heir of the Duke of Grafton.

They were officially met at the station by Sir Trevor Plowden, the Resident, and Sir Vikar ul-Oomra, the Prime Minister, with their respective staffs.

Their Excellencies left the station in the Nizam's state carriage under an escort of the African Cavalry Guards for Chowmahalla Palace, where they remain as H. H. the Nizam's guests.

Many and elaborate were the triumphal arches under which the carriage passed on its journey. The natives of Hyderabad can salaam more profusely than perhaps any other race.

A Ball was held yesterday evening in their honour by Sir Trevor.

A word now as to the ruler and his dominions. The present Nizam, Mir Mahbub Ali, is thirty-five years of age, and as the chief Native Mahomedan ruler in India, is entitled to a twenty-one-gun salute. The extent of his sway is over close on 100,000 square miles. ●

Unidentified Body
in the River

The mutilated body of a woman was found in a sack under the Chaderghat-Oliphant Bridge. Any information on a missing Hindu widow should be given to the City Police at Charminar. ●

Chapter Fourteen

Eight chimes sounded from St George's Church clock as Wilberforce dismounted his horse on the broad gravel path between his office and the stables. The Residency Police operated from whitewashed brick rooms lined up like matchboxes around a courtyard square. Each office had two doors, one leading to the inner courtyard and the other to this path, giving them easy ways to escape a native mob. A hangover from the Mutiny about forty years ago when native soldiers revolted over rumours that pig and cow fat greased their guns. Even if it had been true, which God-fearing Christian was to know that Muslims hated pigs and Hindus worshipped cows? Scores of Englishmen, women and children were killed all over India, as the ruler dithered between the rebels and the Crown. The bloodthirsty natives had even stormed the Residency here. It was touch and go for a while for them, an old timer had told him, before the Nizam saw sense and threw in his lot with the British.

Head Constable Thomas approached him, leaving the shade of the building, as Wilberforce handed the reins to a groom. 'Commissioner Hankin is in your office, sir.'

Not a good sign. It meant interference from the higher-ups. Only to be expected, he supposed, given the prize on the horizon. Hankin, an ex-Scotland Yard man, didn't usually butt in, which suited him just fine. They were all here to lie low, make a pile, and return to a comfortable retirement. Hankin had better not take all the credit for the Ripper's arrest.

He stomped into his office and saluted.

'You are late, Wilberforce,' Commissioner Hankin said, looking up from a note in his hand. He leaned back in Wilberforce's chair and gazed at him with mournful eyes in a bloodhound face, silver glinting from a brown beard and moustache.

Late, my eye. No, he wasn't. Not after spending the whole miserable night stuck in the wet and the mud. He'd seen to the corpses' transport to the morgue, arranged for their post-mortems and stationed patrols in the park. Only at sunrise, he'd popped into his little bungalow for a wash and a change into dry clothes. His eyeballs felt stuffed with grit.

Standing at attention in front of his own blooming chair, he sketched out their progress, dwelling on the Brahmin's interference, Ali Baig as a suspect in the Whitechapel murders and the similarity with last night's killings.

The patent disbelief on Hankin's face told Wilberforce precisely what he was making of the Ripper connection, and the commissioner's words rubbed it in.

'Wilberforce, I would drop that line of enquiry immediately. If you keep poking at that dunghill, we'll find ourselves in a scandal that could implicate Her Majesty's relative. You know the Ripper is dead. For the love of God, man, don't get stuck in the past.'

'But sir, we don't have to worry about the Grand Duke and the Earl, they are in the clear. A woman's mutilated body was found in the river yesterday, and it was likely to have been the same killer. The gents couldn't have done it, not in between touring the city, calling on the Nizam and attending the Resident's ball. The man we are after is a native. Ali Baig is the Ripper.'

His superior's face darkened.

Now what?

'That could be dangerous for us. If those two vouched for this Baig in the Whitechapel murders, who is to say they won't do it again? Then where does that leave us? With mud on our faces, that's where. The Nizam's lot will sacrifice Ali Baig if it means putting Her Majesty in a fix.' He scowled. 'It's unfortunate these murders resemble the Ripper killings, and even more deplorable that the natives know that the Grand Duke and the Earl were questioned then, thanks to those damned newspapers.'

The local English-language and vernacular papers had gone the whole hog, positioning the stories of the visit and the Ripper murders side by side, so that it read as if the Earl, the Grand Duke and their friend, the late Duke of Clarence, had conspired to carry out the murders attributed to Jack the Ripper. In his book, they could have. He hadn't ruled them out in the Whitechapel murders, not with their links to the Hellfire Club. Powerful interests had protected the Ripper then, and the largest manhunt in history had failed.

'So for pity's sake, man, don't mention the Ripper again.' The commissioner's bark snapped him back. 'You find some other native behind these murders. Now, Wilberforce, I have bad news for you. Sir Trevor wants Chief Inspector Soobramania of the City Police to join the investigation.'

'Why?' Wilberforce raged inside at having to make nice after the Brahmin had shown him and his men up like that. 'It's our jurisdiction, not theirs, sir.'

'I agree, but that's an order from the Resident.'

He'd heard rumours about Sir Trevor Plowden's cunning: the man had contrived the suicide of a ruler in his previous post in Kashmir and delivered the principality to the British. How could such a wily man permit any dilution of his power?

'If we set this precedent, they can keep poking their noses into all our investigations,' Wilberforce pointed out. 'How will we take over their police, eh... sir?'

The commissioner rose to his feet. 'I can't see what Sir Trevor's game is at the moment, but rest assured he has a plan. Now buck up and remember whose side you're on. Make sure we are not implicated. That's an order.'

Wilberforce scowled. He was bloody well not going to let it go. The Ripper Investigation Committee had hounded poor old John to his death. If John was the Ripper, then as his partner on the beat, Wilberforce would be guilty of murdering those women, even if he had not cut those throats himself. If he found the native on that committee responsible for the conclusion... He clenched his fists.

–

Wilberforce initially put off going to the City Police. He assigned the roster of constables to patrol the park, heard the night shift's report, and met the spy that Head Constable Thomas had managed to drum up in the Baig palace. Then he dealt with routine matters, signed three chits for leave, one promotion, and tore a strip off a shirker.

When the wall clock chimed nine times, it dawned on him that it'd be better to go now before the fellow turned up in his office. Then he could say he didn't want to leave a message, in case it fell into the wrong hands. He reluctantly stepped out into the biting sun.

The groom brought out his bay.

'I'm going alone, Thomas.' No need for his men to see him make such a degrading request to their despised rivals. Thank the Lord, no interpreter would be needed for the Brahmin, whose fluent English was better than his own. Not that he hadn't tried to tamp down his broad Yorkshire accent in London.

The sun blazed as he galloped across to the fortified city, passing empty carts on their way out. Hyderabad's natives, all 180,000 of them, got their supplies from the countryside, the city producing nothing save a peculiar wine distilled from quails and partridges; the very thought gave him the jimjams.

At the city gate, the soldier, a palace guard whose bright yellow uniform reminded him of a cockatoo he'd seen in the London zoo, returned his identity paper and spat on the ground. Wilberforce gritted his teeth and rode through.

Homesick – that's how he felt every time he set foot in the Nizam's domain. Every native looked like a criminal, all wearing outlandish costumes and armed to the teeth with matchlocks and daggers. Even beggars and vegetable vendors carried sabres. The fumes of red chillies in the very air left a heavy sensation in his head and nose. The only bright spot, as far as Wilberforce was concerned, was the heavenly food. Gobsmackingly delicious curries – thank the Lord only Clara and his cook knew of this secret vice.

He found himself at the police headquarters much too soon. The quiet efficiency of the City Police surprised him. The contingent of wild tribesmen guarding the monument, a grizzled man with fierce moustaches and beard at the front desk, and the pair he'd passed on the staircase – all busy with some work or other. No slouching, beedi smoking or the chatter he'd expected to find.

The Brahmin's office on the first floor was immaculate. Through the open door, he appraised the long room with its view of Charminar's minarets and the square below. If only his room was furnished so luxuriously. A silk carpet, a teak bookshelf filled with books – he'd give that a miss – a long settee in blue velvet with neat cushions on each end to nap after lunch, a large desk and comfortable chairs. It felt clean and fresh, and a cool breeze tickled his hair. He glanced at a palm-leaf fan rustling above the lintel, its rope passing through a hole to the fanner, the punkahwallah crouched in a cubbyhole outside.

Finally he dragged his gaze to the man behind the desk. Seated in a plain wooden chair and writing in a notebook, the Brahmin showed no surprise at seeing him. His bright eyes spoke of a good night's sleep, though that wasn't the case: he'd interfered with every suspect. Wilberforce eyed him with acute disfavour. The man must have somehow instigated Sir Trevor's command. But Wilberforce knew how to fix him. He'd get the Acting So and So to interview the visiting nobs. The scandal might even get the fellow taken off the case, a thought that cheered him no end.

Chapter Fifteen

Soob leaned back in his chair and eyed the bristling Englishman, who said, 'I will, of course, be in charge of the investigation, acting Chief Inspector.'

It was hard not to feel sorry for Wilberforce. Bad enough that he had to make a request to a native from the rival police force, and worse still, it was to him, 'the blooming Brahmin' as Wilberforce had yelled from the Baig palace gate last night.

When he acquiesced in a level tone, Wilberforce relaxed in his chair. 'Your office is a fishbowl.' He jerked a thumb at the square teeming with urchins, beggars, vendors and other pedestrians. 'None of them were there when I arrived.'

'They are wondering why you are here. In any case, we have to keep an eye on the subjects.'

'More like they're keeping an eye on you.' A smile cracked the Englishman's face. 'Acting Chief Inspector, seeing how you aren't in uniform, I'll handle all the interviews. Any reason you don't wear one?'

Yes, because the copious gold lace on the uniform's sleeves lit him up like a chandelier, making it hard to move about unnoticed.

'I'm here temporarily until my predecessor is given the all-clear by his doctor,' he said.

Wilberforce brightened up as if it was the best thing he'd heard in a long time. 'That wraps up everything. You show up at my office and I'll keep you informed.'

'You'll report your findings to me.' He couldn't resist the dig.

'I'll inform you.' Wilberforce glowered. He gripped the chair's wooden arms and began rising to his feet.

'Inspector Wilberforce, the killer is not Jack the Ripper. Someone is attempting to copy the Ripper.' He had to convince the Englishman, who would otherwise hare off on the wrong trail for yesterday's murders, and more women could die.

Wilberforce froze and lowered himself again. 'Here's how I see it, *acting* Chief Inspector,' he said coldly. 'The killer *is* Jack the Ripper. He has used the same method in these murders – the neckerchief, cutting the throat, the mutilations. No doubt the woman you found in the river yesterday had these very same mutilations.'

'Yes, but there were discrepancies between the cuts on the right and the left sides of her body,' he explained in a dispassionate tone, but inside, that wasn't how he felt at all.

'Likely been practising on her, Ali Baig has.'

'You're wrong about him being the Ripper, Inspector.'

Wilberforce stiffened. 'Acting Chief Inspector, Ali Baig was questioned as a member of the Hellfire Club during the Ripper investigation. He managed to wriggle out thanks to an alibi from his two friends, your ruler's guests. I'm not letting him get away this time.'

From the street below came a shout: 'Make way for Nawab Nasrullah, make way.' Swiftly followed by the battalion's full-throated hail.

It was the last thing he needed right now. Soob swivelled his chair so that he faced the door, away from the windows.

'I think that chap wants to speak to you.' Wilberforce jabbed a finger at the window.

He twisted around reluctantly. An Arab chieftain was waiting on a camel outside. At his curt nod, the chieftain stiffened and tilted his head haughtily.

Wilberforce's bemusement turned to delight. 'You'll have to bow and scrape before this lot the whole day.'

Soob eyed the Englishman dispassionately. Sooner or later, he would have to respond to the man's wrath. After solving the murder of a famous botanical artist after his arrival in London, Soob had been roped into a secret Scotland Yard investigation of the Ripper case in February 1893. Despite the fact that he hadn't been able to perform his duties openly thanks to local racialism, a rumour had spread about a foreigner's involvement in John Furlow's death. Wilberforce was a clever enough policeman to work out who it was.

'Inspector Wilberforce, the Ripper was caught three years ago by Scotland Yard's Special Investigation Committee.'

The Englishman went red in the face. 'Those bastards got it wrong and a good man died. Blooming idiots didn't even get the number of murders right – six, they said, when everyone knows it was eleven.'

'No, Inspector Wilberforce, the Ripper killed six women. In the other five, the killer did not display the same pattern of escalating violence.'

'Which six are the Ripper's then, eh?'

'Martha Tabram, Polly Nichols, Annie Chapman, Elizabeth Stride, Catherine Eddowes and Mary Kelly.'

Suspicion lurked in the narrowed gaze. 'Have you shared these thoughts with the Yard?'

Soob gave a nod.

'It was you!' Wilberforce lunged over the desk, kicking back his chair, fists outstretched.

Soob jerked his head away from the hardwood backrest as he grabbed the Englishman's wrists, his thumbs finding and pressing a nerve on the inner side.

'Owww…'

The door burst open. HC Muhammad and two constables plunged in, swords raised, mouths open at the sight of the British policeman slumped on the table, moaning in agony.

'Out,' Soob barked. 'The inspector had a heat stroke.'

They retreated, looking doubtful, as Wilberforce wriggled back using his forearms, and collapsed in the chair.

Soob swung around, reached for a terracotta jug on the console against the wall, poured a glass of water and pushed it across the table. A jolt of pain shot through his ribs.

'Thanks to you, my friend and partner committed suicide.' Wilberforce glared as he slammed the emptied glass on the table. 'John left a wife and two daughters. You accused a man without proof.'

'We caught him in the act, Inspector,' Soob said wearily. They'd got there in the nick of time. Those empty eyes looking at him, the sharp glint of the knife swinging towards the terrified woman, the revolver in Soob's hand, the shot. To protect the police's reputation, the commissioner called it a suicide and that was the story put about.

'Trumped up, I'm sure. Am I a suspect in last night's murders? I was in Whitechapel during the Ripper murders. Go on, say it. Everyone suspected me after your report accused John. They thought I was in on it. People who'd worked with me for twenty years. Bloody well couldn't take it any more. I had to leave England, thanks to you.'

It was true that Wilberforce had been under suspicion. What he didn't know was that it was Soob who had found the one witness able to exonerate him.

Wilberforce leaned forward, jamming thick forearms on the table. 'Go on, then, tell me how you concluded it was John.'

'He timed it brilliantly – that's what made us suspect a policeman who knew the police patrol routes and timings. The six women were killed between 7 August and 9 November in Whitechapel and Spital-fields. Furlow knew how long he had to work on the bodies, which streets would be deserted, and where the constables would be on their beat.'

Wilberforce's face turned blotchy. 'Let's assume you are right. We patrolled in pairs, so how did John dupe me?'

'He didn't. He killed when he was off-duty, except for one time.'

Wilberforce's face darkened. 'When we were in the pub.'

'Yes, and he left early – which you didn't bother to mention.' That omission had made Wilberforce a suspect too.

'He asked me not to, and I covered for him. So what? He was meeting a woman, he said.'

Soob looked him in the eye. 'He didn't lie about that.'

A deep flush suffused Wilberforce's cheeks as he realised what had happened to the woman. He rallied for another attack. 'Tell me this, how did John lure the women? Everyone was scared witless by then.'

'The women spoke to him because they trusted him, Inspector.'

'Rot. After the first two murders, the prostitutes were wary of the police.'

'Only Mary Kelly was a known prostitute,' Soob said, frowning. 'The others weren't.'

'Yes, they were. Are you telling me I don't know a tart on my beat?'

'Yes, that is exactly what I am telling you, Inspector. Those women had been either abandoned or had fled violent husbands. Three, in fact, slept on the streets because they didn't have enough money for a room. That's how they fell into Furlow's clutches. He didn't approach all of them as a policeman. He disguised himself – as a woman for Mary Kelly and as a nobleman for Elizabeth Stride. There were other elements that matched Furlow's background. The Ripper's knife skills indicated surgical training. An alienist whom we consulted suggested he had bad experiences with women: perhaps a mother who'd abandoned him, a fiancée free with her favours.'

Wilberforce's thick fingers bunched into fists. 'You've got it all wrong.'

'John Furlow was handsome, was he not?'

'So were many other men in London.'

'He dropped out of medical school.'

'So did others.'

'His mother disappeared when he was young—'

'No, she died. *And* his fiancée became his wife and bore him two daughters. What do you say to that, eh?'

'His first fiancée, Inspector Wilberforce. *And* his schoolteacher told us his mother couldn't take the father's beatings and had left them.'

Wilberforce raised his hand. 'Stop right there. Not another word of this gobbledygook. You nabbed the wrong man. The Ripper is here. He cut last night's victims' throats from left to right, and left a scarf on their necks, just like the Whitechapel murders. What do you say to that, eh? Every characteristic of the Ripper killings is evident in last night's murders, right down to displaying the body.'

'Niloufer Baig's body was hidden in the grass,' Soob pointed out. 'And the river victim's in a sack that would've smashed on the rocks.'

'The gardener would've found Mrs Baig in the morning. Your river victim may not be the Ripper's work.'

For Wilberforce, Soob thought with pity, defending his former partner and friend was the only option. The alternative was much too horrific, but it couldn't be helped. He needed Wilberforce to accept his old partner's guilt and approach this investigation with a cool head and an unbiased mind. So Soob soldiered on.

'You've pointed to the differences not the similarities, Inspector Wilberforce. Only one of the Ripper's six victims had a neckerchief tied to her throat. Here, two victims had silk cummerbunds coiled around their necks, but not the river victim. Ask yourself why the killer didn't want her found. Also, the victims here were most likely drugged; the Ripper didn't do that. In every murder, the Ripper increased the level of violence; here the reverse has occurred.'

'But—'

He raised his hand. 'Kindly let me finish. The Ripper murdered in public areas like street corners except once, when he killed in a room. Here, the killer chose a locked and guarded park. The Ripper's victims were poor women with children, over forty years of age, either married, divorced or widowed.'

'And here, at least two victims are in their late teens,' Wilberforce burst out. 'Two are poor, and one is a beauty and rich. So what? The cummerbund and the stabs are the same. Can't be too hard to pick a lock.'

'Or the killer has a key. Niloufer's was in her pocket.' He held it out. Surprise flashed in the Englishman's eye as if, were the tables turned, he wouldn't have shared this information. 'I suspect Mrs Templeton also has a key. Who else?'

'Phoebe doesn't have a key.' Wilberforce scowled as he pocketed it. 'But the nawab and sons are bound to have one, they own the whole bloody hill. That's how, acting Chief Inspector, Ali Baig entered a locked park.'

'You see what it means. It narrows down the suspects to a local familiar with some aspects of the Ripper murders, who has access to the park key, and who knows when Mallu used the outhouse.' Soob ploughed on, pausing to wipe the sweat from his nose with a handkerchief. 'There is one more thing. Have you considered that the murderer may have targeted one victim and killed the others to make it seem like it was the Ripper?'

'Like a stepmother.' Wilberforce bared his teeth in a smile. 'Well, acting Chief Inspector, we don't have to look far. We both know Ali Baig fits the picture. He hated his stepmother, so he filched the key from his father and killed her. With or without the help of his younger brother – perhaps even the father. Maybe the gent didn't care for his wife wandering around in the park so late. I'm going to see him now.'

'Nawab Zulfikar Baig is in a coma, Inspector.' Dr Currimbhoy had sent him a note earlier.

'How do you know? We haven't been informed.' Wilberforce glowered. 'Even so, it doesn't mean the two brothers didn't do it, or Ali Baig on his own.'

'But why would Ali Baig copy the Ripper's method and incriminate himself?'

'Means, motive and opportunity: all point to that cocky bastard.' The martial glint in his eye said he wouldn't budge. 'I'll trouble you to keep your views to yourself. Ali Baig meant to kill his stepmother. The other two don't count. They're poor.'

Soob's temper flared. 'Rich or poor, they all count,' he said in an icy tone. 'We are policemen.'

'Oho, so you think I don't care about the poor victims?' Wilberforce surged to his feet. 'I was a constable in Whitechapel, acting Chief Inspector Soobramania. One of London's poorest and most wretched areas. It was my job to look out for prostitutes, thieves, refugees and labourers living there. I lodged there too. Have you ever lived in a slum? Of course not. You make these poor devils fan you.' He jerked his thumb at the palm leaves swishing from the wall.

Soob looked up ruefully. On his first day, he'd packed the punkah-wallas off downstairs to the constables' room. HC Muhammad had hurried in with apologies and asked how they had offended him. So to show they hadn't, he'd let them return to their cubbyhole. And now he was stuck with them.

'Let's put the Ripper conjecture aside for the moment, Inspector,' he said in an even tone. 'What time did Mr Templeton say Niloufer left?'

'Ten thirty. Why?'

'Given the onset of rigor mortis in Mallu's body and the fact she went missing at half past nine, we're looking at nine thirty to ten thirty for her murder, and ten thirty-five to around ten forty-five for Niloufer's. Our suspects must include those in the vicinity: the Templetons and their guests.'

'What earthly reason would the dinner guests have to kill these women?' Wilberforce demanded. 'For your information, I've already checked with Arthur. Colonel Hancock and General Rowbottom live in the cantonment, at least half an hour's drive from Arthur's. They left at a quarter past ten and couldn't have made it back in time to kill Mrs Baig. The Smiths and the Frasers live on Macintyre Road – twenty minutes away from the park. My men have spoken to their coachmen. They were in their carriages when the boy saw the murder.'

'Wasn't Mr Templeton the last to see Niloufer alive?'

Wilberforce scowled. 'Leave Arthur out of it. He had nothing to do with these murders. No motive and certainly no opportunity to kill the first girl, unless you are suggesting he nipped across to the park in the middle of the bloomin' dinner party.'

'Did you ask him if Niloufer Baig looked upset?'

'What do you mean?'

'Her mother said she walked in the park whenever she was upset or worried or annoyed.'

'Rubbish. The woman must've gone there to meet a lover, or maybe she took a shortcut home through that hedge. No need to make up stories about a quarrel with Arthur or Phoebe.'

Though Soob hadn't meant a quarrel, it was another conjecture worth examining. 'Did you ask him?'

Wilberforce surged to his feet. 'If I want your help, acting Chief Inspector, I'll let you know. Remember who is in charge here.'

'And Inspector, there are two more suspects,' Soob said, as if the Englishman hadn't spoken. 'The Grand Duke and the Earl.'

Wilberforce tapped the notebook in his pocket. 'Don't worry, I have them down in my book.'

Just when he'd written him off, the Englishman surprised him.

'Ah, it surprises you.' Wilberforce eyed him with rancour. 'You thought my superiors would warn me off them and I'd meekly give in. For your information, they did, but as you so kindly took the trouble to point out, we *are* policemen. Our job is to hunt down the killer, whoever he or they may be. You, I hope, will be good enough to remember it when your nobs command you to pin the crime on an Englishman. The Earl's name, let me also inform you, came up during the Whitechapel murders. Rumour had it that some Ripper victims knew about his visit to a male brothel and were blackmailing him and the Duke of Clarence. My former superior, Inspector Abberline, raided the brothel. Quite a ruckus it created, but ultimately the scandal was hushed up. By the Palace, it was said, because the Duke of Clarence was involved. A sick bunch, the lot of them.'

That, Soob wholeheartedly agreed with. He paused to carefully choose his words. 'So we are looking at three murders, and perhaps two killers.'

'Ali Baig and his younger brother, or Ali Baig and his two high-up friends. Take your pick, acting Chief Inspector. And since you are so keen to assist me, you can tackle the suspects within your jurisdiction. I'll find out if the Duke and the Earl went missing from the ball last night.' Wilberforce bared his teeth in a smile. 'Seeing how they are putting up at the city palace, you can go and speak to the gents. Find out if they were doing a Hellfire ritual with their friend.'

Wilberforce seemed to be expecting a protest. Looking put out when Soob didn't react, he stormed out.

–

Soob pencilled a few lines on his official stationery, sealed it and shook the bell on his desk. Wilberforce was in for a disappointment, he thought.

Head Constable Muhammad marched in, his hennaed hair a halo in the piercing sunlight. He stamped his feet and saluted, little balls of sweat dotting his broad face. His eyes, though, crinkled with worry, and Soob followed his gaze to the red stains on his khaki shirt. He really needed to get stitched up.

He handed over the note. 'See that this is delivered immediately to Lady Ariel Falloner at Resident Plowden's palace. And ask Sub-Inspector Kamran to join us.'

For a few minutes Soob listened to the muezzin of Mecca Masjid calling the devout to the mid-morning prayer. Though he wasn't a Muslim – or religious at all – there was something soothing about the sonorous chant that, no matter how tense things had been, unfurled a calm space within him.

Then Sub-Inspector Kamran knocked and entered, followed by the head constable. More contrasting personalities would be hard to find. The sub-inspector, a Shia whose Persian forefathers were traders and administrators, had a spry mind and a mischievous tongue, which he often used to rile the stolid Muhammad. The head constable, a descendant of enslaved Africans brought to the Deccan in the seventeenth and eighteenth centuries, was a staunch traditionalist with fixed notions on how things ought to be, which Kamran delighted in flouting.

Now, when he told them to sit, Muhammad remained standing poker-straight – his credo being one ought not to sit in front of one's superiors. Kamran plonked himself in a comfortable chair, turning the HC's expression more wooden.

Soob briefed them on the investigation.

'I never thought to see the day we'd be working with *them*,' Kamran said. 'Do we get a free pass to enter the Residency?'

'I'll arrange the permits for you two. HC Muhammad, you have relatives working for Nawab Baig and the Templetons?'

'My third cousin is a footman in Nawab Baig's palace, sir.'

'Good. Ask him where the three Baigs were last night between nine and eleven thirty. And find out if the sons quarrelled with their father about their new stepmother, and what happened during the lunch they had with Begum Niloufer Baig earlier this week.'

The HC saluted, but did not leave. His agitation was evident from the nervous way his yellowed fingers twirled the tips of his hennaed moustache.

'What is it?'

'Sir, the two foreign royal visitors of our esteemed Nizam. Do I have to see them and ask about Yakub?'

It came as no surprise that Wilberforce's suspicions had leaked. Not in a city that revelled in rumours, the wilder the better. Yakub was the local name for Jack.

Soob scowled at the beatific expression on Kamran's face. The dratted fellow was up to his old tricks with poor Muhammad.

'I'll deal with it. You focus on this case and report to me directly.'

The HC saluted and backed out of the room, looking relieved.

Soob frowned at his deputy. 'As for you, Sub-Inspector Kamran, stop playing tricks on the HC. And no more rumours about Yakub. This information is highly confidential, but the real Ripper was caught three years ago. Someone is copying him. Your task is to talk to the servants in the Templeton house. Find out what happened at last night's dinner, where the Templetons were between nine thirty and ten forty-five, what they say about Mrs Templeton's friendship with Niloufer, and what they spoke of last night when she stayed back. Though if the servants don't speak English, they may not know.'

'You'd be surprised at how little knowing the language matters when it comes to gossip, sir.' Kamran rose to his feet and saluted. 'They'll know.'

Chapter Sixteen

At eleven in the morning, finally done with the last of a full three dozen patients – some with squalling babies, others burning with malaria and typhoid, and worse still, the women with burns and bruises inflicted by their own brutish husbands and fathers – the low murmur in her head turned strident. *Find Niloufer's murderer.*

Shiraz got up from her office chair and paced to the window opening into a courtyard. She breathed in the warm humid air, her agitation gentled somewhat by the red-whiskered bulbul hopping under a gulmohar tree looking for worms in the carpet of flowers. What to do? Should she wait for Soob to tell her what was happening with the investigation? He wasn't one to discuss his cases, even with Cyrus when he was hunting for the Ripper. But she couldn't just sit around and wait – she'd made a promise to Aunt Gul.

'Dr Shiraz.' Dr Dora knocked on her open door, her bun gleaming pewter in the suffused light. 'Can you mind the clinic? One of my harem patients, Mrs Maryam Baig, has collapsed. She isn't normally prone to illness or hysteria.'

Shiraz's heartbeat quickened. 'Is she the wife of Ali or Imran Baig?'

'Mr Ali Baig. Do you know her?'

This was her chance to get into the Baig palace and see Nawab Zulfikar Baig. Like her, he'd be desperate to catch Niloufer's killer, and with his backing, which they would need if his sons had a hand in the murders, they could seize the fiend who'd broken their hearts.

'Do you mind if I go, Dr Dora?'

Dr Dora was eyeing her with a quizzical expression. 'But you hate harems, Dr Shiraz. Are you sure?'

Shiraz nodded and hastened out with her black medical valise. Though she admired the Englishwoman's zeal in setting up this twenty-two-bed women's wing a decade ago, and in the face of great opposition from the clergy and the conservative nobles, their relationship did not encourage confidences.

'We need you,' Dr Dora had pleaded with Shiraz when she had arrived in Hyderabad six months ago. 'The women here are in purdah. They can't be seen or touched by a male doctor. Having you here would make all the difference to them.'

To Shiraz, who'd come to the city to bring Cyrus's ashes to his mother, it made no difference whether she stayed on here or returned to Madras and her parents. She didn't care what she did; there was nothing to live for. Joining Dora's staff, pouring every ounce of energy into healing the sick and infirm until she could barely stand at night – this had become her penance for not being able to protect the fragile life in her womb, and for Cyrus.

She hurried through Afzulgunj Hospital's grand foyer, pausing to pick up a baby crawling on the mud-streaked marble floor and return her to the mother huddled by a granite pillar. Her coachman was waiting by her carriage under a pipal tree. The hospital's location by Afzul Gate allowed swift progress across Purana Pul Bridge to the Residency, and then down Musi River road, passing her home and a handful of vegetable carts. Soon the Baig lake appeared, its still water reflecting the sky, the brown-blue of a medicine bottle.

They bowled past Niloufer's house. It looked forlorn and deserted. She swallowed the lump in her throat.

At the Baig palace gate, hot fury flooded her insides. Why weren't the guards in the white of mourning? How ill was Nawab Zulfikar that he couldn't be bothered to give the ritual respect Niloufer deserved as his wife? Then the significance of the burgundy colour struck her – the colour of the cummerbund wrapped around the young girl's neck. Could the Baig sons have carried out such gruesome murders?

The soldiers allowed them to enter. The horses cantered down a long driveway, looping around to the back where nobles placed their harems – as if housing the women was an afterthought. Through the glass of the carriage window, she glimpsed gracious marble arches adorning the sandstone edifice, and closer to the driveway, a gardener crouched over a bed of yellow cosmos and plucked the spent flowers. This sense of a routine day among the nawab's retainers further kindled her ire. How dare they carry on as if all was well?

The carriage came to a halt by a whitewashed wall high enough that no man standing on an elephant could peer over into the garden it enclosed. Shiraz stepped out onto the blue mosaic-inlaid flagstone and took the two steps to the door. It opened as she raised her hand to the lion's head knocker, a barefoot young girl in a patched kameez and pyjamas standing within. A slave.

A familiar helpless rage welled up in Shiraz at how commonplace it was in the Deccan to own human beings, how uncaring the wealthy were in treating fellow humans as objects, making slaves of them. Slaves in other harems bore scars on their bodies and faces, wounds she had stitched and patched up. That's why she'd stopped going to harems, unable to restrain herself from tearing into the wives and mistresses in the harems, inevitably forcing Dora to step in and pacify the situation. Though this girl's quick and impish smile and unmarred complexion didn't indicate a life of torment and beatings, Shiraz wanted to make sure.

'Do they treat you well?' Shiraz asked.

Looking puzzled at the question, the girl nodded.

'Do they beat you?'

The girl frowned, shook her head, shot her a scared glance and hurried ahead as if to escape a madwoman.

Shiraz followed through the dark corridor reeking of coconut oil and jasmine. Each time she entered these cages, the indignity of the women's lives struck her forcibly: trapped behind high walls, at the mercy of their powerful husbands, and on the man's death, left to the charity of his successor. Until she'd set foot in a harem, Shiraz hadn't realised how important seeing the sky was to her sense of feeling free. Niloufer would have lived entombed behind this door had she followed the tradition. If only she had, Shiraz thought, darling Niloufer would be alive now.

The girl stopped at the corner room and opened the door to a luxurious chamber with indigo and saffron silk carpets. Shiraz breathed in the fresh scent of rose water, the daylight diffused by pale green damask curtains screening a large window.

An older woman and a middle-aged attendant hovered by a four-poster bed with a mosquito net gathered and tied to the rosewood posts with golden tassels. Rarely had she seen western furniture in these harems; the wives usually slept on thick mattresses while the attendants had to make do with the stone floor.

A dryad in the woods – the phrase floated into Shiraz's head as she gazed at the woman, about her own age, lying on the bed. Ali Baig's wife was a beauty with sculpted cheekbones and lush lips, now pressed together as tightly as her eyes.

'The hakim is here, Begum,' the old woman said.

The lady's large eyes flickered towards her as Shiraz came to sit at her bedside and picked up the lady's wrist. 'What's your name?'

'Maryam.'

'Maryam, what's the matter?' No fever, normal pulse rate, cool forehead.

The lady darted a glance at the older woman and closed her eyes, tears leaking from their corners.

Sensing that she would only speak when they were alone, Shiraz told the attendants to step out.

As soon as the door shut, Maryam sat up and seized her hands, a wild plea in her eyes. 'Help me, Doctor. My Mohsin is missing. Only five years old, my only child.'

Shiraz frowned. 'When did he disappear?'

'The day before yesterday. He was playing in the garden with his nursemaid at teatime and when I went to call them for dinner, he wasn't there. Neither was Devi, his nurse.'

'Surely your husband—'

'Don't mention him,' she cried out. 'He is the reason my baby has been kidnapped.' She flung herself back and sobbed piteously into the bolster.

'What do you mean?'

The door burst open.

'Who are you?' The man in the doorway scowled. He had dark hair shot with grey, and a hawk-like nose. He was attractive, with an ease in his bones that told Shiraz he enjoyed the company of women, and not only as sexual objects. How she knew it, she couldn't explain.

Shiraz identified herself, and his expression darkened.

'I know who you are, cousin of Niloufer. My wife doesn't need the likes of you attending to her. Leave now. That woman got what she deserved, wandering about in the park at night.'

How dare this brute insult sweet Niloufer? She opened her mouth to say something cutting, but the thought popped in that this was her chance to find out Ali Baig's alibi.

'Where were you last night?' she asked, swallowing her rage.

'Eh, what?' He looked nonplussed, then realising what she meant, he stormed into the room. 'How dare you accuse me of murdering that woman. Get out.'

She rose to her feet and looked him in the eye. 'You hate Niloufer and there was a burgundy cummerbund on the other dead girl. Was it you?'

'Get out of my house.' He loomed over her, fists clenched.

Maryam's clasp on her hand tightened.

'Where's your son?' Shiraz asked.

'What business is it of yours?'

'Your wife is very worried about—'

'Stop involving strangers, Maryam.' He seized his wife's shoulders, and Shiraz's hand slid free. 'I sent the boy to your father in Delhi. Why the hell don't you believe me?'

Panic braced the anger. What was he hiding?

'I don't believe you.' Maryam's voice trembled. 'Why so suddenly? I didn't even bid him goodbye. Why didn't Devi tell me?'

'She went with him, of course,' Ali Baig said, gazing into his wife's eyes. 'You wouldn't have let me send him, that's why I didn't tell you.'

'But why so suddenly?' She put her face in her hands and sobbed. 'You are lying – our son is in danger.'

'Get out, Doctor,' Ali snarled.

Shiraz picked up her valise, and with Ali on her heels, strode out. The door slammed behind her.

In the empty corridor, the attendants having fled, Shiraz hovered outside the room, ear pressed to the door, ready to rush back in if she heard any sign of him beating Maryam. To her surprise, she heard a low murmur, a cajoling tone. Despite his fury, Ali hadn't raised a hand to his wife. In her experience, the menfolk of her patients were free with their curses and fists. She didn't know what to think of this.

–

Shiraz retraced her steps to the entrance, looking for someone to speak to about the child and about meeting Niloufer's husband. Her instincts told her to believe Maryam.

A door opened to her right, and a wrist tinkling with maroon glass bangles beckoned her. It was a young attendant in a long burgundy tunic and baggy pyjamas.

Shiraz entered, hoping the lady in this room – perhaps another wife of Ali or the younger stepson's – would throw more light on the missing child. She wasn't sure how many wives they had; three were allowed by the holy Koran, but the rich might keep several dozen.

The darkened room and a cloying scent of musk and damp struck her unpleasantly in contrast to Maryam's room. Here, the furnishings were traditional: a perfume box, a silver case for the water bottle, a silver drinking cup and a paan box were arranged around a dark velvet-covered cushioned mattress in the centre of the room. Seating arrangements in this city, she'd noted before, mimicked the sun and its planets, with the most powerful person on this central masnad, and others on carpets placed in a semi-circle.

Candles in a crystal chandelier lit up a voluptuous woman reclining on the masnad, a discontented expression marring her fleshy good looks. Instinct told Shiraz that this young woman would have a firm grasp on the goings-on in the harem.

The lady introduced herself as Parveen, Imran Baig's wife.

'Be seated, hakimji,' she said, breathing fast, as if she'd been running. Glittering necklaces circled her neck, bangles studded with white and red stones jangled as she fluttered her fingers.

Next to her, a floor-length gilt-edged mirror reflected another young girl moving a palm leaf back and forth, fanning her.

Shiraz slid off her shoes and sat on a teal silk carpet, folding her legs under her. No mourning whites on Parveen either. Her lips tightened. Nawab Zulfikar had a lot to answer for, and she wouldn't leave without confronting him.

'What's wrong with Maryam?' Parveen drawled. 'What's her new drama? Always she's making a fuss. Is she going on about her son, my little dervish?'

'Where is he?' Shiraz asked, frowning.

The lady raised the lid of the silver box by her elbow, and taking out a betel leaf from one of its many compartments, began making paan.

Shiraz gritted her teeth while Parveen scooped the pale pink paste of slaked lime and smeared it with her index finger on the leaf.

'She said her son is missing. Is he?'

'Of course not. Mohsin is a real handful, that one.' The warmth in Parveen's tone and the smile playing on her lips shaved off years. 'Nothing has happened to my little dervish. He's gone off to visit his grandfather. Trust that drama queen to carry on like he's been murdered or something. He is very mischievous, you know – we play hide and seek. That ugly nurse of his, she won't let him out of her sight even for a moment, sticks to him like a leech. What does she think I'm going to do? Me, a second mother to my little dervish. Must be Maryam's doing. Just because I don't have children doesn't mean...' Her voice trailed off, sadness creasing her face.

This practice of measuring a wife's worth by the number of children she bore, especially sons, as if the man had nothing to do with it! It was insupportable, Shiraz thought, and her tone gentled.

'Parveen Begum, why did Ali Baig send the child away so suddenly?'

'To protect my little dervish, of course.' The lady continued packing the leaf with areca nut, cloves, cardamom, rose petal paste and tobacco paste.

'From whom?'

'I can't tell you. Ask Maryam. She sees things.'

'What things?'

'You know, spirits, ghosts. Ali sahib is a devil worshipper. Hai, don't repeat it to anyone.' The malice in her eyes said otherwise. 'So what if her husband didn't tell her. She'd insist on going instead of being here, supporting Ali sahib in his troubles.' Parveen folded the leaf deftly, pinned it with a clove and held it out.

'What troubles?' Shiraz shook her head, not caring for the grainy taste.

'Oh, I shouldn't say.' The lady deftly popped it into her own mouth, wedging it against a cheek. 'My husband will be angry with me. Now, tell me, what did the killer do to Nawab sahib's new wife? You are her cousin, no? I heard Ali sahib.'

Shiraz gave her a sharp look. The woman had eavesdropped; that's why she'd been out of breath.

'What troubles does Ali Baig have?' she asked again.

'Oh, I can't say. My husband will be furious. He told me to keep it a secret. I heard your cousin was stabbed in the heart.' Her gaze held an avid gleam. 'A river of blood, they said. Did the murderer take her heart? Was it her lover? Ooh, there was such drama here when they met your cousin. Our husbands told us to send a message saying we were unwell.'

The images conjured by this woman sickened Shiraz. Poor Niloufer, she hadn't mentioned these slights to Shiraz. What else had she kept a secret?

'What drama?' Shiraz grimly soldiered on.

'Ooh, Ali sahib was shouting like a mad bull when we heard about the marriage. He called your cousin all kinds of names. Maryam wanted to wear mourning for your cousin but Ali sahib has forbidden it for all of us. Nawab sahib is in a very bad state, they say – dying.'

Shiraz's heart sank at the news. Zulfikar Baig was her only ally in this palace. Unless… 'Your husband, was he angry too?'

Parveen scowled. 'No. He said it wasn't his business, he is only the younger son. Everything will go to Ali sahib as the eldest son. I was supposed to marry him, you know.' Parveen turned to the spittoon by her elbow and spat.

'Ali Baig?' Shiraz asked, looking away from the stream of red issuing from the woman's mouth.

Parveen nodded vigorously. 'But that woman ensnared him. She's my cousin, you know. So I was betrothed to Imran sahib – my father said he was clever and grew money.' She spat again. 'Little did my father know. My husband has taken all my jewellery. See these bangles?' She shook her wrist, and the metal bits knocked, making a thudding sound. 'I have to wear imitation stones and gold-plated brass bangles like this slave.' She picked up the enamelled stick next to her and rapped the attendant's knuckles. 'Fan faster, imbecile. Now tell me, hakimji, was your cousin naked when you found her?'

Such ghoulish delight in other people's misery! Shiraz rose to her feet, slid on her shoes and hurried out, furious with Parveen – a mad horse who needed to be held in check, an unenviable task for the husband. Shiraz might have dismissed the woman's description of her sister-in-law as a drama queen except that Parveen's fondness for the child was unmistakable. Could Maryam's frantic plea stem from pique that her husband had not consulted her? An overblown response, to be sure... but there was no telling what fancies a woman caged within these walls might harbour. Oh god, stop it... she was starting to sound like Dr Currimbhoy.

In the corridor, Shiraz bumped into a wiry man in his mid-thirties. He had regular features and wore a grey angharkha, bugloos and a signet on his little finger.

He paled. 'How can you be Nilo...' His voice trailed off.

She raised her scarf and covered her head, inwardly completing his sentence. With her pale skin and not dissimilar features to Niloufer, his mistake was not surprising.

'Forgive me, madam,' he bowed, recovering his composure. 'I am Imran Baig.'

His pleasant tone contrasted with the brother's strident voice further down the corridor.

Shiraz introduced herself.

'Why are you still here, Doctor?' Ali said, striding towards them. 'I told you to leave.'

'If I may speak, esteemed brother, you are scaring the lady,' Imran said in a firm tone.

'She's that woman's cousin, here to spy on us. Posing impertinent questions to me instead of asking why our father's new wife was wandering alone in the park at night.'

'You are insulting, sir,' Shiraz snapped. 'How dare you make such vile insinuations. Niloufer loved your father – she was not in the least bit interested in his money. You people don't even have the courtesy to mourn her. I'd never have expected it of Nawab Baig.' She paused, then struck again. 'Tell me, where is your son's nursemaid?'

Ali barrelled into her. She staggered back, cracking her shoulder against the brick wall, and a sharp twinge tore into her as she watched Ali raise his fist. For the first time in her life, she felt utterly helpless. He could kill her, and nobody would raise a finger to help. Her eyes shut of their own accord, and she found herself slipping down, the brick cool against her back.

Fight, a voice said in her head.

She forced her eyes open. Ali's fist shot towards her. She flung out her clenched hands and hit something soft. A cry. Was it from her?

Ali bent over, clutching his stomach.

She shrank against the wall, her eye going to the dagger strapped to his cummerbund. Her hands grabbed it as he lunged for her. The blow never came.

Imran's wiry body blocked Ali and grabbed his arm. 'Esteemed brother, she is our guest. It's dangerous for you.'

Ali stiffened, shock flitting across his face, as if Imran had revealed a secret. Shaking off his brother, Ali turned and stormed back to his bedchamber.

Shiraz released her breath and slid down to the floor.

'Are you all right, Dr Daruwalla?'

She gave a jerky nod, not trusting herself to speak until her heartbeat slowed. Shivers rippled through her. Nobody had ever raised a fist to her before.

'Please accept my heartfelt apologies. My esteemed elder brother is under a great deal of stress.'

Shiraz rose, pressing her back against the wall, hoping her legs wouldn't give way. They held up, though her insides felt like water.

'Please forgive him, Dr Daruwalla.' Imran picked up her valise from the floor where it had toppled to one side and matched her slow pace. 'It should never have happened, and neither should your cousin's murder. Please accept my deepest condolences on her death.'

'I want to see Nawab Zulfikar Baig,' she said, hating the tremble in her voice. He would set things right.

'I'm afraid my father is in a coma and fading fast.' His reply crushed her hope of seeing Niloufer's husband again. It was now up to her and Soob to find the killer without any help from Nawab Zulfikar.

'Then your father doesn't know that his household is not mourning Niloufer,' Shiraz snapped as they reached the carriage.

Imran hesitated and, after a shamed glance at her, opened the carriage door. 'My esteemed brother will not permit it.'

She got in, clamping down her anger. 'Where is your nephew?'

'Have you been talking to my esteemed brother's wife? She makes dramas. My nephew and his nursemaid are in Delhi with his grand-father.'

'But why didn't your brother tell his wife?' She leaned out of the window as he rapped on the carriage side.

He must not have heard her.

The coachman clicked his tongue and the horses started moving. More armed and mounted men had assembled at the main gate. How could a child be kidnapped from this fortress?

But part of her hesitated at dismissing it as a figment of Maryam's imagination. Ali had attacked her when she asked about the child and the nursemaid. What was he afraid of? What was he hiding? The problems hinted at by Parveen? Was it connected with the child's disappearance?

Maryam believed her child was in danger, the panic in her eyes too stark to ignore. Even if it turned out the boy was safe, she would believe Maryam for now. The memory of her own baby would not let Shiraz abandon another mother.

Chapter Seventeen

Soob reined in his horse by a handcart at the Delhi Gate entrance to the city and bought a green coconut. With the fruit's top lopped off by the vendor, and the tender white hollowed out to create a spout, Soob tipped the juice into his mouth, the cool liquid tunnelling down his throat.

A contingent of Rajput soldiers with gleaming shields of polished hide marched past on their way back to barracks after night duty at the city gate. Initially, he'd been struck by the presence of so many races in the city bazaars, until he'd learned that the Nizam and other high nobles hired mercenaries from the north of India, the Frontier Province, Arabia and the Hadramut, a custom from the seventeenth century under the first Nizam, a former Governor of the Deccan for the Mughal Emperor Aurangzeb. It was no small irony, he thought wryly, that these mercenaries were more trusted than the locals, the hope being that they'd engage in empire-building efforts in their own homelands, not here.

Leaving behind the yellow domes of the mosques rising above the grey stone city wall, he rode across Chaderghat-Oliphant Bridge. With Wilberforce hell-bent on seeing the Ripper's hand in these murders, he had little faith that the Englishman would interrogate his friends, the Templetons.

A British soldier scrutinised his identity paper, then a chit bearing the Resident's seal secured between two loose foolscap sheets in a register, and let him in.

Unlike the web of the city bazaars, the Residency was laid out like a chessboard, its squares cut by smooth asphalt roads lined with neem and peepul trees arrowing past small rain-fed lakes. Granite boulders jutted here and there, marring the orderliness the British residents had tried to impose on the chaotic Deccan landscape. He rode past the Residency

Gardens, the Bank of Bengal, the Telegraph Office and the English Post Office, passing stunted white houses with little Grecian porticos lived in by Anglo-Indians and the British. Finally, the sparkling teal of the lake appeared behind the tapering asoka trees.

The bright sunlight revealed what had been hidden last night: the grand sandstone mansions with their gardens and winding driveways, underlining Nawab Zulfikar Baig's wealth. He rode up to the ornamented iron gate of Templeton's house, and a guard emerged from a wooden box framed by a mantle of purple bougainvillaea.

Despite the khaki shirt he'd changed into from the bloodstained one, an avid gleam appeared in the guard's eyes as he saluted, as if recognising an official.

'Is it about Begum Baig, huzoor? I told the constable she left here when the timekeeper at the nawab's palace beat the drum ten and a half times.'

'Did you see her walk towards the park?'

The guard shook his head. 'The sahib summoned me to put out the lamps by the front door.'

'Mr Templeton didn't come to the gate?'

'No, huzoor.'

'You informed him when Mrs Baig's guard came to enquire?'

'Yes, huzoor. He told me to say the begum left at half past ten.'

Something wasn't right about these answers.

'Didn't he help in the search?'

'No, huzoor.'

A slow burn kindled in Soob's chest. Was it because Niloufer was a native? He used to believe racialism didn't matter, seeing it merely as a problem of attitude and manners. But now, as he rode down the curving driveway, past a gang of squabbling jungle babblers on the lawn abutting the hedge, it dawned on him that the smallest inaction arising from racialism could have a fatal result and so ought not to be tolerated, even for a moment.

The sun pinched his face and shone sharp on the silver leaves of the sage and pale blue plumbago flowers – an inspired planting (possibly Phoebe Templeton's doing) that drew bright lines on either side of the driveway in the sunlight and would do the same in the moonlight. Their shared love of plants had drawn the two women into a friendship, Niloufer's mother had said.

If racialism underpinned Templeton's lack of concern for Niloufer's safety, why allow a friendship to blossom with his wife? Or was there a more sinister reason for Templeton's boorish behaviour?

Ahead, the two-storey mansion's facade glittered, painted and toughened from a lime paste mixed with seashells and eggshells. A marble portico divided the half dozen rooms on each floor, their slatted green window shutters firmly closed to keep the heat out.

A stable boy took the reins, and an attendant led Soob through a corridor lined with terracotta pots of fern and money plant.

The study's decor was meant to evoke an English gentleman's sanctuary – two maroon leather wingback chairs by an unlit fireplace with a snarling tigerskin hung above, a writing desk with a comfortable chair in the centre of the room, and a bookcase by the far wall with tomes bound in fine calfskin. The books looked too new to have been taken out and read, though. The furnishings failed to conjure the scent of tobacco and the crackling fire of an English winter, which was surely the intention, exuding instead a mildewy odour in the humid heat of India. Cane and wicker, though more suitable, would be rejected by this breed of Englishman, intent on recreating England in a hot and foreign clime. In his experience, this hankering for home typically marched shoulder to shoulder with a disgust for the native.

Arthur Templeton turned from the sideboard, a snifter of whisky in hand and a sneer on his face. Around Soob's own age, thirty-two or so, but a couple of inches shorter, the Englishman's morning suit in worsted linen, mutton-chop whiskers on a tanned face, and a shiny signet with a diamond on his little finger gave off the aura of new wealth. The nervous energy in his green eyes caught Soob's notice.

'What seems to be the problem? You aren't from the Residency Police.'

'Chief Inspector Soobramania of the City Police,' he said. 'I'm here on the matter of Mrs Baig's murder.'

Templeton scowled and didn't ask him to sit. 'At least you speak English properly, not like some of your fellow natives.' He clicked his fingers. 'Soobramania, now I've got it. Aren't you the chap who stopped the insurrection? Of course you are. We've been trying to get an interview with you. For a native, you didn't do a bad job there. When can I send my chap to you?

'Didn't you hear me?' Templeton raised his voice and spoke slowly, mimicking a local accent. 'When can my chap come to interview you?'

'Mr Templeton, kindly tell me why you didn't escort Mrs Baig home.'

The Englishman's face tightened. 'What for? She lives on the other side of the park. I told her I could summon her guard or send my chap with her, but she refused.'

'Did she have a lantern?'

'Of course, I bloody well gave her one when we said goodbye in the portico.'

Soob eyed him coldly. 'So you didn't walk her to the gate.'

'Who the hell are you to lecture me in manners?' Templeton thumped the mantlepiece, the brush of his fist releasing a moth from the tiger skin. 'She was perfectly safe with my guard watching her.'

'Didn't you call him in immediately?'

'So what if I did? What's it to you?'

It was bad form not seeing Niloufer safely to her home but hardly surprising. The man's defensiveness, though, was ringing an alarm. Might he have called the guard back in deliberately?

'Why didn't one of your other guests drop her home?'

'They'd bloody well left, hadn't they?'

Templeton turned his back and poured himself another shot of whisky from the decanter, sloshing some on the sideboard.

It was a little early in the day for alcohol, Soob thought. He asked what time they had left.

Templeton's cheeks reddened. 'Around a quarter past ten or so. Look, what's the point of asking me these questions? You should be looking for the killer.'

'Why did Mrs Baig stay on?' Soob continued.

Templeton stiffened, then knocked back the drink in a convulsive movement.

Soob waited in silence.

'I don't know,' Templeton said, not meeting his eye. 'Women's talk, I suppose.'

'Your wife and Mrs Baig were friends?'

'No, no, she was a neighbour, that's all,' he said, face paling.

'Kindly call your wife.'

'She's not at home.' Templeton bared his teeth in a smile. 'Out with her companion.'

'When will she be back?'

'Don't know.'

'How long was Mrs Baig with your wife?' Soob persisted.

'About ten minutes or so. I returned from seeing off the others. She emerged from my wife's sitting room, and I escorted her out.'

'Your wife didn't accompany Mrs Baig to the front door?'

'No.'

Surely Phoebe Templeton ought to have seen her visitor out. Rohini had always done so with her guests.

'Then what did you do?'

'I came here and wrote my article.'

'Nobody saw you?'

'What do you mean?'

Soob took a stab at his hunch. 'Did your wife quarrel with Mrs Baig?'

Carriage wheels sounded outside.

Templeton paled. 'What the hell are you implying? Get out.'

Muffled voices in the corridor. The door opened. A lady in her late twenties stood there in a teal blue morning gown with tapered sleeves. A halo of auburn hair, skin that had spent time in the sun, a rangy figure, grey eyes spitting fury.

'Why didn't you tell me about Niloufer, Arthur?'

The same lemony perfume worn by Niloufer tickled his nose as she stormed past to her husband.

Hidden behind her, in a light pink gown, was a plump woman with brown curls, of a similar age. Her fixed pleasant expression was that of someone who had to paste on a cheerful facade regardless of how she felt inside. He'd seen it before in nurses and governesses. This must be the companion.

'Who are you?' Phoebe turned to Soob, her direct tone typical of Americans and those born into great wealth.

Soob introduced himself and said he had questions for her.

'No need,' Templeton snapped. 'She'll tell you the same thing.'

'Mrs Templeton, what did you and Mrs Baig talk about after the other guests departed? Was she upset in any way?'

Blood drained from her face. She collapsed into the armchair. After a moment, she asked in a whisper, 'Is that why she was walking in the park? Because of me? Was she killed there?' A queer intensity flashed in her eyes. 'Was she killed by the fountain?'

'She didn't mean anything by it, sir,' the companion said hurriedly.

'Phoebe, stop talking.' Templeton planted his hand on his wife's arm.

She shook it off while holding Soob's gaze. 'The fountain gave Niloufer the jitters. It was as if death was waiting for her there, she said only last week.'

'My wife doesn't know what she is saying. Get out, sir.'

The companion looked frightened.

'Mrs Templeton, anything you can tell me about Niloufer's mood when she left would help us. We want to understand why she was in the park so late at night.'

Husband and wife exchanged glances. This was the first time she'd looked at Templeton properly since entering the room. It made him think of Rohini; she never looked him in the eye if he'd annoyed her. What had Templeton done to make his wife so angry?

'What did you and Mrs Baig discuss last night, Mrs Templeton?'

Phoebe stared at the shuttered window, gripping the leather armrest so tightly that her fingers gleamed white.

'I told this fellow you two were acquaintances.' Templeton's tone carried a warning. 'You met in the park and chatted about petunias and berries and whatnot.'

Soob tried another tack. 'While riding in, I couldn't help noticing your garden. I'm also a botanist. You've achieved a nice harmony of European structure and Deccani drifts. Made your garden speak in two accents.'

She looked at him as if, for the first time, he appeared human to her. 'You know your plants, sir.'

'Is that what you spoke of?'

Tears trickled from the corners of her eyes, and she closed them tightly.

Templeton grabbed his arm. 'Enough of this, Inspector. I'll be sending a complaint to Ludlow. I know your commissioner very well.'

He set his own grip on the Englishman's wrist, pressed a nerve on the inner side.

'Ow,' Templeton yelled, his fingers letting go.

'Do you have a key to the park's side entrance, madam?'

Phoebe's gaze skittered away. The metallic chitter of a squirrel sounded from outside the window.

He turned to the companion. 'Yes,' she said and flushed when Templeton glowered at her.

'Can I see it?'

'No,' Templeton barked. 'Keep quiet, Edith.'

'Was she... did she suffer?' Phoebe opened her eyes, a plea in them.

'The murderer cut her throat and stabbed her many times.'

Phoebe clutched her head and rocked to and fro.

'Stop badgering my wife, Inspector.'

She was in no state to answer his questions. He dropped Templeton's hand and strode to the door. On the way, he caught a glint of sympathy in the Edith's eyes. He would see the companion separately and find out what the couple were hiding.

He stood for a moment in the foyer to let his eyes adjust to the sun's glare. Clearly Templeton and Edith were nervous about Phoebe, and she was angry with her husband. Was it connected to Niloufer? What did Phoebe and Niloufer discuss, or more likely quarrel about, when she stayed back?

'I'll be lodging a formal complaint against you, Inspector,' a red-faced Templeton said, dogging his heels.

'I look forward to reading it. It is Chief Inspector Soobramania.' Soob spelt his name out, and with each letter Templeton's flush grew deeper, jaw tighter.

The stable boy who'd been watching for him hurried over with his bay. As he rode out, a familiar carriage came towards him from the Baig palace. Shiraz's. He angled his horse into its path.

Chapter Eighteen

The Brahmin's words – that Constable John Furlow was Jack the Ripper – stuck in his craw. He should have known the slippery fellow was the native on the bloody committee.

Wilberforce massaged his wrist, still tender from the man's pinch, and wishing he'd smashed his fist into that smirking face, he climbed up the dozen steps to the Resident's palace door. The mid-morning sun skewered his neck, sent sweat rolling down his temples as he paused halfway to take in the imposing Corinthian columns. His spirits lifted somewhat at this symbol of British might – a colossal sphinx on either side looking down at him – as implacable as Her Imperial Majesty was in ruling her empire. And if that didn't inspire awe in these natives, brute force would undoubtedly do the trick, he thought, noting the imposing cannon at the foot of the stairs. Here, unlike in the Baig palace, Wilberforce didn't feel like some toff's lackey; he saw himself as an essential cog in running the empire.

Up by the magnificent door, he espied Bill Colley standing at attention, guarding the portal. Bill solemnly contemplated the shimmering haze enveloping the river and the city's bastions in the distance. Not a whisker twitched on his face, one that exuded a cherubic innocence at odds with his real nature. Bill never forgot a face or a name, when and where he had seen them and what they had worn. Their shared first name and the Spitalfields connection, Wilberforce's old beat and Bill's childhood home, had forged a firm bond between countrymen stuck in a foreign land.

'I was expecting to see you, Inspector Wilberforce,' the doorman said in a deep baritone. 'Dastardly doings there were last night by them nobs and the nabob.'

'Bill, we've lost a fine policeman in you.'

'Our nobs disappeared with the local one for over an hour, and all the courtiers, the whole hoity-toity lot of them, ran around like chickens looking for their chicks.' He jabbed his thumb at the sky. 'It surprises me them higher-ups haven't warned you to keep your nose out of the nobs' affairs.'

A part of Wilberforce braced at the thought of the inevitable struggle with his own superiors. He'd worry about that when it came to the crunch.

'Was the local Nawab Ali Baig?'

'Wouldn't you like to know.'

Wilberforce didn't have time for this.

Sharp blue eyes sussed his mood, and then out came the nod.

'Do you know where they went?'

'You should see my friend, McAllister, in the stables. Head groom. Not a great admirer of the police, though. Tell him I sent you, otherwise you won't get a word out of him.'

'Won't forget this, Bill, thanks. You don't happen to remember what the nobs were wearing, do you?'

Bill rattled off the descriptions, his eyes following the lazy circling of a kestrel in the sky. When it came to Ali Baig, the mention of a cream coloured jacket, tight pantaloons, a scarlet cummerbund—

'A scarlet cummerbund. You're sure that's what the native chap had on?'

At the nod, the blood pounded faster in Wilberforce's veins. The colour of Ali Baig's cummerbund matched the one around his step-mother's neck. But when Wilberforce had seen him, he'd been togged up to the nines in black and silver.

'When Ali Baig returned, had he changed into a black and silver frock coat?'

'Bull's eye, Bill.' He gave Wilberforce a broad wink and a hearty slap on the shoulder.

At the stables, the head groom, a spare man with a gloomy face, gave monosyllabic answers to his questions.

'Did the Russian Duke and the Earl come to the stables last night?'

'Aye.'

'When did they come?'

'Last night.'

'What time?'

'Don't know.'

Wilberforce tried again. 'Did they come with a native nob?'

'Aye.'

'Who was it?'

'Don't know.'

Bloomin' water out of a stone.

'Bill Colley is a friend. Told me to speak to you.'

'Colley, you say?' The first glint of animation appeared on his face. 'They left in thon nabob's carriage. Must've been around quarter past nine. Giggling like a bunch of wee lassies, they were. Up to no good, if ye ask me.'

Sending up a mental thanks to Bill, Wilberforce asked, 'Do you know where they went?'

'To the nabob's house. Waited around in the stables for their summons, so his coachman says to me lads. Grooms and servants were under orders to keep out of the garden.'

'Did they return before the thunderstorm?'

'Aye, but only just.'

The rain had thundered down around midnight, which meant they'd been in the vicinity during the murders. If only Wilberforce could search the Baig gardens, he'd be sure to find evidence – bloodstains, bits of flesh or bone even – pointing to a Hellfire ritual. He knew it. The sick bugger must have changed his bloodied clothes after cutting the victims' throats. Why hadn't the other two changed theirs? Or did he do it alone, with his friends simply an alibi? It had worked for Ali Baig before, in London.

He shook the Scotsman's calloused hand and strode back to his horse.

Chapter Nineteen

Shiraz leaned out of the carriage window. 'Soob, I'm so glad to see you.'

She looked pale, and her normally neat hair was coming out in untidy strands from a plaited bun. The humidity pressed thick and hot around them.

'Did you know that Ali Baig's son is missing?' she continued in a thin voice. 'The child disappeared two days ago, his wife said. He denies it, says the boy is with his grandfather in Delhi. His brother and sister-in-law say she makes dramas all the time, but what if she's right? Soob, can you check with the Delhi police?'

He stared down at her. 'What were you doing in that harem?'

She didn't meet his eye. 'His wife was hysterical and I offered to go because Dr Dora was busy.'

'I don't believe it. You went there to find out where Ali was last night and to try and talk to Nawab Baig. I told you I would deal with it.' He put his hand on her arm resting on the sill. Didn't she see how dangerous it was?

She winced.

His mind blanked for a moment, unable to fathom the reason. A cold chill gripped his heart. He pushed up her sleeve. Red bruises. As if someone had gripped her hard and shaken her.

'Who did this? Ali Baig?'

She twitched her arm away and retreated into the carriage.

'Suleiman, carry on,' she said.

'No, Suleiman,' Soob said, dismounting. 'Get down and stand by the horses' heads.' The grizzled coachman darted an anxious look at his mistress and complied.

'Tell me, Shiraz.'

Blood pounded his temples at her halting account of the attack. 'I will take it up at the highest levels, you can be sure of it.'

'Please don't. It will make things difficult for Dr Dora and our hospital. They may use this to shut us down, saying it's for our own protection.'

'He cannot be allowed to get away with it. What if he'd broken your arm? Did he injure you anywhere else?'

She shook her head with difficulty. Stiff neck. As if Soob was going to believe her now. His lips clamped in a grim line. He owed it to Cyrus to keep Shiraz safe.

'His younger brother, Imran, came to my rescue, so let's forget it,' she said, a plea in her eye. 'Soob, we have to find out if the child has been kidnapped. Imran's horrid wife Parveen said Ali had problems. She refused to tell me what they were, but what if—'

'Why are you deliberately putting yourself in danger, Shiraz?' he interrupted. 'You loved Niloufer and you want her killer found, I understand that. But let me do my job. I don't want to have to worry about your safety. Anything could've happened to you in that harem.'

'Don't treat me like a defenceless woman,' she snapped. 'I must find out about the child. Ali attacked me when I asked about the nursemaid. What if his troubles are connected to some quarrel with another nawab? They could've kidnapped the boy and killed the nursemaid – she is a Hindu because Parveen called her an infidel.'

'Oh, for god's sake, Shiraz, leave it to me. You were defenceless against Ali.' Even as he said it, he winced inwardly. Rubbing in this fact would eat at her, he knew, but what choice did he have? For her own safety, she had to stay out of the investigation.

She turned her face away.

Was she crying? He bunched the reins in his fist. 'Please Shiraz, leave it to me.'

'I have to find out if the child is safe. I have to.'

'I'll send a telegram to the Delhi police today. HC Muhammad will find out his grandfather's name. Leave it to me, Shiraz. *Please.*'

She knocked jerkily on the carriage side. This time the coachman clambered up to his box, and taking care not to meet Soob's eye, clicked his tongue. The horses set off.

He rode behind them, furious with her for putting herself in danger, and furious with himself for making her feel weak. He hardly saw her as some delicate flower. He'd admired her from the moment they'd met at a dinner in London hosted by a British parliamentarian for Indian scholars. Her grit and intelligence had been made clear, much to his amusement, when she interrupted their host's drunken toast to her fine eyes and comely figure, with a pithy rejoinder from *King Lear*. 'Holla, holla! That eye that told you so look'd but asquint,' she'd proclaimed in a ringing tone. Cyrus had been there too, and a month later, Soob had stood witness to the couple's marriage.

Why couldn't Shiraz see that a woman – and what's more, a *widow* – had little power against any man, much less a nobleman. Her doggedness would make her hound Ali Baig. It was frightening to imagine what might happen if there was some truth to Shiraz's speculation. It wasn't uncommon for these Deccan nobles to use their mercenary-soldiers in feuds to kidnap the sons of their rivals. The city police did not get involved in such matters, the deputy commissioner had warned Soob. And with such an aggressive personality and prickly demeanour, feuds were not unlikely in Ali's case. If so, Shiraz's prying would put her in grave danger.

He drew the horse to one side to allow a vegetable cart to pass.

Soob would make arrangements to protect her.

She would hate what he was going to do, but he'd rather she was angry with him than see her dead.

–

The yellow-and-silver livery of the footman standing outside police headquarters raised his spirits. The note to Lady Falloner had worked. But first, he'd see to Shiraz's safety. Now he was beginning to understand, though he didn't like it one bit, why the men here caged their women. He dismounted and gave the reins to the footman. 'I'll be back in a jiffy.'

'Send the HC up to my office,' he told the duty constable and took the steps two at a time to his office. As he entered, boots thudded up behind him.

'Sir.' The HC saluted, breathing hard.

'At ease, Muhammad. I need two reliable men to shadow Dr Daruwalla, one for the day and another one for the night. Put them on the job immediately, within the hour. And find Ram Rahim.'

'Yes, huzoor.' HC Muhammad saluted.

'Do you know the name of Begum Maryam Baig's father? He lives in Delhi.'

Of course he did. Muhammad's encyclopaedic knowledge of every Hyderabadi nobleman's family tree rivalled none.

'Shabash! Well done. Find out from your footman cousin about the nursemaid who looks after Maryam Baig's boy. What's her religion, what does she look like, is she married, widowed, any children?'

'Yes, sir.'

'And send this telegram to the Delhi Police immediately.' He sat at his desk and pencilled the message on his writing pad.

Chapter Twenty

Soob followed the footman on horseback, cutting through the busy bangle bazaar. Though the city palace was only a few minutes' ride down the avenue, the footman called in excruciating, sonorous tones, 'Make way, make way for the esteemed Chief Inspector.' Everyone – shopkeepers, cartmen, pedestrians – recognised yellow and silver as the ruler's colours, and now thanks to his personal town crier, they knew he was meeting the foreign guests.

'Going to arrest Yakub,' he overheard a shopkeeper say with a knowing nod as he rode past.

Soob gave the reins of his bay to a groom at the ornate entrance to Chowmahalla Palace, the city residence of the richest native ruler in India, who was among the wealthiest men in the world. Wealth and luxury he treated with indifference, having been raised to respect scholarship and spartan living. But even a saint would be impressed, he thought, as he followed the footman towards two guest palaces of white marble flanking a rectangular pond in the courtyard. Beyond, an archway twined with pink damask roses led to the Nizam's living quarters, a labyrinth of houses and pavilions, off-limits to him and the ruler's guests. Half of the seven thousand harem inhabitants were women, including three thousand wives and relatives of the Nizam's father, all guarded by a corps of a hundred women soldiers, known as the Amazons. A dozen flamboyantly dressed courtiers lounged in the shade outside the guest palace, fanning themselves. They observed his unassuming khaki tunic and pants, sneers mingling with avid curiosity and an unspoken question: were the foreign guests involved in yesterday's murders?

A richly garbed chamberlain led him into the hallway. More furnishings of damask and brocade, velvets and silks under crystal chandeliers left Soob with a slightly sick feeling.

Lady Ariel Falloner's presence, while smoothing his welcome, would permit only oblique questions about the visitors' movements last night. It was strange to think that he had known her only for two weeks, having met her on his first day in Hyderabad. Seeing an auburn-haired Englishwoman being mobbed by mercenaries in the bazaar, he'd hurried to the rescue only to realise that this youthful widow of a famous diplomat wished to photograph them for a series on the people of India. They had struck up an easy acquaintance, which had deepened quickly after events had put Ariel in acute danger. Soob had rescued her, and today, he'd shamelessly traded on it.

He glimpsed a glass billiards table and gold and silver statues in one room, and in another, tables with mechanical gadgets and clocks in gold, silver and gilt, each with a different time, chiming different hours. A sentry in each alcove between the rooms saluted as he passed. It would be impossible for the visiting nobles to evade scrutiny in this fishbowl – unless a local had helped.

The chamberlain opened a brass-etched teak door to reveal another large chamber with luxurious furnishings.

'Chief Inspector Soobramania,' the man announced in a sonorous tone.

From a French blue settee in the middle of the room, Lady Ariel Falloner smiled at him, her chestnut hair and cinnamon-coloured muslin gown glowing in the sunlight sloping through the stained-glass windows. A delicate scent of wisteria trailed from her as they shook hands. Above them, a three-bladed ceiling fan – a new invention Soob hadn't seen before – was being plied by an invisible punkahwalla from an alcove outside.

While she looked cool, the same couldn't be said for the two men in the room.

A hawk-nosed man with a cropped beard and a moustache tapered into fine points was seated next to her, wearing a deep red uniform with gold tasselled epaulettes, sweat beading his forehead. She introduced him as Grand Duke Alexei Alexandrovich, her cousin. The other man, in a blue morning coat, dark hair slicked close to the skull, and sporting a bushy moustache, introduced as the Earl of Euston, gave him a curt nod and wandered away without shaking his hand.

Both looked to be in their mid-forties, with a world-weary glint he had seen in other rich men who had indulged in every possible whim. It promised to be a difficult interview.

He sat on a Chippendale chair, took a glass of iced water from a white-robed attendant, and resigned himself to the initial pleasantries.

'Chief Inspector Soobramania, I was telling Alexei about your expedition in the Himalayas,' Lady Ariel said in a low-pitched tone. 'Alexei has climbed the Hindukush mountains with his battalion.'

Her informality with her cousin surprised Soob, the nobility being sticklers for titles, particularly in front of outsiders.

'When was that, Your Excellency?' he asked.

'This very month three years ago. And you, sir?' Deep-set dark eyes examined him with a measured gaze.

'Four years ago, Your Excellency.'

'Alexei, the Chief Inspector wants to talk to you about Grigory Grum Grzhimailo. Such a lovely alliterative name. Did I pronounce it right?'

The Russian entomologist, his excuse for wanting to meet the Grand Duke, wouldn't hold up for long.

'Perfectly, Ariel. Chief Inspector, I did not expect anyone here to know of our great explorer.'

'We met in Chitral. He was also collecting plant specimens.' It wasn't a lie.

The conversation moved to rare plants, and they agreed the search for the elusive Himalayan orchid was like hunting for the Yeti. He was pleasantly surprised by the Grand Duke's knowledge of flora and fauna.

The attendant served tea, coffee, and plates of biscuits and cakes. The supercilious Earl had sloped off and was peering at a horologium in a glass cabinet, which, even from this distance, looked a fine specimen of an astronomical clock.

The Grand Duke began a tale about tracking a snow leopard near Chitral, while Soob sipped coffee and considered how to bring up the murders. When the nobleman paused for breath, Soob asked about his impressions of Hyderabad.

'This ceremonial to-do suffocates me,' the Grand Duke said. 'Give me a gun or a knife and a mountain or a jungle, and I am content.'

'Do you skin your kills?' Soob asked.

'Of course.'

'I don't know how you do it, Alexei,' Ariel said. 'He can peel the skin off a tiger or a leopard without making a single tear.'

Soob didn't doubt it. There was nothing clumsy about this man.

'Spare my blushes, my dear. Sir, would you agree the hunt ought to be fair to the beast?'

Soob inclined his head, though he strongly disapproved of the practice of killing animals for fun.

'It wasn't here. The whole blasted beat was arranged like a military exercise. Men grouped in three lines with an officer in command. Scouts stationed in trees waving a red flag for tiger, white for panther, bear or stags. Once they signalled the game's direction, the senior officer gave the command by bugle call. If the tiger showed signs of breaking back, the beaters fired a blank volley to turn him. Finally, the poor beast was herded to the machan, where we took our shots. I missed deliberately. Bah! What sport is there in this?'

'Your host wants you to go away satisfied, cousin,' Ariel said.

'I'm not,' the Grand Duke retorted. 'Our German cousin boasted he'd bagged four tigers and a leopard here. Didn't say they were served up to him on a platter.' The Grand Duke scowled.

'I, for one, should prefer to leave this place with all my limbs intact,' the Earl of Euston piped up in a querulous voice.

'Alexei, our guest is not interested in your grouse.'

'Tell me, Chief Inspector,' Grand Duke Alexei said. 'How do you hunt your murderers?'

'With stealth and caution, Your Excellency.' He took the opening. 'We had two murders last night in a park near the Residency palace.'

'That's where I'm staying,' Lady Ariel said, clasping her hands and leaning forward. 'Who was killed?'

'Two young women. One was Shiraz's cousin.'

'Oh, that's dreadful. I'll call on her today.'

'Do tell me how they died,' Grand Duke Alexei said, and when Soob described the mutilations and spoke of the silk cummerbund, a strange expression flitted across the nobleman's face.

'Are there any suspects?' The gleam in his eye said he had deduced the reason for Soob's visit.

'The investigation is under the British Residency Police, Your Excellency. I work in the City Police, which answers to the Nizam.'

'These religious savages are the worst sort,' the Earl said. 'I hear they have strange rituals here. They slit their victim's throat and drink the blood. The Devil's devotees the lot of them, thugs.'

'The Thuggees, Your Excellency, are a tribe who strangle their victims and steal their belongings,' Soob said in a bland tone. 'You are confusing them with the worshippers of Goddess Kali, who offer blood sacrifices of a cockerel or a goat. Not human.'

Something about the Earl's cold disdain had set his teeth on edge. Now the nobleman was inspecting him through a quizzing glass, as if he were a cockroach.

'When were they murdered?' Lady Ariel asked.

'Between nine thirty and eleven last night.'

'I was dancing with the fair Georgina at the Resident's ball,' the Grand Duke drawled.

'No, you weren't, Alexei. Everyone was looking for you. Your nawab friend and the two of you had disappeared.'

'Ah, yes. We were in the garden discussing our plan for today's hunt.'

'But they didn't find you there,' she said.

'Would this friend be Mr Ali Baig, Your Excellency?'

'Yes, we belong to the same club.' A martial glint lit his stare. 'You may have heard of the Hellfire Club?'

Soob inclined his head. 'Where did you go, Your Excellency?'

A frown pleated Ariel's forehead, her gaze flitting between her cousin and him.

'I don't see what business it is of yours, sir,' said the Earl of Euston.

'Ali Baig's stepmother was murdered last night.' He looked at Lady Falloner and added softly, 'Shiraz's cousin.' He hoped she'd hear an apology in his tone for having treated her shabbily.

Hurt dulled her gaze as she realised why he had asked for this meeting.

'Is our dear Ali Baig a suspect?' the Grand Duke enquired in a soft tone.

Soob didn't reply.

'I really don't understand why you are talking to us about the murders of native women,' the Earl said, glowering.

The Grand Duke uncoiled himself from the settee. He almost came up to Soob's height. 'I'm afraid you won't catch the Ripper here, Chief Inspector. Come, let me walk you to the door.'

Soob shook hands with Lady Falloner who looked fixedly at a point on his chest.

'I'll be having a word with Sir Trevor and His Highness, the Nizam, about your impertinence, sir,' the Earl said, scowling.

The whiff of lemon came from the nobleman, much like the scent that had led them to Niloufer's body.

'If I were you, Chief Inspector, I would delve into the Ripper investigation and find out what they concluded,' Grand Duke Alexei said at the door. 'But then, you already know all about it.'

Someone had leaked the true story to the nobleman.

Lady Falloner's hurt look stayed with him on his ride back. He would send her a note of apology.

Their absence from the ball could indicate one of three things: they were involved in the murders; they had helped Ali Baig unwittingly; or they had simply spent time with their friend away from the pomp and ceremony. The Grand Duke, whom he would have liked in other circumstances, struck him as a highly intelligent man who craved danger. Would he and the Earl put their neck out to help Ali Baig? Or was Ali using his friends to evade capture?

There was another possibility. These murders could be a Hellfire Club challenge. The transcripts of the Ripper investigation contained gory descriptions of the club's rites: abusing, maiming and even killing young virgins as sacrifices to the god Pan. *Fais ce que tu voudras* was the Hellfire motto. Do exactly what you want.

It galled Soob that their lofty status allowed them to waste his time, and it outraged him that their inability to comprehend the human tragedy arose from a blindness to the victims as fellow humans. Such stony inhumanity, he thought grimly, could very well drive such men to satisfy sick wants.

Chapter Twenty-one

While returning from attending a childbirth in a city slum, a tingling sensation kindled between Shiraz's shoulder blades. She leaned out of the carriage window, but aside from a mounted constable behind them, there was no one around.

'You were defenceless.' Soob's words sounded in her head, brutal and correct. She'd been lucky in where her blow landed on Ali, but that wouldn't have been enough if Imran Baig hadn't decided to intervene. Why hadn't she fought back properly? Why did she have to be rescued? The answer was a simple one: the primal instinctual response to violence was to freeze. All these months, she'd scolded her patients – who'd come with bruises and bones broken by their husbands – for not fighting back. Her exhortations, she'd thought, would make them bolder, little realising that she lashed their sense of frailty and weakness even rawer. What those women had needed was her quiet sympathy and support, something she yearned for herself now.

She took a deep breath and straightened her spine as the carriage reached the hospital. All this was beside the point. The missing boy had to be her first priority. Something in her wouldn't let her sit back. Niloufer would understand, would want it so. She couldn't bring herself to speak about the baby, not even to Soob.

As she crossed the atrium into the zenana wing, her thoughts circled around the moment Ali had struck her. Where is the nursemaid, she'd asked, and it had alarmed him.

She hurried through the dim corridor, past her office, to Dr Dora's, and rapped on the door.

The Englishwoman looked up from a file she had been perusing, a matted grass fan in one hand. The teakwood table gleamed, otherwise empty of files and papers, which were neatly stacked in the bookcase behind her.

Shiraz closed the door.

'Ah, Dr Shiraz, just the person I was thinking of. How did it go at the harem?' The Englishwoman's forehead crinkled. 'What happened?'

Hoping her voice wouldn't tremble, Shiraz described Ali's attack. Dr Dora, almost unconsciously, stroked a scar on her jaw. Their gazes met, and the Englishwoman gave a nod as if Shiraz had uttered the question: *Have you experienced such brutality?*

'My dear, I don't want to talk about my late husband,' Dr Dora said, stepping around the desk. 'Show me where he injured you.'

Shiraz unbuttoned her blouse and pushed the muslin off her shoulder, wincing as it brushed the raw bruise.

Lips clamped in a grim line, Dr Dora dressed it with salve, muttering under her breath.

Now she understood the Englishwoman's reserve, her unstinting devotion to her work, her fervour to start this hospital for women, her willingness to go to her patients at any time of the day or night. It was an angry grief that she hadn't protected herself properly. Not so different from her own guilty grief at not being able to save her baby.

'Nobody from here will go to that man's harem again, Dr Shiraz.'

'Thank you, but please don't do that, Dr Dora. We can't punish them for his behaviour.'

'You certainly must never go there. Promise me.'

She wasn't going to promise. 'Tell me, is Maryam Baig prey to fancies?'

The Englishwoman shook her head slowly. 'She has always struck me as down to earth, a good wife and mother.'

Her heart sank. Maryam's fears could have a solid basis. Then why did her family call her a hysteric?

'Dr Dora, could you do me a favour and find out what the child's nursemaid looked like?'

'Why would you want to know that?'

'I haven't got time to explain right now, but believe me, it's a matter of life and death.'

At teatime, Shiraz's footsteps took her to Dr Currimbhoy's office to request a favour. Much as she disliked relying on his goodwill, it was for Niloufer's sake.

Entering his office was like straying into a battlefield. Books and folders bulging from the shelves, papers piled crookedly on the floor and jars of specimens perched precariously on the stacks. A dozen framed certificates dangled off nails on the walls. Her fingers itched to straighten them. She took a deep breath. Ugh, stale cigar smoke.

'Ah, Dr Daruwalla, been working hard, I see.' The voice came from behind a thick wall of folders stacked on the desk. 'Good, good. Not like these nobles, lolling about in bed all morning after cavorting all night.'

Dr Currimbhoy swept the files aside and beamed at her, his bald pate gleaming in the pale light trickling in through the small window. He needed two cushions on his chair to come up to the level to write comfortably. 'You are just in time for tea.'

'I'd rather not, Doctor. My stomach feels queasy.'

She dusted the chair in front of the desk with a handkerchief and sat down.

Dr Currimbhoy held strong views on the place of women, which was certainly not in a hospital. So he'd decided to treat them as honorary men. Dr Dora he regarded with caution, but Shiraz he lectured, chided and chivvied, much as he would have a favourite pupil.

The kettle began whistling. He bounced up and switched off the kerosene stove stuck between two bookshelves.

'You look faint, Dr Daruwalla.' He poured the water into a colourful teapot set on another pile of books. 'Have you had lunch? No, I thought not. Help yourself to some shortbread biscuits from that tin. My wife made them.'

Past experience said he wouldn't take no for an answer. She opened it and took one.

He cleared his throat. 'Wasn't Niloufer Baig your cousin by marriage? I'm sorry for your loss.'

'Thank you, Dr Currimbhoy.'

He poured the tea into white bone china cups and handed one to her. 'Now, drink this.'

She took it and thanked him. The head doctor had a habit of forcing the drink on his visitors, having acquired the taste as a student in

London. His behaviour was seen as eccentric by Hyderabadis, who regarded tea as an English drink, though it was, in her view, the least of his eccentricities.

She took a sip and asked about Nawab Zulfikar Baig.

'Fading fast, I'm afraid. Won't see the night out.'

Her spirits sank – poor Zulfikar. They sipped their tea in silence. Raising the cup provoked a burning sensation in her shoulder, and she winced.

'What's wrong with your arm, Dr Daruwalla?' he asked.

'I injured it,' she said.

'How?'

'Oh, just an accident.' He'd be furious, and there was no telling what he'd do.

'Let me have a look at it.'

She shook her head. 'I banged my shoulder against the door jamb. Actually, Dr Currimbhoy, I came to ask you for a favour. It's about Niloufer: she must have a Parsi funeral.'

'Didn't she convert to Islam? I heard talk of excommunicating her.'

She gripped the table and leaned in, expecting this objection. 'But she had to for the marriage to be recognised under Islam. A Muslim cannot marry a non-Muslim. But Niloufer was a practising Parsi. Why, last week, she celebrated Navroz with the rest of us.'

'Her husband knew how she felt?'

'Yes, he wasn't bothered by such matters. Please, can you put in a word with the Fire Priest? He is your patient, isn't he?'

Dr Currimbhoy tapped his chin and gazed at the files. 'It can't be done,' he said after a while. 'Once a woman marries out of our religion, even her children aren't Parsis. The Fire Priest won't allow it.'

'But, Dr Currimbhoy, she didn't believe in Islam. Niloufer didn't practise it.'

He shook his head slowly, pity in his gaze. 'No, Dr Daruwalla, it won't pass muster with him. He is a principled man, a stickler for rules. He has to be.'

'Can you please try, Dr Currimbhoy? Her soul won't rest in peace until we perform the Parsi death rites.'

Though Shiraz didn't believe in an afterlife or ghosts, she felt Niloufer wanted this. Parsis considered the dead to be impure and kept the bodies away from fire, water and earth. They couldn't burn the body like Hindus nor bury it like Muslims and Christians. Her community let the body remain in the open, in a rounded structure with high walls and no roof – the Tower of Silence – where vultures and crows consumed the flesh. A few weeks later, the bones were collected and stored in deep wells, the bottom lined with charcoal and lime. Shiraz felt in her bones that Niloufer's spirit would not tolerate any further deviation from the death rituals. Already, her body lay alone in the morgue without being attended by two people. She'd tried to impress this fact on the English inspector, but he'd ignored it.

Dr Currimbhoy seemed nonplussed at her plea. 'Let me see what I can do. Mind, I am not making any promises.'

She thanked him and asked for one more favour. He gave a puzzled nod.

Chapter Twenty-two

'Do have a samosa, Chief Inspector,' said the dapper middle-aged official, impeccably turned out in a black achkan and white bugloos, with a red rose in his lapel and a maroon fez on his head.

'Thank you, but I just ate lunch,' Soob said, resting his head against the wooden backrest in the stationmaster's office, the teakwood panelled walls enclosing them in a hushed gloom.

It had been a quick meal – rice and yoghurt with a mango pickle – at the hotel, a change of the bandage, picking up his luggage, and a forty-minute journey here in a hired carriage. He would be taking his family to a house he'd rented in the Residency.

'My staff did not see Nawab Baig's chamberlain or soldiers here that day, Chief Inspector,' the official said, finally answering Soob's question. 'The child is the heir after his father and would surely be given a proper send-off. I would have been informed. In fact, I had taken leave that day.'

The whistle of the train sounded, coming closer.

The assistant entered, empty-handed. He couldn't find the Delhi passenger list for that day.

The stationmaster frowned. 'It must be there.'

'Show me.' They walked down the platform to a small room tucked away by the canteen, packed full of files on metal shelves, and the assistant retrieved a folder from the bottom shelf. It had about a dozen sheets of paper with pencilled names. Soob sifted through quickly. The manifest was indeed missing.

'Does this happen often?'

The assistant scratched his stubbled jaw. 'No, sir.'

'Is this room locked?'

'Only at night, sir.'

Even an illiterate person could identify the date without needing to know the script, he thought, as cries and yells sounded from the platform. A whistle sounded and the train chugged in.

Soob strode out into the crowd, mulling the question: Why was it important to conceal information about whether the child and the nursemaid had travelled to Delhi? And to whom?

The *Deccan Queen* stood hissing and belching smoke under the arched iron canopy. The air reeked of soot and sweat as he waded through the passengers and their well-wishers, feeling like a prizefighter weaving and ducking blows from their corded blue-and-red-striped bundles. Ahead, an Arab battalion leapt and waved their swords in the air, yelling slogans for their chieftain, a big man in breeches, gaiters and a fez, and Soob slipped into the path cleaved by them.

Spotting his tall grandfather in wire-rimmed glasses standing stiffly by an iron pillar, three stripes of ash on a dark forehead scrunched in a frown, his heart softened. His grandparents *were* his parents, his own having died of cholera when he was five, young enough that all he knew of them were the stories he'd been told. It was his grandmother who had made his favourite dishes for lunch and tiffin and bathed his forehead with a cool cloth when he was burning with fever; and it was his grandfather who had told him stories each night from the Puranas and the Mahabharata.

Only on seeing Tatha in his white cotton vaishti, and a white cambric cloth draped over a bare torso sporting the sacred thread, did he realise how much he had missed them. His tiny grandmother in a mango-coloured nine-yard sari beamed at him as he detached himself from the Arab procession. Clover-shaped diamonds glittered from her nostrils and the large vermilion dot on her creamy forehead stretched with a smile, her cheerful personality a fitting foil to his grandfather's sombre mien.

Natraja stood next to them, goggling at the armed men as they passed. More warmth suffused his chest. His nephew was a miniature version of his grandfather, down to the clothes and hair tuft, though many said it was Soob he resembled.

Natraja's eyes lit up on seeing him, and he surged forward. Then stilled as if recollecting something, and ducked behind the pillar. Soob's heart sank. He had much to make up for with his ward.

'You are late, Subbu,' his grandfather said. 'We have been waiting for three minutes.'

Murmuring an apology, he touched their feet, and then rose and signalled to a porter.

A passenger blundered towards them and his grandfather clicked his tongue and tapped a black umbrella on the sandstone platform. The man jumped back as if stung and muttered an apology.

'Come here, Natraja,' Soob said.

The boy sidled up silently but ducked away when Soob put a hand on his shoulder.

'He is feeling shy,' his grandmother said. 'Natraja hasn't seen you since...' Her voice trailed off.

Soob busied himself with assisting the porter. Losing a father and mother to a revolutionary's bomb simply because they happened to be in the bazaar was hard for anyone, let alone a nine-year-old. He had been stuck in his own grief, with first Rohini and now his younger brother, but how much worse it must have been for Natraja. He should have tried harder to be a good uncle. Deep down, though, Soob knew he hadn't tried at all.

They set off, the stick-thin porter with three holdalls on his head, and two cloth bags on each end of a pole balanced on his shoulder, pursued by his grandfather poking the umbrella at those in his path.

With the remaining two jute bags slung on one shoulder, Soob supported his grandmother with his other arm.

'Natraja, you walk on the other side of Pati.' His nephew complied, but didn't meet his eye.

'Did you have a nice journey, Natraja?' Soob tried again, raising his voice over the hubbub, slowing his pace to match his grandmother's gait.

The boy mumbled something and looked away.

His grandmother winced.

'What's wrong, Pati?' He stopped. 'Is it your gout?'

She gave a nod, but still managed a smile. 'Don't worry, Subbu, it doesn't pain so much.'

He helped her on. He must have Shiraz examine her properly once they settled in.

They bundled into the brougham, Soob next to his grandfather, across from the other two in foldaway seats, and everyone trying to avoid their knees touching the others. An enquiry about their journey drew a grunt from his grandfather while a quiet Natraja stuck his head out of the small window.

'Subbu, you have become thin,' his grandmother said in Tamil. 'You are not eating properly.'

'I'm looking forward to your avial and upma, Pati,' he said, smiling at her pleased expression.

His grandfather cleared his throat as he all too often did before raising a difficult subject. Soob's heart sank. He couldn't face a plea about performing the expiation rite – not just yet.

'What have you been doing in your holidays, Natraja?' he asked hurriedly as the carriage rattled over a rock.

'Nothing,' Natraja mumbled, rubbing his eye.

'Tell Athimber what you've read in the magazines he brought for you from London,' his grandmother said.

By the age of seven, his nephew had learned to read English, Tamil and Sanskrit.

'Sherlock Holmes?'

Natraja bobbed his head and continued gazing out of the window, as four women jogged past with large pots balanced on their heads.

'They are toddy runners,' Soob explained as his grandfather cleared his throat again, 'bringing toddy to the city gate. As a Muslim, the Nizam cannot permit alcohol inside the city.' No need to add that the police were expected to ignore it being smuggled in.

Natraja's eye flickered towards him and then away again.

His grandfather took a deep breath and opened his mouth.

'Natraja, one of my constables saw a purple frog on the riverbank,' the words tumbled out. 'Let's find it this evening, shall we?'

His nephew swiftly turned to him, eyes wide; like his father, his passion lay in studying insects and small animals. Then he seemed to recollect something and turned back to the window, fixing his gaze on the large boulders they passed.

Natraja wasn't making it easy for him. What was it going to take? He decided to try an old game he and Cheenu had played with the boy. 'Can you spot the cracks in those boulders, Natraja?'

The boy gave a stiff nod.

'What do you think they would contain?'

After a pause, a mumble came. 'Water, rare plants… even fossils and insects.'

'Correct. We'll come here next week.' After he'd found the killer. The number of promises he was making. This time, he'd fulfil every one of them, come what may.

'Subbu,' his grandfather said.

His grandmother glanced at her husband. 'Natraja, do you remember the story about those rocks your grandfather told you in the train? Tell Athimber.'

Soob wanted to hug her.

'Giants once lived in the Deccan,' Natraja said, continuing to stare out of the window. 'They kicked and flung these boulders in games of catch.'

'Did Tatha tell you the story from the Hitopdesa?' Soob asked.

'Not yet,' his grandfather said. 'I was going to when we came to Golconda fort.'

'There it is,' Natraja said.

The thirteenth-century citadel rose in the distance, silhouetted against the heated sky above a black ridge.

'Tell him the story,' his grandmother said.

His grandfather took a deep breath and began. 'Once upon a time, a traveller passing by watched some men throwing meat from there into the valley. Many birds – kites, eagles and crows – swooped down, and snatched and flew away with the meat in their beaks. The men began chasing the birds. "Why are you following the birds?" the traveller asked the men. They didn't reply, so the traveller followed them till the birds swooped down to their nests.'

'Why were they running after the eagles, Tatha?'

'My boy, you tell me.'

Soob pointed to his grandmother's diamond nose-ring, and Natraja's face cleared.

'Oh… diamonds. There are diamonds in the valley?'

'Well done, Natraja,' his grandfather said, having studiously ignored the exchange. 'Yes, Golconda valley has veins of gold and diamonds. The nuggets stuck to the meat the eagles carried away to their nests.'

Watching Natraja stroke his chin, looking just like Cheenu, something caught in his throat.

'Interesting, but is it true?' his nephew asked.

It brought a pleased smile to his grandfather's face and to his own.

'Now as to that, I have a theory.'

Natraja yawned. 'Sorry, Tatha. Please tell me.'

'Later. The child is tired,' his grandmother said.

His grandfather gave a nod and to Soob's relief, lapsed into silence.

White stucco bungalows of the Residency appeared on either side and soon the horses slowed to a trot.

'It is a thin river,' his grandfather said, as the Musi appeared before them.

'For most of the year, it is only a narrow stream about an eighth of a mile wide. But we have to be careful this month in the rains. Flash floods can sweep through the gullies.'

They looped right onto Musi River road and the horses trotted past flat-roofed bungalows with Grecian columns and gardens sloping to the river. They passed Shiraz's home, and a dozen houses later, reached a bungalow with a large garden and a low fence. This was his first glimpse of the house Dr Currimbhoy had found for him to rent from a Parsi friend. A slate roof with an overhang covered a verandah, and shadows of the grey stone pillars snaked in long lines on the meadow grass. Cowslips poked up here and there with some other flowers he hadn't seen before and itched to examine.

His grandfather peered at the glowing white wall smeared with chunam – a lime paste made with eggshells and seashells – but to Soob's relief, didn't utter a word of reproach, though such dwellings were polluted for Brahmins who didn't touch either shell.

The coach driver unloaded the luggage on the verandah.

'Wait here for me,' Soob told him and remained there, gazing up at his grandparents who had taken off their slippers and climbed the stairs.

A sack of groceries by the front door smoothed out his grand-mother's worried frown.

Natraja wandered off to the wooden fence, shading his eyes from the afternoon sun as he watched a camel in the river bending its long neck to drink the water.

'Subbu, tell me when you will perform the atonement rite.' His grandfather towered above from the verandah.

'Let's talk when I get back tonight,' Soob said and leapt back into the cab.

'Subbu, your pollution will taint Natraja as your ward, he is a son to you now.' Sweat beading his forehead, his grandfather glowered. 'Why are you making him an outcaste?'

Soob was still trying to find an answer as the carriage entered the High Court.

Chapter Twenty-three

Soob mounted the dusty sandstone steps into the rose-pink granite edifice of the High Court, wove his way past men in white turbans and dhotis and past the husk curtains drenched in water to cool the hot breeze, all the while tussling with his grandfather's question. Why was he depriving Natraja of his birthright?

He found himself outside the lawyer's chamber and knocked on the door.

'Enter,' a voice said.

He stepped in and greeted the old man with a grey hair tuft seated in a cane chair behind a wooden desk.

Tathachari Iyengar, whom he'd mentally dubbed as the Old Brahmin, had asked for Soob's help in the previous investigation that brought him to Hyderabad. A strange bond flourished between them, an outcaste and the chief regulator of the Deccan Brahmins, forged against the backdrop of a disappearance, murders and an insurrection.

'Sit, Chief Inspector Soobramania.'

He cast a jaundiced eye over the wood and cane furniture, the cloth-bound legal tomes – not the polluting leather of an animal's hide – and the absence of mattresses, cushions and carpets: all unwelcome reminders of his former caste's acute fixation on purity and pollution.

'I can wait if those men outside need to see you, Mr Tathachari,' he said.

'Don't worry about them,' the Old Brahmin said, taking off his thick wire-rimmed glasses. His shaven crown, dark complexion, grey hair tuft and spectacles reminded Soob, rather inconveniently, of his grandfather. 'They show up daily to discuss their lawsuits. Hyderabadis, you should know, are the most litigious people in the world. They enjoy lodging claims on property, drumming up imaginary fights, and if all else fails, there is always the anonymous letter accusation. All this, mind you, without any proof. A waste of my time. Thankfully, the recent changes to our justice system are beginning to curb those instincts.

'You don't know what a relief it is to all of us,' he continued, massaging the dark marks where the spectacles habitually rested. 'Ten years ago, in a property dispute, they could gamble on the vagaries of luck and divine intervention. But now, under the new process, they have to show proper evidence of their claims, thank god. Now tell me, how is your grandfather? I hear Madras is reeling under a cholera epidemic.'

Soob told him of their arrival.

'Good, I will pay a visit. I've been longing to discuss the recent translation of the Bhagavad Gita with a Sanskrit scholar of such calibre.'

A peon entered with a silver glass of water on a tray. The silver gave Soob a jolt. It was used by Brahmins because it did not attract pollution, so the taint of a low caste or outcaste's touch wouldn't travel to a high caste person. An odd feeling, this, to experience his excommunication in such a tangible way. It annoyed him that he minded, as did the Old Brahmin's steady gaze. Another realisation dawned on him. He had been able to ignore racialist condescension at Scotland Yard and in the ICID because of an unshakeable sense of self-worth owing to being born as a Brahmin. But this, he saw now, had come at the expense of the dignity and self-worth of those born in a lower caste. It was galling to find that he was no different from men like Templeton. He, after all, had turned a blind eye to the indignities his caste had inflicted on non-Brahmins to create that illusory sense of superiority.

'You are not as uncaring of your outcaste status as you claim to be, Chief Inspector Soobramania,' the Old Brahmin said with a shrewd glint in his eye.

Soob picked up the glass. It irked him more that his upbringing forced him to pour the water into his mouth, instead of sipping it.

Setting the empty glass on the tray, he stretched his legs. This wasn't the moment to brood over the wrongs of his former community; some things could never be set right. 'I've come to ask you about Shia laws of inheritance, Mr Tathachari.'

'I read about the murders. Tragic indeed. I assume you are here about Nawab Baig's Parsi wife, about her rights.'

The Old Brahmin slid on his glasses and got up, went over to a bookshelf and removed a fat volume. Thumbing through the index, he stopped at an entry and then turned to the page. 'The nawab's gifts to her on the marriage day are hers to dispose of.'

'Do they revert to him on her death?'

'Yes, unless her relatives challenge it.' The Old Brahmin raised an eyebrow.

'A mother and three brothers.'

'If they contest it, they stand a small chance. I tackled a case last year where the issue revolved around bride price. Is the gift to the bride her natal property, or is it part of the married estate? I argued it was her own and not part of the estate, and the judge agreed with me. It helped that he was a Sunni and disliked Shias on principle.'

Religion, it seemed, had replaced luck in influencing legal decisions here, Soob thought drily as he posed the question that had brought him here.

'Shias have a different set of rules than Sunnis?'

'Yes. Shia law divides legal heirs into three classes. Class one is parents and children, male and female, and their descendants, with the male child receiving double the inheritance of the female child. Class two is grandparents, brothers and sisters of the deceased and their descendants. Class three is paternal and maternal uncles and aunts and their children. If there are inheritors in class one, they will inherit all of it. Class two won't come into the picture.'

'So in the case of two sons, both receive an equal share?'

'In theory. But I have come across cases among the nobility where the eldest son gets all the immovable properties and a large share of the movable assets.'

'What about the spouse of the deceased?'

'I was coming to that,' the Old Brahmin said. 'The spouse is an heir by affinity, while the children are heirs by consanguinity. The wife, if she outlives the husband, inherits a one-eighth share. But this does not include immovable property or land, only the movable assets.'

Nawab Zulfikar's rapid decline was worrying enough for him to test another angle.

'And in the case of parricide?'

'Ah, so the rumour is right that the nawab is in bad shape, and quite suddenly too.' The Old Brahmin flipped the page and ran a finger down one side, stopping halfway. 'When someone intentionally kills his relative wrongfully, he does not inherit from them.'

'Whom would it go to?'

'The next heir, the murderer's son if he had one.'

'Not to the brother?'

'Inheritance is all about timing. When the father is killed by the son who is the heir, he still inherits, but when his guilt is established, the situation is that the heir's son is now in class one, and the heir's brother moves to class three of the inheritance ladder.'

Soob drummed his fingers on the desk's teak edge. It meant Imran Baig had much to lose from killing his father and little to gain from Niloufer's murder. Ali, however, would accrue a fortune from their deaths.

'Do you know the Baig family lawyer?'

The Old Brahmin smiled. 'I can do better than that. My old pupil is the man you want. I'll send the peon to fetch him.'

While they waited, the Old Brahmin cleared his throat. Soob's heart sank at the determined glint in his eyes.

'I wanted to bring something to your notice that will help your personal circumstances. As you know from your own experience, our caste has not been able to take advantage of the Nizam's scholarships to study in England. Those that have, their families have suffered, like yours.' Sympathy shone in his eyes. 'So we, in the Deccan Brahmin Association, have devised a remedy. These students can atone prior to embarking on their voyage. Then we won't have to excommunicate them. The date for the rite has been fixed for the day after tomorrow. Anybody who has incurred this ritual excommunication in the past can join in.'

'What happened to its sacrosanct nature, then, if a ritual can be changed?' Soob bit out.

'Worshipping the sun from land every morning and evening is the mark of our twice-born status, and will always be sacred. But when the impossibility of performing it arises not from human negligence, but from other circumstances, then we elders must do something. We cannot stand by and see these youths become invisible, non-beings.'

Every aspect of daily life – festivals, marriage, birth, death rites, rites of passage, neighbours, where one was allowed to live – depended on belonging to a caste. This he understood only now. A hollow feeling grew in him. How much Rohini must have suffered, yet not a word of reproach had marked her letters.

A plea and an apology shone in the Old Brahmin's gaze. 'It is a simple ceremony. You only have to chant some hymns and feed the wood fire with ghee. If the elders in Madras had devised a similar method, you would have performed the rite.'

Yes, Soob would have done so. Then Rohini would not have been shunned as the wife of an outcaste. She might not have died. Her susceptibility to malaria, Soob was sure, was caused by the stress of having to bear the shunning.

A knock sounded on the door, and Soob turned, swallowing his anger.

The middle-aged man, Nawab Baig's lawyer, looked like he had been neatly pressed into a white sherwani and bugloos, the maroon fez on his head matching the colour of the rose in his lapel.

Thanks to the Old Brahmin, the man was forthcoming about the nawab's will, which, he said, wasn't a secret from his sons. The Baig lineage valued the heir, and to him went all the immovable assets — vast estates and houses — and movable ones — jewels and gold coins. The late first wife's bride gift had been bequeathed by her to Imran, the younger son.

'An exceedingly handsome amount, if I may add,' he continued, the carrying timbre of his voice excellent for a courtroom and a deaf judge. 'Imran Baig is wealthier than his older brother, that is, until Mr Ali Baig inherits in the event of his father's death.'

'And Mrs Niloufer Baig's bride price? Was it a handsome amount?'

'Nawab Zulfikar Baig gave her a king's ransom in jewels. He told me he didn't want her to be at anyone's mercy on his death, which he knew would come in the natural course, before hers. Though, by god's will, that hasn't happened.'

'What happens to it now? Does it go to her mother?'

'As part of the marriage documents, Begum Niloufer Baig insisted on signing a will bequeathing her bride price to her husband. She asked me to inform his sons, and I did.'

'So the king's ransom in jewels reverts to Nawab Zulfikar?'

'Yes, and after him, to his heir. Then,' continued the lawyer, 'Mr Ali Baig will inherit a fortune.'

Chapter Twenty-four

'Have you seen this?' Commissioner Hankin stormed in and slapped *The Jasoos* on Wilberforce's desk. The late afternoon sun washed over the black print of Templeton's news sheet.

Wilberforce gave a gloomy nod. He could recite the article word for word.

> Informed sources have told *The Jasoos* that Chief Inspector Soobramania of the City Police has questioned the royal guests in connection with the murders. The Russian Grand Duke and the Earl of Euston were at a ball in Resident Sir Trevor Plowden's palace, which readers know is only a ten-minute carriage ride from the Baig park where the bodies of two women were found last night. Murders are not new to our visitors. Other rumours about the Nizam's distinguished visitors are far too blasphemous to be repeated.

'I told you those damned jackals would make it embarrassing for us.'

Wilberforce hadn't thought it possible for his superior's face to grow longer, but it did.

'Isn't Templeton your friend?' Hankin continued. 'What's he doing printing such scurrilous garbage? Whose side is he on, anyway? Why didn't he mention their friend, Ali Baig? What were you doing? You were supposed to keep those two out of it. How did that Brahmin chap manage to see them?'

That was what Wilberforce wanted to know as he morosely scanned the equally nasty *Deccan Gazette*. A report on the Chloroform Commission's successful visit. A headline – DECCAN RAIL SCHEME IN HOT WATER – caught his eye. Praise the Lord, he hadn't been taken in by Arthur's blather and invested in the scheme. A right old mess he'd have landed himself in.

'I'll have a word with Templeton, sir, but I can't promise he'll straighten up. The Nizam's old tutor is the moneybags behind Arthur's newspaper. As for the Baigs, he rents his house from them.'

The commissioner thumped his fists on the desk. 'Threaten him with arrest. Tell him we'll close down his newspaper if he doesn't toe the line.'

A hollow threat, of course. They both knew the blasted newspaper would come off the printer's block in the city and from there circulate to everyone in the Residency.

'And Wilberforce, make sure Her Majesty is not embarrassed by the list of suspects.'

He must have let his scepticism show because the commissioner leaned in. 'Let me spell it out for you. Whatever you find out, best not undermine our prerogative to oversee the Nizam. You know what I mean.'

Raging inside, Wilberforce inclined his head, keeping his face expressionless. To hell with that. He had no plans to exclude the visiting nobs until the evidence said so. But nothing would be gained from getting his superior hot under the collar about their midnight jaunt with Ali Baig. A mention of Baig's scarlet cummerbund and change of clothes would no doubt mollify Hankin, but in Wilberforce's book, the Grand Duke and the Earl could be just as guilty. He wasn't going to let them off the hook until he was dead sure. The burgundy colour of the cummerbund around the fountain lass's neck that matched the colour assigned to the Baig family wasn't enough for him to arrest Ali Baig. The lawyers would bleat that anyone could have pinched it from his wardrobe.

Hankin, who'd been examining him coldly, spelt out the fate that awaited him if he fingered the royal guests. 'You'll lose your job, certainly, and have no prospect of future employment in any police force either here or in any of our colonies. And don't expect the Nizam to employ you out of gratitude. We damned well won't allow it.' With that, he stalked out.

Wilberforce tapped a pencil on his desk gloomily. His eye fell on a chit from the Residency hospital addressed to him. On opening the missive from Dr Hehir, his mood improved. After the blood had been rinsed off, the scarlet cummerbund around Niloufer's neck had revealed the initials H. P. From his time at the Metropolitan Police, he recognised the emblem as being that of Henry Poole, a famous Savile Row establishment in London.

Wilberforce promptly pencilled a telegram to an old colleague at the Met, asking him to check. If the shop's register carried Ali's name as the purchaser, he'd have his man. The murderer had finally slipped up. Just like those jackasses in England who signed the chemist's register to purchase weed killer and rat poison and whatnot – got them nabbed, those blooming wife killers.

He sealed the note. This must surely tighten the case for Ali Baig's arrest.

Chapter Twenty-five

Soob took the only chair in Dr Currimbhoy's office not piled high with papers. Books, papers, certificates all strewn about, and the air dense with the smells of tobacco and carbolic acid – how anybody could work amid such clutter!

'Good you have come, Chief Inspector.' Dr Currimbhoy handed over a file. 'I have two more things to add to Dr Khan's report on the unfortunate widow you found in the river. Have her family reported her disappearance?'

'They may not know.' That is, if Shiraz was right about the nurse-maid being the river victim.

'You mean her in-laws won't report it?'

'They won't bother. One less mouth to feed.'

'Bastards!'

The doctor echoed his sentiments. A widow's lot was so wretched that death often was a deliverance.

'I showed the body to Dr Hehir,' Dr Currimbhoy said. 'Do you know him? No? He is at the Residency hospital and conducted the other two post-mortems. He agrees with me that the cleaner cuts resemble those on the park victims. So at least one of the killers is the same. That is number one.

'Two,' the doctor counted it off, 'is that both park victims were drugged. The laboratory is checking the blood samples of all three victims to determine the drug.'

The doctor's sharp glance suggested he was waiting for Soob to ask the right question. It was always a viva voce exam with Dr Currimbhoy. It would be nice if, for once, he didn't have to work so hard to draw out the information.

'Did the drug kill them?'

Dr Currimbhoy beamed as if his favourite pupil had passed a difficult test. 'This is why I tell everyone the new Chief Inspector is sharp as a blade. Both victims died of heart failure caused by the drug.' He paused and spoke with a dramatic flourish. 'Neither girl had a heart condition. No blockages in the arteries.'

'The mutilations were done after their deaths?'

'Yes, they didn't suffer, Chief Inspector, thank god for small mercies.'

One small consolation for the families, Soob thought, rising to his feet. 'How was the drug given?' he asked.

'We don't know,' Dr Currimbhoy said with a scowl. 'Their stomach contents didn't reveal any traces.'

Whether the drug had been used to induce heart failure or simply to knock out the victims, it was clear that the killer was not the Ripper, a man who had revelled in inflicting pain. Inspector Wilberforce wouldn't see it that way, though. Until this moment, Soob hadn't realised that Wilberforce's passionate denial of his friend's guilt had indeed inserted a sliver of doubt about having shot dead the right man.

'Are you aware, Chief Inspector,' the doctor's voice intruded into his thoughts, 'that your shirt has fresh blood on it? Show me the wound, if you please.

'Tchah, tchah, you policemen are the worst patients,' he continued as Soob reluctantly unbuttoned his shirt. 'Can't you see how deep it is? It could get septic.' He picked up a swab of cotton from a jar and dipped it in a bottle of iodine. 'How did it happen?'

'An encounter with some rocks,' Soob said through gritted teeth as the iodine burnt through the wound.

Mumbling under his breath, Dr Currimbhoy took out a spool of thread and a needle from the drawer and deftly stitched the wound together. 'No use telling you not to do anything strenuous for the next week or so,' he said, firming up the bandage. 'I'm warning you, if the stitches break and become septic, I won't be held responsible.'

'Thank you, Doctor. I hereby promise to absolve you of all such blame.' Soob rebuttoned his shirt with a smile.

–

Back in the office, the muezzin's late afternoon call to prayer floated in as Soob heard HC Muhammad's description of the nursemaid, a middle-aged married woman with long dark hair. Not the river victim, then. Two other pieces of information prodded his notice: Ali's order to the servants forbidding them from entering the Baig gardens the previous night, and a fight between father and son.

'The esteemed nawab, may Allah grant him a long life, shouted at his eldest son about losing money in the Deccan.' Muhammad shuffled his feet, looking uncomfortable about such goings-on among beings he regarded as divine and beyond the judgement of ordinary mortals.

'Is Ali Baig involved in a feud with some other nobleman?' Soob asked, testing Shiraz's speculation about the child being kidnapped by a rival.

'No, sir. The esteemed Ali Baig is a very generous and just man, loved by everyone – and by all his servants.'

Soob leaned back in his chair. At least one of the killers of the river victim had gone on to murder Niloufer and Mallu. The mysterious drug that induced a heart attack – did the killer know it would cause that effect? If the stomach contents didn't show any traces of the drug, how had it been administered?

The killer's personality was taking shape: methodical, detached, willing to do whatever it took, and finding ways to do it quickly and easily. Ali's mercurial personality didn't sit well with such a clinical bent of mind. Unless, of course, the nobleman had had help.

Chapter Twenty-six

In keeping with his promise to Natraja, Soob rode home as dusk approached. Seeing his nephew – in khaki drawers, white undershirt and India rubber boots – standing on the mud verge outside their gate, eyes fixed solemnly on an elephant bathing upstream in the river's silvery waters, warmth suffused his chest. That intent gaze was the same as his brother Cheenu's when observing a lizard, a beetle, or some other creature's habits.

Natraja had been waiting for him, and the relief in the boy's expression said he'd expected to be disappointed. Soob realised that he was doing to Natraja what he had done to Rohini: put his work first, at their expense. He had a lot to learn and make up for, and he didn't know how he was going to do it.

For want of something to say, he pointed to a yellow-and-silver-clad man on the riverbank. 'That's the mahout of the Nizam's elephant. Hope it doesn't get sick from drinking the dirty river water.'

Natraja, who was stroking the bay as it nuzzled and blew into his ear, shook his head. 'It isn't drinking water, Athimber. It is pushing its proboscis down its throat to fill up the bag in its stomach.'

'Like a water bottle in its stomach?'

Natraja gave a nod.

'How long will it take?'

'Ten minutes or so.'

'And then?'

'Whenever it feels hot, the elephant will poke its trunk down its throat, suck some water and squirt it on itself to cool down.'

'Ingenious of nature, don't you think?'

'That's what appa said.' Natraja looked away at the river.

Soob's hand went out to press his shoulder, feeling the tremble in the fragile bones. 'Wait here. I'll change into rubber boots.'

He stabled the horse and strode to the house. The spacious bungalow had three bedrooms, a living room, a dining room, a study and a kitchen. An outhouse at the back took care of his orthodox family's requirement that the toilet remain outside the house. Soob slid off his shoes and, dipping a copper bowl into a pail of water, washed and dried his feet with a cotton towel looped on a nail, then mounted the six stone steps to the verandah.

Sanskrit chants came from one of the bedrooms. Soob, thankful that he didn't have to encounter his grandfather, followed the aroma of roasting cashews to the kitchen. His grandmother squatted by a wood fire, her face shining in the heat as Soob told her about their expedition.

'Don't be too long, Subbu. I am making upma.'

His favourite supper.

Picking up his rubber boots from a wooden box by the entrance, he pulled them on at the verandah's edge, legs dangling to the gravel path. Flocks of birds wheeling around in the pale orange sky preparing for their night's roost and the dwindling pedestrians on the four bridges hurried his stride to the gate. He hoped to find someone who'd seen the killer carrying a sack yesterday at this time. And, of course, the purple frog.

Soob dug a toehold in the slippery mud of the embankment and helped Natraja slide down to the section between the second and third bridges, Afzul and Laik ud-Dowlah. Coconut and tamarind trees flanked them, the coconuts clustering like green balloons and the dark brown tamarind seedpods dangling between lacy fronds.

He tugged on Natraja's arm and pointed to a narrow channel running along the bottom of the embankment. 'See that? Plants can't grow there because there is a rock ledge just below the sand.'

Natraja pressed his boot in, testing for the rock.

The river, swollen from last night's rain, gushed faster as they picked their way through scrub and bush. This bank had fewer dwellings; a lush paddy field rolled to Chaderghat-Oliphant Bridge up ahead.

'Did you know Chaderghat has a double meaning in Deccani?' Soob said. 'Ghat means the place where washermen lave sheets, which are called chadar in Deccani. It also refers to the sheets of water you see there gliding over the granite boulders and crashing down into the waterfall. The cataract here is deep, has dangerous currents. I don't want you to swim here alone.'

'Are there any crocodiles, Athimber?' He squinted at a muddy hump glistening by a boulder in the paling light.

'I haven't seen one, but you never know. Don't come here on your own. Promise me.'

'Is that where the lady's body was found, Athimber?' Natraja pointed at the rock ledge.

'How do you know about that?'

'It was in the newspaper Tatha was reading. Are we looking for someone who may have seen the murderer?'

'*You* will look *only* for the purple frog.'

The eager gleam in the boy's eye dimmed. Though Soob was loath to stifle his adventurous spirit, what with the rains quickening the river and the probability of flash floods, not to mention a killer on the loose, the riverbank was too dangerous. He stopped by a scrubby bush. The boy was trying to dodge making a promise. Perhaps a scientific explanation might do the trick.

'This soil is sandy clay loam and red laterite, not chalk or limestone. What do you think will happen when the rain hits the earth here?'

A gust tugged at his hair tuft as Natraja thought about it.

'Here is a clue: where will the water go in clay and in porous limestone?'

Natraja's face lit up. 'In limestone, it will seep through and collect deep underground, and maybe become an underground river?'

'Yes,' Soob replied with a smile.

'And clay will run overground and flow into the river,' Natraja continued.

'The soil here is?'

'Clay.'

'Correct, which means what in the monsoon?'

'The river's level will rise very suddenly. Dry areas will fill up in seconds.'

'Correct. That's why I don't want you walking here by yourself. Promise me you won't come here alone.'

Shoulders drooping, his nephew reluctantly bobbed his head.

A gust brought the reek of rotting weeds.

'If you see anybody squatting for their toilet, tell me.'

Natraja wrinkled his nose, casting a suspicious eye on the brown rills that crisscrossed their path. He was right to do so: the pits in the city and Residency back lanes brimmed with urine and faeces, carried by the storm drains to the river, where they choked the fish and other wildlife. There were far better ways of disposing of the waste, but catch either side bothering to do them.

'A boy is fishing up there, Athimber.' Natraja pointed to a youth in a loincloth straddling a wooden joist under the Laik-ud-Dowlah Bridge. He had sunk a line into the water below.

Soob hailed him in Deccani and asked if he fished here every day.

'Yes, Chief Inspector.' The boy quickly removed the straw he was chewing.

'Did you see someone carrying a sack yesterday evening or throw one into the river?'

The youth shrugged. 'Always someone is hauling something or the other, crossing from here to there.'

'What about in that rice field?' Soob pointed to a green patch before Chaderghat-Oliphant Bridge, a likely spot for the killer to throw the sack in, considering its position on the weir.

'Funny you should ask, Chief Inspector. It was around this time I saw the grass shake all the way to the river as if someone was creeping in it.'

'Who was it?' Soob asked.

'Not a dog or a pig, huzoor. They like the other side of the river. More food there. You reckon it was the murderer?'

Though he couldn't understand Deccani, Natraja had picked up the gist and was gazing intently at the grass.

Soob sighed. He wouldn't be able to contain his nephew's zeal to ape Sherlock Holmes.

'Get behind me,' he told Natraja, who'd darted ahead and made for the skirting between the river and the paddy grass.

After a few minutes of searching Natraja found it in the wet earth between water and field, the imprint of a shoe lit up by the sun's dying blaze. The tall paddy grass had screened it from the rain.

'Is it the murderer's?' Natraja's eyes sparkled just like they had done before the tragedy.

'Could be. Or a dog or pig.' He smiled, testing him.

Natraja shook his head. 'It isn't a dog's paw. And a pig will leave only two marks. It has four toes and treads only on the middle toes.'

Wishing he had plaster of Paris or Spence's Patent Metal, which he could have poured in and left to set, Soob crouched and sketched the pattern with a pencil in his notebook.

'Does it match?'

A close scrutiny by his nephew, followed by a bob of his head.

Then with his thumb and middle finger, he measured the foot size. 'About nine and a half inches.'

'Ten inches, Athimber.' Natraja copied him. 'I measured the distance between my thumb and middle finger two days ago and it was exactly five inches.'

A warmth filled his insides; a naturalist relied on the hand for a measuring tape.

'Tell me, how tall would the person be?'

'Not your height, Athimber, but not as short as the fisherman.'

'Correct. I would make it between five foot five and five foot seven or so. Though, of course, there are tall people with small feet and short ones with big feet.'

At least the shoe's imprint ruled out a labourer or any barefoot slum dweller. Even if they could afford shoes they wouldn't want to ruin them in the wet. The killer's familiarity with the rhythm and timing of the river crossings, and of the deserted patches like this one, pointed to a local, and someone who was not poor. Among their suspects, the Baig brothers, the Earl of Euston and the Templetons were the right height. The Grand Duke was taller and had larger feet.

He turned to the fisherman swarming up the wooden bars to the bridge. 'Wait. Did you see a rider or hear a carriage at this time yesterday?'

'I didn't notice, huzoor,' the youth said, straddling the balustrade. 'Carriages are always moving up and down that road.' He heaved the sack of fish onto the bridge and, slinging it over his shoulder, disappeared into the gathering grey.

Boots stamped up ahead on Chaderghat–Oliphant Bridge, and at the change of guard, the bagpipers started a rendition of 'God Save the Queen'.

When the bagpipes fell silent, Natraja piped up. 'Athimber, I want to learn Deccani.'

'I'll give you my Urdu textbook. Deccani has the same script, but borrows words from Marathi, Telugu and Urdu. You'll learn faster, though, by speaking to someone.'

'I can practise with the fisherman.'

'You are not to pester him, Natraja.' But he recognised the glint of single-mindedness, a trait the boy shared with his father and uncle.

As night fell, they retraced their steps home. Finding the lone shoe mark was a piece of luck. Now he knew that there was only one killer, not two; the two types of cuts were made by the same person. This was a clinical murder. The murderer had been practising on her.

Silently raging at the killer's inhumanity, Soob helped Natraja clamber up to the road. To practise mutilating like this, stuff her dead body in a sack and throw it in the river, all these actions indicated that the killer didn't want her body to reveal that someone was copying the Ripper. Soob turned towards the bungalow gate. Why, he wondered, was it so important to the murderer to be identified as Jack the Ripper?

Chapter Twenty-seven

Thanks to Dr Currimbhoy, who'd done as she had asked and lured Imran Baig to the hospital on the pretext of discussing his father's condition, Shiraz was able to waylay him in the damp cool of the atrium.

Surprise flashed on his face in the dim flicker from the wall sconces as the lamplighters set flame to wick, though not fast enough to match night's arrival. He made his way to her, stepping aside for two orderlies carrying an injured man on a wooden plank.

He bowed. 'I hope there have been no ill effects, Dr Daruwalla? Kindly accept my deepest apologies again on behalf of my brother.'

An involuntary shiver went down her spine. What if she never forgot that moment of sheer helplessness?

He drew closer, as if her fears were apparent to him. 'It won't happen again, Dr Daruwalla. My brother has given me his word.'

She felt outrage at being reassured like this. Even worse was her relief at Imran's words, as if she'd been dreading another attack. If Ali Baig ever raised a fist, she'd see him in the law courts of Madras. The vow made Shiraz feel a little better, and she broached the questions about the child and the nursemaid.

He repeated that they were in Delhi.

'You are sure?'

He looked surprised. 'Yes, my brother said so.'

That settled it. Ali's word was worth nothing. 'What does she look like?'

'The nursemaid?' His forehead wrinkled at her interest in a servant. 'I don't know. She is always veiled, of course, in front of me.'

Her heart told her to believe a mother's intuition. She ploughed on, ignoring the babble of the patients and the wails of the babies magnified by the dome.

'Maryam thinks your brother is to blame for the child's kidnapping.'

Imran Baig frowned. 'I told you that my nephew is with his grandfather in Delhi, and my sister-in-law likes to make dramas about nothing. These murders have made you look for conspiracies where there are none, Dr Daruwalla. Kindly stop spreading such tales. I may not be able to restrain my brother next time if he finds out about your suspicions.'

He gave a curt bow and strode out into the street.

Uneasiness niggled at her as she retraced her steps to the zenana common room. Did he just threaten her? Or was he simply parroting his brother's words?

The two armchairs and the mattress on the floor by the window were unoccupied. Shiraz bent and inhaled the sweet scent of damask roses in a bowl on the console. Here she, Dora and the three nurses unwound with a cup of tea or a glass of cold sherbet, their haven from the stink of formaldehyde, chlorine, blood, sweat and urine.

A note with her name was propped up by the bowl – from Dr Currimbhoy. She was relieved to read that Niloufer and the other girl had not suffered: death had occurred from heart failure possibly caused by a drug.

Dora bustled in. 'I was about to come to your office, Dr Shiraz. I just got a telegram from Emily Boardman.' She collapsed heavily into an armchair and wriggled her feet out of her shoes, her white stockings sticking wetly to her feet. 'Thank heavens, she is returning next month from England. Also, I found out from the Baig ladies that the nursemaid's name is Devi. She is short, plump, has a dark brown complexion, and long black hair down to her knees. Married to a farm labourer in Maryam's village. Four children. The servants said she left for Delhi with the boy two days ago.'

It couldn't be the widowed river victim. Her spirits lifted – the boy was safe. Ali, astonishingly, had told the truth.

'It was very good of you to have found out so quickly, Dr Dora.' Shiraz clasped her hand. The Englishwoman stiffened, then relaxed and gave a nod.

'I don't know why you wanted this information, Dr Shiraz, but can you please leave it alone now? I don't want you to get hurt again.'

Though it was sweet of her colleague to care, Shiraz could make no such promise. Not that she knew what to do next. If the nursemaid

Devi had been the river victim, it would confirm the kidnapping and perhaps Ali's enemy being behind the attack. Or it could have been Ali himself who'd killed the nursemaid for helping the kidnappers, and then copied the Ripper's killing spree to throw the police off the scent. And also rid himself of Niloufer, a claimant to his father's fortune. But now, all that was moot. Devi was not the river victim.

Shiraz got up and put the kettle on the kerosene stove.

The fact posed a question she did not like. Was Maryam creating a drama over nothing?

Chapter Twenty-eight

Much to his grandmother's displeasure, Soob bolted down his favourite supper of upma and coconut chutney, and rushed out to see Wilberforce and check on Nawab Zulfikar Baig.

If a police station's layout could be said to reflect the personality of its ruler, then the Residency Police was the stark opposite of its city counterpart. Military precision in the way things were ordered – clean, well lit, no hustle and bustle of carriages, no cries of vendors and chatter of pedestrians. All the elements that should have appealed to his spartan tastes. To his surprise, though, he found himself hankering for the whimsical unpredictability that touched his day-to-day dealings with the Nizam's subjects.

With the dour Anglo-Indian head constable keeping mum about Wilberforce's whereabouts, Soob carried on to the Baig mansion, hoping to find the nawab alive and conscious. Two battalions of Sikh mercenaries thronged the gate, their numbers doubling since last night, while groups of horsemen patrolled the boundary walls. The man's angry outburst at his younger brother last night made it clear that Ali Baig feared someone. The connection with the murders, though, was less clear, he thought, handing his identity paper with the Nizam's seal to the chieftain, who let him in.

At the entrance, where a carriage waited, a familiar figure emerged into the light of the torches at the top of the steps.

Soob took the steps two at a time to reach the doctor. 'Is the nawab dead?' he asked in a low tone.

'Yes.'

Soob clamped his lips in a grim line. Zulfikar Baig's death, coming so soon after Niloufer's murder, bothered him. Worse still, Dr Currimbhoy's puzzled frown suggested suspicion of unnatural causes.

'Doctor, is it foul play? Seems too much of a coincidence.'

Shrewd eyes examined him as the lamplighters lit the torch strapped to the marble pillar above. 'It was a simple case of food poisoning, Chief Inspector. Nawab Zulfikar ought to have recovered after ejecting the prawns from his stomach. But he didn't. For a healthy man without a chronic ailment, he faded far too fast.'

'Could the shock of his wife's murder have weakened his will to live?' Soob asked.

'That's what his sons say. Maybe I'm being overly suspicious. It's this city, you know. These people use poison like salt. Only last week, a nawab was poisoned by his retainer with oleander tea, all because the man was scolded for something he hadn't done. But I have no proof and I don't believe in making unfounded accusations. I shouldn't have mentioned it to you, Chief Inspector. Please don't let it go any further.'

Dr Currimbhoy trudged down the steps to his carriage.

'Hakimji.' A turbaned retainer stepped out of the shadows and accosted the doctor at the foot of the steps. 'Is my master dead?'

'Don't answer him, Dr Currimbhoy,' Soob shouted, sprinting down the steps.

Too late. The doctor had nodded.

The man roared and swung a dagger at Dr Currimbhoy's throat. Soob, hurling himself at them, managed to grab the assailant's arm. In seconds the retainer would draw another blade with his left hand, he thought, straining to find purchase on the man's skin slippery with sweat. No help was forthcoming from Currimbhoy, who opened and shut his mouth like a fish out of water, eyes wide in fear. The steel inched closer even as Soob's fingers slid, losing their grip inch by inch. A drop of blood trickled down Currimbhoy's throat, the skin nicked by the knife. Feeling the attacker's muscles flex and shift out of his grasp, Soob grimly hung on, unable to firm up his hold without releasing the arm.

Bewilderment seeped into the doctor's gaze. Soob tugged the man's arm, but it was like wrestling with a wet granite boulder, slippery and unmovable. All the while, Soob stared into the doctor's eyes, at Currimbhoy's dawning realisation of his impending death. The blood drops swelled to a trickle.

'Stop, Muzaffar,' a voice commanded.

The retainer stilled.

Imran Baig strode up and shoved the man away.

'I must kill him,' the assailant said, frowning. 'He killed my master.'

Dr Currimbhoy skipped back. 'Arrest the man,' he yelled, recovering his temper along with his voice.

Soob shook his head. Much as he'd have liked to, the retainer had neither committed murder nor inflicted grievous injury on the doctor. Even if he had, the crime would have been treated as manslaughter under the Nizam's laws, which, though modelled on British ones, also bowed to tradition. As a policeman working for the Nizam, Soob had to uphold the ruler's laws, and custom here dictated that a man who owed fealty to a nobleman was duty-bound to kill whoever had harmed his master. Having failed to save Nawab Zulfikar, in the retainer's eyes the doctor had committed grievous harm.

'What brings you here, Chief Inspector?' Imran Baig asked.

'I am sorry for your loss, Mr Baig. I've come to see your brother.'

'Nawab Ali Baig is not at home,' Dr Currimbhoy piped up.

'I'm about to send my men to Huq's gambling den to fetch him,' Imran Baig said in an expressionless tone.

'Mr Baig,' Soob said, deciding to make the request on the outside chance it might be granted by this more amenable son. 'I'm sorry to bring this up at such a time, but will you allow the doctor to perform a post-mortem?'

Sharp eyes examined him. 'Do you suspect poison, Chief Inspector?'

'In such matters, it's best to assuage all suspicions,' Soob replied as the doctor's face brightened up at the nobleman's mild response.

'If it were up to me, I would agree.' Imran Baig's face was inscrutable. 'Kindly make that request to my esteemed older brother.'

–

London had its gaming hells in Cockford's Club and Brook's, and Hyderabad had Huq's Hell.

Abdul Huq, like other adventurers who flocked to Hyderabad, had mysterious antecedents. He'd made a fortune brokering deals between the Nizam and those wanting to do business in the richest state of British India. If one wanted a mining concession in the Golconda diamond mines, or a deal to sell muskets to the Nizam's army, or to set up a railway in the Deccan, Huq was the man to swing the deal. All these schemes began and ended the same way. With a bang.

Soob reviewed these facts as he rode through dark and narrow lanes, finally arriving at Huq's Hell. By the thatched barn housing it, he spotted an urchin lounging against a lamp post, the sole source of light in the slum, and dismounted.

'Guard her well, and I'll pay you two coppers.'

The boy perked up and saluted with a grimy hand.

Soob entered the gloomy portal. Huq had done nothing to spruce it up, he thought, noting the holes in the straw roof and the sticky mud floor. The effect, no doubt, catered to the upper-class notion that the poor lived in filth. Far from the truth, of course. Soob had visited dozens of poor dwellings, all neat and well swept, with everything in its place.

A motley crew greeted him inside the main room. Fresh-faced British cadets, from the Hyderabad contingent maintained by the British Resident and compulsorily financed by the Nizam, were staring at perfumed and brocade-clad Hyderabadi nobles and merchants, all hobnobbing with mercenaries and other riff-raff.

He cut through the mingled odours of leather, sweat, rotting straw and musk and emerged into a narrow corridor. Jeers and whistles came from the back of the house.

'What's going on there?' he asked a cadet coming towards him.

'Cockfight,' replied the youth, looking surprised that a native spoke his language.

Soob's uniform, which had already sent an attendant skidding around the corner, was attracting ugly looks from a gang of ruffians lounging further down. Gripping his dagger, Soob was about to head towards the cockpit when the scent of expensive lemon cologne stilled his step. It came from the door to his left. Soob knocked on it. It was unbolted from inside and someone opened it. The ADC to the Grand Duke.

Soob bowed, and after a puzzled glance at his uniform, the ADC returned the salute.

'May I have a word with the Earl of Euston and Grand Duke Alexei?' Soob enquired in English. 'I am Chief Inspector Soobramania.'

The ADC shook his head and began to close the door.

'Let him in,' a voice commanded from inside.

Candles in the four wall brackets lit the small room with a deep yellow glow and illuminated the Grand Duke Alexei Alexandrovich. He looked debonair in evening clothes – a long black silk jacket, grey pantaloons and patent leather boots. He lounged on one side of a rectangular wooden table that was heavily gouged and scarred. The Earl sat across the table from him, his features crumpled in a scowl, and bloodshot eyes glared at a pair of bone dice on the table and then at Soob. The Earl had discarded his silver-and-black jacket and was in a black muslin shirt, lace frill at the cuffs. A croupier in a white sherwani and churidar sat at the far end of the table. Black and white counters lay in a heap in front of the Grand Duke.

Soob noted the third chair, which had been pushed back as if the person had left in a hurry.

Two soldiers stood to attention on either side of a dirty and ragged curtain drawn along the window across from the doorway.

'Damn it, Alexei,' said the Earl, ignoring Soob. 'You have the luck of the devil. You've held the dice box since we arrived.'

The Grand Duke, who'd stood up politely at Soob's entry, bowed. 'You've come at a providential time, Chief Inspector. Ali has just left to answer the call of nature. Do take his place and play with us.'

An expression of distaste crossed the Earl's face as if he were smelling something unpleasant when Soob sat in the chair.

Grand Duke Alexei handed him the dice. 'Do you know the rules of chicken hazard?'

Soob shook his head.

'You bet on a number and throw the dice. If your number shows up, you win and you continue to be the caster until you lose. Then the dice pass to me.'

Soob rolled the dice in his palm. 'May I name the stakes?'

The Earl looked affronted at his boldness but Soob didn't care. This was perhaps his last chance to find out if they had conducted a Hellfire ritual in Ali's garden.

Grand Duke Alexei inclined his head.

'If I win, you will answer my questions,' said Soob.

'One question for each win.' The Grand Duke's eyes glinted with amusement.

'Seven,' said Soob and threw the dice.

Grand Duke Alexei cocked an eyebrow at the displayed number.

'Where did you go last night from the Resident's ball?'

'Back to Chowmahalla Palace, of course, my dear Chief Inspector Soobramania,' the Grand Duke drawled.

'I meant during the ball, when you left with the Earl and Ali Baig,' Soob said, cursing himself for squandering the throw.

'Ah, that is a question to which you haven't won an answer,' the Grand Duke murmured.

Soob rolled the dice and the number he called out came up again.

The Earl gave an exclamation, grabbed the dice and examined them closely.

'The dice aren't loaded, sir,' Soob snapped.

The nobleman poured a cloudy wine into a glass tumbler and held it out. 'Do have some wine. It's made from quails, a speciality of your city, I'm told. I've never had anything quite like it.'

Soob shook his head. It was the vilest thing he'd ever tasted.

Before he could repeat the question, the Grand Duke murmured, with a wry twist to his lips, 'We went to Ali's place.'

Cursing himself again for not having been more specific, Soob grimly rolled the dice again, praying that his new-found luck in games of chance would continue, luck that had begun after Rohini's death. Might as well go all out. 'Four.'

The Earl let out a snort. 'You might've met your match in luck, Alexei.'

The Grand Duke leaned forward, an inscrutable look in his eyes as he eyed the dice displaying four.

'Last night, did you perform a Hellfire ritual in Baig bagh, the garden next to Ali's mansion?'

'What the devil do you mean, trying to interrogate us like this?' the Earl exploded, jumping up. 'I'm bloody well taking this up with our host. Get out.'

'Now, now, a bet is a bet,' the Grand Duke said, narrowing his eyes. 'Pray tell me, who has been murmuring lies into your ear, Chief Inspector?'

'Is it a lie? No, don't answer this question.'

'No, we didn't,' the nobleman drawled, staring into his eyes.

Soob didn't believe him, not after noting the Earl's surprise. Of course, they must have performed the ritual in Ali's garden. It wouldn't have taken long to move Mallu's body to the park. And if Niloufer had surprised them there, then it could have been one of them Ram Rahim had seen.

'Seven.' Soob rolled the dice again.

The Grand Duke smiled broadly. 'I wonder how long Lady Fortuna will favour you. My record is four.'

Indefinitely, Soob wanted to say, as the dice slid to the edge of the table.

The Earl bumped into the table, rocking it, and the dice tipped over the edge onto the floor.

The croupier made a dive for them, but the Earl was swifter. He scooped the dice and shook his head. 'Wrong.'

The croupier looked surprised.

The Grand Duke frowned and with an apologetic glance at Soob, said 'ten' and rolled the dice.

'Good show, Alexei,' the Earl said, when it came up.

'Do you suspect us of killing the girls or of helping Ali kill them?'

'That's two questions, sir.'

'Touché.' A smile curved his lips. 'Pray, answer the first one.'

'I'm merely collecting the facts, sir.'

'And here I was,' the Grand Duke said, shaking his head slowly, 'expecting you to play fair.'

Soob eyed him coolly. Clearly, he couldn't strike the trio off the list of suspects for the first two murders.

The door burst open and Ali stalked in, a silver cummerbund gleaming against a black silk sherwani. 'My man said you'd sneaked in here, Chief Inspector. How dare you harass my friends? What lies has he been telling you about me, sir?' His tone had softened when he spoke to the Grand Duke, but his hand crept to the sword at his waist.

So Ali didn't want to lose face in front of his aristocratic friends, Soob thought. 'I merely came to applaud your bravery in attacking a defenceless woman, a doctor who had come to tend to your wife.'

Ali took a step towards him. Then recollected himself as Soob had expected him to. To lose composure in front of a commoner would let the side down.

The Grand Duke raised an eyebrow, but the Earl yawned.

'I didn't hurt her,' Ali said through gritted teeth. 'That woman was rude to me.'

'Rudeness *cannot* be forgiven,' the Earl said. 'That too from a female. It deserves the strictest punishment.'

Checking his urge to throttle the man, Soob regarded the Earl. 'How, may I ask, was it rude on her part to enquire if his son and the nursemaid were missing?'

Ali clenched his fist on the jewel-crusted handle of his sword. 'My son is perfectly safe in Delhi with his grandfather. Kindly stop making a fuss about something that is untrue.'

'Ah, but it's not me making a fuss,' Soob said in a dry tone. 'It's your good wife. It was she who asked Dr Shiraz for help.'

Ali gritted his teeth. The door opened and Abdul Huq walked in with two heavies, big men with bulging muscles. Pathans, Soob thought, as Huq made an obsequious bow, his nose almost touching the curled ends of his gold embroidered shoes. 'My humblest apologies, Your Excellencies. I don't know how this man managed to get in here. I shall rid you of his presence immediately.'

The Grand Duke glanced at Huq as if he were a bad smell. Then turned to Ali with narrowed eyes, a question in them.

'Have you invested in the Deccan Rail Scheme?' Soob managed to get in the question that had popped into his head on seeing Huq, and had his answer in Ali's sharp intake of breath.

The thugs, smelling of sweat and garlic, grabbed Soob's arms, but he barely heeded it. His brain mulling over this new angle. HC Muhammad's nephew-footman had overheard Ali's father berating his son for losing money not in the Deccan, but on Deccan Rail.

'Wait, the Chief Inspector was just leaving.' The Grand Duke rose to his feet and bowed politely to Soob. 'It was a pleasure to meet you, sir, one so favoured by Fortuna.'

Soob inclined his head, shook off the thugs' loosened grip, and turned to Ali. 'Nawab Ali Baig, I am sorry for your loss. Your father was pronounced dead in the past hour. Please let Dr Currimbhoy know if he may perform a post-mortem, a normal practice when someone dies so very suddenly.' Not waiting for an answer, he strode out of the room, his last glimpse being Ali's murderous lunge and Huq's intervention.

Making the fellow lose his cool was small recompense for the man's behaviour towards Shiraz, though. Soob retraced his steps through the dim corridor and the public rooms, mulling over what had occurred during the Hellfire ritual, and Ali's violent reaction to queries about his son and the nursemaid. The troubles Imran's wife had hinted at to Shiraz could be money-related, and the missing passenger list further fuelled

Soob's suspicion that the son was indeed gone, kidnapped perhaps by his creditor. The nursemaid could have been killed by the kidnapper, or by Ali for helping in the kidnap or for not protecting his child. It explained why Ali was taking such pains to hide the kidnapping, and why he hadn't reported it to the police. Hyderabad's 'eye for an eye' dictum sanctioned such kidnappings by the creditor if the debtor defaulted. Considering the Nawab's fury at his son, it seemed more than likely Ali had borrowed money from someone. But who?

Surely not Huq, at least not in the Deccan Rail Scheme, and not with the wheeler dealer's previous record of absconding with the proceeds. Soob stepped out of the main door. If these suspicions were correct, then Ali's ability to repay and save his child depended on his coming into a fortune.

He tossed two coppers to the boy, who beamed and handed over the mare's reins.

Was Ali's anger at the mere request of a post-mortem a son's anguish at losing a father? he mused as he mounted the horse. Or was it a murderer's fear?

Chapter Twenty-nine

Shiraz hurried from the hospital to Niloufer's house to tell Aunt Gul about the post-mortem results. Her carriage passed others trickling in and out of the gate: relatives, friends and acquaintances come to pay their condolences. She didn't recognise the middle-aged and older men huddled in groups on the lawn, some puffing on pipes, looking uncomfortable. Niloufer's brothers should be arriving tomorrow from Bombay and Madras.

In the sitting room, Aunt Gul sat on the settee, still as a doll, her gaze fixed unseeingly on a crystal shepherdess on the coffee table. Shiraz's mother-in-law sat next to her sister and conversed in a low tone with four women seated around the table. The sisters wore mourning clothes as did the middle-aged and older guests who all bore similar expressions of sympathy and relief that it wasn't their daughter or sister.

'Has she drunk any water or eaten anything today, Aunt Friya?' Shiraz asked her mother-in-law who was inspecting her navy hospital clothes with disapproval.

'She refuses to.' Then she whispered, 'I knew you wouldn't change, so I brought a set of white clothes. It is in the guest bedroom.'

This obsession with form she never understood about Cyrus's mother. What did it matter at a time like this? She had hurried here with the news that Niloufer had not suffered, surely that was more important. Of course, she couldn't say it with these visitors all agog for the gruesome details.

'Come with me, Aunt Gul,' Shiraz said, helping her up.

The maid, watching from the door, hurried to lift Shiraz's valise, and together they escorted Niloufer's mother to her bedroom in the back. The maid hovered by the window while Shiraz mixed a thimble of powdered sedative in a glass of water. After Aunt Gul drank it and lay back on the pillow, Shiraz clasped her hand and told her.

The glazed look lifted for a moment. 'My Niloufer didn't suffer? Is the doctor sure?'

'Yes.'

She sighed and closed her eyes.

Shiraz stroked her hand and sat quietly for a while. Then, when Aunt Gul's breathing became steady, she rose to her feet.

'The ribbon was the wrong colour,' Aunt Gul said in a puzzled tone.

'What ribbon?' Shiraz asked.

'On the park key.' Aunt Gul opened her eyes. 'It should have been green, not blue.'

–

'Yes, it is a pity there is no heir to succeed Cyrus,' her mother-in-law was saying to a dowager, not bothering to lower her voice or pretend she had not seen Shiraz, who'd changed into the white clothes.

Gritting her teeth, Shiraz moved towards another group sitting by the garden windows. As she drew closer, she overheard the words 'bad luck' and 'brings death'. The woman who spoke looked discomposed on catching her eye.

Tears choked her throat. They thought she'd brought death into the family, first with Cyrus and now Niloufer. Lips clamped tightly, she signalled the butler to serve the water. She refused to give them the pleasure of seeing her hurt.

Past dinnertime, she returned to her mother-in-law's home alone; thankfully, Friya remained at her sister's side. She shooed off the waiting butler, the cook and the maid, unable to stomach even a morsel, and took solace in the garden. Aunt Gul's words about the ribbon's colour rang in her ears. Whose key was in Niloufer's pocket?

A gentle wind caressed her hair, imbuing it with the sweet fragrance of parijat flowers scattered under a flowering tree. She bent and picked up the small cream flower by its orange stalk and breathed in its heady scent. The grass rustled by her foot, and she jerked back as the sound rolled away from her. 'Grass snakes and rat snakes are not poisonous,' Soob's voice sounded in her head, 'but beware of the saw-scaled viper, a nocturnal snake less than a foot long, it huddles in the niches of palmyra saplings.'

Hoofbeats in the driveway drew her back to the portico. Two horses trotted towards her, their riders a groom and an Englishwoman wearing a khaki divided skirt, a white blouse and a short jacket; auburn hair poked out of her riding hat. She dismounted and introduced herself as Phoebe Templeton.

Shiraz stiffened. This woman, this so-called friend, was responsible for Niloufer's death. She hadn't bothered to see her home safely, and hadn't even apologised to Aunt Gul.

'I'm sorry to visit you so late,' Phoebe said in a low, American-accented voice. 'I have to ask you something.'

Politeness demanded she lead her to the sitting room, where she offered her tea or a drink.

'No, thank you,' Phoebe said, perching at the edge of a paisley armchair. She removed a handkerchief from her sleeve and began twisting it, but still didn't offer an apology or her condolences. The uneasiness in her deep-set grey eyes reminded Shiraz of a patient looking for words to describe a sensation, and mustering up the courage to speak. Shiraz was certainly not going to make it easy.

'You must wonder why I'm here,' Phoebe said finally.

'I only wonder why you haven't come earlier or been to see Niloufer's mother,' Shiraz said, her tone icy.

Phoebe's face crumpled. She pressed the kerchief to her eyes, and her shoulders heaved. But it wasn't grief driving her tears, Shiraz realised when Phoebe whisked away the handkerchief and fury bled from her reddened gaze. It was anger.

'Will you answer me truthfully? Niloufer said you never lie. Was Niloufer having an affair with my husband?'

Shiraz shot to her feet. 'How can you even think that?'

'Was she?' Phoebe asked coldly, fingers clenched on the armrest.

'Of course not. For god's sake, she got married last month.'

'Are you sure?'

'Of course I am. Niloufer wouldn't do such a thing to anybody. You were her friend, and you know how deeply she loved Nawab Zulfikar Baig. And you know how direct and honest she was.'

Phoebe's lips twisted with disbelief.

'Who told you she was having an affair?' Shiraz asked.

'Nobody.' Shoulders drooping, Phoebe rose to her feet.

'I don't believe you. Was it an anonymous note? A letter?' At the lady's start, Shiraz pounced. 'A letter, then. Show it to me.' Then a terrible thought struck her. 'Oh my god! Did you confront Niloufer at your dinner party?'

Phoebe flinched, panic and guilt in her skittering glance as she jumped up and rushed out.

Shiraz gave chase and grabbed Phoebe's sleeve in the portico. 'Is that why Niloufer left after everyone else? You confronted her then. How upset she must've been... that's why she didn't see the killer. It's *your* fault she's dead.'

Shrugging off her grip, Phoebe seized the reins from the groom waiting with the horses. She vaulted on and galloped away.

Shiraz watched her go, fingers curling into fists. Niloufer would never have an affair like this. She was besotted with Nawab Zulfikar. *But how well did you know her?* a voice whispered. *Very well*, another voice snapped, shutting up what sounded like Imran's horrid wife.

She returned to the sitting room and poured a glass of water from the silver jug on the sideboard. Her hand shook as she drank it. Who could be so cruel as to play such a trick on Niloufer?

She glanced at the grandfather clock in the corner. Past eight. Soob worked late, so he might not be home. She'd go across to his office first thing tomorrow, though part of her didn't want to see him.

All the while, Phoebe's strong fingers twisting the handkerchief remained in her mind's eye. Hell hath no fury like a woman scorned. Women had killed for less.

—

Shiraz found herself in bed, having washed and changed into her night-gown and doused the lamp without being aware of it. She pressed her hot forehead against the cool pillowcase, the scents of soap and sunshine doing little to calm her.

Too tired to slide out from under the mosquito net and close the shutters, she lay on the slightly damp white sheet amid the cackles and whispers of night insects.

A scrape sounded outside as if someone had kicked a small stone. Not the gate guard. He wasn't supposed to patrol the side garden abutting her room, not when her window was open.

Was that a shuffle? Ice skittered down her spine. She held her breath and strained her ears for more sounds. Someone was outside her window. The killer? Ali?

With trembling fingers, she lifted the mosquito net and began wriggling out, stilling at the rasp of the sheet. She forced herself to continue, sliding inch by inch to the floor.

Another scrape, as if someone had stumbled.

Rain began plunking down on the open shutters, muffling her rapid crawl to the door on the cool mosaic. She huddled with her back to the wood, watching the sill for the intruder's shadow.

Were those fingers? She couldn't be sure. To her horror, her teeth began chattering. Gritting them, she raised her hand to the latch, palms damp and slippery. Please let it slide smoothly. Please. Carefully, she slid it back.

A thunderclap startled her. Her fingers rammed the bolt back, locked her in. Something moved at the window. She watched the shadow in fright.

'Oi, who's there at the window?' someone yelled from the garden.

She blinked, and the shadow disappeared. Lightning flashed on an empty sill.

With trembling hands she unbolted the door.

'Hakimji, what's the matter?' The guard's voice came from outside. 'I heard a shout.'

She hurried back to the window. 'Wasn't it you?'

He shook his head.

Her heart raced. A whiff of lemon tickled her nose. She'd smelt it by Niloufer's body. Not Kanaga of Japan.

'Stand back and shine your lantern near your feet. Quick, before the rain washes it away.'

With the lantern lowered, raindrops plinking on the metal and his hand, yellow light illuminated the mud. Under her gaze, the fine lines and whorls caved into a puddle. It was the imprint of a shoe.

Chapter Thirty

Rain pelted down steadily, drenching the horses and plastering Soob's hair to his skull. He quickly dismounted at the bottom of the Baig hillock and told the constable to shelter in the residence of Niloufer Baig.

'The bungalow next to the park, not the harem in the palace,' Soob clarified. 'Come to the park's back hedge if you hear three short whistles.'

Soob slipped up the back lane, staying close to the reed grass in the water meadow, the wet stalks muffling his footsteps. His intent to arrive by nine had been scuppered by an anxious deputy commissioner who'd shown up in the office to upbraid him for not cooking up evidence against the visiting dukes. Only his curt request to put it in writing had silenced the rant. It was now 10:45.

He crept on till the asoka trees loomed above like black megaliths and then crossed over to the mansion boundary walls. Not a moment too soon. A snap, a crack, followed by a splintering sound. Through the rain, he glimpsed a tree come down on the other side of the road.

Wilberforce's constables were nowhere to be seen. Unless they were concealed in the meadow grass, watching for the killer? If so, the Englishman was sharper than he looked.

Instinct told him to hurry. Water ran down into his collar as he reached the side road between the park and the Templeton residence. Still no sign of the constables.

The hedge scraped his bandage as he searched for the hole Ram Rahim had made, the one the boy had used to enter the park. Ah, there it was. He bent and checked; nobody was crouching there. No telling if the killer had made another hole; that's what he would have done. So he continued, fingers and arm brushing the hedge to orient himself.

Lightning flashed, silhouetting a shadow up ahead. He stopped and strained his ears. The storm's roar, however, drowned all other sounds.

A stone struck his heel.

Someone was creeping up on him.

He lunged towards where he'd seen the shadow, and staggered. The hedge wasn't there. There was another hole. This wasn't the one leading to Niloufer's garden.

Soob ducked in, the opening big enough for an average-sized person.

A burly body crept past. The whiff of paan, something shining from the man's shoulder – a glint of gold epaulette. Wilberforce's constable. Soob backed into the park.

He emerged onto the grass, the rain coming down hard and fast, a streaking veil over the champa tree grove to the right and the three-foot-high bougainvillaea hedge up ahead lining the gravel path. He squinted, shielding his eyes from the rain, and made out an undulation on the track, like mounds of sand. Was that a woman's cry?

Gut cramping, he sprang forward.

–

After a quick dinner of fried bread slathered with minced meat and egg, Wilberforce galloped back to the park. Leaving his horse with a constable at the entrance, he strode up to a scrubby bush deeper in the park where he'd stationed a constable. The rain had thankfully subsided to drizzle.

'Any movement?' Wilberforce murmured.

The constable rose and saluted. 'No, sir. Nobody has come past me.'

Wilberforce gave a nod and carried on, keeping to the grass verge. Above, lightning flashed, thunder rumbled. Then the heavens opened up just as he reached the crossroads where they'd found Niloufer Baig's body. Making no attempt to hide he cut across the lawn in the general direction of the back hedge. Hearing a cry, his step turned into a sprint.

Luck sent him arrowing directly towards the body, and divine intervention, perhaps, made him trip over her. He crouched in the lashing rain, trying to find her pulse.

A muscular body rammed into him, knocking him face down into the gravel. Wilberforce twisted and punched, connecting with bone.

His face burnt like a fire had started in its centre. The killer was tough and knew how to pummel and kick his weak spots. But Wilberforce, a former boxing champion in his village, had a trick or two up his sleeve. He twisted his body and, heaving the killer off his legs, sprang up.

Lightning flashed as the killer dived towards him. It was the blooming Brahmin. He'd reared back, but Wilberforce swung his fist, managing to put in a good crack on the bugger's shoulder.

Whistles sounded, and his men, led by HC Thomas, pounded up.

'Send men... back lane,' the Brahmin huffed, doubled up on his knees by the body, one hand pressing his chest as if something had broken.

Surely he hadn't punched him so hard, Wilberforce thought, not in the least bit sorry if he had.

'Killer... hole...' The Brahmin pointed a finger at the hedge.

Chapter Thirty-one

Eleven and a half drum beats sounded from the timekeeper at the Baig palace.

'Why in God's name didn't you chase him?' Wilberforce asked, blood oozing from a nostril, uniform sticky with mud.

Soob was furious with himself as he gazed at the lifeless body in the bright light of two lanterns.

A cavity gaped in place of her left eye, the edges ragged, as if the killer had cut it out quickly in the dark. A silk cummerbund, the colour of shells but now soaked with blood, coiled around her neck. More blood pooled under the neck.

'The bastard must have been crouching here, taken advantage of the rainstorm. If you hadn't jumped me, acting Chief Inspector, I could've nabbed him.'

'And if your constable hadn't crept up on me, I'd have caught the killer coming out of the hedge.'

'This is the Ripper's work.' The Englishman was not to be budged. 'You were wrong about John. His death hangs upon you, and now, because of your obstinacy, another poor woman is dead.'

Yes, it was his fault for not taking adequate precautions. His face must have revealed his sentiments because the Englishman's fury drained away, leaving behind a despondent droop of his shoulders.

'No use crying over spilt milk, I suppose,' Wilberforce said, much to his surprise. 'It is a proper dog's dinner you've made of it, but I can't say I'm blameless either. I should've posted more men to watch the hedge.'

Soob gave a nod and crouched by the woman. She was about Niloufer's age and appeared to be Deccani, with a flattish nose, dark brown complexion, lips stained red with betel juice, and heels calloused from walking barefoot. Her black hair, slick with coconut oil and rainwater, plaited and tied with a frayed gold tassel, lay along her torso. Thick wrists still bore a few green and pink glass bangles, the shattered remnants of others on the sleeve of a grey kurta patched in several places. A bloodstained light-green dupatta lay crumpled by her waist.

'Now do you concede it is the Ripper?' Wilberforce looked as grim as Soob felt. 'Those bastards left the ball last night with Ali Baig and must've continued their sickening Hellfire rite tonight.'

'They have alibis, Inspector Wilberforce.' His spies had eyes on the trio's movements: the Baigs were at home – Ali receiving funeral visitors and Imran preparing the burial shroud – and the Nizam's guests were at a banquet in the Premier Noble's city residence.

'Alibi, my foot. Ali Baig could've slipped out through a secret passage or some such.'

A point that had occurred to Soob too. He picked up her hand. Her palms were rough from scrubbing utensils and washing clothes. No bits of skin or leather under the short henna-stained nails.

Around them, the scent of leaves mingled with the rust of blood. He sniffed, but couldn't detect the hospital odour the other victims had. Bending closer, Soob inhaled again.

'What in God's name are you doing, acting Chief Inspector?'

'What can you smell near her mouth?'

Wilberforce dabbed away the blood from his nose and sucked in air through his mouth. 'Not much after your punch. Maybe blood… coconut… garlic.'

'Coconut hair oil and probably her dinner. Nothing sweet and antiseptic?'

Wilberforce shook his head.

'I think it is the drug.'

'Who told you?'

'*You* should've informed me,' Soob snapped, fed up with these games of one-upmanship.

Wilberforce gave him a measured look and then a nod. 'Check with the servants in the street and see if they are missing any women, HC Thomas.'

The head constable, who'd been standing on the gravel path, blew a whistle. Half a dozen constables trotted over from different parts of the park.

'This lady is a Muslim, so focus on a Muslim household.' At Wilberforce's raised eyebrow, Soob explained that Hindu women wore a vermilion dot on their foreheads, and would be in a sari or a half sari, not a kurta-pyjama.

The Englishman grunted and changed his instructions, and the constables hurried off to conduct a door-to-door search.

A large fruit bat, a flying fox judging by its size, glided silently above them towards the gaunt stalks of a papaya tree at the lawn's edge. Soob picked up the cummerbund and examined it. A monogram was embroidered on one end.

'What have you found?' Wilberforce asked, leaning forward.

Soob held it out.

'Henry Poole of Savile Row,' they said simultaneously.

'The cummerbund around Mrs Baig's neck had these initials. It must be Ali Baig.' Wilberforce slammed his fist into his other palm. 'We've got him now.'

Soob shook his head. 'You do realise that there are other suspects: the royal guests and Arthur Templeton.'

'I've sent a telegram to the Metropolitan Police asking them to check with Henry Poole. If we find Ali's name in their register, we have a watertight case.'

Soob was less sure about the evidence. It seemed too blatant a mistake for the killer to make.

'Beats me, though, how that bastard managed to make a hole under the noses of my constables.' Wilberforce turned a gloomy gaze at the opening.

'You had a man patrolling the back lane the whole day?'

'And the side lanes and the front too. Summon the patrol constable for the back lane, HC Thomas.'

'How long does it take the sentry to walk from this end to the other?'

'Three minutes. Some four strokes with a sharp blade would've been enough to do it, right enough. Take less than a minute. How in God's name did my man miss the killer making this great big hole?'

A middle-aged constable came over, looking anxious, then paled at the sight of the woman's body.

'Tell me what happened yesterday evening,' Soob said in Urdu.

The man dragged his gaze away from the dead woman. 'The rubbish cart man came, huzoor, then some servants wanted to see where the murders had taken place. I had to shoo them away.'

'Dogs?'

'Of course, sir, and a herd of pigs too. They charged towards me. I almost didn't see them because it was getting dark. I ran there.' He pointed at the lane abutting Templeton's house. He'd alerted the others, and together, with their matchlocks, the constables had dispersed the animals.

Dr Currimbhoy jogged up, out of breath. He squatted and examined her. The rain thankfully had abated.

'She died under an hour ago,' Dr Currimbhoy said. 'The blood hasn't clotted.'

Wilberforce let out an angry snort. 'See, if you hadn't butted in, we'd have the Ripper in chains.'

Soob ignored the comment. He retrieved his time piece from his pocket. Eleven forty-five. Wilberforce and he had heard the cry around eleven and had found the body immediately afterwards.

Soob picked up a lamp and shone it on the gravel.

'Bastard didn't leave any other clue apart from his calling cards: the cummerbund, the slit throat and the mutilations,' said Wilberforce.

'I found a shoe print on the riverbank yesterday evening.' Soob took out his pocket book, unwrapped the oilskin and flipped the page to the sketch.

Lips pursed, Wilberforce joined in the search, but all they could see were the scuff marks of the constables' boots.

A flurry of whistles sounded from the main gate. They exchanged a glance and moved in that direction. Moments later, a lantern bobbed jerkily on the lawn as a constable dashed towards them with a young Deccani in tow.

'Sir, this man says his wife is missing.'

'I told my men to inform all the households in the vicinity to guard their women.' Wilberforce said.

The man made for the body on the ground and sank to his knees. A guttural cry wrenched out of him. 'Fatima!'

Wilberforce's face showed the same guilt and rage that Soob felt. It was their fault, there was no getting away from it.

'Your stitches have broken,' Dr Currimbhoy said quietly in his ear.

'Not now,' he replied.

They waited in silence and when the husband had regained his composure, Soob drew out the story. Fatima was his wife. He was a gardener to Brown sahib, and they lived in the servants' quarters on the other side of Templeton's bungalow. Nineteen-year-old Fatima knew about Yakub. She would not have stepped out into the back lane so late at night.

'Yakub took her from the outhouse.' The husband clutched his head. 'Anyone could've scaled the boundary wall.'

She always used the outhouse at half past ten or so before sleeping. The children were asleep, so nobody saw her go. The rain had woken him, and he'd realised Fatima wasn't there.

'Hindu, Muslim and Parsi, rich and poor. The killer is making no distinction apart from the sex,' Wilberforce said. 'Of the four victims, if we count your river one, three were poor, and two were related to gardeners. Those two were friends, you reckon?'

'Not a Muslim and a Hindu woman.'

He explained that they couldn't mingle because their religion forbade a man who was not a relative from seeing them, which could happen if they visited each other.

'They were chosen because they live on this street,' Wilberforce said. 'But it was chance that these two were taken.'

Soob shook his head. 'They were chosen deliberately. The killer knows this street well.'

'Which brings us back to Ali Baig.' The Englishman bared his teeth in a smile.

Whistles sounded from the Templeton side of the park. The side entrance. Wilberforce's eyes widened with the same fear Soob felt.

He sprinted, ignoring the pain in his ribs, Wilberforce on his heels, his boots slapping the wet green.

A constable stood by the side entrance, and on seeing them, opened his fist. Glittering on his palm was a cloverleaf brooch clustered with rubies and diamonds.

Wilberforce's sharp breath and the glance towards the Templeton bungalow told him who the owner was.

'Where did you find the brooch?' Soob asked the constable in Urdu.

'Right here. At that edge.'

'Is it Mrs Templeton's?' he asked.

Wilberforce stiffened, then nodded.

No one had been allowed into the park since the first murders. And the Residency Police's thorough search meant that the brooch must have been dropped here in the past hour or so, not before.

He looked Wilberforce in the eye. 'We have to see Mrs Templeton right now.'

Chapter Thirty-two

Three fat candles shone from the mantlepiece on Phoebe Templeton as she clutched the marble ledge, the cheerful pink and mauve spring-flower print of her cotton robe accentuating her gaunt, hollow-eyed gaze. It was her hair, though – wet and plastered to her scalp – that had him exchanging a glance with Wilberforce.

'Arthur has taken a sleeping draught,' she said in a monotone, her eye on his bloodstained shirt.

At Wilberforce's 'We've come to talk to you, Phoebe,' she tottered and crumpled into the Chesterfield chair. 'What's happened?'

'Where were you this evening?' Wilberforce asked.

'Here.'

'The whole evening?'

'I went for a ride before dinner.'

'Where?'

She paused. 'Just a ride along the river.'

A lie.

'What time did you get back?'

'A little before half past eight.'

'Then?'

'We ate. I looked in on my children. I knew the thunderstorm would frighten them, so I sat with them for a while, then tucked them in. I went to my sitting room where I read till eleven or so.'

'This was what time?' Wilberforce asked.

'Just past nine. Why are you asking me these questions?'

'Did anyone see you there?'

The sizzle of the flame as an insect died in it was the only sound in the room as the import of the question sank in. She sat up, spine stiffening.

'What do you mean? Why are you asking me these questions? What has happened?'

'Mrs Templeton, did anyone see you in your sitting room?' Wilberforce switched to the formal language of official enquiries.

'No,' she said, narrowing her eyes. 'The servants retired except for the night attendant who comes if we ring the bell. Arthur was asleep.' Her gaze darted between them. 'Oh, I forgot, Edith popped her head in to say goodnight.'

'When?'

'Just after eleven.' She glanced at a cuckoo clock pinned to the wall between two bookcases. It was past midnight now.

They would find out soon enough if she was lying.

'Isn't your sitting room by the back garden, Mrs Templeton?' Wilberforce asked.

It surprised him that the Englishman knew the house's layout, as did his friendship with a social climber like Templeton.

'Why are you treating me like a suspect, Bill? What are you accusing me of?'

'Please show us your sitting room, Mrs Templeton,' he said at Wilberforce's silence.

She took them through a corridor overflowing with pots of palms and ferns to a room facing the back garden. More plants in jam jars trailed down a glass cabinet filled with dried specimens. The walls carried sketches and watercolours of plant skeletons and flowers and fruits – all exquisitely detailed.

She indicated a silk settee and two armchairs grouped around a coffee table, but neither policeman sat. Soob walked over to a writing desk by the bank of glass doors along one wall, drawn there by a dark leather-bound book entitled *Sermons of the Children of God*. It lay next to an open notebook and a cheery bowl of sunflowers.

'May I?'

'No,' she snapped. 'It is my prayer book.'

'Are you a Christian?'

A fire lit her gaze. 'Of course, we are the true Christians. I prefer not to discuss my faith.'

His eye snagged on a list in the notebook: *Duranta erecta*, oleander and angel's trumpet. 'These are poisonous plants.'

'For an article in my husband's paper, Chief Inspector.' Her tone was glacial. 'It will be in today's paper – on poisonous plants in the Deccan gardens. The next one is on botanical paintings.'

Above the desk hung a watercolour of a gladiolus signed 'Phoebe'. She had captured the peach-red flower's luscious curves and vibrant colour.

'Is that your work?'

She inclined her head.

'It is exquisite.' Religion and plants seemed to be her passions.

Her face relaxed somewhat.

He went over to the glass doors. Small circles of white phlox and stocks glowed like ghosts in the four corners of the lawn, and a bougainvillaea bloomed against the far wall, its white bracts merging with the whitewash.

'Is your back door there?' He pointed to the boundary wall.

She nodded.

Wilberforce glanced at him with an expressionless face, but Soob could read his thoughts: how easy it would be for Phoebe to cut through the lawn, pop out, grab Fatima, drug her and carry her to the park's hedge. She could have used gardening shears to cut the hole when the constable was at the other end of the lane, or at dusk when the pigs ran across.

Fatima was petite and would be easily carried by someone used to lifting terracotta planters and tugging out tough weeds. Phoebe's fingers, wiry and strong, were those of a seasoned gardener. The leather bits under Niloufer's nails could have come from a gardening glove.

'Phoebe, are you all right? I heard—'

It was her companion, who Soob now knew was called Mrs Edith Whittaker. She was yawning as if she had just woken up. A floral muslin scarf covered hair set in curlers, and a pink muslin robe, belted loosely, exposed her nightgown. 'What's the matter?'

'Edith, come in and tell them you saw me last night.'

'I did,' Edith said, clutching the lapels together. 'At ten, just before I went to bed.'

'No, it was at eleven, Edith. I heard the clock.'

'But I counted the cuckoo's cries, Phoebe.' Edith inspected their faces. 'Oh, I may be mistaken.'

'Do you keep this door open or shut when you are here?' Soob asked Phoebe.

'Open. I close it when I go to bed.'

He opened the glass door. The noise of the cicadas became louder, and the fresh, dewy scent of rain-washed grass blew in, along with wails.

'Something's wrong at the Browns' servants' quarters,' Edith said.

'Do you know their gardener's wife, Mrs Templeton?' Soob asked.

'Her children play with Sam, our labrador.'

'Did you see her tonight?'

Phoebe shook her head, but with growing horror on her face.

'Did you walk in the back garden?'

She shook her head again as if her mouth couldn't shape the word.

'Mrs Templeton, please show us your brooch – the one shaped like a cloverleaf,' Wilberforce said.

'I don't know where it is,' Phoebe said.

'It's in your jewel box, Phoebe,' Edith said helpfully.

Phoebe glared at her and left the room.

–

Wilberforce stepped into the garden and wandered to the back door, leaving Soob to question Edith Whittaker.

'Please sit, Mrs Whittaker,' Soob said. 'You are her companion? What do you do?'

Her duties involved writing letters, dealing with the staff, organising dinners and teas and lunches, and looking after the boys. She'd come as a governess initially. Her husband was in Bombay and would be joining her soon.

'What did you do last night, Mrs Whittaker?' he asked.

'Dinner was late because Phoebe had gone out for a ride. After that I read to the children. Phoebe usually does it but she had a headache and came here. Arth— Mr Templeton took a sedative and went to bed.'

So Phoebe had lied about reading to the children. 'What time was this?'

'A little after half past nine. By ten, I had tucked in the children and thought I'd check on Phoebe. So I popped my head in here.'

'So you saw her at ten, then.'

'Yes. Oh! No, it must have been eleven as Phoebe said.' Her fingers nervously clutched at the robe's front.

He revised his earlier impression of a nondescript woman. Edith had a fine figure, one Wilberforce, who'd returned to the room, was eyeing with a frown.

'Chief Inspector, has the murderer struck again?'

His silence she took for a yes and carried on.

'Then I must tell you, I heard a noise in the back garden last night. My room is on the other side of this corridor, and overlooks the back and side gardens. It must've been the killer. You see, I thought it was Phoebe. She often wanders in the garden at night.'

'What time was it?' Soob asked.

'I'm not sure. I fell asleep and woke up to a squeak. The back door hinge squeaks. I thought the servants had forgotten to lock it. With a killer wandering about, I couldn't sleep until I had checked. I lit the lantern and took my umbrella for protection. But fortunately, the latch was bolted from inside, so I came back.'

'Why didn't you go to Mr Templeton?' Soob asked.

'Oh, he'd taken a sedative.'

'And Mrs Templeton? Was she up?'

She hesitated.

'Was the light on in her study?'

She gave a nod.

'You went in and found the study empty.'

'No, no, it is as Phoebe said. She was there.' Her eyes darted to a money plant on the writing console, but not before he glimpsed fear. Why was she afraid of Phoebe Templeton?

'Tell me, was there any unpleasantness during the dinner party?'

'On the night Mrs Baig was killed?' Her glance skittered back to him and then away again. 'Of course not. There was no quarrel between her and Phoebe, if that's what you are asking.'

'Then why did Mrs Baig stay back?'

'She told Phoebe she wanted to speak to her.'

So it was Niloufer who had something to say to Phoebe Templeton. 'About what?'

She went pink and began fiddling with the tie of her robe. 'I don't know. They came here. I tidied up in the drawing room and went to bed.'

'Which is across the corridor from here, you said.'

He was quite sure from her flushed cheeks that a quarrel had occurred and she knew all about it.

'Did you see Mr Templeton?' he asked.

'No, he had gone out to see off the guests. I went back to my room.'

Something told him she had hurried there to eavesdrop on the conversation.

'And did you see Mrs Baig before she left?'

'No.' She looked him in the eye.

Phoebe walked into the room. 'Edith, I can't find my brooch.'

'You wore it yesterday.' Fear returned to Edith's face.

'No, it was the day before at the dinner party.'

'Is this yours?' Wilberforce opened his palm.

'Where did you find it?' Phoebe asked, reaching out.

Wilberforce closed his fist. 'In the park.'

'How did my brooch get there?'

'You tell us, Mrs Templeton,' Wilberforce said.

'I can't account for it,' Phoebe whispered. 'I just don't know. I have a key, but I haven't used it.' She fumbled in her dress pocket and drew out a small iron key with a green ribbon. The colour, Soob noted, was different from the one in Niloufer's pocket.

'What happened in the park?' Edith spoke up, staring at her employer. Her expression, which Soob couldn't pin down, contained fear and something else. Hope?

'A woman has been murdered,' Wilberforce said.

Phoebe gave a deep sigh and fainted, conveniently managing to collapse onto the silk settee. Soob glanced at Wilberforce and found a scepticism that matched his own.

While the lady of the house was being revived, Soob examined the back door. It was bolted from inside. He slid the iron latch and pushed the wood. No squeak came from the hinge; it had been oiled. So what had Edith heard?

A dog yelped and hared away, startled by his sudden appearance. Tiny pinpricks of light twinkled up at him, the eyes of spiders in a heap of leaf litter by the wall. Smells of decaying fruit and meat came from the rubbish heap on the other side of the lane. The water meadow lay there, shrouded in smoky grey mist.

It would be easy for Phoebe to step out unnoticed. The Templeton servants, the butler had said, lived in rooms along the side of the house, far from the back door. She could have heard Fatima in the outhouse through the high hedge, a duranta that must have been planted when the house was built. Strange, though, that a gardener like Phoebe would keep a plant whose leaves and berries were poisonous to pets and children.

He followed the wails to the house next door. The thatched roof of the outhouse was visible over the low wall, and shadows squatted near it. On seeing his lamp, a shadow peeled off and burst out of their back door.

'Who are you?' A young bearded man with agitated eyes accosted him, knife in hand. 'Why are you spying on us, on our women? Did you kill my sister?'

The other shadows converged on them. Fatima's relatives.

'Was your back door unlocked?' Soob asked, after identifying himself.

'Yes,' the brother said, lowering the knife.

'Would your sister have opened it?'

'Of course not. We all knew about Yakub roaming here and there. I made sure it was bolted. What are you implying?' He raised the blade. 'Fatima was a decent woman.'

'I meant no disrespect,' Soob said. 'Could your sister have helped a stranger? Perhaps the killer pretended to be injured, and she came out to help him?'

'Are you saying she was duped?' The brother stroked his unkempt beard. It framed his sister in a good light but had the troublesome feature of her being with a strange man. 'No, she would have come to her husband or me.'

'Do you live here too?'

'Yes. I help my brother-in-law in the garden.'

'So you and your families know the people living next door?'

'Of course. Our sons play with the gardener's children, and with the dog. A big black dog.'

'The English people don't mind?'

He heard Wilberforce call his name.

'The memsahib told her gardener it was fine. But the other English person, who wants to be the memsahib, scolded our sons. The children didn't understand her language.' He spat on the muddy ground.

He meant Edith Whittaker. Did Edith want to supplant Phoebe Templeton and become the memsahib? Soob mulled on this as he slowly retraced his steps to the Templetons' back door.

Chapter Thirty-three

They sat in leather wingback chairs in Cosmopolitan Hotel, drinks in hand, a small fire in the fireplace drying their clothes. The steady gush of rainwater in the storm drains sounded from outside the shuttered window.

'You are bleeding,' Wilberforce said curtly. His nose had swelled up to twice its size.

Soob wryly examined his khaki tunic now suffused with red. He'd been trying to ignore the fiery burn each time he took a breath. He'd have to stop at the hospital on his way home.

'An earlier wound.'

Wilberforce lapsed into silence, his finger stroking the rim of his glass filled to the brim with whisky and soda. Then he looked up, clearing his throat.

'Are you still of the mind that someone is using the Ripper's method, Chief Inspector Soobramania?'

No 'acting' or a snide tone, Soob thought. A first.

'Yes, the Ripper is dead, Inspector Wilberforce.' He well understood the demons chasing Wilberforce, especially from a case that had blighted his career, his friendships and his personal life.

The Englishman downed the drink in one long gulp. 'The nobs are off our suspect list then.'

'Not quite. They know the Ripper was caught and committed suicide.' He mentioned the Grand Duke's parting shot and his subsequent meeting in the gaming hell.

Wilberforce brightened. 'Then they could've helped Ali. Maybe not to kill, but certainly with an alibi.'

'Perhaps. But why would Ali, who presumably knows about the Ripper's death, copy the Ripper? Why incriminate himself?'

'Maybe Ali wanted to incriminate his nob friends.'

'Of course.' Soob slapped his forehead. 'Inspector Wilberforce, the killer doesn't know the Ripper was caught. We are looking for someone who knows a few details of the Ripper murders, but for some reason thinks all those murders had the same characteristics – the left eye and the neckerchief.'

'How did the killer come to have that idea? The London papers didn't report it that way.'

'The newspapers here may have. I'll check with the *Deccan Gazette* editor tomorrow and you do the same with Templeton's paper.'

Wilberforce leaned forward, hands gripped into fists. 'If they've reported these details, then our killer is a local.'

'Not necessarily a Deccani, though.'

Wilberforce drew a sharp breath. 'You think Phoebe had something to do with the murders?'

'Her behaviour has been very suspicious. Fatima could have opened the back door to Phoebe, someone she had seen working in the next-door garden. Edith's evidence puts Mrs Templeton in the garden at the time of the murder. But there is a problem. Mallu—'

'But surely, if Phoebe is the killer, then Mrs Baig should have died first,' Wilberforce interrupted. 'She was killed between ten thirty-five and ten fifty, and the other girl was killed between half past nine and ten. Phoebe didn't have the chance to kill the first girl, as she was at the dinner party.'

'Yes, I was coming to that. Mrs Templeton was in the house at the time Mallu was killed. I checked with the butler. But we both know she is hiding something. Where did she go before dinner last night? And what did she quarrel about with Niloufer? Her companion, I think, is aware of it. Then we have Mrs Templeton saying she wore the brooch at the dinner party but not yesterday, though Mrs Whittaker disagrees. You must know Mrs Templeton well.'

'Phoebe doesn't mix with us, so I rarely see her. But if she is telling the truth about the brooch, then someone took it from her jewellery box and dropped it in the park after seven yesterday evening, most likely to frame Phoebe. Why? And even if she dropped it at the dinner party, the guests are most likely off our list. I'll get a constable to check on their alibis. We can also write off the servants. The cook had a toothache and she was in bed in her quarters. The maid had the night off, and the butler had been sent to the city to deliver a package for Arthur. The carriage wheel came off on his way back, and he had to get it repaired. So we are back to the question: who would want to frame Phoebe?'

Soob shifted, wincing at the pain across his ribs. 'How are relations between Mr Templeton and his wife?'

Wilberforce's fingers tightened on the glass. 'Why would Arthur frame his own wife?'

'Isn't she rich?'

'Swimming in it. Her father, that is. Owns oil wells in America. But it doesn't make sense. The money is the father's. And from what Arthur let slip, he is barking mad. The father-in-law, that is. They belong to some strange religion. Beats me why they can't stick to the normal Catholic or Protestant line.'

Wilberforce got up and refilled his glass from a bottle labelled 'sherbet' at the soft drinks table. Since consumption of alcohol was banned for religious reasons within the city, it was common practice, Soob knew, for hotel proprietors to smuggle in alcohol this way for their European guests. After the events of the night, the Englishman deserved a drink, he thought.

'What happens if Mrs Templeton is convicted of murder? Does he get her money?'

'I don't know. Arthur boasted to me that the old man settled a sizeable sum on her when they married. But unless they hang her, he won't get his hands on it.'

'Does he have his own money?'

'Does now. The native bigwigs are well disposed towards him, and he managed to make nice with a powerful courtier.'

'Mr Templeton, I presume, isn't a nobleman.'

Wilberforce gave a snort and winced, clapping his kerchief to his face. 'Third son of a middling silk merchant,' came the muffled response.

'Has he made any bad investments lately?' Soob asked.

'He advised me and some others to invest in the Deccan Rail Scheme.'

'The one that went bust today?'

'Yes,' Wilberforce said grimly. 'Arthur must've lost money in it. I'll find out. Then, what you are thinking makes sense. These moneylenders are a bloodthirsty lot. To save his skin, Arthur would do anything, even frame Phoebe.' He gave a slow nod of his head. 'It would be like him to take advantage of someone else's murders to get out of a fix.'

Soob drummed his fingers on the armrest. 'There is something odd about Mrs Baig staying back to speak to Mrs Templeton. Mrs Whittaker looked flustered when I asked her about it. My hunch is they quarrelled.'

Wilberforce scowled. 'Wouldn't surprise me if Mrs Whittaker flung the blooming brooch into the park to incriminate Phoebe. She claims to have heard a door squeak and was in the garden checking on the back door. What's to stop her from entering the park then, eh? Also, the back door doesn't squeak, the side door does. And with a storm blowing through, how did she even hear the noise? But what motive could she have?' He gazed at the golden liquid in his glass glimmering in the candle's flame.

'Is there something going on between her and Mr Templeton?' Soob asked, thinking back to Fatima's brother's comment – *that English person who wants to be the memsahib.*

'Hah! Not bloody likely. Not with that mousy woman. Arthur goes for beauties. His current flame is a dancer in a brothel. Chandini.'

'I was thinking more along the lines of Mr Templeton using her.'

'As a cat's paw? String her along? Not with the marriage—' Wilberforce broke off abruptly.

Soob raised an eyebrow.

'With his marriage on the line,' the Englishman continued, not meeting his eye. 'Phoebe wouldn't stand for it.'

That wasn't what Wilberforce was going to say, Soob thought. He would find out soon enough when he interviewed Edith Whittaker.

Wilberforce downed the whisky in one and slammed the glass on the table. 'Where does all of this leave us? I'll tell you – no suspects, that's where it leaves us if we follow this line of enquiry. Acting Chief Inspector, the only motive we need to focus on is who stood to gain from the death of the rich Mrs Baig. I'll be seeing their lawyer today.'

And they were back to 'acting'. Soob's lips twitched. 'Inspector Wilberforce, I've already had a word with him. You did say we should interview those in our own jurisdiction.'

He told him about the provisions of the Baig will, ignoring the Englishman's chagrin.

'See, everything points to Ali Baig,' Wilberforce bit out. 'He stands to gain most from his stepmother's murder.'

'Well, the Templetons don't come out too well either. I will be seeing Edith Whittaker to find out about the quarrel.'

Wilberforce glowered. 'It seems to me that the murderer put the brooch there deliberately to frame Phoebe and throw us off the scent. I know who else lives at the top of this hill who could have made an excuse, sneaked out from some secret tunnel into the park or the back lane, murdered the poor lass, and slipped back in the pelting rain. It wouldn't have taken Ali Baig more than ten or so minutes. Even if he was away for two short periods, once to grab the lass and the second time to murder her, he could bloody well do it.'

Soob didn't reply. The brooch's presence in the park still didn't make sense. Why frame Phoebe Templeton? A possibility rose, evoked by something he'd heard a little earlier.

He stared into the fire.

What if the brooch had nothing to do with the murders?

Chapter Thirty-four

The black of the night sky had lightened into a smoky grey when Soob gave up on catching any sleep. He rose to his feet and rolled up the rush mat. After his ablutions he donned an old pair of trousers, a faded bush shirt and rubber boots and wandered into the garden with a notebook and pencil. Filling his lungs with the scent of cold grass, dew droplets wetting his boots, he gazed at the dark turrets of the city wall flattened against a sky turning silver, his brain still tussling with the conflicting clues.

'What are you doing, Athimber?' Natraja stood in the verandah, rubbing the sleep from his eyes. A sleepy chitter came from a bakul tree.

Soob's spirits lifted. It was the voice of the old Natraja, the curious-minded boy he'd been before the tragedy. 'Do you want to help me identify the plants?'

Natraja nodded and moved towards the steps, his white vaishti flapping in the breeze.

'Wear your boots. There may be snakes in the grass.'

'They won't harm me unless I step on one, Athimber. I want to feel the grass, nice and cold under my feet.'

'Go and put on your boots.'

When Natraja returned, Soob told him to stand still and observe.

'Observe everything – the plants, the breeze, the sound, the scent, the insects. See if you can describe the feeling you have. Then close your eyes and do it again.'

'I can smell grass and a fishy smell, feel the cold dew, hear little rustles… insects and birds waking up. I heard more things when I closed my eyes.' Natraja opened his eyes. 'How is this useful for finding plants, Athimber?'

'Think about how you study animals. Don't you look at what its surroundings are, what it eats, how and where it lives?'

Natraja bobbed his head.

'It's the same with plants. We understand it through its interactions with the air, temperature, soil type, weather, which other plants are near it, what bees, insects, birds and other fauna come to it or stay away from it.'

'Like us, plants also live in communities.' Natraja clasped his hands behind his back and rocked on his heels – Cheenu's mannerism.

Soob nodded, swallowing the sudden constriction in his throat.

'What happens if a plant is bad for other plants? How does the community react?'

'Give me an example,' Soob said, liking how Natraja's mind carefully considered every element of a topic, testing it in different situations and predicaments. That's how one came to perceive the behaviour of a plant, an animal or even a human.

'Like when the banyan tree doesn't let other plants live in its shade. The banyan needs water and if there is another plant, it won't have enough water. It is killing to protect itself, but isn't it harming the community?'

'Good example. So what do you think the community would do?'

Natraja contemplated the trunk of a banyan tree on the far side of the meadow grass.

'I'll give you a hint. What can humans and animals do, but plants can't?'

'Move,' Natraja said. 'They can't throw out the banyan tree as we can with bad people. And animals can leave the place where the bad animal lives. But plants have roots stuck to one place.'

'So the solution is?'

'The banyan lives for a very long time, no? Over a hundred years?'

'Much longer.'

'So it won't die unless a big storm uproots it. They will let it be, and nothing will grow under it, so it can't kill anything.'

'Correct. Now fetch the encyclopaedia from my room.'

As he watched Natraja slip through the doorway, feeling a warm glow of pride, the boy's example sparked an idea for a new motive. Natraja returned while he was mulling over the implications.

'First you must identify its family, then the similarities and differences with the others in that family. Have a go with those light blue flowers.' He pointed to a plumbago clump by the verandah. 'Find it in the book.'

It had become light enough to see the drawings. Natraja spotted it in a few minutes. He had a botanist's eye for finding characteristics – like a painter for angles and lines. A valuable asset for a naturalist, Soob thought, and felt his lips curving into a smile.

'Remind me to give you Alexander Von Humboldt's *Essay on the Geography of Plants*. He was a German naturalist, and came up with this method about forty years ago. Now note down what I describe. These plants we won't find in the book.'

As sunrise flooded the sky with orange and pink, two sparrows hopped in the grass looking for worms, and jingles sounded from the gate. It was the milkman and his buffalo with bells tied to its curled horns. He milked directly into the pail Soob brought from the kitchen.

His grandmother, who'd already bathed, stepped out of the kitchen by the small back garden. She held a wooden bowl of rice powder.

'Where is the tulsi plant, Subbu?'

He dragged a sandstone pedestal from a corner, and found a potted basil plant in the back garden to put in it.

Taking a pinch of rice powder, his grandmother drew a geometric design on the grass below the pedestal. She would light a diya, an oil lamp with a cotton wick dipped in ghee, and facing east, would pray to the sun god for a harmonious day. Rohini had done this every morning too. What a good mother she would have made…

His steps had taken him back to the verandah where his grandfather, having completed his prayers to the sun, was sprinkling water from a copper bowl on the grey stone. Knee-deep in the grass at the far end, immersed in his task of identifying plants, Natraja had not noticed the rites.

Soob still didn't know what his nephew thought of his outcaste status or what the boy expected of him – and wasn't looking forward to finding out. He filled his lungs with the comforting scent of ash and camphor and girded himself for a difficult conversation with the grandfather to whom he owed everything.

'I waited for you last night, Subbu,' his grandfather said reproachfully. 'You came very late. We need to discuss when you will perform the atonement rite and remove your outcaste taint.'

'Tatha, I'm not going to do it,' Soob stated baldly, unable to approach it in a less hurtful way.

'But, Subbu, you will remain a polluted Brahmin. We won't be able to be with you or meet you. Our community has been very generous in granting us a reprieve for so long.'

'I'm sorry, Tatha.' Soob stared at the bowl his grandfather was gripping tightly, the bones in his knuckles pale, veins arching.

'Don't you understand the implications, Subbu? An outcaste has no community, and without community, you have no identity in our society. You will cease to exist for us. Why can't you adhere to these few rules even if you think those priests have wronged you?'

All the questions Soob had posed to himself many times, and he had come up with the same answer. 'Tatha, it's not simply a question of returning to the caste. If I perform the rite, it would be a travesty of what I stand for.'

'What do you stand for?' His grandfather's voice rose, and Soob caught Natraja's glance from the corner of his eye.

He replied softly. 'For the principle that we are all born equal, but possess different skills. At birth our basic nature is similar and what we choose to add or subtract from it is the product of our choices. You are asking me to return to a hierarchy that caste imposes at birth itself.'

'That is not true, Subbu. The concept of karma is precisely about the choices you've made in your previous lives. Those deeds and actions are responsible for your birth into a caste in this life, but the merits and demerits of the previous life are exhausted in this one. We—' He stopped as his wife bustled up with rice water in steel tumblers.

Soob thanked her with a smile.

His grandfather took a glass and poured the rice water into his mouth, raising the glass two feet above his head. Soob followed suit. By mutual consent, they did not speak until she returned to the kitchen.

'Subbu, we have the freedom to choose better moral and spiritual actions in this life,' his grandfather continued. 'And be reborn in a higher caste the next time. When you deprive Natraja of his caste, think of its moral implications for your next life and for his present life and subsequent ones.'

'Tatha, I don't believe in an afterlife or in previous lives. I think the Carvaka school was right.'

'Bah!' The round steel wire frames flashed in the pale sunlight. 'Don't talk to me about those materialists. No god, no afterlife, only this world matters – what rubbish they speak. And even if we take your

186

view that only this life matters, should you not do your best to be an ideal guardian for Natraja? You are making him suffer.'

His grandfather put the tumbler on the stone floor and glanced at Natraja, who had wandered over to the picket fence abutting the road. 'Subbu, how long will you remain angry with our priests?' He raised his hand when Soob opened his mouth. 'It does not matter whether your stance comes from principle or anger. What matters is Natraja's happiness. The boy looks up to you. He wants to be like you. See what he reads, see his mannerisms. He copies you in everything.'

Soob took a deep breath and stared at the horizon. How to explain that he felt guilty each time he looked at Natraja. That was why he'd left Madras immediately on his return from London, taking long assignments in other cities.

'You are Natraja's guardian,' his grandfather pleaded. 'It is your duty to perform the boy's upanayanam, Subbu.'

A compulsory rite for a boy, the donning of a white cotton thread worn diagonally on the torso signified a Brahmin male's passage from boyhood to studenthood, and would officially bestow on Natraja the status of a Brahmin, a member of the twice-born caste.

'Can't you and Pati perform the ceremony for Natraja like you did for us?'

'No, Subbu. It is your duty. By performing the expiation rite you will show the boy how much you care for him. It will soothe him for his loss, make him feel more settled with us. Do not put your anger above the boy's well-being.'

A mosquito sang and struck his arm. Soob absently rubbed the sting. It dawned on him that the choice was not between following his principles or submitting to his caste's rules. It was between his own best interests and Natraja's.

'Huzoor,' Ram Rahim yelled from the gate.

Soob beckoned him in. 'Excuse me, Tatha.'

He strode down the steps and up the short gravel driveway.

Ram Rahim's report that a man had tried to enter Shiraz's bedroom around ten the previous night quickened his heartbeat.

'Are you sure it was a man?'

'Huzoor, it was the shadow I saw killing the begum. He ran away when I yelled. I remained there until now, as you had asked me to.'

'Shabash, Ram Rahim.' He patted the boy's back. 'Have you eaten? No? Wait here.'

To face a deadly killer not once, but twice – such bravery was commendable for one so young. Ram Rahim deserved a fistful of gold mohurs, Soob thought, as he retraced his steps to the bungalow for his money pouch. Though the boy was convinced the killer was a man, again he had only seen a shadow.

Soob slowly mounted the verandah steps.

It looked as if his idea about the new motive was being borne out. Several improbable and seemingly unconnected events had already occurred. But to get the evidence and catch the culprit he would have to plan carefully.

Chapter Thirty-five

Her mother-in-law hurried in with the newspaper. Shiraz raked the hair off her face and sat up in bed. Aunt Friya had never entered her room, Cyrus's childhood room.

'Another girl has been murdered in Baig park, a gardener's wife.' She tapped the news sheet. 'It seems she lived next door to the Templetons. The murderer had the audacity to send a note to the newspapers.'

Shiraz ran an eye over the front page – the collapse of the Deccan Rail Scheme, the war in Abyssinia, the Ripper Strikes Again. As she read the horrific details, the previous night's terror flooded back. But for her mysterious guardian angel's yell, this could have been her fate. She glanced at her mother-in-law's anxious face. No need to add to her worries.

'The audacity of that fiend to send such a letter,' Friya continued. 'Poor Gul. I must go to her before she reads this.'

Shiraz read the gloating words of the foul letter printed in full.

> I have struck in Whitechapel, and now I have struck here. Grand work, the last job was. I gave the lady no time to squeal. My knife is so nice and sharp I want to get to work right away. I leave clues, but you fail to find me. I give you fair warning about my next kill. Tonight it is. Catch me but I don't think you can.
>
> Yours truly, Jack the Ripper

The article explained that the letter, inked in red, had arrived at the *Deccan Gazette* office sometime during the night. It hinted that the letter writer must be an Englishman, since few natives spoke the language, and ended with several pertinent questions to the authorities: *What are the Residency Police doing to save poor Deccani women? How do they plan to protect them in their own homes? Is the madman angry with gardeners?*

Surely it couldn't be Jack the Ripper, Shiraz thought, frowning. Soob had caught him. Memories of Soob brooding silently with Cyrus in their London flat, grieving for the victims and the Ripper's wife and two daughters flooded in.

'Could you find out more about this new murder from the Chief Inspector?' her mother-in-law said.

Shiraz nodded. She threw off the cotton sheet and slid out of bed, glancing at the cuckoo clock on the wall. Ten past seven. An early riser, Soob would be at his desk by now.

–

After a quick wash, a glass of cold milk, and a change into her hospital clothes, she set off in her open phaeton, bowling alongside the river, a jagged line of silver in the oppressive sunlight. It was one of those humid days when everything she touched left a damp mark. The buckram collar of her blouse and its muslin sleeves were already sticking to her skin.

An uneasy knot massed in her stomach as she stared at the river, barely noticing an ibis waiting to lance a fish, the shallow waters lapping against its stick legs. If she'd informed Soob last night about Phoebe's accusation, could last night's murder somehow have been prevented?

'Hakimji, the Chief Inspector is coming towards us.' The coachman clicked his tongue and the horses stopped as Soob rode up.

Fine lines crisscrossed at the edge of his eyes. He must have been up the whole night tracking the killer, she thought, her heart softening, and the unpleasantness of their previous encounter melted away.

'What happened last night?' Both of them spoke at the same time.

'Soob, I read about the murder. Is Phoebe a suspect?' She had meant to begin with Phoebe's story about the love letter and then lead up to her own near escape.

'I told you not to investigate,' he bit out. 'Don't you understand how dangerous it is? The killer is dead set on killing more women. Didn't last night teach you anything? Why are you sleeping with the window open?'

Fury flooded in. Soob was having her watched. 'How dare you! It was your constable at my window. I thought it was the killer.'

'But it most likely was, damn it.' His grip on the carriage door tightened, knuckles gleamed. 'Fatima was murdered last night in the park. It could've been you. From now on, you mustn't go alone to any of the slums. I'll have a word with your guards to patrol the entire house and arrange for the Residency constables to be out on the street. And Shiraz, keep your window locked. We are dealing with a very dangerous killer.'

Her gorge rose at his assumption that she would do his bidding.

'How would you like it if I forbade you to investigate because I wanted to protect you? You are no different from these nawabs, wanting to lock me up. You don't see me as an equal.'

'I'm not going to argue with you, Shiraz. *Do as I say.*'

He'd never used such a cold tone with her before. Why couldn't he see that his fussing deepened her sense of vulnerability?

Fine! If he was going to behave like this, she would investigate on her own. There was no need to tell him about the shoe imprint, which in any case had been washed away; it would only bolster his argument. Not a word would escape her lips about Phoebe's visit or about the wrong colour of the ribbon on Niloufer's key. She'd get the evidence from Phoebe, check her park key, and only then tell Soob when she thrust the letter in his hand. That would show him what a helpless woman was capable of.

'Suleiman, drive on,' she snapped.

The coachman's glance at Soob, who gave a nod, irritated her no end.

'Promise me you won't investigate any more,' he said urgently, but she turned her face towards the river.

She couldn't shake him off until they reached the hospital. Once he'd ridden on, she instructed the coachman to take her to the Templeton residence.

–

'Is Mrs Templeton in?' Shiraz asked the man in a white uniform who'd opened the door. 'I am Dr Shiraz Daruwalla.'

He bowed. 'Madam has gone out for a drive with her father, hakimji.'

'Dr Shiraz.' A woman bustled up from somewhere deep in the gloom of the corridor. 'I am Mrs Edith Whittaker, Phoebe's companion. She should be back soon. Do come in. Open the door properly, Thomas.'

The butler stepped back and opened the door wider, but his rigid frame and the sideways glance at the companion spoke volumes. Though Shiraz had little patience with these hierarchies, she knew what he was thinking: that though Edith's skin colour made her part of the ruling class, her profession did not – she was a servant like him, and ought not to put on airs.

Edith could tell her more about Phoebe's accusation, Shiraz thought, entering a corridor with green palms arching from terracotta pots and urns. They entered a sitting room bright with sunlight streaming in through a bank of French windows. She turned to the companion. Even in such a short acquaintance, it was clear to her that the two women couldn't be more different from each other. This lady's comfortable air and quiet presence contrasted starkly with Phoebe's suppressed rage and unnerving intensity. Edith's blue eyes held a pleasant expression and she wore her brown hair in a soft, neat bun. A duff-coloured cambric gown subtly revealed plump curves. But something familiar about how Edith Whittaker moved, almost with a rolling gait, and in the slightly parted lips when she took a breath, caught her attention. What was it...?

'It came to me just now that Mrs Baig is your cousin,' Edith said, showing her to the settee. 'You bear a resemblance. I'm so utterly sorry about the tragedy. Please accept my condolences.'

Angry words caught at Shiraz's throat. She wasn't going to thank this woman who could have prevented Niloufer from leaving alone. A part of her, though, knew it wasn't Edith's fault.

'Were you at the dinner party?' Shiraz asked.

'Yes, of course, I organised it. That is one of my tasks.'

'Then perhaps you can help me. It would give solace to our family if we could get a sense of Niloufer's last hours. Were they happy?'

'Your cousin was a beautiful lady. Her wit and charm were admired by all of us.'

'Was she her usual self at the dinner?' she asked in a curt tone.

'Actually, Mrs Baig was rather quiet that evening. And so was Phoebe.' Edith had an odd expression, something between a plea, guilt and sadness.

'Why? Were they not speaking to each other?'

Edith didn't meet her eye.

'Mrs Whittaker, I know all about the quarrel.' Shiraz was fed up with these lies.

'Oh.' Edith shifted and stretched her feet. Little mounds of flesh swelled out of the shoe buckles. Water retention, Shiraz noted automatically. 'It was about that letter your cousin wrote to Mr Templeton.'

Shiraz frowned. It wasn't a poison pen note but an actual letter from Niloufer. 'Did you read it?'

Edith looked away, then nodded. 'It said that she loved him and was counting the hours before she could see him again.'

Such overwrought nonsense didn't sound like Niloufer at all. Something relaxed deep within her. But how did Edith know what the letter said? Shiraz found it unlikely that Phoebe would have shared such personal information with someone who worked for her.

'Did you find it?' Her wild shot hit the mark.

Edith Whittaker lowered her voice. 'It was among the papers Mr Templeton gave me to type. I was horrified when I found it. Phoebe walked in just then, and I tried to hide it. She became suspicious and snatched the letter from me. Believe me, Dr Daruwalla, I wouldn't for the world have shown it to her.'

The woman had become more animated and she seemed to be enjoying relating the gossip.

Shiraz frowned, eyeing the companion's avid expression. Had Edith wanted Phoebe to find out? 'When did this occur?'

'At teatime on the day of the dinner party.'

'How did Mrs Templeton react?'

'She turned pale and walked out clutching the letter. It was quite frightening really.'

'Did she confront her husband?' Shiraz asked in a tight voice, seething at the person who'd concocted such a horrible lie.

'I don't know. But Phoebe was very cold to Mrs Baig and Mr Templeton at the dinner. When everyone was saying their goodbyes, Mrs Baig told Phoebe she wanted to speak to her.'

'And did you hear their conversation?' She would bet that Edith had eavesdropped.

The lady hesitated, her gaze skittering away towards the sparrow hopping outside the window. 'My room is opposite her study and they were speaking loudly. Your cousin denied writing the letter. That's all I heard. Later, Arthur walked her to the door and returned immediately.'

'How do you know?' Shiraz pounced. 'You were in your room, weren't you?'

Edith flushed. 'Oh, I came out for a glass of water.'

The door opened, and a good-looking man with green eyes strolled in.

'Edith, where is— Oh, sorry, I didn't know you had a visitor. Hello, I'm Arthur Templeton.' He thrust out his hand.

Shiraz didn't shake it. She had nothing but contempt and rage for this man.

He withdrew his hand, unsure of how to proceed.

'Dr Daruwalla came to see Phoebe,' Edith said brightly.

'I'll leave you to it, ladies,' he said and turned, but Shiraz's 'I'm Niloufer's cousin' made him twist around. He gave a jerky bow.

'I'm sorry about Mrs Baig's death. I should've insisted on dropping her home. I—'

'Her murder, you mean,' Shiraz interrupted coldly, her ears catching the crunch of carriage wheels in the driveway. 'Yes, you should have.'

A maid entered with a tray of tea and biscuits. Shiraz had been about to decline refreshments, but Phoebe Templeton's panicked gaze from the doorway as their eyes met changed her mind. She picked up a cup of tea, to prolong her visit.

The dark pouches under Phoebe's eyes spoke of a sleepless night, but sleep was for the innocent, Shiraz thought grimly. Not for a so-called friend who'd tortured Niloufer's last hours.

Still pale, Phoebe came up to Shiraz. 'How do you do. I'm Phoebe Templeton. You must be Niloufer's cousin, Dr Shiraz.'

Shiraz put her cup down and shook hands silently, not trusting herself to speak in a calm tone. Part of her wanted to say they'd met last night, but she refrained from doing so, curious about the lady's motives.

'Did I interrupt something?' Phoebe asked, her gaze skittering between her, Templeton and Edith Whittaker.

'Yes, Nilou—'

'I was telling Dr Shiraz about your religion, Phoebe,' Edith Whittaker interrupted. 'Do tell her the commandments of the Children of the Sun.'

After an inscrutable glance at her companion, Phoebe sat on the settee and spoke about her religion in a monotone. The commandments sounded the same as the usual Christian ones, but what was the point of knowing them, Shiraz brooded, if these people couldn't follow a simple love thy neighbour? Phoebe looked away to the window and continued. 'Do not covet your neighbour's wife, do not procreate out of wedlock, do—'

'I came for the letter,' Shiraz interrupted, unable to bear it any more.

'What letter, Phoebe?' barked Templeton, who'd been pacing in the room.

His wife's fingers twisted her wedding band.

'Phoebe, it puzzles me as to what happens if there is a child from the affair,' Edith spoke up in a coaxing tone from her chair by the window. Back to her job of being a peacemaker, Shiraz thought.

'Life is sacred,' Phoebe said quickly. 'It must be cherished above all other ties. If the man or the woman is from our religion, they have to divorce, and the guilty party has to marry the mother of the child.'

Life was precious, Shiraz thought, turning a cold eye on Arthur Templeton, who flushed. The vein throbbing at his temple pleased her. He deserved to suffer. They all did.

She glanced at Phoebe, whose formerly blank expression had been replaced by something else. A realisation perhaps? As if she'd solved a mystery.

'Do they have to marry for the child?' The annoying companion went on wasting their time.

And Phoebe's continued responses were plainly to avoid discussing the letter with Shiraz.

The clock above the door chimed the half-hour between nine and ten.

Shiraz rose to her feet impatiently. She had to get Phoebe away from the annoying companion and the glowering husband.

Phoebe shot up and followed her out. 'Thank you for not mentioning my visit, Dr Shiraz,' she said at the front door. 'Did Edith tell you about the letter?'

'Mrs Templeton, give me the letter. I can prove to you it's a forgery.'

Phoebe reluctantly took it out of her dress pocket. It looked creased as if it had been opened and read many times. Shiraz pocketed it before Phoebe could change her mind.

'Now please show me your park key?' She couldn't be bothered to circle her way to it through pointless chit-chat.

Looking puzzled, Phoebe slipped her hand into the pocket again and took out a key, its top tied with a green silk ribbon.

'Is Niloufer's husband's tied with a blue or a green ribbon?'

Phoebe looked puzzled. 'I don't know. Same as mine and Niloufer's, I suppose.'

How was that possible? Shiraz had seen the blue ribbon on the key in Niloufer's pocket, but Aunt Gul had said it ought've been green. Could someone have changed the ribbon? Or was Niloufer carrying her husband's key?

Shiraz stepped out into the porch where her carriage was waiting.

Or was there another key?

–

Shiraz told the coachman to stop on the roadside at the foot of the hillock. She opened the carriage door and read the letter in the bright sunlight.

> *Dearest Arthur,*
>   *I am counting the minutes till we can meet again. I love you. I am pining for you. I cannot eat or sleep. I close my eyes and all I can see is you. I want to be with you all the time, my dearest Arthur.*
>
>   *Your ever loving Niloufer*

It looked like Niloufer's handwriting but this was definitely a forgery. Niloufer would never write such melodramatic rubbish. Soob, she was sure, would be able to expose it.

Very well, she'd write up her conversation in the manner of a medical note – record her impressions and observations – and send it to Soob along with a dinner invitation. First, she'd confirm from Maryam whether Nawab Zulfikar's key had a blue ribbon. If so, Niloufer's could have dropped out in the struggle and Ali had slipped the wrong key into her pocket.

All this while, something about Edith Whittaker had been tugging at her. Shiraz leaned back against the leather seat and half-closed her eyes, summoning a picture of Edith in her mind, and tried to pinpoint what it was. The way Edith breathed through her mouth, how she flexed her swollen feet.

Edith Whittaker was pregnant.

Chapter Thirty-six

No one looking at this run-down street would guess it had been a fashionable address just a century ago, Soob thought, trying to tamp down
his temper at Shiraz's stubbornness. He dismounted by a marble fountain and tied the horse to an iron post outside the office of the *Deccan
Gazette*. The newspaper was housed in a mansion, lodged between an
ironsmith and a tea shop. These run-down shops selling rusted nails and
iron were a far cry from the area described to him by the newspaper
editor as possessing gracious mansions, ponds filled with lotuses and
fish, exquisite gardens with flowering trees and marble fountains.

Turning his thoughts away from his encounter with Shiraz, he
stepped into the newsroom. Several walls must have been removed to
create the large chamber that resembled a railway platform, its air dense
with curses and tobacco smoke, with desks occupied by half a dozen
men, stationed one behind the other and pounding out stories on their
typewriters.

'Why are you taking sides between the Nizam and the British, huh?'
cried a man at the centre of the room, ash flecking his chubby chin,
wild tufts of hair growing from his ears. 'Let them fight it out. Have you
forgotten our first commandment: reporters must be impartial. Tchah!'

Though newspapers had been censored in Hyderabad since 1891, it
was possible for a clever editor with high connections to evade these
restrictions. The editor of the *Deccan Gazette*, Vahid Baig, a canny old
soul under a gruff exterior, possessed both qualities along with a third,
a credo to lay the facts before the public, which had endeared him to
Soob.

'Sorry, Vahid sahib,' the hapless recipient of the lecture said, ducking
under the red-hot tip of a beedi careening towards his nose. 'I only
thought we Hyderabadis should help the Nizam to keep control of the
city.'

'Bloody fool! That's not our job. Let his ministers do theirs.' Vahid Baig shook his head sorrowfully. 'But you are right, my lad. Not a strong man, our Nizam. Capable when he puts his mind to it, but that's as rare as sighting the Id moon. Freud is right, my boy, everything we do now has its origins in our childhood. What can we expect of a child who lost his father at the age of three and was cosseted by a pack of women? Bah!'

Soob steeled himself to face a lecture on the Viennese psychoanalyst. In the short time he'd known the man, Vahid Baig had flitted from the German Marx to the Englishman Hume to the Frenchman Montaigne.

'Ah, Chief Inspector Soobramania.' Vahid Baig beamed. 'The man of the hour. The Ripper Hunter. Come to give us the scoop! Peon, quick, bring Rooh Afsa and biscuits for our honoured guest. Raju, bring your notebook, take down every word. Note the reaction when he sees the letter.'

Even a lecture on Freud was preferable to gracing the paper's front pages again, Soob thought, as he shook his head. 'No interview at the moment, Vahid sahib. I'd like to speak to you alone.'

Amid a clutter of papers and books in his office, Vahid Baig handed over the yellowed notepaper. The top portion, which might have contained a crest or some such mark of identification, had been neatly scissored off.

The wording and the use of red ink mimicked the real Ripper's letter to the Central News Agency. Furlow had sent the letter on 27 September 1888 – the first time he'd used the name 'Jack the Ripper'. It confirmed what Soob already suspected, that the killer was educated, spoke English, and knew about the real Ripper's letter to the newspapers.

'Your view, Chief Inspector Soobramania?' Vahid Baig barked. 'Are we dealing with Jack the Ripper?'

'Did you print the original letter in your article on the Ripper?'

'Not much grass grows under your feet, Chief Inspector.' He cleared his throat and spat in the spittoon. 'Printed it last week. Think it is copied from there?'

'May I see it?'

'Pah! That bloody fool of a reporter took the description of the Ripper's murders from that scoundrel Templeton's rag.' He hauled out a news sheet from a drawer and slapped it on the table. 'Didn't realise that it pertained to only one murder. Is that any place to find out the truth? These young men are all the same. Looking for shortcuts, not willing to put in the hard work.'

Soob read the article. Now he knew why the killer had carved out the left eye and left a cummerbund around the victims' necks.

'Suspects, Chief Inspector?'

'We are still investigating, Vahid sahib. Tell me, is Nawab Zulfikar Baig related to you?'

'Third cousin on my father's side.'

Soob offered his condolences. 'Can you tell me about him?'

'Passionate, loyal, steadfast, razor-sharp intellect. Kept him one step ahead of those snakes in our ruler's court. We weren't close, but we respected each other.'

'A one-man woman? Is that why he didn't have several wives?'

'Yes, you've hit the nail on the head, Chief Inspector. When his wife died from malaria five years ago, he was inconsolable. Then last month he met the Parsi girl and married her. Acuity undone by his passion. No fool like an old fool, they say. Quite a ruckus it kicked up in the two communities. And now both are dead.' Vahid Baig shook his head sorrowfully.

'How did his sons take their mother's death?'

'Badly. Especially Imran, her favourite. Used to be a rapscallion. Wouldn't say that looking at him now, would you? When he came back from London, he turned sombre and reserved. Ali went to the other extreme. Gambling, opium, women, wild friends. You know about the Hellfire Club? Complete scoundrels that lot. Tragedy, as Freud says, shapes our character more than good fortune.'

That was certainly true for him. Rohini's death had made him more secretive and detached, less willing to allow others to affect his emotions.

'Zulfikar was worried about Ali,' Vahid Baig carried on. 'He hoped marriage would steady him. Put him in charge of their spy network, that's what Ali wanted. For some time it seemed to calm him.'

'Imran Baig managed the estates. Isn't that unusual?'

The editor picked up a bell and shook it violently. 'Imran has the head for making money. The boy has spun handsome profits. Ali has the spendthrift's insouciance.'

'Did Ali invest in the Deccan Rail Scheme?'

'Don't tell me the bloody fool sunk his money into that rascal's scheme? I warned him not to, as did his brother and father. Fellow running it is a gunrunner, a slippery Afghan named Abdul Huq. Brings ruin to all except himself. The fellow connived with unscrupulous bankers from England and has gone underground.'

'Imran knew about Huq?'

'Yes, and he warned Ali in front of me when I met them at a soiree. Knows that scoundrel's true colours. Told me the fellow tried to dupe him in a property transaction. That boy knows how to make money. Doubled the family fortune. Ali is a very lucky man. I can tell you from my own experience how galling it is to see a dissolute firstborn run through the family wealth. Where's that fellow?' He shook the bell violently.

'Does Ali Baig have a feud going on with another nawab?'

Vahid Baig shook his head. 'Ali is a very popular man among his peers and their fathers. He may be hot tempered, but he is kind and very loyal to his friends.'

So the trouble mentioned by Imran's wife was not a feud, Soob thought. As he'd suspected after hearing of Ali's quarrel with his father, it involved money and a ruinous investment. 'Tell me more about the Deccan Rail Scheme.'

Vahid Baig hawked and spat again in the spittoon. It was a familiar tale of promissory notes, forged documents, false promises, and bribes to high officials in London. Not just that, Huq had been implicated in previous scandals too. 'Made a fortune brokering deals. A mining concession in the Golconda diamond mines, selling muskets to the Nizam's army, now this. How people can be such credulous fools, tchah!'

A peon entered with a tray of sherbet, water and a plate of biscuits.

'Bloody fool, what's taken you so long?' The editor picked up the plate. 'Chief Inspector, you must taste Golconda biscuits, our speciality.'

Soob took a golden biscuit and bit into its flaky centre. He was famished, and going by the number of interviews he had planned for today, this might well be his lunch.

'Would the list of investors in the rail scheme be with Huq, Vahid sahib?'

'Yes, but you won't find him.'

'Who is Huq's patron?'

'Now you are asking the right question, Chief Inspector Soobramania.' Vahid Baig beamed. 'That's the first thing you must ask a Hyderabadi.'

'Who is yours?' Soob retorted with a twinkle in his eye.

'I have none,' the editor uttered grandly. 'I am my own patron. There are very few, and I count you among this number, who owe nothing to anybody. Huq is completely beholden to the Premier Noble. Isn't Nawab Khurshid Jah favourably disposed to you after you thwarted the insurrection?'

Soob ignored the editor's attempt to discover whether the Nizam's brother-in-law owed him a favour. Poker-faced, he asked if Huq lent to his investors.

'He would be foolish to do so. All his schemes go bust like the Deccan Rail. How would they repay him? Your best bet, Chief Inspector, is a jeweller. They are the moneylenders here.'

'Whom would Ali Baig borrow from, if he needed to?'

'That fool! So that's your line of investigation. I think you are wrong. Ali is a gambler and quick-tempered and could kill in the heat of the moment. But not these murders. He doesn't have that cold streak you need for such clinical dispatch.'

Though the editor had correctly identified the murderer's personality, he was too close to the Baigs to have an impartial mind.

'Who?' Soob tried again.

'Try Mukesh Lal, our family jeweller.'

A familiar name to Soob from having helped the Lal family during the insurrection attempt. That, he hoped, would help in loosening his tongue. Jewellers were notoriously secretive about their clients.

'But if I were you, I'd look at that Templeton.' Vahid Baig spat again. 'A scoundrel through and through. Prints the most scurrilous rumours if he is paid to do it. Gives us all a bad name. Ask him how much he has sunk into the Deccan Rail Scheme. Knowing the wily rascal, he'll somehow wriggle out of that mess. Pah!'

'How do you know he invested in the Deccan Rail Scheme?' Soob asked, stiffening.

Vahid Baig tapped his nose and smiled. 'Now tell me, when do you plan to arrest his wife? Wasn't Mrs Templeton's brooch found in the park?'

Soob rose to his feet smoothly and thanked the editor.

'Ah, so you won't confirm it. Never mind, Chief Inspector. The lady definitely knew about the Ripper murders, having been in London then, my sources tell me. As for the left eye being gouged out, her mistake comes from her scoundrel husband's sensationalised account.' He rose to his feet and bowed. 'Mark my words, it is Templeton. He needs his wife's money after sinking so much into Huq's scheme. How convenient it would be if he could frame his wife and pocket her fortune.'

With these words ringing in his ears, Soob strode out through the newsroom, into the dim corridor and out into the sharp bite of the noon sun. He bent and untied his horse, which had been sheltering under a canvas awning hoisted for that purpose.

If Templeton had unknowingly made the mistake about the left eye, then another improbable event had come to pass. Soob knew now that he was on the right track.

Chapter Thirty-seven

Even a lunch of his favourite spicy fowl curry, fried bread and mutton cutlets failed to improve Wilberforce's mood. He wasn't looking forward to questioning the editor of the *Deccan Gazette*. Plucking the Ripper's letter from him was going to be like pulling hen's teeth. The letter's gleeful tone and even its words were identical to the Ripper's missive to the London broadsheets. Wilberforce planned to shake the letter under the Brahmin's nose: *See, I told you that you were wrong about John Furlow.*

Chittering birds flew in and out of the leafy boughs in the compound of the Residency Police station as he mounted his horse. Now for the torture.

By the time he'd pushed through the crowd jabbering and haggling away in the brocade shop lane and emerged into a broader street with scent shops, it felt like biting red ants were running up and down his back. He tethered his horse to an iron post outside the *Deccan Gazette* office. Taking a deep breath, he stepped into the gates of hell.

All the nasty articles the paper had printed about the Residency Police ran through his mind, making his blood boil. At least the fellow didn't spare the Nizam's lot. Though how he managed not to be clapped up in the dungeons was a mystery, Wilberforce thought, as he marched up to the editor's desk.

As he had foreseen, the man refused to hand over the Ripper letter and gave him that supercilious look perfected by these high-born types. His threats rang hollow; both men knew he had no authority in the city.

Wilberforce was forced to speak to a reporter and admit they had made no arrests. Why not? the fellow had the temerity to ask, and added that everyone knew about Phoebe's brooch. He had to restrain himself from wiping the smirk off the oily fellow's face. The final indignity came after his reluctant promise of an exclusive when they caught the Ripper.

Vahid Baig coolly informed him the letter was with Chief Inspector Soobramania, that the killer had copied the Ripper's method from an incorrect article in *The Jasoos*, and, to add insult to injury, told him in a kind tone to do his job and arrest Phoebe.

The Brahmin was back to his old tricks of grabbing the evidence, and for all he knew was the one who'd blabbed to them about the brooch, Wilberforce thought gloomily as he stomped out. His spirits sank further – if the killer had copied a newspaper article, then he couldn't be the Ripper.

He mounted his horse. It could still be Ali, though, he thought, urging his horse into a trot. He'd give the wretched Brahmin a proper good bollocking. But the fellow was out somewhere, not in his office at the Charminar Police Station. The sticky heat did little to improve Wilberforce's mood on the ride back.

Chapter Thirty-eight

Shiraz attended a complicated childbirth in a slum on the Residency side of the river. When the baby finally came out, a thin cry drawn from his chest, she gathered the newborn in her palms, her spirits lifting. Soob would be furious that she'd come alone but she didn't care. This little one was the most important thing in the world right now. A perfect baby boy. She tried to ignore the hollow feeling in her stomach.

The hut stank of straw, cow dung, sweat and vomit. As usual, the single window and the door remained shut. No matter how many times she and Dora told them about the benefits of fresh air and sunlight, they wouldn't listen. Sick people were also shoved into a dark corner in these airless rooms. This time Shiraz got a window opened, but the moment she left, she knew it would be shut.

It was too late to have lunch, and she still wasn't hungry. But there was one thing she had to do, if only she could summon up the nerve.

–

Shiraz marched into the Baig harem, having fibbed to the gate guard that Maryam Baig had summoned her. In and out quickly, she told herself, having already removed the rubber stopper on a syringe loaded with a sedative. The young slave girl opened the door, and this time her glare said everyone in the harem had been warned about Shiraz.

'Here, this is for you.' Shiraz handed her a packet of flaky sugary soan papdi, Hyderabad's speciality. 'Is Begum Maryam alone?'

Delight mingled with surprise on the girl's face as she gave a quick nod. She hugged the packet to her stomach as if nobody had ever given her a present.

Shiraz pressed the girl's arm and quickened her step to Maryam's room.

A dark room with drawn curtains greeted her. Maryam lay in bed, head against a paisley bolster, a slender arm flung over her eyes. It angered Shiraz to see her clad in the white of mourning – for Zulfikar but not for Niloufer.

She marched up to the bed. 'Maryam, does your husband have a key to the park?'

The lady sat up quickly. 'What are you doing here, Doctor? If my husband comes in… Have you found my Mohsin?' She eyed her with nervous hope.

Shiraz repeated the question.

'Which park?'

'Baig bagh.'

'I don't think so. Why do you want to know?'

'Where is your father-in-law's key?'

Maryam frowned. 'I don't know. Why are you asking these questions?'

'Your husband must have it now. Does it have a ribbon tied to it?'

Maryam stiffened. 'I don't know. Wh——?'

'Did you trust your son's nursemaid?' Shiraz interrupted.

'Devi? Of course. She adores him. Is she involved? Did you find out something? Are you thinking she helped his kidnappers?' Maryam seized her hands so tightly that it hurt.

'I don't——' Someone collared her throat from the back.

'Ali sahib, don't!' Maryam screamed.

'I told you not to interfere.' Ali's hard tone matched the press of his fingers.

Shiraz clawed his wrists but her clipped nails found no purchase on his skin.

Dark motes danced in front of her eyes, blood rapidly ebbing from her head. She couldn't breathe. Wiry strong fingers. Maryam's mouth contorted, but Shiraz couldn't hear the scream.

'Don't strain against your attacker.' Soob's calm voice spoke in her head. 'Remember what I taught you. Lean into the movement. It will catch him off guard.'

She did, and Ali's grip relaxed, as if in surprise. She twisted away, head to the side. He pushed her into the mattress, choking her in a sea of white. Her hand flailed and slapped a cylinder. The syringe. Her fingers curled around the glass, thumb somehow on the plunger, and she swung it in. He yelled. She'd jabbed the needle into his arm. His hold loosened. A heavy weight slumped on her, pressing her into the mattress.

'You killed my Ali,' Maryam screamed and shoved her to the floor, freeing her.

'No... not dead,' Shiraz croaked, gulping air into her lungs as Maryam pounced. 'Sss... sedative.'

Maryam jumped up and swooped on Ali, pressing her ear to his heart.

While she stroked her husband's cheek and forehead, Shiraz struggled to her feet, then pitched forward onto her valise, falling again on her knees. She took its support to rise and, pulling the handle, dragged it along the floor as she lurched out of the room.

Chapter Thirty-nine

The ferocious mid-afternoon sun seemed not to bother the patients and their relatives milling about outside Afzulgunj Hospital. Soob thrust Shiraz's note, which had been delivered to him earlier, into his saddlebag. He'd galloped here to tick her off, but she was out on a call. What galled him more was that she had discovered vital evidence: the love letter, the quarrel, the wrong key, and possibly a kidnapped child and a missing nursemaid.

'Make way, make way.' A footman dashed in front of an entourage, escorting a nobleman on a camel, the umbrella above his park bench doing little to stop the sweat rolling down his rotund face.

Soob let the cavalcade pass, their spurs clinking, matchlocks thumping, careless about hitting a pedestrian's limb or foot as they thundered towards the river. In the mood he was in, he'd arrest the lot if they hurt a single pedestrian, nawab be damned. He followed them to the river where they parted ways, the cavalcade thundering on towards the High Court.

At the Residency gate, the British sentries waved him through after cursorily inspecting his identity paper.

The hurly-burly of the city gave way to deserted lanes and an occasional caw and chirrup. A trio of purple moorhens bustled about in the water hyacinth at the Baig lake's rim, looking to feed on small fish, algae and tadpoles. The usual clutch of gawkers huddled at the park gate in the burning sun, mouths open, drinking in the guard's embellished telling of the murders.

At Templeton's mansion, the butler led him down the side garden to a grove of mango trees. Squeals drew his eye to a banyan tree beyond, and a smiling Edith pushing a young boy on a swing.

They reached a grove by the side of the house. There, in bamboo chairs encircled by terracotta pots of marigold, larkspur, mignonette and corncockle, with cups in hand, sat Arthur Templeton and a man with dark brown hair and regular features. A silver coffee urn gleamed from a glass-topped table. It struck Soob forcibly that silver could have such different meanings. For lower-class Englishmen like Templeton, silver was a symbol of their ascendance to a higher class. For Parsis like Shiraz, silver was a metal that infused purity in water and was therefore good for health. And for his own caste, silver's purity meant that it would not transmit the impurity of a non-Brahmin's touch.

Templeton bent and knocked the ashes of his pipe among the marigolds. Soob had seen before this disdain for nature in men in a hurry to get ahead in life.

On seeing him, Templeton scowled and remained sprawled in his seat in silence. After a quick glance, the other Englishman stood up and introduced himself as Eardley Norton, a barrister from Madras. Soob had heard talk of the lawyer in the corridors of the ICID, of his shark-like ability to make mincemeat out of witnesses in the courtroom. They shook hands; Templeton glowered.

'Where is Mrs Templeton?' Soob asked.

'We've already answered your questions, Chief Inspector,' Templeton snapped. 'No need to pester my wife again.'

'Some more information has come to light, and I want to confirm it,' Soob said, eyeing the green swathe of potted palms coiling around the bungalow. He was in luck. Phoebe Templeton stepped out from the back of the house, mud clinging to the pale border of her gown and gardening gloves, wisps of hair wet on her forehead.

She came over. 'Is it about the love letter Niloufer wrote to Arthur? Dr Shiraz must've told you.'

Templeton jumped up. 'Phoebe, stop it. You know it's a lie. I didn't even see the bloody letter, and I certainly didn't do anything to encourage Mrs Baig.' A vein throbbed in his forehead; his face had turned the colour of a blister.

Soob's eye flickered to the lawyer, who was now gazing raptly at a pot of larkspur.

'Be quiet, Arthur.' She brushed a strand from her eyes wearily, her gardening glove leaving a muddy streak on her forehead. 'You've done enough damage already. Chief Inspector, how can I help you find Niloufer's murderer?'

The glove's chocolate-coloured leather made him put out his hand. 'May I see those gloves, madam?'

She drew a sharp breath and stepped back.

'Certainly not,' the lawyer said firmly. 'Best if you say nothing, Phoebe.'

'Here.' She ripped them off and thrust them in his hands.

As he examined them, she furiously proclaimed, 'I did not kill Niloufer. My religion forbids the taking of a life.'

It was a lighter shade than the fragments under Niloufer's nails. He gave them back and asked about the love letter. 'What did Mrs Baig say?'

It was a forgery, Shiraz had written, but he had to check for himself. Dratted Shiraz. If only he could have seen it before coming here.

'She said she had not written it,' Phoebe replied. 'But why would anyone forge such a letter?'

He could think of several possibilities.

'This is ridiculous, Phoebe,' Templeton burst out. 'I had nothing to do with Mrs Baig, and I've no idea how it came to be with my papers.'

The lawyer shot a glance at Templeton; he didn't believe him. Neither did his wife, Soob thought, watching disgust flare in her eyes.

'I would've settled a good sum on you regardless of our agreement, Arthur. You didn't have to do this to me or our children.' She turned on her heel and marched away, her gown swishing and snapping at the terracotta pots.

Soob followed her to a damask rose flower bed in a far corner of the back garden. She bent by a straw hat and picked up a pair of secateurs.

'Mrs Templeton, what did the letter say?'

She eased aside a thin green branch and deftly snipped the cris-scrossing stems to create more air for the rose bush.

'Dearest Arthur.' She spat out the rest of the words in the letter as if they had scoured her memory. Then snipped a healthy branch that did not need to be cut.

'Did it sound like Niloufer?' The letter's melodramatic tone didn't match his impression of a forthright and no-nonsense woman.

'That's what she asked when I confronted her. How could you think I'd write such tripe, she said. But why would anyone forge such a letter? I thought we were friends, and I don't make friends easily. But with her,

I felt like I'd known her for years. How could she do this to me?' Her lips wobbled, and she continued removing healthy branches.

'Don't kill the rose bush, Mrs Templeton,' he said.

She dropped the secateurs and fumbled for a handkerchief in her sleeve.

As she composed herself, he mulled over Niloufer's personality. She had come across as an adventurous and stubborn daughter, a sparkling and affectionate friend, and a mischievous and lovable cousin. In his experience, one usually repeated a pattern in the choices one made. In her friendships, she had been drawn to rebels like Shiraz and Phoebe, and in her intimate life she would have been attracted to the same type of man. From all accounts, though, Nawab Zulfikar and Arthur Templeton were dissimilar.

He wanted to understand how Phoebe saw Niloufer. 'What did you and Mrs Baig talk about?'

'Plants, our families, my faith. I told her about our way of living. We believe in creation and life, not taking a life. We believe in fidelity and loyalty. We trust our fellow beings to behave with us as we would behave with them. We tell the truth.'

'Always?'

'Yes.' She looked him in the eye.

But he wondered: this woman who pretended to faint when things got tough.

'What happens when someone abuses your trust?'

Kneeling on the grass to gather the cut pieces, she twisted and shaded her eyes from the bright sun.

'You think I killed Niloufer because she was disloyal to our friendship, Chief Inspector? You are wrong. She was very dear to me. But now it's too late.' She bent and picked up the thorny stems, the leather stretching over her knuckles.

'What does your religion say about punishing those who betray you?'

'We believe the punishment must fit the crime.'

'The Old Testament's eye for an eye, or in the biblical manner of turning the other cheek?' Or the Hindu way – they expected fate and karma to dole out the punishment either in this life or in the next. His view was that one paid the price in this life, there were no past or future lives.

212

The heated air shimmered in the silence, her fingers fidgeting with the sharp curve of the secateurs, dislodging flecks of leather. She did not answer.

'And your husband, is he a member of your religion?'

The question snapped her out of her reverie.

'Of course not. We aren't Mormons. Whoever joins us does so by choice, when they experience an awakening. Arthur has not.' And he never would, her tone said.

He'd pegged Templeton as the sort to want his ego stroked, and a wife to dance to his tune. He couldn't see this lady doing any of that. In fact, her earlier outburst indicated she held the whip hand in the relationship.

'You, I suppose, experienced one?'

'Yes, but I cannot speak of it,' she said coldly. 'Excuse me, Chief Inspector, I have to see to tea. I'm afraid I can't escort you out. Please follow the side of the house and you will come to the front.'

Soob retraced his steps past the grove; the two Englishmen had gone indoors. It made little sense for Templeton to embark on an affair with his wife's friend and risk losing his family and fortune. And if the letter turned out to be a forgery, it wasn't clear who'd want Templeton to lose everything. Mrs Whittaker might be able to clarify the terms of the marriage contract, he thought, searching for her among the trees. The swing was empty.

At the front of the house, her voice hailed him.

Edith Whittaker hurried out of the front door. 'Chief Inspector, can you come to the racecourse later this afternoon? I need to tell you something but I can't talk here.'

Chapter Forty

A message from the deputy commissioner was waiting for Soob in the office. He rode over to the nobleman's palace. They had a saying in Tamil for this type of sun – scissor-sharp – but the sharpness paled when compared to Mir Akbar's cutting words on seeing him. Even the obligatory fifteen minutes of pleasantries had been dispensed with.

Mir Akbar paced about in his sitting room. 'What pains me is how incompetent you have been, Chief Inspector Soobramania. You have the evidence against Mr Templeton's begum. Her brooch was found near the murdered woman, so why haven't you arrested her? That inspector is their friend, so of course he cannot dishonour his friendship. You, on the other hand, have no connection with them.' And so he carried on.

Soob waited till he ran out of steam. 'Sir, firstly, I don't have juris-diction in the Residency. Secondly, it is better to have a watertight case against the lady, she is a wealthy heiress and has the expertise of a fine lawyer whom you have no doubt met. It is Mr Norton from Madras.'

'Oh!' Mir Akbar's countenance paled.

He'd been subjected to the lawyer's cross-examination in a bribery case before the Madras High Court, and as Soob knew from sensation-alised reports in the dailies, the nobleman had not escaped unscathed.

Then the toothy smile made a reappearance, much to Soob's misgiv-ings. 'I will send a note immediately to the British Resident demanding why they have not arrested the culprit.'

A relieved Soob left him to the happy task of composing a stroppy note, which would be couched in the politest terms and contain the sharpest of rebukes, something Mir Akbar excelled at.

Back he rode again to the Charminar Police Station, sweat rolling down his temples. There he instructed the duty constable to send Sub-Inspector Kamran to Irani's hotel.

Soob would rather have sat on the cool stone verandah of his new home and eaten dosas prepared by his grandmother, but the thought of another argument with his grandfather had stopped him.

He rode down the avenue to Mahbub Chowk, a square with a clock tower and a flower garden fenced in by low iron railings.

There, he reined in his horse by a newspaper vendor next door to Irani's, his eye caught by the headlines in a special afternoon edition of the *Deccan Gazette*. He handed over a coin and took the paper. True to his word, the editor had splashed news of the imminent arrest of a prominent Residency inhabitant. Short of mentioning Templeton's name, every other detail about the couple was splayed on the single page of the news sheet.

Irani hurried out from the hotel. 'Chief Inspector, welcome to my humble establishment.' He bowed, his nose almost touching the stone floor, and ushered Soob in.

A Persian whose forefathers had come to the Deccan a century ago, Irani had made a name for himself in a city renowned for its biryanis and kebabs. Irani's was the place to go for a biryani and a kebab at their most sublime.

As usual, the long room was packed with soldiers, shop assistants and footmen, all squatting cheek by jowl on floor mattresses, the air redolent with fumes of frying garlic and onions.

For his European clientele – mainly adventurers and cheats who'd fled from the British police to shelter under the Nizam's protection – Irani had set aside two tables by a window overlooking the square. That's where he escorted Soob.

Soob recognised the burly German at the next table tucking into a biryani: an adventurer who'd fleeced a dozen princes in central and north India with a mythical goldfield in the Congo. The Nizam liked to offer these men refuge simply to annoy the British.

The crook gave a quick nod and continued eating, his spoon moving faster now between plate and mouth.

Though Soob didn't begrudge the ruler these little rebellions, he could do without having to hobnob with cheats and forgers. He gazed out of the window at the clock tower, its dark granite reminding him of the bits under Niloufer's nails. The laboratory had confirmed they were leather. His surmise had been right: the murderer had worn gloves for protection against being scratched. As he waited for lunch, two contradictory motives jockeyed for his attention.

The vegetarian biryani arrived with dal, mirchi ka salan and raita, and its fragrant aroma made his mouth water. He set aside his concerns and gave his full attention to lunch. He scooped a spoonful of rice, added a dollop of raita to douse the fiery chilli, and began eating.

Halfway through the delicious repast, Sub-Inspector Kamran walked up and saluted. He was in an Arab costume and ribbons poked out of the canvas bag slung on his shoulder.

Soob gestured to the other chair. 'Have you eaten?'

Kamran shook his head. 'I managed to speak to Mary, an ayah at the Templetons', he said in Deccani as the German pushed back his chair and got up. 'She thinks I'm a button seller.'

'Good.' Soob signalled the proprietor who was pocketing a coin from the German.

Irani bustled up and Kamran ordered a mutton biryani with the same side dishes.

'Mary has been with the Templetons for about a year,' Kamran reported. 'The servants all detest Mrs Whittaker. That woman calls herself a madam, but she is just like us, Mary said. It seems that ten days into her employment, Mrs Templeton asked the butler to lay one more cover at dinner. The servants were all miffed about it.'

Fatima's brother had made a similar remark about Edith Whittaker, 'that white woman who wants to be the memsahib'.

'Anything going on between Templeton and Edith Whittaker?' Nothing in their demeanour had indicated an affair.

'She thinks there is. Otherwise, why should a servant eat with the employers?'

'What did she say about the Templetons?'

'Mrs Templeton is a very good memsahib, keeps an eye on everything, doesn't scold them for no reason. You know how servants are. They despise employers who are too lenient. But they also dislike those unjust to them. Mr Templeton is like that, he accuses them of stealing if he misplaces things, and never takes the blame even after finding it. She went on about some vase he broke and blamed Mary. And today, he was in the pantry fiddling with an empty teacup, looking for cracks in it to blame her.'

The attendant brought a terracotta matka sealed with dough. Kamran opened it with a knife and inhaled the fragrance of the biryani with eyes closed.

'What are the relations between husband and wife?'

'Mrs Templeton has stopped speaking to her husband,' Kamran said, tucking in. 'The servants say he is afraid of her.'

'How can they tell?'

'He jumps when they enter the room.'

'Is it recent?'

'Since the day of the dinner party, sir. They quarrelled bitterly just before the party. Mrs Baig's name was mentioned several times.'

'You've done well, Sub-Inspector Kamran.' He told Kamran to order dessert. Unlike him, the sub-inspector had a very sweet tooth and never failed to coddle it.

Chapter Forty-one

Two women helped a petite middle-aged woman into Shiraz's clinic, bleeding from her nose, her arm at an unnatural angle. The collarbone looked broken.

'Her husband, a drunk, accused her of sleeping with her cousin,' the woman's older sister said. 'He keeps her locked up. Where would she meet our cousin?'

Shiraz grimly set the bone and stitched the wounds while the poor woman stoically bore the pain. Chloroform would have helped in rendering her instantly unconscious. She decided to see Dr Lawrie for some vials. The Chloroform Commission, in town to evaluate his claim that it was safe to use the drug in proper doses, had signed off on it today.

By two in the afternoon, her head throbbed, and the thought of dealing with the reports and files on her desk was more than she could bear. She trudged across to Dr Currimbhoy's office to ask about the Fire Priest's response.

He looked up from a chart, the ash dropping off his cigarette. 'Nawab Zulfikar Baig is dead. He died yesterday evening.'

She didn't feel anything. To her it seemed like he had been dead since Niloufer's murder. Soob hadn't bothered to tell her this morning, and it upset her. At least, Zulfikar didn't have to live without his beloved Niloufer, she thought, recalling from the wedding celebrations his adoring gaze at Niloufer, and the look of wonder as if he'd been bestowed with an unexpected and precious gift.

'Was he murdered?'

Dr Currimbhoy grimaced. 'We won't ever know. The sons won't allow a post-mortem. Against their religion, they say. He will be buried today in the family grave.' He jabbed the cigarette in an ashtray brimming with stubs.

Parricide would be child's play to a man who had attacked her twice, and who was suspected to have killed three women. It sickened her that they couldn't prove it, not without an exhumation. She could do little about Zulfikar's death, but she would fight for Niloufer's right to be buried as a Parsi.

'Have you spoken to the Fire Priest, Dr Currimbhoy?'

At his pursed lips, her heart sank.

'I am sorry. He said as soon as a conversion occurs, the woman is no longer a Parsi. Niloufer married the nawab and was living with him, so she is—'

'No, no, she stayed in another house given by him.' A wild idea struck her. 'What if we pretend she never married him? Her husband is dead, so he won't mind. Neither will his sons, who would be more than pleased to wipe out Niloufer's name from their family history.'

'But—'

'Please, Dr Currimbhoy. Can you at least ask the priest if that would work? Please.'

'Doctor Currimbhoy, please come quickly,' an attendant exclaimed breathlessly from the doorway.

He jumped up and grabbed his medical valise, and without answering her, hurried out. She remained sitting, gripped by hope that her solution would work with the High Priest. A conjecture clamoured for her attention. Niloufer's murder and Nawab Zulfikar's poisoning, if proven, raised the question: was the timing of their murders connected to the Baig fortune?

–

The butler bustled into the sitting room. 'A lady is here, hakimji.'

With a sigh, Shiraz set her teacup on the coffee table, wishing she hadn't come home to change before going over to Niloufer's. She was in no mood for social chit-chat with one of her mother-in-law's friends, all agog for the gory details.

To her relief, it was Lady Ariel Falloner, looking cool in an elegant dove grey cambric gown, a string of pearls circling her slender neck. Next to her, Shiraz felt like a frump in her sweat-dampened hospital clothes, hair in untidy wisps.

She got up and held out her hands. 'Ariel, how lovely to see you.'

The butler drew a sharp breath at her familiarity, but he wasn't to know that danger had a way of bringing people closer. She and Ariel had met through Soob earlier this month and had found common ground in the fact that both had been widowed young. They were alike in another way: they would do whatever they could for a cause they believed in.

Ariel clasped her hands. 'I am so sorry to hear of your cousin's murder, Shiraz. Do accept my deepest condolences for your loss.'

Shiraz thanked her, lips trembling as she tried not to burst into tears at the genuine sympathy.

'Do you want to talk about it?'

Looking into Ariel's calm grey eyes, Shiraz found the words tumbling out: the gruesome mutilations, Ali's attack, the missing child, the encounters with Phoebe, the timing of Niloufer's death. 'I don't know if Phoebe killed Niloufer, or if Ali did. Or his friends...'

The butler entered with a maid, each carrying a tray with sherbet, tea, iced water, shortbread biscuits and slices of seed cake.

'My cousin Alexei is not a murderer,' Ariel said after they left the room. 'I have known him since my childhood. But I'm not too keen on Henry. There is something repulsive about him. But it doesn't make him a murderer. Soob, though, thinks like you. And now they are angry with me.' Her lips tightened.

'What happened?' Shiraz asked, her spirits rising at Ariel's explanation. Soob had not hesitated to tackle such powerful men.

'Soob, I suppose, is being a good policeman and following all the trails,' Ariel said. 'My cousin was furious with me. I had to apologise profusely.'

'So where were they that night?'

'They refused to tell him, of course, but it isn't what Soob suspects. I expect they were doing something connected to that tiresome club of theirs. The Hellfire Club. Why are grown men such schoolboys!' She sipped her tea.

Shiraz, however, knew from Soob that the Hellfire was hardly an innocent schoolboy club.

'You also think my cousin is involved.' Ariel correctly read her thought. She tapped a long pink-tipped finger on the gilded armrest, then began pulling on her tan gloves. 'I'm having tea with them and the Commander-in-Chief Sikandar Khan of the Nizam's army. Come with me, and you can ask them yourself.'

The white Corinthian columns and pink stucco facade of Nawab Sikandar Khan's palace glistened in the late afternoon sun. Shiraz eyed the guests – courtiers all, clad in silks and brocades, jewels encrusting their turbans and fezzes. Hovering at the edge of the sloping lawn, they examined her and the others seated in chairs – Ariel, Grand Duke Alexei, the Earl of Euston, the interpreter, the host and his horse – with expressions ranging from superciliousness to downright envy.

Below stretched the city wall and, beyond, the riverbank's green-and-brown patchwork of shrubbery and bare earth. In the distance, the marble dome of the Resident's palace shimmered in the heated air, framed by the coconut palm groves. Two punkahwallas fanned them, dipping the large palm leaves in pails of iced water.

'Why aren't the others speaking to us?' Ariel murmured in her ear.

'It is a sign of respect,' Shiraz said. 'Important guests are sequestered and displayed like paintings.'

'Or animals in a zoo.'

Their host, who cut a splendid figure in his uniform copiously laced with gold and sporting two rows of medals on his chest, poured more oolong tea from a silver teapot into a Sèvres china saucer. Commander-in-Chief Sikandar Khan was reputed to be a trifle eccentric, something she could well believe, seeing the horse sipping the tea from the saucer as delicately as a debutante.

Ariel exchanged an amused glance with Shiraz and her cousin.

A page knelt ceremoniously in front of Ariel and held out a silver salver with a scroll. Ariel picked it up. 'It is in Persian.' She gave it to Shiraz. 'Can you read it?'

'It is from the ladies of the house,' she said, perusing it. 'They personally supervised the cooking of the delicacies served to us, and have invited us to the zenana after tea.'

'Wonderful,' said Ariel. 'Please tell Nawab Sikandar that we shall be honoured to visit his wife.'

'Wives,' Shiraz murmured.

The interpreter, a young man in his early twenties who had graduated with honours in English from Nizam College, bowed and translated Ariel's words.

The host beamed and spoke again.

'The esteemed nawab,' the interpreter said, 'wishes to enquire as to the relationships Your Grace and the esteemed Earl of Euston and Lady Falloner bear to Her Imperial Highness, the Queen of England.'

Halfway through the Grand Duke's reply, the interpreter stood up and bowed hurriedly. 'I have to make toilet, Your Excellency,' he said and fled.

Shiraz wondered if she ought to step into the breach but decided not to. These noblemen had queer ideas about speaking to a woman, especially a native.

'The chap must have the runnies.' The Earl frowned at the interpreter's rapidly disappearing back.

The host poured more tea on the saucer with an expressionless face and held it out to the horse, who slurped it down politely.

'We've been outranked by the horse,' murmured Grand Duke Alexei. 'I hope he doesn't expect us to bow and converse with the animal.'

The Earl, who gave Shiraz the chills with his reptilian gaze and clammy hands, looked put out.

'Hush, he might hear us,' said Ariel.

'He doesn't speak English.'

Shiraz was not so sure, noting the flash of amusement in Sikandar Khan's eye. Many nobles pretended not to understand the language in order to eavesdrop on their British counterparts.

Ariel smiled apologetically at their host.

Nawab Sikandar Khan bowed and spoke to Shiraz. Speaking Farsi, not Deccani, as was the custom among the high nobles of the Deccan, he told her he would return after seeing his horse to the stables. 'Madam Daruwalla, would you be kind enough to translate for me?'

Shiraz nodded and told the others as the nobleman strode away, the horse taking mincing steps by his side.

'By the way, you two forgot to curtsey to the horse when it got up,' remarked the Grand Duke, stretching his booted feet on the grass.

'Well, I didn't see you two bow,' Ariel retorted.

The Grand Duke turned to Shiraz. 'My dear Dr Daruwalla, please allow me to offer my condolences.'

'Thank you, Your Excellency.'

'Alexei dear, do put us out of our misery,' Ariel said. 'Tell us where you two were with Nawab Ali Baig.'

'Why all these questions, my dear? Is it for your policeman?'

Shiraz latched on to an angry undercurrent in the Grand Duke's tone. It suggested a new complication: was he Ariel's suitor? They had never discussed their hopes for the future, and she could not say if Ariel, like herself, had no intention of ever marrying again.

'Alexei, be serious for once. It is important. Did you perform one of your club rituals?'

Her firm tone sobered him, and he leaned forward in the chair. 'I don't want you to think badly of me, my dear. I know the club has a bad reputation, but believe me, it was in the past. We don't countenance such behaviour. There were no women involved at the ceremony in Ali's garden.' He clasped Ariel's hands and looked into her eyes with an undeniable sincerity. 'I give you my word of honour.'

Chapter Forty-two

The top two tiers of the Malakpet Racecourse brimmed with nawabs, dark faces, rich turbans, rubies, sapphires and emeralds sparkling like fireflies. In the lower rows, pink and white faces bobbed under straw boaters and flowery parasols. Of course, nobody who was anybody was going to miss the Exhibition Race run by ostriches, Soob thought, noting the high nobility lounging in the upper tiers on either side of the Nizam's box. The ruler's box was clothed in yellow and silver damask. There, the fifteen-year-old heir perched on a golden throne, solemnly listening to an interpreter translate the Grand Duke's remarks.

There was no sign of the Nizam, such an avid racegoer that he had moved the racecourse here, within an easy ride of his city palace. Soob could well imagine the huddles and secret councils of courtiers required to craft this carefully considered snub to the Grand Duke and the Earl of Euston, a prelude to the arrest they expected Soob to orchestrate. A forlorn hope, though. They had rock-solid alibis for the murders of the river victim and Fatima.

He found Edith Whittaker in the second row of the marquee-shaded stand, scribbling in a notebook, while next to her, Arthur Templeton held forth, jabbing a finger at the ostriches lining up at the starting gate. Her sallow complexion, mud-coloured gown and simple hairstyle stood out among the muslins and chiffons and hats adorned with ornate folds of silk. She reminded him of a diligent sparrow among a bevy of swans.

'The first race will start soon,' the town crier announced. 'Please take your seats.'

The punters scrambled to the ropes, and seeing Templeton rise to his feet and dash down to the track, Soob cut through the crowd to Edith's row.

Her face lit up on seeing him, and she patted the empty chair.

'Thank you for coming, Chief Inspector,' Edith said. As the pitch of conversation increased, excitement mounting at the upcoming race, she leaned closer, bringing a whiff of lavender.

'I couldn't speak to you in the house, not with Phoebe around. You see, last night, she passed my window carrying a forked stick. I think she came from the side door, the one opposite the park.'

'What time was it?'

'Around eleven. The clock's chimes sounded then.'

If she was telling the truth, it put Phoebe in the garden when Fatima was killed, sometime between ten forty-five and eleven fifteen.

'Wasn't it raining?'

'Yes, but I could see her clearly. She came close to my window to shelter under the eaves.'

A drumbeat rolled.

'Chief Inspector, do you mind? I need to watch the race. I help Arth— Mr Templeton write the stories. I act as his secretary because I can type and write shorthand,' she added, following his gaze at the notebook.

So much effort, and yet, Soob thought, this woman would never be treated as an equal by the Templetons. She lacked what society prized: wealth and pedigree, which, in his book, were not a patch on hard work and striving. It must gall her that Phoebe and Niloufer had it all despite doing nothing to merit it.

The starting gun went off. She leaned forward in her seat, eyes wide and excited. A cheer went up in the crowd as the ostriches shot forward like racehorses. Each man put his legs under the wings and locked his feet below the breast. The birds thundered out at a tremendous pace, kicking like horses.

'The sharp right-handed course tests the best jockeys,' she said.

He wouldn't have marked her out as a gambler, but the gleam in her eye and the clenched fists told a different tale.

The crowd roared as two ostriches ran neck and neck on the home stretch. The leading ostrich with a white halter was the Nizam's brother-in-law's bird. Shadowing it was the ruler's yellow-and-silver haltered one. At the last moment, the rider of the Nizam's ostrich leaned forward and struck the spindly hind legs, spurring its lunge past the chalk line.

'The ostrich of His Exalted Highness, the Nizam of the Deccan Dominions wins by a beak,' the announcer cried.

The band struck up a tune as the punters, Templeton included, hurried to the betting window to collect their winnings. Was the outcome really such a surprise, the cynic in him wondered.

'Arthur will be back soon, Chief Inspector. He won't like what I'm about to tell you. Shall we take a round on the grass before the next race?'

She glanced at her neighbours, some leaning in sideways or forward, blatantly eavesdropping.

They descended the wooden steps to the mown grass by the pavilion, but the gossips dogged their footsteps. He led her further on the green, his forbidding frown finally staying the pursuit.

'Phoebe frightens me, Chief Inspector,' she said, turning to him. 'Ever since I found Mrs Baig's letter, she has been acting strangely. I've caught her glaring at me when she thinks I'm not looking. She lied about losing the brooch. I saw it in her jewel box yesterday when she sent me to fetch her bracelet.'

'Have you told Mr Templeton about your fears?'

'Yes.'

'What did he say?'

'He is afraid of her.' She hesitated.

'I know about her marriage contract,' he said, espying Arthur Templeton from the corner of his eye.

'Oh, then you know he can't divorce her because he would lose everything. I found the agreement in Arthur's papers and read it before I realised what it was.' She looked him in the eye.

'What does it say?'

'Edith,' Arthur called out.

She turned her back on him. 'If Arthur commits adultery, Phoebe gets a divorce, the children and all his money. If she strays, Arthur gets it all. Her father settled a fortune on her after the wedding. Don't be taken in by her religious fervour, Chief Inspector. She is a cunning woman.'

'Edith.' Templeton stomped up. 'Why are you talking to that fellow? Come away right now.'

At the entrance archway in the dust swirling from the landaus and broughams trundling in to collect their passengers, he glimpsed the two

Baigs enter a well-appointed carriage. He must have missed seeing their box.

Taking his bay's reins from the groom, his thoughts turned to the Templetons. The forked stick was a specific detail. It could have been part of a sling used to throw the brooch into the park from the garden. But why would Phoebe incriminate herself?

Or Edith could be lying. As he mounted his horse, set his feet in the stirrups, and flicked the reins, the question weighed on him. Fatima's brother's words pointed to Edith's desire to supplant Phoebe Templeton. If he was right, with her rival out of the way, Edith could become the new Mrs Templeton.

Chapter Forty-three

'Sir, an old Brahmin is here to see you.' Kamran stepped aside and Soob's grandfather hurried into the office.

'Natraja has run away, Subbu. Come quickly.'

Soob shot up and rushed around his desk, putting his hand on his grandfather's trembling forearm to usher him to the chair. 'When? What happened, Tatha?'

'Half an hour ago.' His grandfather's legs gave way, and he collapsed into the chair. 'I received a letter from Tathachari Iyengar this evening asking when he could come and see me. He mentioned the expiation rite planned by the Deccan Brahmin Association. Natraja overheard me tell your grandmother about your decision not to perform the ceremony. He ran out of the gate. By the time I got there, he had disappeared.' Panic, guilt and an accusation lodged in his grandfather's gaze. 'I hailed a passing cab and got here quickly.'

Soob forced himself to meet his grandfather's look, a sick feeling cramping his stomach. What must the poor child be thinking: that he would be an outcaste, shunned by his friends, alone and miserable?

'Subbu, hurry. It is getting dark. What if he had an accident? All these carriages and horsemen going so fast.'

'Tatha, I'll find him, don't worry. You go home and wait. What was he wearing?' He ushered his grandfather downstairs as the description poured out. After seeing him off in the police carriage, he turned to HC Muhammad and Sub-Inspector Kamran, standing by for his command.

'Organise five teams, four constables each. They should look for a nine-year-old Brahmin boy with a hair tuft, wheatish brown complexion, in a white lungi like what my grandfather wore. He has been missing for half an hour. Search near Purana Pul Bridge and the city side riverbank.'

'What if he is in the Residency, sir?' Sub-Inspector Kamran said. 'The HC and I can go across with our permits.'

'All right, but first see to the search parties on our side. I'll ride across and begin from the Purana Pul section. You two start from the Chaderghat-Oliphant Bridge end. I suspect he is hiding close to the house.'

A constable hurried up with Soob's bay and he swung up into the saddle. Daylight was fading rapidly as he galloped to Purana Pul Bridge.

The lamplighters were lighting the bridge lamps amid a steady stream of carriages and men crossing over. He reined in his horse and scrutinised the shrunken riverbank. Thanks to last night's rain, the river had risen, lapping at the three-quarter level of the timber piles. Twilight's smoky grey lurked over the undergrowth below. Hard to make out if anyone was there, but he doubted it. Natraja had promised not to walk there alone.

'Salaam, huzoor.' Ambling towards him was the previous evening's fisherman.

'Have you seen my nephew?'

'The boy you were with? Yes, he spoke to me, but I couldn't understand him.'

'When?'

'A little while ago, just after the sun set.'

'Did you see where he went?'

The boy pointed with his thumb behind his shoulder.

Soob expelled a breath he hadn't realised he was holding. Natraja had retraced his steps home.

Horse at a trot, he searched the dirt side path alongside the Musi River road. To his left were the large bungalows of his neighbours, officials like him. He stopped at the first house, belonging to a British official in the Nizam's treasury.

'Did you see a boy walk past in the last half hour?' he asked the guard standing to attention, his matchlock held in the crook of his arm.

'Yes, sir. He was on the river side. He kicked a stone and it came onto the road. I was about to warn him that a carriage was coming, but he turned his face away and began crying.'

Something caught in his throat. 'Where did he go?'

'He went that way.' The guard pointed towards Soob's home, halfway down the street.

Soob wanted to gallop there but forced himself to stop at the next bungalow. He had to do this systematically in case Natraja had slipped down the embankment or suffered some injury; every moment could count. He shouted Natraja's name at intervals and crossed over to the embankment side and back again at the next bungalow. The guard there had not seen Natraja; his mistress had called him in to issue instructions around that time. Two houses away though, the guard *had* seen Natraja shuffling along.

His neighbour's house was empty, and the guard on the other side said he had not seen Natraja. Now it was safe to assume his nephew had returned home. With relief came fury. How could Natraja put them through this? Especially his old grandparents.

The bird cries fell silent as the last flock turned in to roost. He dismounted and tethered his horse to an iron post inside the gate and lit the lantern hanging from his saddle.

'Natraja,' he shouted, ears straining for a human voice. All he could hear was the whirr of wings, the rustle of leaves and the muffled gush of the river.

Soob stilled. The guard's mention of a carriage raised a terrible possibility connected with the new line of enquiry triggered by the morning conversation with Natraja. Could the murderer have seized his nephew because they were worried by him speaking to Edith Whittaker at the races?

Chapter Forty-four

Wilberforce rode alongside the river, passing the large bungalows of the British and Parsis working for the Nizam or the Resident. Nice if he could live in one of these mansions, but the money he saved by renting a smallish bungalow helped pay for his sons' boarding school. Dusk was when he liked to be out: its greyness made him feel like he was back home. As long as he didn't see anyone or hear the local chatter, he could pretend he was riding alongside the Ouse.

Thunder thrummed in the sky, and he scented a sure rain on the river breeze. About time. Bring some relief from the sticky humidity.

A carriage flashed past, almost pushing his horse down the steep embankment, the gold rim of its wheels glinting before it disappeared into the dark. Cursing loudly, he reined in, the horse struggling to keep its balance on the crumbly mud. He had a good mind to pursue the carriage and give the coachman a piece of his mind, but the dark had swallowed it.

He continued past Chaderghat-Oliphant Bridge and on until, as he neared the Brahmin's house, someone cried out from the roadside.

'Inspector, huzoor,' the cry came again, and someone yanked at his stirrups.

Wilberforce stopped the horse.

It was a small boy with a mud-streaked face. The urchin witness to Niloufer Baig's murder.

The little chap jabbered a series of incomprehensible sounds and kept pointing in the direction Wilberforce had come. Finally, the words 'Nawab Baig' made sense to him. Of course, the gold wheel rim sparked in his memory. He'd seen it when he went to question the fellow on the night of his stepmother's murder.

'You saw Nawab Ali Baig? What about him?'

The boy jabbed his finger and babbled. The words 'Huzoor' and 'Brahmin' also made sense. Was the Brahmin chasing Ali Baig?

Wilberforce leaned down and lifted him up in front of him. A vile smell came from the grime on his bare shoulders, as if the urchin had rolled in refuse. He wheeled the horse around and galloped after the carriage.

'N… raja,' the boy kept saying urgently.

Something was up with the carriage. Had Ali struck again? That would be asking for too much, to catch him red-handed. The horse lengthened its stride, a thoroughbred chestnut with racing in its blood. Soon, the rattle of carriage wheels sounded ahead.

The scrub became denser and blacker on either side as the gaps between houses became longer. They were coming to the outer limits of the Residency. It was pitch black now, and Wilberforce wished he had the time to stop and light the lantern.

Ahead, a bulky shadow loomed. The carriage's pace increased as if Ali Baig knew he was being chased. Definitely up to no good. Might even nab him with another unfortunate soul, surefire evidence even the Nizam's lot couldn't dispute.

Something tumbled out of the carriage. Wilberforce whipped his horse, and it surged ahead. The urchin yelled and tugged his forearm, jabbing a finger at a bush they had just passed.

'Raja… Raja…' The boy was hysterical and swung his leg over the horse's back to jump off.

Wilberforce grasped him with one hand, but undeterred, the urchin bit him.

He yelped and his fingers tightened on the reins. The horse ploughed to a halt.

'You little bugger.' He thumped his free hand on the boy's shoulder, but the urchin bit him again and dived for the asphalt, crashing on his knees. Before Wilberforce could bend and collar him, he'd scurried to the bush.

Wilberforce hesitated at the sight of the boy crouching by a sack. His brain had caught up with his vision. What if it was another body?

He looked over his shoulder for the carriage, but it had disappeared into one of the side streets. Damn!

'…Raja.' The boy shook the sack and kept repeating the word.

The sack started moving.

Wilberforce swung off the horse. As the first raindrop hit his wrist, he lit his lantern, illuminating a small boy, the same age as the urchin.

Wearing a muddy skirt-like toga and a hair tuft Wilberforce had seen on Brahmins. The boy's eyes were closed, and he mumbled something.

The silver silk in his hand sent Wilberforce's blood racing. He recognised it. Ali Baig had worn it on the night of the first murders. Wilberforce tugged the cummerbund from the boy's fist. It was faintly damp, and on sniffing it, his head got woozy.

Now he knew which drug had incapacitated the victims, and the cummerbund gave him proof enough to arrest Ali Baig.

–

'How is he, Dr Currimbhoy?' Soob asked, crouching and stroking Natraja's hot forehead as he lay on the rush mat in the bedroom. A kerosene lamp hissed, its fumes leaving through the open window above into the verandah. From a corner, his grandparents quietly watched Dr Currimbhoy read the thermometer.

'Just a light fever. Nothing to worry about. The boy got off lucky. I don't think he inhaled too much chloroform. How long do you think he was in the carriage, Inspector Wilberforce?'

'Possibly five or six minutes,' said the Englishman looming in the doorway.

'I expect the child to regain consciousness soon, within the hour. Give him plenty of water. Food will hasten his recovery.'

'Is his heartbeat fine?' Soob asked, putting a hand on Natraja's chest to reassure himself that the beat was steady and even.

'Yes, Chief Inspector.' Dr Currimbhoy put his stethoscope into his valise and rose to his feet. 'He has been lucky. Despite being asphyxiated, the chloroform has not entered the heart through the trachea. He will be all right. Just keep him comfortable and let him sleep it off. Rest and simple food should pull the child through.'

His grandfather thanked the doctor, and explained the instructions to his grandmother while Soob ushered the two men to the verandah.

'Inspector Wilberforce, allow me to thank you properly for rescuing Natraja,' Soob said, holding out his hand. 'I will be forever in your debt.'

The Englishman shook his hand, red-faced and mumbling something under his breath, and lowered himself into the rush hammock. Soob looked for Ram Rahim, but couldn't see him on the lawn. Dr Currimbhoy silently occupied the other hammock, but in the verandah lamp's light hanging from the wooden beam above them, Soob noted the puzzled frown creasing his forehead.

Leaning against the pillar, Soob asked the question that had been bothering him about the speed with which the chloroform had taken effect.

'That's been worrying me too. My colleague Dr Lawrie has been experimenting with chloroform for the last seven years. He found it takes about three minutes and forty seconds to produce full unconsciousness.'

'Huzoor,' Ram Rahim called from the shadows of the garden.

Soob strode down the steps and pulled Ram Rahim into his arms. 'Thank you, Ram Rahim. I won't forget what you've done. Neither will Natraja.' He led him up to the verandah. 'Tell me what happened.'

'Huzoor, I was coming to report to you. I was walking from there,' he pointed at Chaderghat-Oliphant Bridge, 'and saw your nephew standing on the other side of the road. A carriage came past and stopped next to him. Then the carriage started again, and your nephew wasn't there. I thought he'd gone down the slope to the river, and I ran up to warn him that it was dangerous. He wasn't there. I immediately thought the killer must've taken him. So I started running after the carriage and saw the firangi inspector on his horse.'

'Then he must've administered the drug for less than a minute,' Wilberforce said after Soob translated the words. 'But your nephew has been unconscious for far too long. Does body weight matter to the speed of the reaction?'

'It seems so,' Dr Currimbhoy said with a slow nod of his head. 'My colleague's experiments showed that unconsciousness occurred in one minute seventeen seconds in children below the age of four. But your nephew is older. Unless...'

The doctor gazed into the darkness.

Soob went into the house and came out again after a few minutes. He put a hand on Ram Rahim's shoulder and led him to the gate. There he handed over a gold mohur and a fistful of coppers and told the boy to get himself dinner from Irani's.

If he'd asked his grandmother to feed the boy, she would have, though it would have been vegetarian fare. Soob was convinced they would set aside their caste dictates for someone who had rescued their beloved grandson. A thought occurred: *If they can do it, go against their convictions, why can't you?* He pushed the question away.

The boy's eyes widened at the gold mohur among the coppers. 'Huzoor...'

'Thank you, Ram Rahim. We will never forget what you have done for us. Come back here afterwards, and you'll have a place to sleep.' His grandparents wouldn't object.

As Soob walked back to the verandah, it struck him how birth could determine such different lives for a boy. There was Natraja, sure of his place in the world, now perhaps in danger of losing it through Soob's intransigence. And here was Ram Rahim, blithely making a place for himself with the little he had. He'd planted a foot in each religion by choosing the names of a Hindu God, Ram, and a Muslim prophet, Rahim. It wasn't that Natraja paled in comparison to Ram Rahim. Both were intelligent, kind, loving and enterprising. But Natraja had never faced the question of who he was, about his place in the world. Ram Rahim had, and had given a strident ringing answer.

'I think I know how the effect of chloroform was hastened,' Dr Currimbhoy said, coming to the edge of the verandah and peering through the dark at Soob. 'If I recall correctly, with dogs, my colleague found that stopping the airways produced quicker unconsciousness, in thirty seconds. And with the addition of phosphorous, the stoppage of the respiration and slowing of the heart occurred almost immediately on applying chloroform to the face. So, I think the abductor used phosphorous with the chloroform.'

'Who else would know these details?' Soob asked, rinsing his feet and drying them. 'And who would have access to chloroform and phosphorous?'

'Certainly the medical fraternity. It was reported in *The Lancet* several times in the past three years. And this week the newspapers had much to say on the subject because of the Royal Commission's presence here.'

'And access?' Inspector Wilberforce asked, hand on chin. He had been watching Soob's ablutions with amused interest.

'Both can be found in any of our medicine cabinets. I don't lock mine, and I would hazard a guess that neither do my colleagues. The locals tend to keep away. They think it is poison.'

'Are the Baigs and the Templetons your patients?' Wilberforce asked.

Putting aside his gratitude to the Englishman, Wilberforce's question was that of a seasoned, hard-working and dogged investigator. Soob's respect grew for the man's investigative prowess.

'The Baigs are, but the Templetons go to Dr Lawrie.'

An owl hooted nearby.

They had enough to arrest Ali Baig, Wilberforce's expression said as he rose to his feet, clutching the silvery silk.

Soob disagreed: they couldn't charge Ali with the murders or even slap a kidnapping charge on him since all they had was his cummerbund, which he could claim had been stolen from his closet. But he remained silent. Even an arrest, Soob thought, would be sufficient. Once Ali was in prison, the killings would indeed end.

Chapter Forty-five

The Brahmin's nephew, praise the Lord, had the presence of mind to grab the silver cummerbund they'd seen on Ali Baig on the night of the first two murders. That and Wilberforce's slightly embellished eyewitness account as well as the Musi River road guards who identified Ali's carriage sufficed for an arrest. The clincher came in the Metropolitan Police telegram on his desk. Ali Baig's name was indeed in the books of Henry Poole as the purchaser of the shell coloured cummerbund found on the gardener's wife and the scarlet one coiled around Mrs Baig's throat.

He galloped to Commissioner Hankin's residence for the arrest warrant and arranged with him to have the nob drawn out of his palace. Sir Trevor lured the man to the Residency for a drink. A bloodbath with the Baig army of ruffians would have been a sure thing had they shown up at the Baig palace with the warrant. Thank the Lord he'd taken these precautions, he thought, trotting over to cut off his quarry dressed in traditional costume studded with golden bits and bobs, whose contingent was mincing up to the cannons at the Residency gate.

His three dozen soldiers surrounded Ali's dozen. Even so, it could be a close thing, he thought, as steel rang, their swords and muskets grabbed by the ruffians now encircling their employer.

'Ali Baig, you are under arrest,' Wilberforce shouted. Damned if he'd give him a bloomin' title.

The Ripper had the gall to smirk. 'What's the charge?'

'For starters, the murders of your stepmother and the two innocent young servants living in your lane.' He'd been dissuaded from mentioning the killing spree in London.

'And your evidence?' the Ripper asked, looking down at him as if he were a cockroach.

'Don't you worry about that,' Wilberforce said through clenched teeth. 'An open and shut case, that's what it is. You killed your stepmother, Niloufer Baig, because you hated her. She stood in the way of you grabbing your father's full fortune. You thought it was clever, didn't you – murdering those poor girls, using the Ripper's method.' How Wilberforce longed to say 'You are Jack the Ripper'. He controlled the urge and carried on. 'You were in the vicinity for the three murders, Ali Baig. You had the means, motive and the opportunity.'

'Ah, but you are mistaken, sir,' the man had the gall to drawl. 'I was with my two friends Grand Duke Alexei and the Earl of Euston during that woman's murder, and I was receiving mourners at my palace when the gardener's wife was murdered.'

A cool customer, this one. The whiff of lemon wafted over as the man turned his horse. The same scent he had left behind with the murdered women.

'You do know, don't you, my dear Inspector,' he drawled over his shoulder, 'you cannot arrest me without permission from our esteemed ruler. I know all about your obsession with the Ripper. But I wonder whether it is simply a smokescreen. For all we know, you might be him.'

Fury flooded in. These long years of smarting at the insults, grieving for his dead partner, his exile to foreign lands where he and his family neither felt at home nor wanted to be, all of it surged up.

Before he knew it, a cry rolled up from deep within, and Wilberforce found himself surging ahead, his hands grabbing the nob's shoulders, pulling him off the horse, tumbling down himself, still holding on, barely feeling the metal bits cutting in, drawing blood.

All hell broke loose, but Wilberforce had eyes only for the man lying next to him, struggling to get up. He pounced and pummelled him, blind to the swords clashing above his head, muskets, stirrups and boots banging into his side, hooves kicking his ribs and face. When the red veil lifted, he realised blood flowed from his nose and oozed down from his temples to his jaw. It didn't bother him in the least as he gazed with satisfaction at the man on the cobblestones by his boots, curled up and groaning.

As they led Ali Baig away, the madman moaned that his arrest would put his family in danger. Pah! It was him putting everyone else in danger, more like. The confession could be got out of the nob now that Wilberforce had him under lock and key. He'd see to it.

Thank the Lord, their superior numbers had let his men get away with superficial wounds. Not so with Ali's lot. Two dead – and several badly injured, he hoped.

When he arrived at the Baig mansion, two battalions of seasoned soldiers in tow, the younger brother commanded the mercenaries to stand down. He even let them carry out the search warrant, the first time he'd set foot in a nabob's palace. The splendours: all gold and crystal and whatnots everywhere, glittering in the candlelight, enough to give a man a headache, he thought. Finally, in Ali Baig's bedroom, Wilberforce laid eyes on the syringe in the drawer. Stuffed inside a sock it was. Satisfaction flooded in. Head Constable Thomas, whom he'd despatched to search the garden, came hurrying in. Wilberforce quickly followed him to a folly in the garden. A constable stood by a flat-topped boulder, his lamp illuminating fresh blood stains.

They'd got their man.

Chapter Forty-six

HC Muhammad hurried into his office, where Soob had returned to finish his tasks.

'Sir, they are here.' Muhammad's eyes were wide with terror.

Boots clattered on the stairway and four soldiers stormed in.

He'd been expecting them ever since Wilberforce rode off to arrest Ali Baig. Leaning back in his chair, he waited, hoping that the faith he had in his superior's wiliness would be borne out.

The officer in charge, copious gold lace gleaming from olive green sleeves, shoved Muhammad aside and strode around the desk. 'V. S. Soobramania, are you going to come quietly or do you want to be hauled out in chains?'

Soob rose to his feet. The officer seized his arm and marched him down the stairway, spurs clinking on the wooden steps. A small part of him softened at the sight of the mercenary-constables crowding the small lobby and outside, clasping their swords and daggers, anxious and determined, waiting for his signal to attack. Of course, he wouldn't issue such a command. It would be their death sentence, either under the lethal swords of the palace guards, or worse, a public execution as traitors under an elephant's foot.

'Mount your horse,' the officer barked at him as the Arabs sprang onto theirs.

They rode under lit lamps, pedestrians and vendors gaping up at him, murmurs rising over the buzz of kerosene lanterns and their noisy passage as they made for Afzul Gate. When they carried on past the city gate, Soob let out a breath he hadn't realised he'd been holding. His faith had been borne out, he thought with satisfaction, when they slowed down and turned into the grand entrance of the deputy commissioner's palace.

His superior was pacing in the audience chamber under the rosy sparkle of a handsome chandelier. On seeing Soob being marched in, all four of his gold teeth flashed in a smile.

'Mr Soobramania.' Mir Akbar jerked his head, and the soldiers retreated to the door.

'You have woefully disappointed me, Mr Soobramania,' Mir Akbar said sorrowfully, shaking his head. 'To think, I had such high hopes for you. We are grieved at your betrayal.'

'I've betrayed no one,' Soob said in a dry tone. 'The investigation is under Inspector Wilberforce, and if he has arrested Nawab Ali Baig, he must have reason to do so.'

'Tut, tut, Mr Soobramania, surely you do not think us such fools. If the others had their way, you would be hanging from iron hooks in the Golconda dungeons. But I appealed to our Exalted Highness on your behalf.' He gazed meaningfully at him. 'I put it to him that your training at Scotland Yard must make you see that the killer was still at large. To give you a chance to right the wrong you have done to us, in his munificence and magnanimity, our Exalted Highness has decreed that you will be expelled from the city.'

Soob eyed him with amusement. This was what he'd hoped would ensure his safety: Mir Akbar's unending efforts to make Soob his man. The ICID must have weighed in, forcing the Resident's hand, but this wily courtier had appropriated the British command as his own plea to the Nizam. He'd convinced his liege lord that leaving Soob free to investigate, and putting him under an obligation to them for having spared his life, would evoke gratitude and make him biddable. A grateful Soob, Mir Akbar must have said, would contrive to pin the murders on a British subject.

The nobleman, who'd been watching him closely in the bright glow of the Venetian chandelier, gave a pleased nod at Soob's bow, thinking, no doubt, that the message had been understood and accepted.

With a toothy smile, Mir Akbar enumerated the penalty. 'Be warned, Mr Soobramania. If you are found inside the city, I will personally escort you to the execution ground.'

As the soldiers led him to the city gate on foot, shackled and bound in chains for all to see, Soob realised that a key piece of evidence still remained to be tracked down from the Baig jeweller in the city bazaar. He would have to enter the city and brave the danger.

Chapter Forty-seven

Shiraz didn't return home till a quarter past nine. Her mother-in-law was in the midst of eating soup, and looked irritated. The crystal chandelier had been lit and a place had been set for Shiraz at the other end of the six-seater table, along with an additional one for any unexpected guest.

'Chief Inspector Soobramania has sent a message that he will be late.'

'Aunt Friya, Ali Baig has been arrested for Niloufer's murder and for the other murders.' She lowered herself into a chair.

The lines at the corner of her mother-in-law's mouth deepened, and the chandelier's light hung dark bags under her eyes.

'The devil! May he rot in hell. What misery he has brought. Poor Gul. She has just heard from the Fire Priest. He won't let Niloufer be given Parsi rites.'

The butler entered and served her mulligatawny soup from a tureen. Her mother-in-law's frown eased, signalling that no more talk of the tragedy would be tolerated during dinner. 'I think the monsoon has begun in earnest today. The garden will begin to bloom again.'

Shiraz, who'd been forcing herself to swallow the soup, glumly eyed the sparkling crystal and silverware, polished every day regardless of whether a guest joined them or not. So much effort, for what? Why did she live with someone who had no warmth for her? Each meal was like eating in purgatory, a self-inflicted punishment. Yet, she couldn't leave Aunt Friya to mourn Cyrus's death alone.

They had finished the first course when the butler announced Soob.

'Ask him to come in, Nathan, and bring a basin of water and a towel,' her mother-in-law said. Though Soob had met her only ten days ago, she'd taken to him immediately because he was Cyrus's friend.

Shiraz dabbed her lips with a starched white napkin while Soob apologised for his lateness. His grim glance at her said he was furious about the letter.

'Don't be silly, Chief Inspector Soobramania,' her mother-in-law said. 'You are doing a very important job. You must build up your strength. We will discuss your investigation over coffee.'

There could be no talk of murders at dinner, even if the victim was her beloved niece.

If they'd been on good terms, Shiraz would have rolled her eyes when Soob glanced at her.

He washed and dried his hands on the towel and took a seat near her mother-in-law. He refused the soup and the main course, dhansak, was served. Her mother-in-law took a spoonful, and noting Soob's doubtful examination of the dish, reassured him that it was a vegetarian version made of lentils, rice and vegetables.

'Oh, like a south Indian dish, pongal, but with vegetables,' he said after eating a spoonful with relish.

If she weren't so emotionally fraught, it would have been amusing to watch a Parsi dowager play mother to Soob. Aunt Friya didn't much care for women, or possibly her coldness was reserved only for her daughter-in-law.

After Soob declined the almond pudding dessert, they repaired to the sitting room. The muslin drapes swayed in the cool breeze coming through the mosquito netting of the French windows.

Only when they were sitting with cups of coffee did her mother-in-law finally ask about Ali's arrest.

'Why did Zulfikar's son kill Niloufer?'

Soob explained about the inheritance Ali stood to lose to Niloufer. 'That devil.'

Shiraz fidgeted with a cream-coloured tassel of a cushion, willing her mother-in-law to leave.

Finally the lady got up, and Soob steadied her as she staggered. 'It must have been a long and traumatic day for you, Mrs Daruwalla. I need a quick word with Shiraz.'

Her mother-in-law shook his hand and left the room without bidding Shiraz goodnight.

She doesn't dislike you, Niloufer had told her when Shiraz wondered what she had done to merit such treatment. *She dislikes the concept of the daughter-in-law who has taken away her son.*

'Have you any news of the child?' she asked, when the door closed.

'Bring the letter, Shiraz.' His tone was icy.

'There might be one more piece of evidence against Ali. I asked Maryam if he has a key to the park. But Ali Baig interrupted us. I'm sure—'

'You went back there again?' Soob stalked up to her. 'Don't you understand the danger you were in? Did he injure you again?'

Shiraz's hand involuntarily went to the silk scarf around her neck.

He bent and gently drew the silk down, eyes narrowing at the livid fingermarks on her throat.

'I had to find out about the child and the nursemaid.'

'Show me the letter,' he said in an implacable tone, one she'd never heard him use before.

She frowned. 'If I hadn't told you about Ali's son, you wouldn't have found that out. If I hadn't told you about Phoebe's visit, you wouldn't have known about the letter.'

'Just get the letter.'

'It can't be Niloufer's handwriting, Soob. Someone forged it.'

He stared at her stonily.

She stormed out and went to her bedroom at the end of the corridor. There she sat on the bed and took deep breaths. Only the child's safety matters, she told herself, and went over to the writing console. Picking up the letter and a note written by Niloufer, she returned to the sitting room.

'Do you have a sample of Niloufer's handwriting?' he asked, and scowled when she promptly handed over the note and letter.

After comparing the handwriting, he slipped them into an oilskin pouch.

'It's a forgery,' she said, incensed at his silence.

He hesitated and then nodded.

'Tell me what I couldn't see.'

'The G is different. The curve is a fraction wider in the letter.'

'Soob, we must find the forger. That person is as responsible as Ali Baig for killing Niloufer. I thought at first it was Templeton, but it makes no sense for him to accuse himself of having an affair with Niloufer. I think it is Edith. Maybe she's having an affair with Templeton and wants him to leave Phoebe and marry her. Phoebe said her religion viewed infidelity as a sin that called for an immediate divorce. If Templeton is caught having an affair with someone else, Phoebe would have to divorce him, but Edith wouldn't be blamed.

244

With a baby coming, she needs the job. She must think that, once free, Arthur would marry her.'

'What baby?' Soob stiffened.

She told him her suspicion. 'So you see, nobody else will employ her here. Phoebe would see to it. So Edith could have decided to use Niloufer's name in the letter.'

Soob paced up to the window and gazed out at the dark.

'Is there something in it?' she asked. 'Soob, I want to help. Please let me.'

'What about Phoebe?' Soob asked, to her surprise.

'As the forger? Why?'

'What if their marriage agreement says if one of them is caught in an affair, the other one gets all the money?'

'Then Phoebe is very much in the picture,' she said, shocked that people would sign such agreements when they were in love and anticipated only happiness in their future. 'If it was Phoebe – forging the letter, quarrelling with Niloufer, driving her in her agitation into the park... I'll never forgive her.'

A riveted glint appeared in Soob's eye as if he finally understood something.

'What is it, Soob?'

He shook his head and began walking to the door.

'Soob, we have to find the child.' She clutched at his arm. 'I'm sure he has been kidnapped. You think the mother is hysterical, but you don't know what it's like to lose a child.'

'And you do? If you go back there—'

'Yes, I do. We were going to have a baby. I lost both of them because of my negligence. I argued bitterly with Cyrus. He'd forgotten my birthday, such a silly thing to fight over. I am responsible for him being in Bond Street that morning, he went there to buy me a gift. He was killed because of me. If I hadn't behaved badly, he wouldn't have been there. He'd still be alive, Soob.'

She found herself clasped in Soob's arms, his hand patting her head gently.

'No, don't.' She reared back. 'I don't deserve it. It gets worse. I was resting at home when the constable knocked on the door. He told me Cyrus was dead and gave me his wallet. I don't know what happened for the next few hours. I must've wandered about in a daze. The next thing I knew I was in the hospital, and my baby was dead.'

She couldn't look him in the eye, couldn't bear to see the anger and disgust, the accusation.

He stepped in and held her close to him again. For a few moments she felt comforted.

'It isn't your fault,' he murmured, stroking her hair. 'Shock does that, your mind doesn't sense the cold and the rain.' He gently cupped her head.

'I should've been more careful,' she mumbled into his shoulder.

A sound came from the door. Shiraz moved back, thinking it was the butler. But on looking over his shoulder, she couldn't see anybody in the doorway and heard only the rapid beat of footsteps hurrying away.

'Stop blaming yourself, Shiraz,' Soob said in a calm tone. 'Both were unfortunate accidents. Nobody blames you. Cyrus certainly wouldn't.'

But his mother would, she thought, spirits plummeting even more at the suspicion that her mother-in-law had overheard them. She prayed it wasn't so, as Soob led her to the settee. That trauma, at least, she hoped to spare Cyrus's mother.

Soob poured a glass of water from the silver jug on the sideboard and brought it across to her. He pulled up a chair and sat by her. 'I know what it's like to feel guilty. I left Rohini here and when she was grievously ill, I couldn't return. The investigation was at a critical stage, and the trap had been set for the Ripper. I thought Rohini would recover, or that's what I told myself.' He looked into her eyes.

Shiraz straightened up, hands clasped on her lap. He'd never spoken of Rohini before, not to her, not to Cyrus.

'Do you think I was fooling myself?' His direct gaze demanded truth from her, not false comfort.

'Yes,' she said, staring back, willing him to see that she didn't blame him for acting according to his nature. 'You could've returned, Soob, but you chose not to.'

He swallowed hard, still holding her gaze. 'Go on.'

'You have to tell me why,' she said in a gentle tone.

'Because... I didn't want to.' She saw dawning horror in his eyes. 'I valued my job over Rohini's life. I could've saved her.'

No, that's not it... how could you feel guilt at being who you are? she wanted to shout. It was because of his nature, he saw himself as a saviour of the weak and vulnerable. In choosing to remain in London to catch the Ripper, he'd chosen to save future victims over saving his wife. It was written into his personality, and given another chance, he'd make the same choice. Though she desperately wanted to say it aloud, she couldn't. Soob would have to work through his guilt to arrive at this truth.

But she could prod him with her questions. 'Do you really think you could have saved her by returning?'

'Yes.' He frowned, still staring at her. 'No... perhaps. It was my duty as her husband to care for her, be at her bedside. I didn't. I pandered to my ego, felt satisfied at saving those poor women from John Furlow.' He clenched his hands on the silk armrest. 'I sacrificed Rohini.'

'Don't you see, Soob,' Shiraz said, 'your wanting to save those poor women from the Ripper drove you to it. Wouldn't you make the same choice again?'

He looked struck, and she, feeling encouraged that he was finally beginning to see the truth, waited in silence.

'Yes,' he said in a low tone, after a long pause. 'That's why I feel guilty. 'That's why I'm punishing myself. But now, I'm also punishing Natraja – my guilt about Rohini won't let me perform the expiation rite. But not doing it will harm Natraja's future – make him a pariah unless... I... let him go. I...' He choked and put his head in his hands.

She stroked his back. 'Would Rohini want you to make amends like this, Soob? Would she want you to abandon Natraja? Of course not.' Shiraz hesitated, knowing that her question would hurt him even more. But she had to ask it. 'Is that the real reason for your refusal to perform the rite? Or is it you?'

He looked at her, a blank, puzzled gaze. Again, horror dawned. 'It is me. I'm a monster.'

'No, no, Soob,' she said. 'That's not what I meant at all. You are principled. You believe in standing up for the weak and the vulnerable, even if it endangers your personal life, your loved ones. You can't perform the expiation rite, not because of Rohini, though that's what you've told yourself. It's because of who you are as a person. Returning to your caste, to those hierarchical customs and the inequality it imposes on outsiders, it goes against your entire moral fibre.'

'But surely all these principles can go to hell for Natraja? His happiness means everything to me.' His gaze pleaded with her to agree.

Shiraz's lip quivered. 'If you perform the expiation rite, will you be the Soob Athimber he looks up to?' she asked in a gentle tone.

He stared at her, the mute answer in his eyes saying his response was unutterable, unacceptable.

'Your refusal to bow to your caste's dictates stems from the same quality that made you stay on in London and finish what you promised to carry out.'

'My saviour complex, you mean,' he said bitterly.

'No, Soob, that's not what I meant. You never leave a task unfinished. Your assignment in London, you couldn't leave it half-done. It would've put more women in danger, victims who had nobody but you to save them. Rohini would have wanted you to save them.' As Shiraz spoke the words, she knew they were true for Rohini. Even though she had never met Soob's wife, she had a sense of the lady's qualities, gentle but strong, kind but firm, and above all as principled as Soob. These she had gleaned from the few times he'd spoken of his wife. 'She must've told you to remain in London?'

He nodded slowly. 'That's what she wrote when I offered to return. And I seized it.' He looked away at the curtains drawn on the bank of windows.

'Tell me, if you'd returned and Rohini had lived, wouldn't you blame yourself, and to a certain extent her, for making you sacrifice your principles? Especially if John Furlow had murdered more women, which he would have most certainly done.'

'Of course not... I...' His voice trailed away.

'Just as you will blame Natraja and yourself if you perform the rite,' she carried on quickly before his anguish struck at her courage.

'So my course of action is what? Live with my guilt and continue adding to it by striking at Natraja's future?'

Shiraz shook her head. 'No, Soob. It is to value yourself as I and so many others value you. Guilt erodes that, makes you devalue yourself.'

The words, she saw, made an impression on him, relaxing some grooves in his forehead. He took a deep breath and turned to her.

'Then perhaps you should also take your advice,' he said. 'Treat yourself with respect, see how kind you are, how fiercely you protect those who are weak. See how willing you are to risk being hurt to find the child and his nursemaid whom you don't even know. How bravely you call out an injustice. How—' He broke off as a shuffle sounded in the corridor.

The butler entered with a note.

It was a message from Phoebe Templeton, saying, 'Come quickly, Dr Shiraz. Edith is dead.'

Chapter Forty-eight

This was a room for a guest, not a paid companion, Soob thought, taking in the handsome furnishings: a teak dressing table, a writing console, a silk carpet, a brightly upholstered armchair. He hastened to the four-poster bed in the centre. Edith Whittaker lay on a white sheet mottled with blood, her employers looming on either side. His relief at the absence of knife wounds was echoed in Shiraz's expression.

While she examined the dark flecks crusting Edith's mouth and cheeks, Soob turned to the couple. 'What happened?'

Templeton's pale face and stony silence told of a deeper relationship with the dead woman. Shiraz had it right.

'Edith complained of a pain in her stomach when she returned from the racetrack,' Phoebe said, her tone steady, uncaring almost, suggesting that a similar realisation had dawned on her. 'I told her to lie down and the maid made her a cup of hot cocoa. Arthur offered to take it to her. At dinnertime I sent the maid to check on her, and she screamed. I hurried here and saw Edith curled up. Blood was leaking onto the bedclothes. I sent for Dr Lawrie and sat with her. About an hour ago she vomited suddenly and became still. Dr Lawrie still hadn't come, so I sent Dr Shiraz a note.'

'What time did you go to her room?' Soob asked.

'Half past eight.'

It was past ten now.

'Please wait for me in your study, both of you.'

'I think it is a miscarriage,' Shiraz said after they left. 'Too much blood is seeping from the womb. But we won't know for sure until the post-mortem.'

'All right?' He pressed her shoulder thinking how traumatic it must be for her to be reminded of her own loss.

She bit her lip and nodded.

On the bedside table, a teacup lay on its side, brown dregs on its lip and the saucer.

He bent and sniffed. Cocoa and something else.

'Do you have an empty test tube?'

She removed one from her valise and handed it over.

He tipped the cocoa into it and asked her to get it tested. His instincts told him something wasn't right about her death.

The butler entered. 'Doctor, the memsahib has fainted.'

Again? He'd have told Shiraz not to bother, but she picked up her valise and rushed out.

A sweet scent of magnolia wafted in from the open window, striking an incongruous note in the vomit- and blood-infused air. He approached the writing console by the window. From here, he could see the back door and a bit of the side garden. She would have seen Phoebe coming from the side door with a forked stick.

He raised the walnut top of the console, the movement causing a piece of paper to flutter inside, a half-finished letter to a woman called Gladys. It spoke of a gay life of fetes and dinners and balls, a social whirl a companion could only dream of.

Wilberforce rushed in. 'Was she murdered?'

Soob explained about the miscarriage and his suspicions about the cocoa.

Wilberforce shook his head. 'Poor thing. Who would blame her for wanting to further herself? She struck me as one of those women who miraculously gains a husband during her voyage to India. Nobody has seen Mr Whittaker. You know the type: once they entrap a rich fool, the husband suddenly kicks the bucket, leaving her free to marry the deluded sod. I suppose Templeton fell for her.'

Soob opened a drawer. A bundle of fluffy pink wool lay there, which revealed itself as a half-finished baby frock.

'Templeton's?' Wilberforce frowned.

Soob picked up a notebook from the writing desk and flipped the pages. Stopped. The writing in cursive script repeated a phrase, one he had seen in the forged letter. And the handwriting, to varying degrees, resembled Niloufer's.

'It doesn't make sense,' Wilberforce said, his frown deepening on learning about the forgery. 'Why would Edith make up a false affair?'

Shiraz's conjecture – that Edith desired Arthur Templeton to be set free but didn't want to be blamed for it – found a willing ear in Wilberforce.

A King James Bible stuck out of a pigeonhole. Soob flipped its pages in case she'd slipped other letters or notes in it. Close to the book's centre, the middle bit had been hollowed, and a pocket diary in red leather nestled in it. On the flyleaf was written 'R PLAN BOOK'. Eleven tick marks against dates matched the exact dates of the Ripper's Whitechapel murders.

'What's wrong? What have you found?' Wilberforce grabbed the diary. 'Mother of God, man, you don't think she is the Ripper? Surely not. We have the Ripper. Ali Baig.' His voice rose to a bellow.

'Inspector Wilberforce, calm down. Edith is not the Ripper. Neither is Ali Baig. Constable John Furlow was the Ripper and he is dead.'

But the Englishman, trapped in fear, heeded him not. 'The dates match. She was in London then. Think she killed herself?'

'Inspector Wilberforce, we weren't suspicious of her so there was no need for her to kill herself. Hear me again: we are not dealing with the Ripper.'

'Who the hell knows what happens in such a diseased mind? Had us on a merry dance she did. Jill the Ripper. I would never have thought it. Has she left a letter confessing to the murders?' Wilberforce's trembling hands rummaged in the pigeonholes.

Soob knew how to get the Englishman to calm down and at the same time reiterate his point. 'Inspector Wilberforce, count the number of tick marks. Eleven. It means the person who wrote this diary didn't know that the Ripper was responsible for only six murders.'

Wilberforce frowned and, after checking, stared at him, a hopeful glimmer in his eyes.

'And the diary is too convenient,' Soob continued. 'Anybody could've written down those dates. And even if she had done so, Edith Whittaker strikes me more as a blackmailer than a murderer, someone who hoarded secrets.'

'But she could still be the Ripper,' Wilberforce said.

'My god, Edith was the Ripper?' Templeton said, wide-eyed, from the door.

Soob frowned. How long had Templeton been standing there, and what else had he heard? Wilberforce looked panicked as if he had the same thought, that they couldn't hush up the diary's contents. With Edith branded as the Ripper, Ali Baig would have to be set free. But all his instincts said Edith's death wasn't an accident or even a suicide, not when she had been knitting a frock for her baby. She was being framed.

–

Looking as if a weight had been lifted off his shoulder, Arthur Templeton sprawled in a wingback chair in the study, his eyes glittering in the oil lamp's light. 'Edith came to us a couple of months ago.'

'Where was she working before?' Soob asked, leaning against the mantlepiece.

'My wife will know the details. She found Mrs Whittaker for the boys, as a governess. They got along famously, and my wife made her a companion.'

'When?' Soob asked.

'A week or so after she joined. It was Phoebe's idea. Edith began taking her meals with us and joined us for dinners and other entertainments. Phoebe treated her like a younger sister. If we had known she was a killer, and the Ripper at that, my God! What a narrow escape.'

By mutual consent, neither policeman mentioned Edith's possible pregnancy, though both were fairly sure that if she was pregnant, Templeton was the baby's father. As Soob stepped into the dimly lit corridor, his gut told him that Arthur Templeton knew about the baby.

Soob tracked down the butler in the dining room. He was standing by the sideboard, rubbing a silver chalice with a rag.

'Where is the saucepan you made the cocoa in?' Soob asked.

'Washed and put away, sir. By Mary, the maid.' The man looked unruffled.

'Summon her.'

'She's run away, sir. These illiterate people think they'll be blamed. They're all like that.'

Sub-Inspector Kamran would find her.

'Take me to Phoebe Templeton.'

She was on the back verandah, huddled in a cane armchair. Next to her was a table with an oil lamp whose flickering light accentuated the dark circles under her eyes. In the garden, fireflies flew in arcs around the nocturnal white blooms of ipomoea.

Soob took the other chair.

'Do you believe Edith is the Ripper?' she asked in a steady voice.

'Do you?' Soob asked. Too late now to stifle the news.

'It's hard to believe that of someone you have trusted with your children. Edith was so good with the boys. That's why I hired her. She had the knack of engaging their attention and making them obey her. Not many can do that. I can't, and Arthur simply shouts at them and makes it worse. Edith only had to command in a quiet voice, and they promptly did her bidding. They're going to be so upset. How am I going to break it to them?'

He thought back to the scene of a smiling Edith pushing her squealing charge on the swing. She clearly enjoyed being with the children.

'Were you friends?' he asked, wanting to understand why she'd made Edith her companion.

'We were very different people. She never came out and said anything to one's face. Everything was squirrelled away furtively. She reminded me of a secretive mouse.'

'Why did you make her your companion?'

'Arthur suggested it. In my faith, we help deserving souls. I felt sorry for her. She'd had a tough life, or so she said. I suppose that was a lie too.'

He didn't think so. Edith had struggled in life, and she had worked hard to acquire skills. She was the English equivalent of a low caste, and he admired her drive and willingness to put in the effort to move up the hierarchy.

'Your husband said you found her.'

'Did he?' An unreadable glint appeared in her eyes. 'I don't know why he said that. He told me our lawyer, Eardley Norton, had recommended her as a governess for our two boys. She seemed pleasant enough, and as I said, she had a way of managing them.'

'What did she tell you about Mr Whittaker?'

'Nothing much. Just that he would join her soon. As I said, we weren't confidantes.'

'Did she mention she was pregnant?'

He shifted his chair to see her expression, but she turned her face away into night's shadow.

'No. Was it a miscarriage?' When he did not reply, she asked, 'How many months? Three or less, I suppose.'

Her question revealed she thought her husband was the father. Or was she sure of it?

'We will know after the post-mortem. The love letter, though, was forged.'

'Did Edith forge it?'

Again, the undertone wasn't one of surprise. Soob stared steadily at her. 'How long have you known?'

She met his gaze, her face inscrutable. 'You just told me.' Her grip tightened on the armrest, and her knuckles gleamed white. 'Chief Inspector, she is not the Ripper. The diary isn't hers. Edith never kept one. She was afraid if her charges found it, they'd stop obeying her.' She closed her eyes. 'I accused Niloufer and I can't undo it. I am responsible for her death. I wished for it.'

'For God's sake, Phoebe, stop talking.' Templeton charged out into the verandah. 'Inspector, she did not mean anything by it. I know for a fact Edith had a diary. I saw her writing in it.'

Chapter Forty-nine

Wilberforce rubbed the itch in his eyes. It was close to dawn, and he hadn't slept a wink, not bloody likely with his backside glued to the office chair, with periodic forays to the cell to question Ali Baig.

Much to his disgust, his superiors had forbidden physical violence; a good fist in the face would have loosened the bastard's tongue soon enough.

'Best it stays on a civilised level,' the commissioner had said. 'Their lot could revive the scandal about the Earl of Euston and the Hellfire Club, and even worse, send that Brahmin to arrest them. We've promised them not a hair on the nawab's head will be touched. You'd better keep our word if you still want this job tomorrow.'

Sweat ran in rivulets down his neck and dampened his buckram collar. The uneasy feeling in his gut wouldn't go away. What if the Brahmin was right that Edith was being framed by the Ripper? Ali couldn't have done it; he had not entered Templeton's house.

Wilberforce had been so sure he was on the right track, but what with Phoebe's brooch and now Edith's sudden death and the diary, he couldn't make head nor tail of it. Though it was close to four in the morning, he needed to speak to the Brahmin.

'Sir, this note has come from Commissioner Hankin.' Thomas saluted and handed over a sealed missive.

The order he had been dreading: 'Release Nawab Ali Baig immediately.'

–

The Brahmin sat cross-legged on his verandah, contemplating the night sky. Thick thunderclouds lodged there. A lantern illuminated his peculiar night attire: a cotton skirt-like thing wrapped around his waist and a white kurta.

He didn't look surprised to see Wilberforce at such a late hour.

'Don't bother with a chair,' Wilberforce said when the Brahmin got up. 'I would prefer to pace on the grass as we talk. I've come to discuss the case. How is the boy doing?'

'Worn out from the excitement. Dr Currimbhoy has given him a sedative. Thank you, Inspector Wilberforce. I will never forget what you have done for him. For me.'

Wilberforce didn't know what to say. He would have saved any child. After all, it wasn't the boy's fault he had this fellow for an uncle.

'It would be better if we walked on the path,' the Brahmin said, coming down the steps to join him. 'Snakes.'

Wilberforce eyed the tangle of black bushes and knee-high grass with disfavour.

'Chief Inspector Soobramania,' he plunged in, anxious for reassurance, 'you are absolutely sure Edith is not the Ripper?'

'Someone wants us to think she is,' the Brahmin said, matching his stride up the short driveway. The trees on either side arched their boughs to create a tented effect.

'The person copying the Ripper?' Wilberforce said, the words wrenched from him. It cut too close to his affection for his old partner and raised grave questions about his ability to judge a man's character. What kind of a policeman was he if he couldn't recognise a killer by his side?

'Not necessarily.'

'You mean someone found her dead and decided to incriminate her? But why? To protect the killer? Like a younger brother? No, strike out the Baigs. I was with Imran Baig till ten at night searching the gardens. Found evidence of the Hellfire ritual.'

The gravel murmured under his boot and the Brahmin's slippers as they turned at the front gate and retraced their steps to the house. By now his eyes had adjusted to the dark and could make out the shimmer of the pale gravel illuminating the path.

'Are we sure Edith Whittaker died of natural causes?' the Brahmin asked in an expressionless tone.

'She was pregnant and it looks as if the foetus has aborted. Do you suspect murder?'

'Suicide and an incriminating diary in the desk are far too neat and convenient. It certainly wasn't suicide. Why would she bother to knit a frock for her unborn baby if she planned to kill herself? And I saw no sign of illness when I met her at the races yesterday evening.'

'You didn't think to mention that to me?' Wilberforce scowled. 'What did you ask her?'

'She told me about the Templetons' marriage contract, which you know already.'

'I didn't want to gossip about Arthur's personal life,' Wilberforce said, annoyed at the defensive note in his voice.

With an impassive face, the fellow continued. 'She said she saw Phoebe Templeton come from the side door with a forked stick in hand.'

'What the blazes was she doing there? Surely not gardening? Even Phoebe isn't so mad. All this is driving me bonkers.' He tugged his hair. 'If Edith was murdered, then Arthur would be my best bet. He found out about the baby and decided to get rid of her before his wife discovered their affair. A vindictive Edith would be sure to tell Phoebe. As for the forged diary, I might as well tell you Arthur was sent down for forging a cheque at university.'

They'd reached the verandah now. The Brahmin turned to him, the lamp casting a glow on his face. 'Is it your view that Arthur Templeton committed all the murders? Or only Mrs Whittaker's murder?'

'That's what puzzles me.' Wilberforce punched his right fist into his left palm. 'We've already gone over his alibi for the earlier murders. He couldn't have killed that gardener's daughter even if he killed Mrs Baig, not while hosting a blooming dinner.'

'Mallu,' the Brahmin said.

'Eh... what?'

'Her name is Mallu.'

'Yes, well... Edith could have helped him kill *Mallu*. Went missing from the dinner, didn't she, for half an hour, claiming she had things to organise. She could've popped down the street, drugged the girl, and using Phoebe's key, dragged her to the copse and killed her. Arthur tells Mrs Baig to meet him in the park and then kills her. And *then* he kills Edith to shut her up. To take the heat off himself, frames her as the Ripper. Either of them could've taken the chloroform and phosphorous from Lawrie's clinic. Not to forget that his newspaper had sensationalised the left eye business.' He scratched the back of his neck meditatively. 'But his motive is a problem. The love letter was a forgery, so why would Arthur need to kill Niloufer and the other women?'

'Or we could look at the facts differently,' the Brahmin said. 'Edith's death, or more likely murder, isn't the work of a killer copying the Ripper. It could be someone else framing her for the Ripper murders.'

'To throw us off the scent, you mean? Who?' The trees shivered in the breeze and dead leaves floated down onto them. What the blazes was the Brahmin implying? Wilberforce found himself more confused now than when he had arrived. 'The Baigs and the dukes didn't have the opportunity. Which brings us back to Phoebe and Arthur.'

The Brahmin didn't reply.

They had reached the gate again. Wilberforce lifted the iron latch and stepped out. If he stayed any longer, his head would be in even more of a whirl. Best to sleep on it. 'Let's wait for the post-mortem results. No use putting the cart before the horse. I'll come round to your office tomorrow.'

'I've been dismissed from service, Inspector Wilberforce.'

His spirits ought to have lifted, finally the fellow had had his comeuppance. But to Wilberforce's surprised annoyance, they sank. It told him how much he had been relying on the Brahmin to come up with the goods. 'What are you going to do?'

'Can you do me a favour? Can you ask Sub-Inspector Kamran to find Mary, the Templeton maid?' The Brahmin told him the information he needed from her.

'How will that help?'

A horseman slowed to a halt by the gate. 'Are you expecting someone?'

In the light of the fellow's lantern he recognised Imran Baig. What did he want? Wilberforce mounted his horse, after un-looping its reins from the iron post, and rode away reluctantly. In all this, he'd forgotten to mention that Ali Baig was a free man. Well, the Brahmin would know soon enough.

Chapter Fifty

Having tied his horse to the iron post vacated by Wilberforce, Imran Baig stepped up to the gate, his dark angharkha merging with the night. A civet cat ducked into the embankment on the other side of the road, the line of its back arched and alert, eyes glistening green.

'I am sorry to intrude at such an early hour, Chief Inspector.' Imran Baig bowed. 'I heard about the death of Mr Templeton's companion. If I were you, I wouldn't take that blue-eyed Englishman's word. He is a rotter and a social climber, and it wouldn't surprise me if he is involved.'

That he'd got Templeton's eye colour wrong wasn't surprising. Like other Deccani nobles, Imran had little time for Englishmen like Templeton, whom they considered social inferiors and illegitimate usurpers.

'Though thanks to the news that she is the Ripper, my brother is free.' These words angered Soob as he opened the gate wider. Why hadn't Wilberforce informed him? Didn't he realise how dangerous a free Ali was to Shiraz's safety?

'I won't come in, Chief Inspector. My brother is waiting for me. I have disturbing news about my nephew. He has been kidnapped by my brother's creditor whom my brother refuses to name.'

Though he had been expecting this, having another improbable event confirmed made his heart sink. But if he was right about the motive, and it looked all too likely that he was, the child's death wouldn't suit the kidnapper just yet. He would have to tread very carefully. 'When?'

'The morning his friends arrived from England. The child was playing with his nursemaid in the garden.'

'But you have an army protecting you.'

'Not then. Only one guard was posted outside the harem door. When he saw the nursemaid following my nephew, he thought they would be fine. Also, I had summoned him just then. The kidnapper must've been hiding in the bushes. The ransom note came that evening. My esteemed brother thinks the body you found in the river is my nephew's nursemaid. Can I see it?'

'The lady's face and body were mutilated. And her hair was shorn like a widow's.' Soob paused. 'Devi is married, isn't she? And she has long hair.'

'How did you know? Oh, your friend, Dr Daruwalla, I imagine.' Imran Baig's jaw tightened. 'I hope her meddling hasn't harmed my nephew. Are you certain she isn't the nursemaid?'

'Mr Baig, did Devi have any distinctive marks or scars?'

The nobleman tapped his chin and gazed at the mist rising from the river.

'She had a tattoo. A Hindu religious sign on her inner elbow.'

'Aum?'

'Yes.' Imran Baig examined his face. 'Was that on the victim?'

Soob nodded.

'Then she is the nursemaid. I don't know why her hair was cut short. Maybe the murderer did it to make it difficult to identify her. Do you think she helped the kidnappers? My nephew couldn't have been taken from the garden unless they had inside help.'

'Tell me, did you see much of Devi?'

'Of course not. She was a female servant. I may have passed her once or twice, fully veiled of course, when I came to visit my wife.'

Dawn's silver suffused the slice of sky above them.

'When and where will you pay the ransom?'

Imran grimaced. 'My brother refuses to tell me.' He turned away and set his foot in the stirrup.

'Who has your father's key to the park?'

'What key?'

'To the side entrance. There are three keys, and each has a piece of silk ribbon tied to it.'

'Oh, that one. My esteemed brother has it.'

'What colour is the ribbon?'

'Green, I think. Why?'

'Not blue?'

'No, I saw my father give it to my brother.' Imran bowed and took his leave.

As Soob retraced his steps to the verandah, he mulled over the possibility of a fourth key. Even if the killer had forged their own key, why tie a silk ribbon to it? And why a blue one, rather than green like the other three? Something Imran had said about Templeton tapped at the edge of his consciousness. But he couldn't pinpoint it. And the nobleman had asked a question: 'Why was her hair cut short?' Suddenly Soob realised the significance of those words.

Chapter Fifty-one

At ten in the morning, when the guards at Afzul Gate switched from the Arab to the Rohilla contingent, Soob strode up, dressed in the yellow turban and navy blue uniform of the former.

'Permit,' the Rohilla guard barked, and eyed the chit Soob handed over.

'Name and regiment?'

'Abdul Qureishi, Qureishi contingent,' Soob said in a quiet tone.

The guard grunted and continued examining the Nizam's insignia, a round bread loaf. A palanquin passed by on the city street, its four bearers chanting, a beat for each step as they marched on. Finally, after one more hard stare, the guard gave the paper back and stepped aside.

Hoofbeats rang on the granite cobblestones. To his dismay, it was the officer who'd arrested him. He'd have to brazen it out. Shoulders back, his chin angled up towards the wall, he saluted and marched past. The officer gave a nod and reined his horse in, as Soob stepped out from the shadow of the gate into the sun. He made a sharp right turn. Behind him, the officer's voice boomed.

'Have you seen the Brahmin Chief Inspector? Or anyone who looks like him – tall, light skin, hawk nose?'

'That's who he reminded me of,' the guard said. 'You just missed him. That Arab in a yellow turban. Oi.'

Soob didn't hang around. He hot-footed it for the grain market, diving into a lane, keeping an ear out for sounds of a chase. At the yells and hoofbeats, he raced past the canary yellow shutters that were not yet open, and finding no other pedestrians on the street, had little choice but to dart into another lane. Not quickly enough.

'There he goes,' someone shouted.

He sent heartfelt thanks to the Persian architects who'd designed the web-like pattern of bazaars linking the four avenues of the city.

And to his night walks in this rabbit warren that now oriented him. He ran, weaving his way through the maze, the street with brocade shops, the English goods bazaar, the silversmiths. Nearly there. Mukesh Lal's jewellery shop stood just around the corner. The metallic ring of hoofbeats on the asphalt drew dangerously close. Down a lane, he caught sight of a flutter of black cloth. A burkha hung on a bamboo trellis outside a shop, the only one open in the street. He grabbed it, flung his turban at the stocky shopkeeper hurrying out, and raced on, away from his destination.

A clatter of hooves. A shout from the shopkeeper. 'That thief stole a burkha. Catch him.'

He had to somehow circle back to the jeweller's shop. If he hid in any of these houses, they'd just hand him straight over to the Nizam's guard. He hurried on, taking a circuitous route, keeping to needle-thin lanes that a horse couldn't squeeze through, while his hands tore a wide strip off the petticoat of the burkha. He wrapped it like a turban around his head, discarding the rest of the burkha in a doorway. As he emerged into the avenue leading to the Nizam's city palace, he slowed to an amble, eyeing four Arab soldiers loitering under a gulmohar tree, one of them haggling with a birder.

They gave him an idle glance, one of the men's eyes narrowing at the uniform. Behind him, Soob heard shouts and cries, and – thankfully – the soldier's attention shifted to his pursuers. He ducked into the metal-workers' lane and in a few minutes was back in the silversmith street, his bounding steps taking him around the corner to the jeweller's lane. A carriage bowled down the street, accompanied by four outriders, and Soob flattened himself into a shop doorway, only just in time as his pursuers halted at the head of the street.

He tensed, the wood hard and unyielding behind his back, and prayed they would move on. But no such luck. The clip-clop of horses drew closer. He took a deep breath and was about to step out when the door yielded. Someone grabbed his shoulders and pulled him back-wards, the grass stifling the sound of his stumble. A youth in a white kurta-pyjama quickly shut the door behind him; a fraction of a second later, the horses trotted past.

He turned to thank his saviour, a middle-aged man with the build of a wrestler, also in a white kurta-pyjama.

The man put a finger to his lips and bowed. Soob bowed back and mouthed 'thank you'. They were in a grassy courtyard with a small sandstone pedestal in the centre containing a tulsi plant. The grey slate roof of the residence stood to the right, a silver-haired man in its shadowed doorway. Mukesh Lal, the Baig family jeweller. Soob realised that the shop fronts hid the bungalow, the jeweller's shop-cum-residence.

They exchanged bows silently. From the half pitying look in the jeweller's eye, it was clear he knew of Soob's dismissal. By mutual and silent consent, he followed the spare-framed jeweller down a corridor.

Through an open door to his left, he saw two men seated silently on a white mattress, face to face and holding hands as if they were betrothed. An assistant draped a white sheet on the clasped hands. A transaction. Soob had heard of the custom. As many times as the buyer pressed the seller's palm, the base amount would multiply that many times. The sheet's cloak ensured only the buyer and the seller would know the price.

The jeweller stopped at the next door, and now they entered a cool room with two high windows near the rafters, barred with iron rods. A mattress with a white cotton sheet stretched from end to end, and white bolsters rested against the wall. Soob slipped off his shoes at the door.

They sat with the obligatory glasses of sherbet and water and made polite enquiries about one another's health. For the first time, he saw the reason for the Hyderabadi custom of engaging in initial niceties. The pleasantries created a comforting rhythm to the meeting and put both parties at ease. Not that he needed it here, any man who had rescued him from the dungeons had his sincere gratitude.

'I have come to find out if Ali or Imran Baig approached you for a loan recently,' Soob said, when it was time for business.

The family jeweller would've been Ali Baig's first port of call. Jewellers like Mukesh Lal ran a lucrative trade, lending money to princes, nobles and merchants at steep interest rates to finance wars, coups and other ventures.

'That I cannot tell you, Chief Inspector.' The jeweller's tone was regretful. 'It would betray my clients' trust.'

If word got out that Mukesh Lal had revealed his debtor's identity, the coup-makers would avoid him like the plague.

'Can you at least tell me if you loaned large sums in the past six weeks?'

The Deccan Rail Scheme had opened for just two days in mid-May and the money had to be deposited within that period.

The jeweller shook his head. 'I'm sorry, I cannot.'

'What happens if the person doesn't repay?'

A hard expression seeped into the jeweller's face. 'The risk is theirs. They have to find the money. We don't forgive debts; otherwise, I would go bankrupt.'

'Can you at least confirm you did not lend a large sum to Ali and Imran Baig in the past six weeks? Our conversation will be strictly confidential.'

Mukesh Lal narrowed his eyes and shook his head. 'I cannot reveal anything about my customers.'

'A child's life is at stake, Mukeshji.' He wasn't leaving without the information.

Though the man's face gave nothing away, Soob knew what was going through his mind. Soob had been of service to the jeweller's family in the previous investigation. Though he saw it as simply doing his job, custom here viewed it as a favour owed to him by the Lal family. Part of that favour had been returned a few minutes ago, but the full price had not yet been repaid.

'Let me repeat the question. You did not lend to the Baigs in the past six weeks, correct?'

The danger that Soob could demand a more difficult favour in the future decided the jeweller's course of action. Mukesh Lal inclined his head.

'Thank you.' Then whom did Ali borrow from? His instinct made him ask another question. 'Would Abdul Huq have lent money to Ali Baig?'

Mukesh Lal gave him a sphinx-like smile. It was hard to gauge if it meant a yes or an amused no. Rationally speaking, it made little sense for Huq who'd made off with his investors' funds in the Deccan Rail Scheme, to lend to an investor in that very project. Yet, his instincts urged him to continue with that line of enquiry. Perhaps he could ask...

Soob rose to his feet and padded to the door. 'One final question: do you have British customers who've taken loans from you?'

'Of course.'

'Arthur Templeton?'

Mukesh Lal gave him a level look.

He had his answer. Templeton had borrowed from the jeweller to invest in Huq's scheme. And had lost it all.

'My carriage can take you to the city gate, Chief Inspector.'

Soob bowed and thanked him. Before he left, he wrote a note and asked the jeweller to have it delivered to the Premier Noble. All he needed now was confirmation from Huq's patron of the gunrunner's involvement in lending to Ali and in the boy's abduction. And perhaps a little more if his hunch was correct.

He told the coachman to stop at the Ashurkhana by the river, and made his way inside to a hole in its back wall, the one Ram Rahim used as a handy exit from the city.

Chapter Fifty-two

Shiraz was about to step into the phaeton in the portico, having come home to change her shoes, when the gate guard hurried up.

'Hakimji, the Chief Inspector's nephew was kidnapped by Yakub yesterday. Thanks be to Allah, he was saved by the firangi inspector and a street urchin.'

Why hadn't Soob told her? 'Suleiman, take me to the Chief Inspector's home.'

'Shiraz, I want a word with you.' Her mother-in-law's glacial tone sounded from the front door.

Leaving her valise in the carriage, Shiraz followed her to the sitting room, wondering what she had done to offend her this time. She shut the door and turned around. Friya stood by the settee, fingers curled into fists, her bloodshot eyes pointing to a disturbed night.

'You killed my son and my grandson,' she burst out.

Shiraz's stomach lurched. 'You heard what I said last night?' It was her mother-in-law's footsteps she'd heard hurrying away.

Cold opaque eyes bored into her. 'You killed them both.'

'It was an accident, Cyrus's death. And our baby's... it was shock. Hearing about Cyrus's death caused me to miscarry.' She found herself repeating Soob's words.

'Don't try to excuse yourself. Your taunts drove my poor Cyrus to that accursed street. And your deliberate negligence killed my grandson, denied me my only link to Cyrus. I do not want you staying here any more, Shiraz. It would be best for you to leave the city and return to your parents. I don't ever want to see you again.'

Relief surged up. She wouldn't have to put up with her mother-in-law's dislike any more. A part of her wanted to rush to her room and pack straightaway. She could be on the afternoon train to Madras, to her parents. Then Maryam's anguished face hovered in her mind. Maryam's child… finding him mattered right now, nothing else. Despair and pain knit the wrinkles in her mother-in-law's face. Her heart softened. This was another grieving mother. She found herself reaching out to clasp her mother-in-law's hand.

The lady stiffened and made a gesture as if to ward off an evil spirit. 'Don't. Just leave.'

'I'm going to stay in Hyderabad until I find the murderer, Aunt Friya. Either here or in a hotel.'

'It won't make up for what you've done,' came the cold response. Then after a pause, the lady continued, 'For Gul's sake, I will let you stay here till then. Do not cross my path in this house.'

Shiraz stalked out into the portico and, through angry tears, saw Soob on a horse trotting up the driveway.

'What's wrong, Shiraz?' he asked, dismounting quickly.

She shook her head, clamping her lips to curb their wobble. Then spoke, hoping her voice wouldn't betray her. 'Is Natraja all right? Why didn't you tell me about his abduction?'

'He is fine. I'm sorry, I didn't want to worry you.' He explained about Ram Rahim's bravery and Wilberforce's help, and Ali's arrest and release.

She ought to feel angry at how he kept making decisions for her but he looked exhausted, and it made her want to comfort him instead. He must have been up the whole night.

'But it was Ali Baig's carriage, so why did they release him when everyone saw how he had kidnapped Natraja?'

'Wilberforce and Ram Rahim and some of the guards saw gold-edged wheels. Ali Baig's carriage isn't the only one with such trimmings.'

'Then who abducted Natraja? It must've been Ali. Edith couldn't have.'

Soob told her what Imran had revealed about Ali's child's kidnapping and the events surrounding the ransom payment. Ali's violent behaviour, she realised, was of a frantic father, ready to kill even. A sharp pain prodded her chest. 'But why didn't the kidnapper release the child when the ransom was paid? Who is he?'

'Ali Baig point blank refuses to tell us. That's why I've come to you for help.' The glint in his eye said he'd treat her as a fellow investigator.

'Can you ask Maryam the name of the man who lent Ali the money? Check if it is Abdul Huq.'

She got into the carriage. Outside the gate, a bullock cart filled with vegetables angled across the road, stuck in the mud. Soob took the reins from the cartman and with small clicks of his tongue moved the buffaloes to one side. They raced to the Baig lake, Shiraz perched on the seat's edge, as dreadful images flashed through her mind.

At least forty soldiers, some mounted and others on foot, gathered at the Baig palace gate. Lithe, wiry men, eyes alert, some with nicks and scars on their faces. In this fortress, the kidnapper had inside help, she thought. Not poor Devi, no matter what others thought.

She tensed as Ali Baig strode up to her carriage, the light glancing off the rifle slung over his shoulder.

'My begum is frantic, Dr Daruwalla. I would be obliged to you if you could calm her.' His eyes were bloodshot, hair awry as if he had been clutching and pulling at it. 'I owe you an apology for my behaviour. My son's life was at stake, and I thought if you meddled, the kidnapper would kill him. But I won't forget your concern and kindness to my wife even though you don't know us.' The depth of his bow was worthy of a queen.

She wasn't about to forgive him so easily. His innocence in the murders and Natraja's kidnapping had yet to be established. Turning to the coachman, she told him to proceed.

The horses began to trot.

'Stop,' she said, espying Imran Baig sprinting towards them.

'They sent a message about the ransom,' she overheard him tell Ali. 'Says we were late with the payment.'

'How much does he want?'

The sum shocked Shiraz.

'My inheritance from our mother is at your disposal, esteemed elder brother,' Imran said.

Ali gripped his brother's shoulder.

Soob, she realised, had dismounted and had been watching them. He came up to the brothers.

'You will be able to keep your money and your son if you follow my advice,' she heard him say as they walked away into the garden.

A nightingale's fluting call followed her carriage to the harem.

She found Begum Maryam pacing in the bedroom, twisting a ruby-and-diamond ring on her finger, her embroidered silk slippers slapping against the carpet. Three attendants watched her anxiously from a corner.

On seeing her, hope bloomed in Maryam's eyes, then dimmed.

'Is he dead?'

'No.' Shiraz told her about the new demand she had overheard. If it were her, she'd want to know the truth.

Maryam clutched her hand with burning hot palms. 'My Mohsin is going to die. The spirits say only you can save him.'

'Lie down,' Shiraz said, and told an attendant to open the windows. Birdsong floated in, and as Maryam curled up on the white bedspread, Shiraz asked about the spirits.

'The spirits talk to me. They can see into the future. You must save my son.'

For a moment the glazed and unseeing veils parted and Shiraz glimpsed a cool intelligence watching her. 'Maryam sees things' and 'she knows more than she is letting on', Parveen had said.

Though Shiraz had not suspected Maryam so far, she did now. What if this frantic mother helped her husband murder Niloufer, Zulfikar and the other women? Or had even done it on her own, to clear the path to her husband's accession to a fortune that would save her son. Shiraz eyed Maryam's arms, slim yet with a wiry strength evident in the lady's grip. Could she be play acting, lying still, eyes closed, pale as marble?

The silence stretched around them. It was almost as if the inhabitants had stripped off their anklets and bangles in preparation for the child's funeral. If this mother was involved in the murders, then she'd definitely know the identity of the kidnapper.

'Maryam, whom did your husband borrow from?'

Maryam's eyes snapped open – again the intelligence shone through for a moment. 'I don't know. Ali sahib doesn't discuss such matters with me.'

Shiraz stifled a snort. Such a desperate mother would have somehow found out. Women in the harem had their own spies among the maids and washerwomen.

'The spirits can tell me,' the lady suddenly said in a sonorous voice.

Though seances were all the rage with the upper classes here and in London, Shiraz put little faith in the supernatural. In medical school, though, when she'd dissected dead bodies to learn about the muscular and nervous systems, she had, it must be confessed, been petrified of their ghosts. She'd asked a woman friend in the boarding house to sleep in her room to ward off the angry ghouls. But three weeks of slicing tendons and examining arteries, and not a single ghost in sight, had succeeded in firmly banishing such thoughts. Still, something in Maryam's cool gaze told her that the answer would come this way, ostensibly through the spirits. Especially if it would absolve Maryam of breaking a previous promise to her husband.

'All right, then, let's ask them,' she said.

Maryam eyed her suspiciously to see if she was making fun of her.

Shiraz gazed back in polite enquiry. She was half-serious. The spirits could do some useful work for a change instead of speaking in riddles.

The lady closed her eyes. A humming sound came from her like a far-away swarm of bees.

She bent to hear Maryam's whispers.

'Borrowed so much money. I told him not to... wouldn't listen. He didn't want to depend on Nawab sahib. Rail... Mohsin... poor, poor girl. Duped... sober.'

'She keeps saying Niloufer was duped,' a nasal voice said in her ear.

Shiraz jumped.

It was Imran's horrid wife come to gloat. She'd slipped in silently.

'Maryam utters prophecies. They have several saints on her mother's side.' Parveen cast a glance at the door and whispered, 'She is a bit gaga, screw loose. I'm not supposed to say anything about it but how would you like to live next to a crazy woman? I'm always frightened. One day she may curse me. Then what?' For once, Parveen looked genuinely fearful.

'Do you know who her husband borrowed from?'

'Huq... right...' Maryam mumbled.

'Keep quiet, Maryam,' Parveen said, putting her hand on her sister-in-law's mouth.

'Abdul Huq?' Shiraz asked, heart beating fast. Soob had been right. Parveen didn't meet her gaze.

'You know. Tell me.'

Parveen shook her head and backed away. 'My little dervish will be killed. I love him like my own son.' Tears brimmed in her eyes.

Parveen seemed suddenly shorn of all ill will. Its source, Shiraz realised, lay in unhappiness at not bearing a child, let alone a son. This woman would have faced the taunts of other women in the harem and in her maternal home. And seen the sister-in-law who'd taken away her intended husband also becoming a mother – a future Parveen could have had with Ali Baig.

'Who told you the child would be killed if the police became involved?'

'Ali sahib.'

'What are you doing gossiping while your sister-in-law is prostrate with grief?' Imran Baig barked from the doorway.

Parveen scuttled away, and Imran, after a quick bow, followed.

Ali Baig entered the room. 'How is she?'

Maryam stilled.

Shiraz tapped the powdered sedative into a copper glass and poured water into it from the bedside jug. She administered the drink, managing to get most of it into the now quiescent patient. 'Let her sleep. I will come later.'

As she left, with Ali Baig hurrying to open the door, she glanced back. Maryam's eyes were open, surveying her with detachment, almost coldly. 'Take care of yourself, Dr Shiraz.'

A shiver went down her spine and she found herself almost running out of the harem.

Soob was waiting for her at the main gate. She lowered her voice and reported Maryam's spirit-talk and the mention of Abdul Huq when she'd asked about the creditor. But she didn't reveal her suspicions about Maryam, not wanting to subject the poor mother to unsubstantiated allegations.

He thanked her, saying she'd been of great help.

As her carriage trundled down the hillock, she wondered at Maryam's parting words. Had Maryam threatened her?

Chapter Fifty-three

At half past five in the afternoon, Soob rode into the Baig driveway, passing men on foot in white traditional dresses and turbans, and a camel carrying a nobleman and mahout, all keeping a respectful silence. Not the birds, though, which were shrieking and wheeling about, jostling for a place in their roosting trees.

The white-robed chamberlain ushered him to an elegant reception room where distinguished guests were received. Its large square windows along both walls opened into a verandah encircling the room. Portraits of long-dead Baigs, clad in brocades, silks and jewels, gazed at him with shrewd eyes in calm faces. One bore a striking resemblance to Imran and another to Ali.

Ali Baig was pacing in the room, circling other tastefully displayed treasures in small glass cabinets. In his white angharkha and with a cloud-like mansubdari turban resting on his head, he looked older and every inch a nawab. Gone was the devil-may-care glint and the cocky arrogance; a crosshatch of grooves lined his forehead and the corner of his eyes.

'You've arranged the venue with the kidnapper?' Soob asked, shaking his head at the chair the nobleman had gestured towards.

Ali inclined his head.

Soob asked him one more question, which he could see puzzled Ali: the colour of the ribbon on his father's park key. Ali's answer solved the final riddle of the case.

An elephant stopped outside the window, its back covered with white brocade, the colour assigned to the Premier Noble, the Nizam's brother-in-law. The chamberlain entered and whispered in Ali's ear.

'Do excuse me, Chief Inspector Soobramania. I have to greet a dear friend of my father's.'

The dear friend in question was the reason for Soob's presence. Being in disgrace with the Nizam, he could not meet the Premier Noble in the city, so he had sent a message fixing this time and place.

Soob left through the back door, stepping into the verandah, which was twelve feet above the ground. He went across to the corner where he was visible to the Premier Noble. The Nizam's brother-in-law stepped off the elephant's back straight onto the chequered floor, his gaze boring directly into Soob. The nobleman inclined his head, the silvery motes of his hair glinting in the sun.

Soob expelled a breath. Huq's patron had confirmed that his client had kidnapped the boy and that he would aid Soob.

He turned around, and in front, beyond the tops of the trees, the lake stretched a blue finger into the sunset. A dozen marble steps led into a gloriously wild garden, and his feet followed nature's call.

'Wait, Chief Inspector Soobramania.'

Imran Baig hurried towards him from the house, clad in white. 'Have you spoken to my brother? We have fixed the time for the exchange. Eleven tonight in the Ashurkhana.'

They stepped on a cobblestone path that led to a grove.

'Was your father fond of the garden?' he asked, as Imran kept pace alongside.

'He liked it this way, unkempt, with absolutely no order. I think a good garden should have properly laid out paths, symmetry in the placement of its water channels, and a few well-chosen shrubs. Something like the gardens of Taj Mahal.'

And tarnish this wild beauty? The man had no poetry in his soul.

'Where is the folly?'

Imran led him down the path lined with flowering trees: pink cassias, red cordias and the dusky pink of crepe myrtle. Here and there stood shrubs, their fragrances sweet, woodsy, musky and floral. Like wandering into a delightful scent bomb, he thought, spotting a turmeric-coloured flower he couldn't name and promptly itched to examine. His eye lit on a white lily in a little pool they passed, hedged with small rocks and boulders. It was a new variety, one he hadn't seen before. A lotus flower floated on the water, and pale sunlight splashed on tadpoles swimming in it. As they passed, a host of dragonflies rose off the water, startled into flight.

They entered a grove of *Mimusops elengi* trees blooming with pale yellow berry-like flowers that exuded a pleasant aroma of bark and nectar. But a heavy sense of violence lurked in the deep shadows, where a flat-topped granite rock jutted from the earth, close to a small marble pavilion topped with a cupola. The downpour had washed away the blood that Wilberforce had found on the rock after arresting Ali.

'You saw them perform the ritual that night.'

Imran pursed his lips and nodded. 'I knew they'd be here when I heard that my esteemed brother had forbidden the servants from entering the garden. He did that each time his foreign friends visited us.'

'But his son had been kidnapped. Yet he carried out the ritual?'

'Yes. I asked him and he said the kidnapper had instructed him to attend the ball and carry out the ritual with his friends. Otherwise his son would die.'

'Did you speak to your brother that night?'

'Yes. He was furious and rushed towards me but slipped in the mud there.' He pointed to a slushy patch at the grove's edge.

'Did you see any women?'

Imran shook his head. 'I'm sure the blood is of a cockerel.' Conviction coursed through his voice.

'What time did you see them?'

'Must have been about half past eleven. Believe me, Chief Inspector Soobramania, my brother had nothing to do with these murders. He belonged to a fast set in London and remained a member of that club despite my father's express disapproval. But he is not a murderer.' Again, conviction rang in his voice.

Inside the grove, he couldn't hear birds, not even the drone of a bee. Then a faint noise started and grew louder. Someone was screaming.

He hurried out of the grove with Imran close behind. A servant sped towards them, howling and wringing her hands.

'In the compost... a dead body.' She wailed and collapsed, hitting her knee with a thud on the cobblestones.

Imran sprinted back down the path and Soob followed. They took the turn away from the house where it forked, bringing them to a clearing. A wiry man in a loincloth held a spade in a sinewy hand. At his feet lay a woman's body, half-submerged in a black mound of compost. Maggots crawled out of an empty eye socket, the left eye.

Soob crouched and stroked her forehead – streaks of brown mud stuck to his fingers. She was Mallu's age and had dressed up to meet someone. Scarlet bangles, a silver anklet, a bright gold brocade border on a maroon kurta, and pink lac-etched feet with silver anklets. Hennaed hands with long painted nails indicated a profession that did not include menial work.

'Where was she?' he asked, feeling heaviness in his chest. He had known that with Ali's release, another murder was on the cards.

'I told my wife to pile compost in that wagon,' the gardener said. 'I needed it to dress the beds. As soon as she dug the spade into the mulch, it hit the body.'

'How often do they use the manure?' Soob asked.

'Every morning,' Imran replied.

She couldn't have been dead for more than a day; the maggots suggested she had been killed sometime yesterday. Before Ali Baig's arrest, and before he had been certain of the killer's identity.

'Do you know her?' he asked Imran, who had a puzzled frown on his face as if he recognised the dead girl.

'She looks like Chandini, a dancing girl my brother likes.' With a dawning horror, his puzzlement seemed to shift focus. 'But all that stopped when he got married.'

There was only one path to incontrovertible proof. Though he would set up strong protections, it would put in grave danger someone he cared for deeply. But there was no other way to catch the killer.

Chapter Fifty-four

Thick cumulus clouds were gathering above, and a balmy late afternoon breeze whipped Wilberforce's face as he dismounted by the stables.

'You were right, Chief Inspector Soobramania,' he said, plonking himself into a chair on the verandah. The Brahmin sat cross-legged on a rush mat and gazed at the meadowgrass where yellow-and-black butterflies hovered over the daisies and whatnots. The grandma brought a silver glass of water to the doorway and gave it to the Brahmin who handed it over, all the while eyeing the silver with dismay.

Wilberforce drank it down, sweet and cool well water it was. 'Edith was poisoned with *Duranta erecta* berries. The cocoa dregs from the cup had enough poison to fell an elephant, they said. And you, it seems, had told the laboratory chaps to test for the berry. How in the blazes did you know?'

'It was listed in Phoebe Templeton's article on poisonous garden plants, and forms a hedge in their back garden.'

'Then I would definitely put my money on Arthur being the murderer. She must have been nagging him to marry her. He needs Phoebe's old man to bail him out now that the Deccan Rail Scheme has gone bust. The bugger almost got me to sink my savings in it too. Wonder who he got the money from.'

'He borrowed from a jeweller, Mukesh Lal,' the Brahmin said and recounted his interview.

Once again, Wilberforce found himself admiring the fellow's thorough and efficient approach. He stroked his jaw, scraping his finger on the stubble. Must shave when he got home. 'Edith's forged letter must've socked it to him. When Phoebe didn't believe his denial of the affair, Arthur must've decided to dispose of Mrs Baig. He knew the suspects of the Ripper case were in the city and decided to use what he thought was the Ripper's method. He could've used Edith to kill the other women, and then once she started blackmailing him, he killed her too. What do you think?'

The Brahmin gave him a measured look. 'I agree with some parts.'

'Which ones?'

The Brahmin told him.

The devilish plot made his blood run cold.

He took out the blank arrest warrant from his pocket, the one the Brahmin had requested in a note he'd sent Wilberforce earlier. By now, he had come to a point where he just wanted to arrest someone who would stay put in prison. Each time he'd come close to nabbing a suspect, someone else had gone and got murdered and mucked up the case.

'I sure as hell hope you're right. I'm going out on a limb on this one, Chief Inspector.'

—

Arthur Templeton tottered into the study where Wilberforce and the Brahmin had already shown themselves. The servants seemed to have decamped en masse.

'Now what?' Arthur sounded fed up. He had pouches under his bloodshot eyes, unkempt hair and a hoarse voice, probably from pleading with Phoebe. The stench of stale tobacco and whisky rolled off him.

'You are under arrest, Arthur Templeton, for the murders of Niloufer Baig, Mallu, Fatima, Edith Whittaker and Chandini.' Wilberforce clapped his hand on his shoulder.

'What do you mean?' Arthur blanched. 'I had nothing to do with the murders. Edith is the murderer. She is the Ripper.'

'We know all about your affair with Edith Whittaker. We know you used her to lure Mallu and Fatima to the park. When Edith forged the love letter, you were furious with her. You'd borrowed heavily from Mukesh Lal to invest in the Deccan Rail Scheme and lost it all. You needed Phoebe's father to bail you out, and now Phoebe was threatening to divorce you. He would have cut off your funds and taken his daughter and your children away. You'd have been left without a farthing in your pocket. So you used Edith to help you kill the women, and then you killed her so that she wouldn't reveal your affair. You put the poison in a teacup and got the maid to pour the cocoa in it, and you personally took it to Edith. The poison came from the berries in your garden hedge. The laboratory has confirmed it.'

'I didn't kill anyone. I know nothing about plants and berries. You can't pin the Ripper murders on me. The baby isn't mine.' His eyes skittered to the door where the Brahmin had positioned himself.

'For the love of God, man, a two-month-old foetus was aborted. Tell the truth. You are the father.'

'I didn't know about the baby.' Templeton collapsed into an armchair, releasing a whiff of mildew. Bug-eyed and red-faced, guilt came off him in waves.

Wilberforce wondered how he could not have seen Arthur's real nature. Just like he'd failed with the Ripper, bloody John Furlow.

'It was clever of you to use the Ripper's method. Wilberforce would chase it like a hound after a fox, you thought. Well, you made a mistake there. You removed their left eyes, which wasn't the case with the Ripper's murders.'

'But that should clear me of these charges,' Templeton shouted. 'I knew the Ripper's modus operandi but chose to take the most horrific one and sensationalise it? You go and find someone who read my piece and made that mistaken assumption. If it was me copying that bloody killer, I'd have done it his way.'

'Or you might have thought yourself to be too clever by half and done it to bamboozle us,' Wilberforce continued in a cold tone. 'Yours was a devilish plot, Arthur Templeton. Very clever of you to incriminate Nawab Ali in the murders. Phoebe told you he hated Niloufer. You also knew from the articles you researched on the Ripper that the members of the Hellfire Club had been under suspicion. When you found out Ali Baig was in that club, you made a scapegoat of him.'

'I'm innocent, I tell you. I'm not the Ripper.' Templeton clutched his head. 'I didn't know about Ali. Edith wanted me to leave Phoebe and marry her. She threatened to tell Phoebe that she was pregnant with my child. With all those silly religious commandments, Phoebe would have divorced me, and I'd have lost all the money and the children. I didn't touch that damned Edith. Believe me, Wilberforce. She hinted very broadly she was open to a liaison. I could've taken her up on it, but I didn't. The baby isn't mine.'

'Have you ever been accused of forgery, Mr Templeton?' the Brahmin asked.

Apart from stiffening, Templeton didn't show any other emotion. He cleared his throat. 'Er... there was a bit of a misunderstanding about a cheque. It happened a long time ago.'

'At university,' Wilberforce said.

Arthur stared at the empty fireplace. Carriage wheels rattled on the gravel outside the study window. Phoebe was back.

'You forged the diary and hid it in Edith's room,' Wilberforce said.

Templeton's eyes darted between them. 'I'm not the Ripper. You can't tie those murders around my neck. Yes, Edith was blackmailing me to marry her. I didn't know how to stop her. I had the idea of forging her handwriting and hiding the diary in her console so that you would think she was the Ripper and arrest her. When she died so suddenly, I hid the diary in the Bible. She'd already forged the love letter and given it to Phoebe. I didn't know what she would do next. But I swear I didn't kill her.'

'You killed Edith Whittaker,' Wilberforce said. 'We have a witness.'

'You couldn't have. I was care—'

'Careful, were you?' The Brahmin completed Arthur's sentence when he stopped abruptly. 'Not quite, Mr Templeton. The maid saw you smear the poison in the teacup.'

'You dirty native—' Arthur lunged at the Brahmin, fingers stiffened into claws.

The Brahmin nimbly hopped aside, and Arthur smashed face forward against the door hinge.

'Not so fast, Arthur Templeton.' Wilberforce stepped up and, seizing Arthur by the collar, gave his skull a few knocks on the wall. 'You are under arrest.'

Chapter Fifty-five

The moth's wings banged against the clear glass of the oil lamp as it tried to reach the flame. Fully dressed, Shiraz perched on the edge of her bed, fingers gripping each other tightly. The flame flickered low, gasping and bobbing, sucking up the last drops of oil as the night maid knocked and entered her bedroom.

Shiraz leapt to her feet. 'Is it the Chief Inspector?'

'No, hakimji, a mute man has come for you. Something about a baby.'

She hurried to the entrance. A wiry man squatted in the portico, his forehead obscured by a smoke-coloured turban, one end coiled around his nose and mouth. The crickets began their shivering chatter around them.

He jumped up on seeing her and bowed, his gaze respectfully slanting to her feet. Inarticulate and muffled sounds emerged from his mouth as he made a rocking movement with his arms. Mud on the backs of his hands made it hard to tell his age, but they didn't seem wrinkled. A labourer, perhaps.

'Your wife is having a baby?' she asked in Deccani.

The man bobbed his head.

Shiraz told the attendant to fetch the coachman and the carriage while she collected her satchel. She would need both hands to lift her sari-skirt from the dirt and litter on the path into the slums where this man probably lived.

Their guide, who had climbed up next to the coachman, pointed towards Chaderghat-Oliphant Bridge.

Blustery air currents whipped around her face as the carriage shot out of the gate. She removed the scarf to cool her head. Something brushed her hair. Her heartbeat stuttered as she ducked. Looking up, she caught the jagged shadow of a bat's wings gliding away.

'Hai Allah!' The coachman clapped a hand onto his turban and stopped the horse. 'A bad omen, hakimji. The touch of their wings brings death. We shouldn't proceed.'

The man made loud, inarticulate sounds and jabbed his finger at the riverbank.

She told the coachman to carry on, having little patience with superstition. He grunted and set the horses to a gallop past Chaderghat-Oliphant Bridge and reached the Chaderghat rock weir from where the gush of the waterfall sounded. There were fewer houses here. Below, the wide riverbed was not yet fully flooded.

A dog howled from the other bank as the carriage halted amid dark scrub and bush. No more houses.

The man pointed to a lone hut on the riverbed; a pinprick of light shone there.

'Shall I come with you, hakimji?' the coachman asked, glancing at the man with a frown.

Now that Arthur Templeton had been arrested for the murders, she didn't have to worry. 'No need, Suleiman. It's not far. Give him the lantern, and he can lead the way. You stay with the horses.'

She lifted her skirt and stepped on the footstool placed for her. Then she gingerly moved down the shallow incline, crunching dead twigs and pebbles under her shoe, the man leading the way with the lamp. She caught a whiff of lemon and thought of Niloufer. Not perfume, more like oil from rubbing the peel on the skin. Mosquitoes and other biting insects hovered around. Those little beasts would find a way to draw blood; they always did.

The mud caked as they neared the riverbed, and the lamp caught two glittering eyes in a shrub. A cat or a jackal.

She stopped to draw a breath and get her bearings. In front, shrubs and paddy grass grew waist to shoulder high; her guide cut through, leaving a dark gap in his wake. A balmy breeze stroked her skin as she gazed at a shadow that flickered above the ancient turrets on the other side of the river. Moonbeams danced on the thick line drawn by the black water to her right.

Though her guide had drawn away, for the first time since Niloufer's murder, she felt safe in the rhythmic quiet only nature could evoke: the gentle sound of gushing water, a chirrup from a sleepy bird, the shiver of air from the hunting owls.

Her guide, she realised, was near the hut, whose outline she could just about make out in the light of the bobbing lantern. She took a step to catch up. Something tugged her skirt. Her heart leapt in her chest. A rat? Bandicoots here were the size of small dogs, with vicious, razor-sharp teeth. She had seen one near her house tearing apart and gobbling up a dead crow. Her fingers brushed wood; a dead branch.

She called out to the man as she pulled the cotton skirt. It ripped. Gathering the cloth in a fist, she hailed him again. But there was now no light ahead. Where was he?

She looked over her shoulder but couldn't see the road. The dark pressed in on her from all sides. Tendrils of dread spread in her stomach, burrowing deep. Her skin prickled, the nerve endings quivering as if someone's gaze was tracking her. It felt familiar; it had watched her these past two days.

She shuffled forward, and with each step taking her closer to the guide, dread loosened its grip.

A sound came from behind her.

She froze. Metallic, as if someone had drawn a knife from a sheath. A slum dweller doing his business in the bushes, that's all. Not the killer. They've caught him. But what if it wasn't Arthur Templeton? What if the real killer was stalking her right now?

Blood fizzed in her veins. She blundered through the undergrowth, ignoring the bites and the rips on her ankles and arms, wanting to flee from the eyes hunting her.

Something rustled behind. She looked over her shoulder in fright. Inky shadows leered back, the bushes twitching as if human. A giant fist rapidly punched her chest from the inside. Be careful, Dr Shiraz... Maryam's warning. The satchel slapped her thigh, and brought her back to her senses. The syringe case, she thought, slipping her hand in, and her fingers closed over its comforting bulk.

A flash ahead oriented her. Thank god.

'Hey, you left me back here without a light,' she shouted in Deccani.

The lamp flickered, the wick struggling to hold the flame. Then she realised her mistake. No one held the lantern. What she had thought was the man's turban was the top of a small tree; the bobbing lantern in the guide's hand was a swaying branch to which the lamp was tied with a blood-red cummerbund.

She tried to recall her guide's face. Did she know him? Was that why he had muffled his face? He was the same height as Ali Baig. They had made a horrible mistake. Ali was the killer after all.

A foot crunched a dead shrub.

She forced herself to stand still. Don't run. He would chase her and once she tumbled onto the rubble, she stood no chance.

Don't breathe in the chloroform. Struggle, then go still. Don't take a single breath for twenty seconds. She could do it.

Shadows of bushes in front, behind and to her left. A pebble slithered somewhere to her right in the river's direction.

She whipped towards it even as her brain told her the killer couldn't be there.

The attack came from behind.

Hands gripped her neck. Silk suffocated her nose and mouth.

She gasped. The chloroform tunnelled through her windpipe. She didn't have to pretend to faint as her final thoughts tumbled through a mist. A man with wiry arms who smelt of lemons... She knew him.

Chapter Fifty-six

'Huzoor.' Ram Rahim pelted down the driveway. 'The killer has hakimji.'

Soob, who'd been pacing with his horse, waiting for this very summons, seized the boy by his shoulders and lifted him to the saddle, and then swung on behind him. Wilberforce and the dozen-strong battalion of Residency Police constables scrambled onto their mounts.

'Make the horse go faster, huzoor,' the boy shouted as they streamed out into Musi River road.

Soob's heart thundered louder than the drum of the hooves on the asphalt, a prayer on his lips: *let Shiraz be alive*. If anything happened to her, he didn't know how he would bear it. He had deliberately put her in danger, even if it was for a short time and with a rescue plan in place. He should have told her the killer's identity. But he was afraid her expressive face would reveal it. With only his hunch and no evidence, this was the only way to catch the killer.

'There, huzoor,' Ram Rahim cried out. Her carriage stood on the roadside at the outskirts where the Residency banks sputtered into shrub and vegetation, and the city wall coiled away on the other side of the river.

He hadn't known whether the killer would lure her to the park or the riverbank, so he had waited at home, halfway between the two locations.

'They went to that hut, huzoor.' The coachman pointed to a dim light swinging to and fro as if held by someone walking. 'I shouldn't have let her go with that man. I had a bad feeling about him.'

Soob leapt off and lifted the boy down. 'Stay here, Ram Rahim. The constable will protect you.'

He and Wilberforce, along with four constables who were keen huntsmen, crept down the embankment.

He breathed in lily of the valley, Shiraz's perfume, and attar of lemon, the killer's scent. A muffled cry came from further ahead.

Soob barrelled through the bushy undergrowth, cursing the constable who'd been shadowing her. The man ought to have protected her. His boots kicked up mud and foul-smelling refuse, scarcely registering the slaps of the wet leaves as he plunged into the paddy field. He drew his knife and slashed at the vegetation, his eye searching for the narrow channel bringing the river water to the crops that would give him a clear path through the plants. His boots found it, slipping into the shallow water, and he picked up speed, all the while willing for another scream to sound so he would know that Shiraz was still alive. Ahead, in the inky gloom beyond the underbrush, two shadows coiled and twisted. Metal glinted in their midst.

'No, stop.' He lunged at them. 'Don't kill her.'

A shadow peeled off, leaving a pool of ink on the silken soil. Soob's heartbeat stuttered. Dead... Shiraz was dead.

Murderer! a cold voice rang in his head. *You killed her. You put her in danger.*

With a guttural cry he sprang at the killer, hit muscle and cloth, a ripping sound, and the killer sprinted away into the night. Soob dropped the rough cotton in his fist and tumbled to his knees. Pale silver flashed above where her face would be, the blade jutting from her throat, blood pumping out. His hand slid under her head, and it tipped to one side. The texture of the cloth on his palm stilled his breath – a turban. Hope flaring, he touched the face and felt the wiry hair of a beard. It was the constable who'd been guarding her, not Shiraz. Where was she? He cast his eye about wildly as Wilberforce and his men pounded past.

'Here, sir,' said a constable crouched by a bush.

With a prayer on his lips, Soob dived towards Shiraz, fingers feeling for her throat. Not cut. He put his cheek by hers, his palm cupping her cheek. Soft breath brushed his lips. She was alive. A deep warmth filled his chest as he gathered her in his arms.

'The bastard is getting away, sir,' the middle-aged constable exclaimed.

Recollecting where he was, Soob leapt to his feet. 'Stay and protect her.'

The constable gave a nod and gripped his matchlock.

Soob tracked the shadows bobbing above the low undergrowth. The killer was way ahead, another figure, probably Wilberforce, ten paces behind, and the three constables further back – and their pace was slowing. They must have stumbled into the deep gullies crisscrossing the riverbed. Only luck seemed to have kept Wilberforce upright, he thought, as he cut through to the foot of the embankment, hoping to find the rock base beneath the shallow sand, which he'd pointed out to Natraja wouldn't allow plants to flourish. From the corner of his eye he caught the Englishman's stumble as his feet found and sprinted on the invisible path.

A loud curse came from Wilberforce. His shadow dipped as if he'd fallen into a gully. Soob crouched as the killer, after glancing back, checked his speed, and swivelled towards the embankment. He had not noticed Soob hidden by a line of bushes.

Soob lost sight of Wilberforce as he raced on, bending low, his feet sure of their tread and balance.

The killer, now about ten paces to his right, was looking the wrong way, over his shoulder towards Wilberforce and the constables rather than diagonally to where Soob was.

Something squeaked and darted across his path. He jerked back, tipping off the killer by his sudden movement. His quarry whipped around and raced away on the mudflat, through puddles, stones and small shrubs, now making for the river. At the river, the killer doubled back towards Chaderghat-Oliphant Bridge, using the slip route at the river's edge, a shallow bar of mud and sand deposited by the meandering river.

'There, he's there, going towards the weir,' Soob yelled, twisting towards Wilberforce, who was back on his feet but sprinting in the wrong direction.

The river gushed past; streaks of silver froth gleamed in the half light. The killer made it to the rock ledge and plunged in, the line of boulders and stones strung across the water acting as protection from the twelve-foot waterfall. The water came up to the killer's neck; when Soob jumped in, the level reached his waist. His long stride and the momentum gained from placing his palm against the rockface and shoving off brought him much closer.

The killer's turban, which had somehow remained on his head, kept dipping into the water and tipped his head to one side when he glanced over his shoulder at Soob. The yards of muslin, heavy from the soaking, knocked the man off-balance, cracking his shoulder against a boulder. The river's sudden heave splayed the killer face-down on the ledge. Water sheeted over him.

Soob pounced and grabbed the killer's shoulders as his body tipped into the cataract.

'I'm coming,' Wilberforce shouted over the river's roar.

Wedging his boots into a niche in the rocks, his back taking the heavy slam, Soob hung on.

'Pull,' Wilberforce said, seizing the killer's arm.

They hefted their quarry back over the ledge and dragged him to the Residency bank and the waiting constables.

A constable lit a match as Soob whipped off the killer's turban.

'Imran Baig, you are under arrest for the murders of Devi, Mallu, Niloufer, Fatima, Chandini and Constable Afridi.'

Chapter Fifty-seven

It was two minutes to midnight when Soob entered the Badshahi Ashurkhana, alone and unarmed. He passed half a dozen black-robed Shias leaving the house of mourning for the son-in-law of Prophet Muhammad, in their view his true successor. He had chosen this venue built by a Shia ruler in the sixteenth century because weapons were not allowed in this place of worship; and for a second reason, which he devoutly hoped would work.

In the large compound in front of the dome, more black-robed devout were circling an incense pit and chanting a prayer. Soob strode past towards the dimly lit tomb, a prayer on his lips that the child was still alive, that Imran's cold declaration that it'd be too late, that he had instructed the mercenaries to kill the child, was a lie. In his pocket he carried the promissory note of a Bombay agent who was authorised to pay the ransom amount to the bearer of the note. His dependence on Imran's hubris, on the nobleman's belief that he was cleverer than everyone else, was what drew Soob's steps to the stone wall abutting the river.

The gush of the river was louder than yesterday, so swollen that it lapped the city walls. Thank god for small mercies, Soob thought. It would allow Sub-Inspector Kamran's boat to come close enough to the back wall of the Ashurkhana for the exchange.

He reached the designated spot between two pillars. It was empty as he'd expected. A wiry Habashi mercenary appeared silently from behind a pillar.

'Where is the boy?' Soob asked.

The man snapped his fingers.

Two dark shadows stepped out from behind a stone column ten feet away. Sobs came from the smaller one.

'Stop your whimpering,' the larger shadow said and slapped the child's head.

Soob's fingers curled into fists and he surged forward.

The first mercenary intercepted him. 'The ransom.'

'Here it is,' Soob said in a ringing tone and as he handed over the promissory note, a group of black-clad Shias glided up to them.

Soob shoved the mercenary into their arms and barrelled into the shadow, desperate to catch the man's wrist and stop the dagger's descent into the child's throat. He caught it with inches to spare and shoved the boy away, the steel now inches from his own eye. It moved inexorably closer. But Soob had one more weapon.

With his left hand he pinched a pressure point on the man's wrist. He squealed and released the dagger. Soob kicked him in the groin and left him to the tender care of the head constable who'd rushed up.

In the clash of steel and fists behind him, Soob pushed the child into a hole in the back wall, and into Kamran's arms reaching in from the other side.

Chapter Fifty-eight

They sat in bamboo and wicker chairs in Shiraz's garden: he, Shiraz, Ariel, Inspector Wilberforce, Vahid Baig, Sub-Inspector Kamran and Dr Currimbhoy. HC Muhammad, though pleased by the invitation, had declined. The evening river breeze wafted over the tea, cake, biscuits, samosas and sandwiches set on a picnic table.

'Soob, when did you know that Ali was being framed?' Shiraz asked, passing a plate of buttery biscuits to him.

'My suspicions grew when too many signs – the Ripper method, the Hellfire ritual, and the choice of victims – pointed to Ali,' he said, picking up a biscuit. 'Each murder was timed to coincide with when Ali was in the vicinity, and most times he didn't have an alibi. What clinched it was my nephew's kidnapping. Vahid sahib, your evening edition hinting at the imminent arrest of one of the Templetons and my conversation with Edith at the racecourse made Imran panic into kidnapping Natraja. Ali's cummerbund in Natraja's hand when Inspector Wilberforce rescued him, and the syringe with the dregs of the phosphorous and chloroform cocktail left in Ali's closet for Wilberforce to find signalled to me the killer's desperation to return our suspicions to Ali. That made me absolutely sure someone was framing Ali. My heartfelt thanks to you, Inspector Wilberforce.'

Wilberforce flushed, a small smile on his lips. 'Chief Inspector Soobramania told me at the beginning of the investigation that only motive would lead us to the killer, and he was right. Beats me, though, how you put your finger on Imran.'

'I began with the question of why copy the Ripper, and why now?' Soob said, stretching out his legs on the grass. 'The murders coincided with the visit of the Grand Duke and the Earl. But of the first three victims, only Niloufer's death benefitted someone, Ali Baig. Their lawyer said Imran didn't stand to gain and, in fact, he was wealthier than his brother. And the consensus was that Imran didn't hate her, only Ali did. Then Imran made mistakes in his hurry to implicate his brother when we began to focus on the Templetons. He sent a note to the *Deccan Gazette* duplicating the words in the Ripper's letter to the London broadsheets. He hinted to Shiraz and me about Ali's worries and, for good measure, told his wife about Ali's debts. He knew she had a loose tongue and would tell Shiraz who, he thought, would inform me. But he couldn't control his wife's anger about her jewellery being confiscated. She complained to Shiraz about having to wear glass bangles like her servants. I found it odd given his wealth and the sizeable dowry he would've received from his wife's father. I initially put Imran's behaviour down to miserliness.'

'Why did he take her jewellery?' Ariel Falloner asked, leaning forward in her chair.

'To deposit it with Abdul Huq as surety for his brother's loan.'

'Surely Imran didn't invest in that rascal's scheme?' Vahid Baig said with a frown.

'No, he invested in his future as the nawab. You put me on the right track when you said Imran had doubled the family fortune. He considered it his hard-earned money, and when we arrested him, he said he was merely taking what was his.'

'Greed was his motive?' Shiraz asked.

'Not precisely greed,' Soob said slowly. 'He thought his brother was the usurper, had done nothing to multiply it. It worried Imran that Ali could well fritter it all away on Huq's scheme.'

'But surely that blasted Huq could've pocketed Imran's jewels,' Wilberforce said.

'Yes, but Imran was playing the long game. He was willing to forgo the amount if it meant that he inherited the Baig lands and the title. He had enough faith in his ability to swell the family coffers again.'

'How can you say it wasn't greed?' Ariel asked. 'That rotter murdered those poor women and kidnapped the child, all for money.'

'The Chief Inspector is right,' Vahid Baig said in a sombre tone. 'In his mind he was taking what was his. Fruits of his labour, that's how he saw it.'

'Good thing then that things didn't go according to his plan,' Currimbhoy said, refilling his teacup. 'Lovely aroma this Darjeeling has, Dr Daruwalla.'

'Some things didn't,' Soob said, brushing crumbs from his tunic. 'Imran had planned to kill Mallu, leave her by the fountain, go through the gap in the hedge and seize Niloufer from her bedroom when she returned from the dinner party. That's why the hedge screen was set aside that night. He planned to drug her, carry her into the park and kill her by the fountain. But Niloufer, who was very upset by the forged love letter, entered through the side entrance. Imran had just finished with Mallu and was heading towards Niloufer's house. He saw her lantern and grabbed the chance, but Ram Rahim witnessed it.'

'That's when he made another mistake,' Shiraz said. 'The key.'

'Yes, he pocketed Niloufer's key, which had dropped on the gravel, and put the wrong one in her pocket on realising he had two keys. Her mother later remarked on the ribbon's colour. Phoebe and Niloufer had green ribbons on their park keys. When I asked Imran on the night Edith Whittaker was murdered, he said his father's key had a green ribbon. He also tried to divert me from Templeton, said I shouldn't bother with the blue-eyed English newspaper proprietor. Templeton's eyes are green. Green and blue, though, look alike to those who are colour blind − it's a rare form. Most colour blind people cannot distinguish between red and green. When Ali confirmed that his father's key had a blue ribbon, it made me suspect Imran had this rare type of colour blindness. Since Imran thought all three keys were tied with green ribbons, he wasn't suspicious about being questioned about the colour.'

'But why did he have to kill five innocent women?' Shiraz burst out. 'Did he show any remorse at all?'

'No.' Imran's clear-eyed gaze when confessing to the murders showed no guilt or regret. Like John Furlow, Imran seemed not to have a sense of right and wrong.

'For someone with such a devious mind, it surprises me that he could have made such an egregious mistake in his imitation of the Ripper,' Dr Currimbhoy said.

'There we were aided by Templeton. Imran consulted *The Jasoos* for the Ripper's method, and double checked in the *Deccan Gazette*. What he didn't realise was that Templeton had decided to take the most gruesome details and write it up as if all the victims had been subjected to such atrocities.'

'My reporter, lazy fellow, used the *Jasoos* story.' Vahid Baig scowled.

'That rotten bugger – excuse me, ladies – practised on the river victim's body then,' Wilberforce said.

'Yes, Imran was methodical and clinical. But my finding Devi's body was a piece of bad luck for him. Even so, he'd made sure that nobody would be able to recognise her. He cropped her hair so that she'd be mistaken for a Hindu widow. The two types of knife cuts, though, misled me into thinking there were two killers.'

'That's Imran for you,' Vahid Baig said in a sombre tone, gazing up at two kestrels circling above in the fading light. 'Systematic, thorough and a fast learner.'

'What a terrible, terrible man,' Shiraz said. 'To think I believed in him because he saved me from Ali.'

Soob shook his head. 'Don't be hard on yourself, Shiraz. We were all fooled. Thanks to you, though, we found out a lot. You stuck to Devi's trail, and your questions raised Ali's suspicions that she could be the river victim. When he was arrested, he asked Imran to check. That's when Imran made two bad mistakes. He mentioned her tattoo, which only the killer could have seen. The second slip he made were his words – the victim's hair had been cut off. How did he know the hair had been cut, as Dr Khan had pointed out to me, not shaved off? I was now sure Imran Baig was the killer. Their lawyer had already clarified to me the order in which the brothers would inherit. If Ali died, his son would inherit. If the son died, then Imran would inherit. Something Natraja said about a banyan tree killing things under its roots brought it all together for me. For Imran, Ali was like the banyan destroying his family's wealth. I realised then that six improbable things had to occur for Imran to inherit.'

'Which were?' Shiraz asked.

'Niloufer's death, Zulfikar Baig's death, Ali's son's kidnapping, the refusal to return the boy despite the ransom being paid, Ali's arrest and conviction. And finally...'

'The child's death,' Shiraz said in a hushed tone.

Soob gave a nod. He'd seen to the boy's safety up until the ransom exchange through Huq's patron, the Premier Noble. In return, Soob had promised a favour to the wily nobleman. He'd do it again, though, for the child's life.

'I knew no murders would occur while Ali was behind bars. But Edith's murder and the forged diary made it impossible to keep Ali in prison. I had two men tailing Imran, and inside the palace, the footman kept an eye on him. But Imran spotted him and drugged him before killing Chandini, although he didn't realise she was Templeton's favourite too.'

'Poor Chandini,' Ariel Falloner said. 'Did you find her family?'

Soob shook his head. 'The brothel owner was very upset, though. Chandini was her star and drew a lot of rich customers. She had bought her from a slave trader six years ago.'

Vahid Baig cleared his throat. 'We have launched a campaign to abolish that disgraceful practice.'

'About time,' Shiraz said. 'Please say that Imran didn't kill his own father, Soob.'

He couldn't prove it, but deep down he was certain of it.

'Thanks to you, the child is safe,' she added at his silence.

'Was Huq involved in the murders too?'

'No, but he told us he kidnapped the child with Imran's help. Once the ransom was paid, he released the boy to Imran who made up the story about increasing the ransom.'

'Surely Huq would have told everyone about Imran,' Ariel said, tapping the teacup's rim.

Vahid sahib shook his head. 'These fellows have a peculiar sense of honour. Once Huq released the boy to the family, it was no concern of his what happened to the child.'

'Chief Inspector, how did you free the child?' Dr Currimbhoy asked.

'There are three loose stones at the base of the Ashurkhana back wall. Ram Rahim used that route to enter and leave the city. With the river rising from the rains, it was easy enough for Sub-Inspector Kamran to get there by boat and take the child when I handed the boy to him. Well done.'

Kamran blushed and looked away at the river.

'But Soob,' Ariel said. 'This means Imran was plotting all this as soon as his father married Niloufer.'

'Well, not then. But soon after, when he discovered his brother's plan to invest in the Deccan Rail Scheme.'

'Whose blood was on the rock at the folly?' Shiraz asked in a quiet tone.

'A cockerel's,' Soob said. 'Another mistake. He wanted us to think the victims had been killed during a Hellfire ritual. But it had been pouring that night and on subsequent nights, and no trace of blood ought to have remained on that rock. He killed Devi elsewhere.' He didn't look at Shiraz.

'He killed Devi in the hut where he was taking me,' Shiraz said in a small voice. 'How frantic and terrified she must have been. How could I not have seen the evil in him?'

'None of us suspected him, Dr Daruwalla,' Vahid Baig said. 'Evil came from the choice he made to grab the fortune and the title for himself.'

'His poor wife,' Ariel said.

'Yes, Parveen, poor thing, is distraught,' Shiraz said. 'Maryam is with her. She's told her to remain in the harem as her sister and a second mother to her son. She is still young, so they will marry her to someone of her choice and provide a dowry.'

'What will happen to Imran now, Soob?' Ariel asked.

Imran had been given no choice by the ruler. Being crushed publicly under an elephant's foot would have brought shame to the Baig name and to the native nobles.

'He took cyanide and died,' Soob said. 'The victims' families have been informed that justice has been done.'

'You mean only we and a few others know it was Imran?' Shiraz scowled. 'I wanted him to suffer. Poor Constable Afridi. He saved me. I want to send money to his family, Soob.'

'I'll get it delivered along with the Nizam's reward. He has given a pouch of gold mohurs to the constable's family.' Soob had added his contribution and ensured that the man's family did not suffer financially. The constable's younger brother was given his job. None of it, though, would assuage Soob's guilt that he had sent the man to his death.

After a moment's silence, Ariel spoke. 'What will happen to Arthur Templeton? And how were you so sure Phoebe or Edith or Arthur weren't the killers?'

'Niloufer's death didn't benefit them,' he said. 'Edith Whittaker forged the love letter, so in reality, there was no affair.'

'How sneaky of him to smear the poison in the empty cup and take it to the maid and get her to fill it with the cocoa.' Ariel set hers on the cane table. 'It was clever of you, Soob, to figure that out.'

'Oh it was Kamran who found out – he reported to me that the maid had seen Templeton fiddling with the cup earlier. Later, when he tracked her down, she told him she'd drunk the dregs of the cocoa from the saucepan, and she was fine. It confirmed to us that the poison was indeed in the teacup.'

'At least his wife is smart enough to divorce him and move back to America with the children,' Shiraz said. 'I never understood what Phoebe saw in him. I didn't like Edith, but her murder shouldn't go unpunished. I hope they find him guilty.'

'He isn't the only guilty one,' Soob said in a sober tone. He told them about his encounter with Phoebe Templeton.

–

Standing among packing crates in the study, she'd informed Soob that they were sailing back to America.

'You put the idea of murdering Edith in your husband's head,' Soob had said.

A faint smile had played on her lips. 'Arthur was perfectly capable of coming up with the idea on his own.'

'Not the poison. You made a mistake with the duranta berries. Your husband told me the article on poisons from the garden was your idea. You thought of using it to influence Arthur after Shiraz said the letter was forged. Your suspicion fell on Edith. You knew she was pregnant, and you realised it was Arthur's baby. You couldn't kill her yourself because of your religious scruples. But if you fed Arthur the information on how to do it, and made him think that Edith was trying to frame you for the murders, Arthur would act. You could see that he was tiring of her. So you used a sling and shot your brooch into the park. But you didn't know the killer had killed Fatima that very night. The coincidence worked in your favour. Arthur thought Edith was gunning for you, so he decided to get rid of her quickly. You were unlucky that Edith saw you with the sling.'

'You have no proof,' Phoebe had said coldly.

He could have told her the evidence was in her eyes, empty and dead. 'Whoever sheds the blood of man, by man shall his blood be shed, for God made man in his own image. That's the dictum you were following.'

'God made her pay, not me. I was simply the instrument. She was indirectly responsible for Niloufer's murder. Arthur's stupidity isn't my fault.' The lady had turned on her heel and walked out.

–

'You mean to say Phoebe Templeton put the idea in her husband's head and the poison in his hand,' Ariel Falloner said when Soob narrated the events. 'Lady Macbeth is not a patch on her. How diabolical!'

'She got away, then?' Wilberforce scowled.

Soob wasn't so sure. It had left a mark on Phoebe Templeton, and she knew it. What she would do with the knowledge was a question only she could answer.

'Soob, Niloufer will be buried in the Tower of Silence,' Shiraz said, detaining Soob when everyone made their goodbyes. 'The Fire Priest has agreed to ignore her marriage.'

'Good.' Soob clasped her hands. 'I'm so sorry for putting you in danger, Shiraz. I should have told you to beware of Imran.'

'You should have,' she replied, eyeing him coolly.

'If I had lost you…' His voice softened.

Chapter Fifty-nine

Soob drew in the comforting scent of ash and the clean whiff of an evening bath, well aware that the expiation ceremony organised by the Deccan Brahmin Association would take place in a few hours, at dawn. Next to him Natraja sat cross-legged on the verandah floor. They gazed out at the river, a rolling and gushing mass below tiny flickering dots of light, fireflies twinkling from the city riverbank. Somewhere in the distance, a dog howled.

He gazed at Natraja, so tiny, so vulnerable, and his to protect and cherish. Yet as with Rohini, his dear Rohini, he was about to fail again.

He told himself that if Natraja was old enough to perform the rite of passage and don the sacred thread, he was capable of understanding Soob's decision. He took a deep breath and turned to his ward. 'I want to tell you why I have remained an outcaste.'

He explained his anger with the priests for not performing Rohini's last rites, his own nature and principles, that they wouldn't let him do what could be so easily fixed. To do the expiation rite would kill all that made him who he was. His work defined him as a person – or was it that he had chosen this work because it suited his temperament? Whatever it was, he knew of no other way to carry on as a person. Would Natraja understand? Was he old enough, mature enough to see that a man's principles defined him as a person?

Natraja's clear gaze drilled into him and he met it. 'If I had to make these choices again, I would do the same thing. I would have gone to London, chased down the Ripper, not come back, even knowing that your aunt was very sick, returning only after I had completed the job. That is who I am.' He'd remained an outcaste and deprived himself of his family because, in his mind, he didn't deserve one. Thanks to Shiraz, he understood now that he was punishing himself because he would always choose delivering justice to the victims above the well-being of his family.

He got up, unable to sit still, and began pacing. 'But what use are my principles if they hurt you, Natraja? I don't want that to happen. But on the other hand, what am I without my principles? Principles, perhaps, is the wrong word. It is that sense of justice, calling out what I think is wrong: that's at the core. If I return to a caste that assigns value and dignity on the basis of one's birth, not one's chosen deeds, then how can I be true to who I am?' He lapsed into silence and looked at his nephew.

'Are you asking me to choose for you, Athimber?' Natraja asked, gazing up at him.

Was that what he was doing? Yes, he was – but this wasn't Natraja's choice to make.

'No, I have to choose.' Soob turned away, the answer sticking in his throat.

'Do you even have a choice, Athimber?'

'We always have a choice, Natraja. Always.' His gaze snagged on a dusky eagle owl circling the stone rampart and shadowed its dip and glide and weave until it sank behind a lotus-shaped battlement.

'I understand, Athimber.' Small arms encircled his waist and hugged him tight.

Historical Note

Hyderabad

Hyderabad stands on the south bank of the Musi River, six miles in circumference and surrounded by stone walls flanked with bastions. It was created by a Shia ruler in 1591 as the capital of the Deccan Sultanate, part of the Bahmani Sultanate (1357–1650) and conquered by Sunni Mughals in the mid-seventeenth century. The administrator (Nizam-ul-Mulk), appointed by the Mughals, seized control of the Deccan and established himself as the first Nizam in October 1724, giving his name 'Asaf Jah' to the dynasty. Subsequently, Hyderabad State became the largest state in India ruled by a native ruler under the aegis of the East India Company prior to 1857, and under the suzerainty of the British Crown from 1858–1948.

The Nizam's position was that of a sovereign prince, and a protected ally of the Queen, Empress of India. The state's external affairs were controlled by the British Viceroy, while the Nizam retained autonomy over the internal affairs. A cantonment of British troops was established in 1798 north of the capital, and five years later, the British Residency was constructed on the northern edge of the walled city. British Residents were expected to extract the state's resources and manipulate the rulers for the East India Company and later the British Crown's military and policy purposes. Persian was the lingua franca of the Nizam's court and administration until 1887 when it was replaced by Urdu, while the language of the street was Deccani – a mix of Urdu, Marathi and Telugu.

The Whitechapel Murders

As far as the public is concerned, the Ripper was never caught. However, there are several theories about the Ripper's identity, one of them being that the Ripper was a policeman (see casebook.org) and that the authorities hushed it up. I've used that theory in this book and created a fictional constable, John Furlow, as the culprit.

Though in the public's imagination, the Ripper was responsible for eleven murders, more recent studies suggest that only six murders can be attributed to the Ripper. Here, for the Ripper's modus operandi and victims, I have adopted the theories portrayed in Robert D. Keppel et al., *The Jack the Ripper Murders: A Modus Operandi and Signature Analysis of the 1888–1891 Whitechapel Murders*, an analysis that states that only six of the murders carried out between 7 August 1888 and 9 November 1888 can be attributed to the Ripper. While Keppel et al. say the Ripper victims were prostitutes (which is Wilberforce's point of view), I adopted the views of historian Dr Hallie Rubenhold in *The Five* (which focuses on Nichols, Chapman, Stride, Eddowes and Kelly) for Soob's claims that they were not sex workers.

Paul Halter's *The Crimson Fog* and the articles in *The Ripperologist* and on casebook.org were also of great help.

For the purposes of the story, I created a secret committee set up by the Metropolitan Police, based in New Scotland Yard, to investigate the Whitechapel murders, and put Soob in it.

Other historical figures

The Earl of Euston was a controversial figure and a friend of one of the Ripper suspects, Albert Victor, Duke of Clarence and Avondale (see casebook.org). He was an aide-de-camp to Edward VII in 1901. While in real life he was a prominent Freemason, I've given him membership of the Hellfire Club, a club started in 1746 by Sir Francis Dashwood with aristocratic hedonists who practised pagan rites and bacchanalian orgies. It continued with these practices in the nineteenth century, and the club members came under suspicion during the Ripper investigation.

Grand Duke Alexei Alexandrovich, a brother to Tsar Alexander III of Russia, visited Hyderabad in the 1890s. I've taken the liberty of making him a member of the Hellfire Club too and combined his visit with that of the Earl of Euston.

Inspector Frederick Abberline was in charge of the Whitechapel investigation, and my fictional Inspector Wilberforce served under him.

Some characters in the book are based on real historical figures, namely the Nizam of Hyderabad, the Premier Noble Sir Khurshid Jah, the British Resident Sir Trevor Plowden, Arthur Templeton, Edith Whittaker, the Commander-in-Chief of the Nizam's army, Deputy Commissioner Mir Akbar, Commissioner Colonel Ludlow and Commissioner Hankin, although any descriptions of them and their actions are my own invention.

To get a feel for 1895 Hyderabad, I consulted the National Archives in New Delhi, Claude Campbell's *Glimpses of the Deccan* (published in 1895), Nawab Mehdi Ali's *Hyderabad Affairs* (9 volumes), the diaries of the Nizam's tutors, and scholarly biographies of important people from that period. It has been more than a decade-long process of soaking in the period, the politics and the mood of those times.

I also created two fictional streets – Baig palace hillock and Musi River road – but the other elements of Hyderabad are faithful to the nineteenth-century map of the city.

Acknowledgements

My publishing journey couldn't have happened without my fabulous agent, James Wills. Thank you, James, for being a wonderful advocate for my book and a reassuring presence all through.

I am grateful to my superb editors at Canelo Crime, Kit Nevile and Craig Lye, who have made *Blood Caste* a far better book. A big thank you to the fantastic team at Canelo, especially Louise Cullen, Kate Shepherd, Kate Berens, Vicki Vrint and Jet Purdie.

A special thanks to my mentor, the brilliant Hal Duncan, who taught me how to conjure and neatly stitch a story.

A huge thanks to my mother, Kalyani Shankar, who was my first reader. My late father, who loved Westerns and Hitchcock films, would have been very proud of me. I wish he could have seen this.

I couldn't have done it without my friends: Sangeeta Goyal, whose advice helped me with the story and plot, Annabel Grey, for the psyche explorations, and Zakiyah Razvi for helping me simplify the narrative.

It took me ages to realise that writing is also a craft and not simply some God-given talent, and when I did, I joined The Novelry. I am grateful to Louise Dean, Kate Riordan and Tash Barsby for their encouragement, advice and suggestions. I also learnt a lot from Tasha Suri, Jack Jordan, Harriet Tyce, members of the noir group and the wonderful writing community.

I was lucky enough to win Adventures in Fiction's Spotlight First Novel award in 2022 and my prize was Marion Urch's thoughtful engagement with the manuscript. Thank you, Marion. Thank you also to Sophie Hannah's Dream Author Programme.

A big thanks to those who were part of my writerly journey: Mita Kapur, Rajni George, S Prasannarajan, Helena Maybery, Victoria Sautter, Anant Maringanti and Deepak Suryavanshi.

I experienced first-hand the Hyderabadi *tehzeeb* and generosity. In particular, I want to thank Inspector Karan Kumar Singh, whom I met for the first time at the Charminar Police station. He was extremely generous with his time, advice and encouragement.

Thank you to my family and friends who cheered me on throughout this long and arduous journey: Dilip, Annika and Rebecca Shankar, Kanta Reddy, Meenakshi Dewan, Suman Dewan, Pip O'Keefe, Neepa Chatterjee, Elizabeth Hopkins, Shandana Khan, Ruth Ben-Artzi Lund, Pratap Bhanu Mehta and M. R. Madhavan – and to my cat, Puchka.

Finally, I owe a lot to my husband, Bharat Reddy, who has been quietly supportive all through my absences into the story world, often bringing me books from the library on old Hyderabad. Bharat, I couldn't have done it without you.

Glossary

Achkan: Knee-length jacket worn by men

Angharkha: A fitted robe that billows out into a skirt. The longer the skirt, the higher the status. Servants wore angharkhas that ended at their hips.

Amma: Mother

Appa: Father

Athimber: Uncle (father's brother)

Avial: A thick stew made with vegetables and coconut

Ayah: Maid

Begum: Lady (a nobleman's wife)

Bugloos: Formal fitted pants worn below an angharkha

Bungalow: In the Indian context, this is a large mansion

Churidar: Tight fitted trousers with folds at the ankle

Dhobi: Washerman/woman

Dupatta: Shawl-like scarf

Ghee: Clarified butter

Hakimji: Doctor

Huzoor: Sir

Kameez: Long shirt or tunic

Kurta: Loose collarless tunic

Mansubdari turban: Elaborate turban worn in the Nizam's court

Mirchi ka salan: Large green chilli and peanut curry

Nawab: Title given to a Muslim nobleman

Pati: Grandmother (father's mother)

Punkahwallas: Attendants who fanned with large palm leaves

Rohilla: Afghan migrant soldier from northern India

Sahib: Sir, Master. Used as a term of respect when addressing a racial or social superior, and also someone whom one respects regardless of status.

Shabash: An Urdu exclamation of praise or admiration

Sherwani: Formal fitted long jacket

Soan papdi: Crisp and flaky sweet made of gram flour, sugar and milk

Tatha: Grandfather (father's father)

Upma: Thick porridge made of semolina flour, vegetables and tempering spices

Vaishti: White unstitched cloth wrap for the lower body worn by men in South India

Zenana: The part of the house in Muslim households reserved for women